DARWINISM

Mark Fuson

Darwinism

Copyright © 2011, 2014 Mark Fuson

All rights reserved. No part of this book may be used or reproduced by any means, graphic, electronic, or mechanical, including photocopying, recording, taping or by any information storage retrieval system without the written permission of the publisher except in the case of brief quotations embodied in critical articles and reviews.

This is a work of fiction. All of the characters, names, incidents, organizations, and dialogue in this novel are either the products of the author's imagination or are used fictitiously.

iUniverse books may be ordered through booksellers or by contacting:

iUniverse LLC
1663 Liberty Drive
Bloomington, IN 47403
www.iuniverse.com
1-800-Authors (1-800-288-4677)

Because of the dynamic nature of the Internet, any Web addresses or links contained in this book may have changed since publication and may no longer be valid. The views expressed in this work are solely those of the author and do not necessarily reflect the views of the publisher, and the publisher hereby disclaims any responsibility for them.

Any people depicted in stock imagery provided by Thinkstock are models, and such images are being used for illustrative purposes only.

Certain stock imagery © Thinkstock.

ISBN: 978-1-4620-7032-9 (sc)
ISBN: 978-1-4620-7033-6 (hc)
ISBN: 978-1-4620-7034-3 (e)

Library of Congress Control Number: 2011961650

Printed in the United States of America

iUniverse rev. date: 08/25/2014

To all the crazy cat ladies in the world…
Don't change a bit!
M

CHAPTER 1

Darwin watched the moon rising just above the tree line; the change would be coming soon. It had been three months since his life had been turned inside out and he was still no closer to an explanation of how it had all begun. He was very much aware of what he had become but he had no recollection of how or when the gift had been passed to him.

Darwin Foster had lived a life plagued with tragedy; friends and loved ones had all been arbitrarily taken from him one by one. Each departure left a scar on Darwin that, over time, would culminate into his being. Standing under the light of the moon Darwin began to see long forgotten images of his youth, drifting in and out of his mind.

The youngest of four children, Darwin was the crowning jewel in the Foster family tree. Darwin's arrival came at a time of much needed joy in the Foster family. Darwin was born into a family of chaos; nothing he did could have changed that, it was as though he was marked from the beginning.

His sister, Marta, was the eldest, ten years Darwin's senior and a definite problem child who would ultimately set the cornerstone of Darwin's persona. Marta had been stillborn but was revived shortly after birth; her umbilical cord evidently found its way around her fragile little neck. The doctors had been confident that Marta had suffered no permanent ill effects, but her behavior throughout her childhood had always left doubt with her parents.

Marta spent much of her childhood with her imaginary playmates, which were made up from her stuffed animal collection. Tea in the afternoon and sleepovers in the evening were a common routine. For a little girl her imagination had conjured up some remarkably wicked characters. Sabu was a stuffed bear, and according to Marta, claimed to be the demon that lived under the bed. Fronella, a renamed Cabbage Patch doll, had a tendency to make things break, or so Marta said. And then there was Jack, a sailor doll with goggle eyes and an odd grin. Marta never spoke of Jack, even at her parent's request. It all seemed harmless for the most part, but as the years passed Marta's behavior became more and more erratic.

Shortly after Darwin was born Marta became withdrawn from her family, and she became a habitual liar. Items from around the house would disappear, only to be later found underneath Marta's bed; of course Marta knew nothing about it. On one occasion her bedroom window was broken from the inside out, a teatime chair was found on the front lawn surrounded by shards of glass, but Marta knew nothing.

One autumn a foul odor began wafting up through the heating ducts. A repairman investigated only to report someone had been urinating down the heating pipes throughout the summer. After inspecting the entire duct work the repairman concluded the urine had originated from within Marta's room, but Marta was again baffled at the accusation.

Around the time Marta had her first period things took a turn for the worst. Marta had become emotionally and physically violent towards the family. Punching, kicking and slapping became the standard greeting given by Marta. Her younger brothers learned to stay away from their older sister; one too many kicks to the groin had taught them a lesson or two. But Marta's parents bore the brunt of the verbal abuse.

"You fucking cunt! Why did you stop loving me, why?!?"

"Burn in hell you mother fucking bastards!"

"Why don't you give it to her up the ass dad, that's the way bitches like it, isn't it?!?"

The profanities flowed through the house like the smell of a bad dinner charring in the oven. The Foster's could only do so much to prevent their younger children from picking up the foul language, but it was a futile battle they were fighting. Even the neighborhood youth were learning all they needed to know about cursing, enough to last them the rest of their lives. The whole community was aware of the Foster's problems, and it had become a major embarrassment.

One afternoon Marta took out her frustrations on the family pet, a small Beagle named Skip. Marta became enraged at the animal's incessant barking; she began chasing him around the house until she cornered the dog. Once trapped, Marta began beating the defenseless animal until her parents managed to restrain her. Skip suffered a broken paw in the attack and severe trauma, which he never recovered from. After the beating, Skip would cower and piddle at the approach of any human, and he never gave more than a muffled bark from then on.

Marta began counselling sessions immediately following the incident with Skip, with her parents at first then one on one with a child psychologist, a Dr. Giddon. She had been going to therapy for months and had begun taking anti-psychotic medication and a heavy dose of Lithium to help level out her mood swings. Life within the Foster home was more normal than it had been in a long time, though Marta's underlying oddities still persisted. Afternoon tea never really ended.

It was just prior to Marta's thirteenth birthday when the walls of reality collapsed in the Foster home. Marta still isolated herself from the rest of the family, but her violent outbursts had all but ceased. It was early September when Marta relapsed, and emerged from her cocoon a demented protégé of sinister forces.

Marta was the first to arrive home from school that Tuesday afternoon, ahead of her two younger brothers who were at basketball tryouts. Her father would not get home from work until sometime after five o'clock, which meant it would be just her mother and baby Darwin in the house. It all seemed like a dream, the unimaginable, it all happened so fast but yet at the same time it became frozen in time.

Marta entered the house through the back kitchen door dropping her school bag to the floor. She proceeded immediately to the kitchen counter and removed a long, narrow carving knife from the magnetic knife strip that was mounted above the kitchen counter. Marta walked ever so quietly into the living room where her mother and baby brother sat watching the afternoon talk show circuit. Marta approached her three-year-old brother and very calmly she stabbed the child in the upper right shoulder. Darwin screamed in terror at first then it elevated to a shriek of agony and panic before his mother could even realize what was happening. As the knife slid into the child's chest Marta did not retract the knife for another blow, instead she began a sawing motion, slicing through the tender flesh and bone of her baby brother. Her mother did whatever she could do to reach her frantic baby; she had barely stumbled to her feet when she reached her daughter. Marta felt her head lunge backwards as something, someone, yanked her long blond hair back hard. She lost her grip on the knife and collapsed backwards onto the floor. It was all over within seconds; Marta reached her feet and without emotion walked to her room where she stayed until *they* came to take her away.

Darwin bled excessively and one of his ribs had been fractured but his lung had not been punctured. Overall he was in good health; after only a few days of observation in hospital he was returned home with only a three-inch scar on his chest. The home was much quieter now, much more somber than it had ever been before. Even with Darwin's return there was little to celebrate. Marta had been taken away to a *special* hospital the evening of the attack, or so the children were told. No one knew if she would be coming back.

*   *   *

Standing in a clearing deep within the forest Darwin began removing his clothing with the tangled images still in his mind. Darwin enjoyed the feeling of bursting through the fabric when the change came but he found it to be quite expensive.

It was early December and it was cold, damn cold; even if the frigid temperature could not physically harm him, it was very uncomfortable to say the least. He toyed with the notion of buying cheap clothes he could wear for a "one time use" for his change nights, but for now he was left undressing in the glacial air. He unbuttoned his shirt and dropped it to the ground, his nipples stood at attention at their exposure to the crisp night air. Now standing erect they looked like two little mountain peaks amidst a valley of small little brownish trees that stretched all the way down into his pants.

Darwin's body looked chiseled in the moonlight; he stood five foot-ten with light brown hair and baby blue eyes. He had always kept good care of himself and he had developed a solid muscular build including his prized six-pack. Darwin had always been extremely mature for his age. He had been given an "under the table" job working at a nursery when he was fourteen and when he was sixteen he graduated to an income tax paying job at the Caprice Theater. Cinema work was hard for a teenager, which included every Friday, Saturday and Sunday but he never skipped a shift and never complained about missing out on all the ritual high school activities. In retrospect the theater probably held back his educational opportunities, but he was insistent on working, a value that had been passed down by his father. During the summer months Darwin worked more than full time at the theater, which included evening and matinee showings. The management had been so impressed with Darwin that he was offered an open-ended promotion to assistant manager. Darwin had hoped to one day attend college and escape the town of New Haven but a lack of money made that dream seem all but impossible. At the same time, theater hours had become an inconvenience with his new life. He had a few more weeks to contemplate his options, but the theater would want an answer before the busy Christmas holiday.

After all these years the scar his sister had inflicted upon him was still very much visible on his upper chest. Memories of Marta were vague and unclear; even details of the attack were sketchy at best. If it were not for the scar he would likely have forgotten all about her. There were no pictures on display at home of his sister, not even one in a family portrait or from a school photo day. All evidence of Marta's existence had been effectively buried; his family refused to acknowledge the evil sister. Darwin was not even sure if Marta was still alive, or if she ever had been. If not for the scar, he might have actually believed Marta had never existed, but part of him knew better.

Darwin placed his left hand over his disfigurement and gazed up at the moon, which was much more prominent in the night sky. His lunar trigger was rising fast; he could already feel the pull on his spirit. His time as a human was drawing to a close, at least for tonight. Darwin became comforted watching the night sky, a sky he had become familiar with long before this night; a further addition to his foundation.

*   *   *

Darwin's older brothers Zack and Cornell had always been a big part of their younger brother's life. Zack was six years older than Darwin and Cornell was four years older, though the age difference did not seem to matter. From the time Darwin was able to ride a bike the brothers seemed to be connected at the hip. Almost every weekend the brothers would ride their bikes all the way to McCarran Park, clear on the other side of town, with the understanding that Zack was in charge.

Zack would create amazing adventures for his younger brothers: searching for lost gold mines, looking for signs of the elusive Bigfoot or forging a new trail to lands unknown. It was all in good fun of course and the boys were always close to a major find, Zack would tell them. Darwin and Cornell always followed the lead of their older brother without dispute; they looked up to him and admired his sense of adventure, or at least his vivid imagination.

The incident with Marta had happened when Zack was nine years old. Perhaps in some way he felt an obligation to his younger brothers to be more of a role model than his sister had been. Zack remembered all too well what Marta had done, even things his parents were not aware of. Zack had been forced to attend afternoon tea which was more like a session with Dr. Mengele. Like his parents, Zack never spoke of Marta; it was all he could do to try to provide his brothers a happier childhood.

Zack always tried to out do himself with his adventures, and one summer he nearly did. According to Zack, in the woods far north of town, beyond McCarran Park and the old quarry there lived a creature of immense power, part man, and part beast. The creature had only ever been seen at night time, especially on a night of a full moon but no one had ever been able to photograph it. Zack explained to his brothers if they succeeded in photographing the beast, they would be famous. Of course this mission would be more dangerous than any they had ever attempted before. This would be a nighttime mission, one that would require their full attention throughout the night; their very lives would be on the line. Zack could not even guarantee their safe return, but he assured his brothers it was well worth the risk. Convincing the parents to allow the expedition would be the biggest challenge of the mission.

Ben and Marie Foster were exceptional parents. As parents went, they hovered in the category just below the designation of "cool" but slightly above "lame". A product of the drug and hippy culture both Ben and Marie had taken a more trusting approach to parenting, much more so than their own parents had. Both had sworn before they had married that they would never judge their children nor discourage imagination, and that they would encourage their children to become their own individuals. Marta tested the limitations of Ben and Marie, but sticking true to what they believed, they never judged Marta, even in the end. Ben and Marie spent some time reevaluating their positions on parenting after Marta but decided the boys should not have to suffer because of problems that belonged solely to Marta. They decided to stick to their values and raise their boys the way they had always intended to, with a wide berth of trust.

When Zack approached his father with the idea of an overnight camping trip into the woods, the reception was less than lukewarm.

"Please dad, I'm almost sixteen, I'll be driving in a few months. I've never given you a reason to worry before, and I've always brought Dar and Corn back in one piece." Zack paused and looked earnestly into his father's eyes. "They get a kick out these adventures, and you're too busy to take us camping. I just wanted to do something above and beyond for them." Zack stopped. He had made his plea, but he had a definite feeling it was going to fall on deaf ears, his father had barely looked at him during his appeal. Too busy fixing that damn mower again.

"I'll talk to your mother Zack, but I make you no promises, you know how she feels about *the bears*." Rolling his eyes he went back to his workbench looking for his flat head screwdriver.

"Dad, there are no bears in those woods." Zack looked in astonishment; his father knew there had not been a bear sighting in those woods for decades, and no attacks, of any kind.

"I know that!" He barked at his son. "Try getting your mother to believe that, she has the weirdest ideas about what lives in those woods. Zack, frankly I doubt she'll go for it." His father sighed and dropped what he was doing. "Son, I'm sorry I haven't been around much, I won't try to make excuses for it. Maybe I can get a few days off at the end of summer and I can take you guys camping, just the four of us. I'm sure your mom could use the time off from us guys." Ben was looking at his son for the first time, in a long time. He had barely noticed how grown up Zack was beginning to look. His son was as tall as him, maybe slightly taller and in definite need of a shave. "I'll see what I can do with your mom Zack, but no promises." He threw his son a little smirk and grabbed him by his shoulder.

"Thanks dad, it means a lot to me." Zack turned and began to leave the workshop.

"Hey, Zack?" Ben shouted at his son who was nearly out the door. Zack stopped and turned to his father but said nothing. "Do me a favor? Scrape that thing off your face?" Referring to his son's sorry excuse for mustache and side burns. "You're starting to look like a hippy. Might win you some brownie points with your mom too."

"Sure dad!" And Zack left the shop to begin the waiting process for the answer, which he feared he already knew.

A full three days passed and Zack had still not heard back from his father. Zack had seen his father on many occasions over the past few days, mostly in the workshop continuing to work on various fix-it projects. It appeared as though his father had given up on the lawn mower, which now sat idly in the corner of the workshop. His latest project was the up-right vacuum, which there was actually nothing wrong with aside from a minor blockage in one of the pipes leading into the bag. His father was a good union man, always appeared busy but never seemed to get anything done. Zack often wondered if his father just did not know how to fix things or if his father was actually hiding in the workshop. On the surface his parents seemed to get along very well, compared to some of his friends' parents. Alcoholism, physical and verbal abuse was common among his friends' families. His parents were good to each other, aside from the lack of time they spent with one another; things seemed okay. His father spent night after night in the workshop working on unimportant projects never finishing a single one. His mother on the other hand, had become a slave to cable TV and the variety of news media shows that were forever introducing the latest Hollywood scandals. Only recently had Zack begun to notice the growing void between his parents, possibly because he had never watched his parents' interactions so closely. Zack had watched his parents intently over the previous few days; with each interaction came the possibility of a discussion on his camping trip proposal. When are we going grocery shopping? Are you going to get a new mower soon, the lawn needs to be cut? Are we going to the Claytons for dinner on Saturday? Each discussion came and went, with no indication that Zack would ever get an answer. There was only one thing he could do.

Zack went out to the workshop just after eight o'clock. He knew his father would be wrapping things up and going to bed soon and Zack wanted an answer. If Zack chickened out, he would have to wait another full day to ask his father. He could always ask his mother directly, but Zack considered that the suicidal option. If he got a favorable answer out of his dad, it might still be possible to get ready and go camping this month. It was an integral part of his planned camping experience that the moon be full. If he missed this full moon then the next one would not be until late August and he just didn't want to wait that long.

"Dad?" Zack only poked his head into the shop without actually setting foot inside it. His father looked up him and smiled.

"Well, come in damn it, I was starting to wonder if you were ever coming back to speak to me. I'm glad you're here though, I have some things we need to talk about." A wave of relief swept over Zack and with it brought new confidence. Zack stood upright, tall and strong and marched over to where his dad had pulled out a stool for him to sit on. His father was about to instil a trust within him, one he had never held before. Zack was proud, and just a little excited.

"Do you notice anything different about me, dad?" Zack smirked and turned his head from side to side attempting to draw attention to his newly smoothed out face.

"Actually that's part of what I wanted to talk to you about. You're not a child any more Zack, you're not quite a man yet, but you do all the man things. I don't want to embarrass you son, but we should talk about it a little."

The relief that had filled within Zack had been blown away by sheer terror: THE TALK! After all these years why now? Zack knew how it all worked, though he had never discussed it with his parents, surely they knew that he knew there was no rational reason to have: THE TALK. His parents had even caught him having his private moments; there was nothing he could learn now from: THE TALK. Terror turned into panic and panic quickly evolved into discomfort and discomfort rapidly changed into what his father had already stated he did not want to cause, EMBARASSMENT!

"Zack, I'm sorry your mom and I haven't been there for you. You've done a lot of growing up on your own. Frankly I don't know how you've done it, I'm so proud of the person you've become. You are an excellent role model for your brothers. If you didn't realize it, they look up to you. In many ways you have raised your brothers, and that wasn't right. I'm not upset that you spend so much time with Darwin and Cornell, but I am upset with myself. I should have been the one taking you guys places; I should have been giving you the adventures." Ben Foster paused. "There's something I want to share with you, but for God's sake don't tell your mother!" Zack nodded but appeared to be completely lost as to where his father's conversation was going. Relief once again began filling Zack as he realized it was A TALK, but not the dreaded; TALK. Ben Foster walked over to an old fridge in the corner of the shop and

Darwinism

returned a few moments later with two cans of beer. Ben handed a can to his son. "Here, just make sure you brush your teeth and use some mouth wash before you talk to your mom."

Zack felt more like a man than he ever had before. For the first time Zack saw himself as an equal to his father, not as the child who required strict guidance. Zack cracked the beer immediately; the can gave a loud "pisst" that seemed to echo throughout the room. This was not Zack's first beer, he had been drunk before, several times in fact, but never had he drank with his father. Zack thought for a moment he should act "new" to the culture of beer drinking, but decided against it at the last moment. "Thanks dad, but why?"

"I want you to start doing more teenage things. I don't mean that I want you to stop hanging out with your brothers, but I want you to start having a life with people your own age. I want you to start dating, and I want you to go to parties. I want you to have the teenage years that all teenagers should have. You've learned responsibility, I don't doubt that. I want you to go learn about what the rest of life has to offer, things your brothers can't teach you. Your mother and I feel you are responsible enough that we don't need to worry about you getting some girl pregnant, or doing drugs, or drinking and driving, but we do worry that you are going to miss out on some very important years in your life. And we don't want you to be bitter about your youth in later years. We want you to spend more time doing things boys your age are interested in. Your mom and I have not been doing our job raising your brothers. We weren't there for you like we should have; the Marta years really fucked things up. And your mom and I have had some problems coming to terms with that period in our lives. If it's not too late we want to try to make things right for everyone, if that's possible?" Ben Foster looked solemnly into his son's eyes; behind the adult mask his son wore was a child screaming for recognition. The eyes of his son spoke a thousand and one words. His father had told him exactly what he needed to hear, but he never truly expected to hear his father say them. Zack looked to the ground, his eyes drifted over the floor to every inch of the rooom, looking for the words to respond to his father, but none came.

Time ceased in the workshop for a while. Neither man spoke for a time; neither made eye contact. The next words to fill the room would be the beginning of the new bond that had been arbitrarily forged between them. Neither man knew where to go from here. The anticipation in the room grew with each second that passed. It was only when Ben Foster realized he was sucking on an empty can of beer that it occurred to him how nervous he really was.

"I don't want to dwell on this Zack. I just want you to know, it's okay to

9

let go of your brothers a little. You can do whatever you want, but you don't have to put your life on hold any more." Ben went to the fridge and grabbed another two cans of beer, this time with the plastic harness still attached. He gave the first can a tug and it slipped off the plastic strap with ease. "Psst!" The sound of bubbles could be heard from within the can upon its opening. Ben handed the now open beer to his son. "Now let's talk about what you came out here to talk about."

"You mean…" Zack paused, leaving his sentence to hang in mid air to avoid a presumption he was not willing to make. He wanted the sentence to complete itself. Everything his father had said left some doubt in his mind. *I trust you son, but spend more time being a teenager.* Zack wanted to do this trip; he wanted to do more things like his father had spoken of.

"You can go." Ben spoke softly to his son.

A moment of confusion set in with Zack. Could go where? Leave the workshop; go camping, where? "You mean I can take Darwin and Cornell camping?" The nervousness spilled out onto each word that Zack spoke.

"Yes, your mom thought it was a great idea. She surprised even me. I'll help you gather the supplies you'll need, and we can go into town and buy what we don't have tomorrow." Ben stopped for a moment, realizing that after two beers, his son, aside from a glaze on his eyes, was holding up quite well. Ben himself was feeling mighty fine after consuming the two beers with his son and the four beers before his son arrived. "Why don't we start as soon as I get home from work tomorrow, I'll come home early. Besides you better go lay down, you might have a hang over by morning if you're not careful."

"Sure thing Dad!" Zack hopped to his feet and began to move towards the door. "And Dad, thanks for everything."

"Don't thank me Zack, you've got no one to thank but yourself." Zack shot a smile at his father and went into the house. Ben Foster remained in the workshop for another hour that evening. Zack could see the shop light on from his desk next to his bedroom window. Zack sat up for a while wondering what his Dad was doing. Eventually Zack nodded off at his desk and by the time Zack awoke, sometime past 2:00 a.m. the shop light had been extinguished.

*   *   *

A long time had passed since the days with his brothers and his father. In reality it had only been eight years, but time passes more slowly when you are younger. Eight years felt more like twenty years. The images of his brothers and father were still vivid in his mind. Darwin had to strain to remember what their voices sounded like, he could see their faces, but their voices had gone silent. Darwin could remember the words they spoke, but not how they spoke them.

Darwin stood at the spot where his brother Zack had taken them to camp. Nothing remained to say that they had ever been there before, but Darwin remembered the place well. It offered the best view of the night sky. The campsite was the largest and grassiest around. There was a rock that protruded out of the ground that was shaped like a double humped camel. A tall maple tree was a few feet away from the campsite. It was the only one amongst a forest of cedar and firs making it look out of place. The campsite was never easy for a person to locate, the trail was grown over badly in parts, but Darwin seemed to have no problem finding the spot. He had spent years avoiding this spot, but now it was as close to home as he could possibly feel. Only within the last year had Darwin started visiting the campsite with some consistency, but this was his first time he had been there at night. He wasn't sure what had made him decide to come up to the campsite for the full moon. Perhaps just for variety, perhaps for closure or maybe just to say hello to some old ghosts.

Darwin began to kick off his shoes and socks. Time was running short; he could already feel his heart rate increasing, only a few more minutes until he lost control. If it were not for the cold night air he would not undress so close to the change, another reason to buy some cheap clothes. With his shoes off to the side Darwin undid his jeans and dropped them to the ground, using his feet to free his legs. His motions became quick and clumsy; his mind was beginning to race with images of the past and the present - and future? His father, Zack, Cornell, the moon, meat, blood, faces. Faces he could not quite see. He knew them, he could sense them, but he could not bring their image to clarity.

A surge of energy rushed through Darwin Foster's body. It was the ultimate adrenaline rush. He could feel his body coming alive with power, his cares began to diminish, and his control was fading. Standing in the clearing wearing only his boxers, Darwin looked to the moon, the rays of light floated down from the sky injecting into his body. He closed his eyes and took in a deep breath of cold mountain air; he was ready to give himself over to the beast. Darwin grasped his boxer shorts at the sides with both hands and tore them from his body. The fabric split down the center of Darwin's crotch and buttocks. He raised his arms to the sky holding the remains of his underwear and screamed with delight.

He was feeling extraordinary, standing naked in the clearing, as his body was awakening. Gawking at his own nudity, he took pleasure in the sensation of strength that was filling his muscles. He loved what he had become; he loved the gift that had been thrust upon him. And it was a gift...Darwin had accepted it from the moment he realized what he was.

Darwin had dabbled with drugs, mostly weed, but nothing could compare with the high he got when he transformed. The change brought on a euphoric state, his body tingled with anticipation, and every sensory area of his body began to run on overdrive. He could smell the pheromones of teenagers having sex in a car two miles away. Darwin could see the life force emanating from the plants; the colors that poured from their leaves and branches became an intense array of dancing illumination that traveled through the night air. A primal knowledge would grow from within, an intelligence that had not existed before, but one that he trusted. Darwin craved the flow of strength that filled his muscles before the change. It was primitive, it was a strength hidden deep within the soul. It was more than adrenaline, the strength was beyond the limitations of what adrenaline could achieve. The sensation brought by the blood could only be described as an arousal of the spirit. What was pumping through his veins stimulated his body from the inside out. The muscles in his entire body experienced their own orgasms. Small spasms not visible to the naked eye would erupt just under his skin. Each pulsation felt like a release of sexual energy, but with each pulse his muscles began to change, increasing their capabilities beyond that of a normal human. It was the purest of sexual experiences. It was a need far greater than he had ever experienced as a mortal. For Darwin, his final indicator that the change was arriving came from his groin. Pointing away from his body was a larger than normal erection, that seemed to develop from the feeling of strength.

It wasn't a curse. How could it be when it was pure pleasure?

The moon was about as high as Darwin would see with his human eyes; this would be the last clear moment in his head until he awoke in the morning. Gazing down at his groin he could see an ever-expanding piece of flesh extending from his body. His body was at the threshold.

* * *

The boys set out after six o'clock on the second night of the full moon. They had tried to wait for their father to get home from work, but a telephone call just before five-thirty delivered the news of that impossibility. A meeting between the union and senior management was not going well; it never went well. Ben Foster spoke briefly to Zack on the phone, but Zack never told his brothers exactly what was said.

"Dad says good luck photographing the beast; it might just be what makes us all millionaires." Zack said to his brothers upon hanging up the phone. But in some way Zack's eyes spoke a different story. His eyes were not that of a happy person, or even an upset person. He seemed more discouraged than anything. His message from *Dad* was clearly a lie, but it didn't really matter. Zack shot a smile at his younger brothers and then spoke. "We're not going to get any pictures of the beast here are we, so let's get going!"

Their mother had meticulously prepared enough food to last them for more than three days, even though they would be home by noon the next day. Each boy had a backpack that was filled with equipment, food and a change of clothing; weighing in excess of twenty-five pounds. Marie Foster had labored in the kitchen for five hours preparing food to feed a small army. There were four types of sandwiches packed: ham and cheese, beef, turkey, and egg salad. None of the boys really cared for egg salad, but fortunately only four of the thirty sandwiches were egg. Their mother had tried for years to get them into egg salad, mostly because their father was a real egg salad fan. Making lunches for her men would be a lot easier if they all liked the same things. The boys knew what fate those sandwiches had; firmly planted on the side of a tree or the back of a passing truck.

"Mom, we've gotta get going, it's going to take us more than an hour just to get there." Zack was cramming the last of the campout feast into his backpack hardly noticing his mother.

"Zack, aren't you forgetting something?" Mrs. Foster was standing in her worn housedress covered with a heavily floured apron. Standing looking at her son as he thoughtlessly continued to pack she began to clear her throat in a disapproving manner. "A-hem," followed by a brief pause, "Zack, you won't have much of campout without this."

Zack turned to find his mother holding a stainless steel Zippo lighter. How could he have forgotten? She was right; a campout without a campfire would not only have been cold but even a little scary, even for a boy of almost sixteen. Zack reached out for the lighter and took it from his mother's palm. He smiled, clasped the lighter with his hand momentarily, and shoved it into the top of his front jean pocket. He turned back to his backpack and continued arranging the last of the sandwiches, which he now had all but the last four packed. Of course the egg salad had to be the difficult ones; if his mother had not been hovering so closely those sandwiches would have been accidentally left behind.

"Do I need to remind you about being careful with fire, Zack? Or maybe you should just take extra flashlights instead..." The comment was thrown out into the open as a response generator. Her son, her young man, seemed more focused on the task at hand - more focused than most adults ever get. The room was filled with the sound of wax paper ruffling, shuffling and crumpling. But nothing was spoken.

"That does it, I think. I'll see if Corn or Dar has some room in their bags for these last few sandwiches." Zack turned to his mom. She stood not more than a few feet from him. Her eyes swelled with sadness, sorrow, happiness and joy. "Are you okay Mom, you look upset?"

"Zackeria, you make me so proud, your brothers could not have asked for a better role model." She extended her arms and Zack moved in for an awaiting embrace, dropping the egg salad sandwiches on the kitchen counter. Standing in the kitchen, mother and son shared a hug of thanks, a hug of remembrance and a hug for losing sight on what was really important. It lasted forever. When so few moments between mothers and sons are shared, sometimes-even forever isn't long enough. "Now you get your ass out of here! You don't want to be setting up camp in the dark."

"Okay, we're outta here." Zack left the comfort of his mother's arms but holding onto the warm feeling it had given him. He picked up his backpack and moved toward the kitchen door. Stopping a few feet from the door, he realized the egg salad sandwiches were still on the counter. He spun around doing a complete 180-degree turn, grabbed the sandwiches and was back to the door before his mother even had a chance to remark. Again at the edge of the kitchen, he remembered he had one more thing he had forgotten. "I love you Mom." Returning ever so briefly to his mother, Zack planted his lips on his mother's cheek, barely enough to be felt, but enough to be appreciated. He couldn't remember the last time he had told his mother he loved her. He couldn't remember the last time he had even given his mother a kiss. For the first time in recent memory, closeness existed between the two that had not been there in a very long time. It was comforting.

Zack found his brothers out on the driveway putting on their backpacks. Cornell was already sitting on his bike waiting to leave, but young Darwin struggled with his bag. The red and blue backpack swung freely off of one shoulder, Darwin's arm chased, in a rather futile effort, the other shoulder strap which seemed to be one step ahead of him. Twisting and turning, the boy twirled, getting close to the strap, and sometimes even brushing it, but never hitting the hole with his arm. Zack ran over to Darwin to lift the bag while Darwin put his arm through the strap.

"Dar, why did you take the heaviest bag?" Zack hoisted the bag up and Darwin slid his tiny arm through the slit.

"I can do it." Darwin, being the defensive child moved away from his brother and hopped onto his bike. Even with the backpack squarely placed on his shoulders, Darwin continued to wobble from side to side. He was a small boy, barely four-foot-seven, and he weighed a meek 85 pounds.

He was the smallest boy in his class, which had caused him significant grief throughout the years. Zack could remember countless times when Darwin would come home in tears from being picked on about his size and lack of athletic ability. The previous year was one of the worst for Darwin.

Darwinism

After a particularly bad basketball game Darwin was found hanging by his jockey shorts from a steel hook in the boys' change room. For more than an hour he hung helplessly. His frail little legs were almost blue from the lack of circulation by the time he was found. When asked who had done it to him, Darwin remained tight lipped. His brother was not a snitch and Zack respected him for that. Of course the school decided that to make a point; the whole gym class was punished for the incident; one hour after school for a week, doing push-ups. *This kind of behavior was not acceptable*; the class had been lectured. This did not help Darwin make any friends. Zack knew his brother had it tough, but even Zack knew it was probably worse than his brother had ever let on. Despite whatever schoolyard tortures awaited his brother, he had one thing going for him, self-determination. His strength of character and his inability to give up despite the elements working against him made him a remarkable boy.

"You think you can carry these egg sandwiches mom made or do you have more than you can carry?" The answer to which, Zack already knew.

"Egg salad!" Darwin shouted in disgust.

"Shhh! Mom made them for us; we should at least take them with us. We don't have to eat them. You don't want to hurt her feelings, do you?" Zack undid the zipper to the top of Darwin's red and blue backpack expecting his brother not to contest the contestable.

"Okay, but I'm not eating it!" Darwin proclaimed.

"I wish you would at least try it, I'm sure you'd love them! They're great for camping. Great, rotten egg FARTS!" All three boys turned in horror as they realized who had just given them the greatest suggestion of all time. "I thought that all boys loved to have farting contests, I may find them disgusting, but as long as you're not in my house, I guess it's okay."

"Mom, you'll say anything to get us to eat those things." Cornell belted out in laughter. "Like moms know anything about that kind of thing." Cornell, giggling, was the first to begin to ride away. As he rolled down the drive, he continued to chuckle. "Bye Mom! Good try anyway!"

Zack and Darwin snickered to themselves at what their mother had said, but attempted to maintain some form of composure. Zack moved to his bike and straddled the seat and almost instantly began to push off. Following the path of his younger brother, Zack began to roll away from the house down the long driveway. Cornell was already on the road continuing to move away from his brothers, slowly but constantly. All that remained near the house was the calm breeze and the silence that passed between Marie and Darwin. Mother and son took a moment to look at each other one last time.

"Darwin, you better catch up with your brothers." Marie walked over to her son and gave him a kiss on his head. Before saying anything more she turned away, to wipe a tear that was forming in the crevasse of her eye. It was a bittersweet moment for her. Her children, her men, were leaving her side. It gave her pride to see how well her boys had matured despite the odds that had been working against them. Before Marie retired to her kitchen to clean the remnants of the camp out feast she turned to give some encouragement to her baby boy. "Get some good pictures of that beast *hun*! She paused for a moment to hear her son's response, but rolling away, his response was drowned out by the sound of the wheels. As an afterthought Marie added. "And watch out for the bears!" But again, her words seemed to evaporate into the evening air, never reaching Darwin's ears.

CHAPTER 2

The wind was picking up; restless fall leaves from the Maple tree tumbled across the ground at the bare human feet of a very naked and cold Darwin. The edge of the wind struck the tops of the trees pushing them side-to-side making them moan and creak with pain. The sounds echoed through the woods unobstructed. A musical chorus played through the treetops, changing at the speed of the wind. The sounds in the woods grew. The sky was about to release its will on the forest.

EEEEEECHHHHH! Swooping down from the nearby maple a large barn owl flew towards Darwin's head; claws extended, eyes focused and the sound of intent emanating from its beak.

"Ah AHH!" Darwin shrieked, hitting the ground barely able to avoid the attacking owl. The large, gray, feathery object passed over Darwin within a foot of his naked body. The owl continued shrieking, off into the southern woods looking for more manageable prey.

Darwin focused for a minute; his heart was racing. Remaining on all fours he caught his breath. His senses were heightening; he could feel it. He could almost sense the owl's emotion. The impressions from the bird were unclear and yet familiar. Was the owl trying to attack, or was the owl trying to flee from the coming wind?

On the horizon of the northern sky, light clouds were beginning to move in, maybe the owl knew something he didn't. And then it hit him. It began as a few flashes of white light, and then imagery began to take form from the shadows within the light. The pictures flared in and out of his brain as though it was a nightmare, the pictures were familiar. The images came to him faster. A tree, a shred of blue cloth, a presence in the night, a forest coming alive, something watching, something stalking. The flood gates in his mind were opening wider, the images were coming alive; he had lived them before. His mind began to show him what he had forgotten.

*   *   *

"What was that!?!" Cried Cornell who now cowered in the shadow of the rock. Something was in the woods. It had been there for a while. It lurked, waiting to make its move. Somewhere, to the north of the camp, beyond the Maple tree, a sound could be heard, almost indistinguishable. The more the three boys focused their ears on it, the less it could be heard. The weather was changing and so was the forest. The sleeping giant deep within the darkness was growing angry. It was just before one in the morning.

Much of their evening prior to this uninvited disturbance had been spent in traditional camping fashion. Darwin and Cornell had erected the three-man dome tent, in record time, even before the sun had set. Zack, as holder of the Zippo lighter, had set out on building the campfire and gathering wood. By nine o'clock that evening the boys were seated around a raging fire, doing boy things.

First gorging on the sandwiches, they had consumed more than twenty within the first hour. A daring contest, with the egg salad sandwiches as the center of the torment, became a source of great fun for the boys. Run through the woods bare-assed or eat an egg salad sandwich, this was the decision that faced young Darwin. His mother would have been proud; the boy ate the egg sandwich without making one EWWWW or ICCK! More typical boy conversations floated around the fire that evening: What would you do if a girl kissed you? Who would you like to kiss the most? Have you ever gone number two outdoors and it wasn't in an outhouse? Have you ever wondered why Superman chose to be good, rather than evil? It was all very simple and innocent.

Around eleven, a foul odor erupted from Darwin's behind which prompted his brothers to wrestle over the remaining egg sandwiches, their mother would have been proud. When the air cleared enough and the silence grew around the camp, the boys began relating ghost stories. The stories themselves were not frightening in any way. A dark desolate road with an unknown hitchhiker, an escaped mental patient, a haunted house, and an alien abduction: every story, although attempting to be scary, usually ended in laughter as someone else let out one more long juicy egg fart. Oddly, Zack never tried telling the story of the beast.

Darwinism

It abruptly ended around midnight when a loud, moan moved through the camp. It was first blamed on Zack who refuted the accusations; but the moan returned. They realized it came from the woods. Each boy quieted, directing one ear to the northern woods, where each had agreed, the noise was originating. Their attention had been drawn to the sounds that continued only quietly, but their fears were rising, and Zack knew he had to do something.

"It was probably a bat." The confidence had drained from Zack's voice having suggested it was a bat more times than he cared to recall. He had heard the noises too, but he had to assure his brothers that nothing was there.

"But what if it's the creature?" Young Darwin whimpered.

"I don't think it's the creature, I've heard it before, it's definitely not him. I bet it's a couple of deer; I'll go scare them off. " Terrified as hell, Zack rose to his feet to begin his journey into the darkness. Holding the largest flashlight, he left the comfort of their blazing fire, and began to edge ever so slowly north. Each step away from the fire made Zack realize how unready he had been, to camp over night, to care for his brothers and to be *the man.* In his mind he secured himself with the fact that sunrise was only four and a half hours away. If he could just prove it was a deer, or a branch or nothing at all he was sure he could convince his siblings there was nothing to fear. If only he could convince himself.

Briefly, an hour before, after the sounds had started, he was certain he had seen something. His certainty did not stretch into the specifics: a shadow, a figure, a movement, a haze, but he had seen something. It appeared only for a second; and maybe it had been less than a second. Next to the bikes, around seven feet in the air, something hovered. Red. Yellow. The colors he saw were brilliant against the moonlight, two small penetrating orbs. They were gone as soon as he had laid eyes on them. *Were they eyes?* There were no animals in these woods, with the exception of some avian, marmots, squirrels and the occasional deer. As Zack edged his way towards the woods he could hear the sounds much clearer. On the edge of the doorstep of darkness an intense fear began to dwell within him. The light from the fire dimmed with each step, adding to his unease.

Darwin and Cornell remained at each other's side and watched as their brother's image began to fade into the darkness. Neither boy uttered a sound. All that could be heard was the sound of a crackling fire, a weak whimper and the rumble of the forest's stomach.

"Go away!" Was all Zack could think to say to the on looking woods. His feeble attempt at frightening the shadow had done more to increase his own anxiety. The flashlight swung from left to right in an attempt to keep light on the entire forest in front of the boy. Every sound, real, fake or imagined brought a new direction for the torch. He had seen nothing, nothing at all, but the sounds continued to grow. Under his feet the sounds of the pebbles shifted and scraped against one another. Every attempt to walk slower and quieter created more noise making the indistinguishable sounds more illusive than before.

Zack realized he was now within a few feet of the maple, where he had seen the glowing *eyes*. His fear began to diminish, replaced with a curiosity. The directions of his beaming torch began to focus on the tree directly ahead. The maple stood in front of him, at the base were the tightly secured bikes. Zack stopped. Something was different; something had changed. The bikes had one continuous chain looping in-between the wheels, weaving in and out circumventing the entire tree. Each bike leaned against the tree, the front wheel of one bike touching the rear wheel of the next bike. The bikes were as they had been, still chained, and still secured. What was different? Something had been disturbed, and yet everything looked as it had before. Leaving the bikes he began edging his way forward passed the clearing of the camp and entering the woods beyond. He knew the sound was near.

The sound was breathing, labored breathing. Crackles of the fire were now gone, and the pebbles under his feet had silenced; the sound from the woods was becoming clear. Sputtering; a weak cough; a gasp for air, a wheeze as it was exhaled. Zack was certain what he was hearing was alive, and injured. The darkness of the woods remained surreptitious. Now standing just beyond the Maple tree, he gazed onwards into the piercing wind that flowed from deep within the woods. The wind had begun as though a door had been opened allowing a punishing current through. It pushed against Zack, harder and harder with each step. But his drive past the maple could not be prevented. In the distance he could see.

Zack again shone the torch from left to right illuminating even deeper parts of the woods. Behind him, the campfire and his brothers were but a speck in the distance and the maple was growing smaller too.

RED! YELLOW!

The teen froze; within twenty feet he could see the eyes of something. The color was mesmerizing, almost hypnotic: red and yellow, blue and orange. The orbs hovered within two feet of the ground, and they did not motion. The sound of the injured could still be heard. It was nothing more than a stammering, still labored, but more so than before. The two points of brilliant light began to sway back and forth, no longer focused on the movements of Zack. Something within him said it was safe to press forward, he felt assured of his own safety. Another part of Zack, asked, pleaded and begged to turn back to the camp. It was his feet that decided to press on, in a shuffle, ever so slowly, propulsive.

Two sounds; a new sound entirely, hidden beneath the breathing. Zack

Darwinism

was near, but not close enough for him to describe it. The flashlight pointed directly at the orbs, which were now appearing and disappearing, moving slowly from side to side, up and down. The energy of the torch dispersed, shattering, unable to illuminate its target. Zack strained his eyes and ears to block out all other stimuli, even the punishing wind was being ignored. Nothing would stop his advance deeper into the woods. Nothing would stop him from gaining the knowledge he was within a few steps of.

A dog? Was it a dog he could hear? The sound was growing clear. Slurp. Snort. Grunt. Was this animal eating? Eating? What?

An object revealed itself to Zack, very slowly an outline of something under the glowing eyes, something large, appeared. Another animal. The labored breathing was coming from this other animal.

SNAP! And a second later, CRASH! Wind was attacking fiercely from within the woods. Branches from nearby trees gave at the force of the breeze, one after the other. Zack hardly noticed the sound of the falling limbs, but he did take notice to the change in the wind direction. Once blowing in his face, the potent wind was now blowing from underneath, from the ground up. It was passing under him, up between the trees, acting as a wedge creating a hole into the night sky. Moonlight drifted through the opening in the sky bringing up the brightness. A glow around the trees was developing as the light bounced from branch to branch. And an outline began to appear, the eyes of color had begun to gain dimension.

Two feet. Three feet. Four feet. Five feet. The eyes moved upward, higher and higher. Six feet. Seven feet. The creature was immense, towering over the animal below. The moon illuminated the beast. Cold and numb, Zack extended his arm and aimed the torch at the rest of the towering creature. The orbs were affixed to a head of an animal, unlike any normal animal he had seen before. The creature, covered in hair, had a canine shaped head with a snout nearly a foot long. The head of the animal was a solid two feet wide, maybe more. The ears protruded five to six inches into the sky. A set of brilliantly white teeth gilded the snout, long, sharp and in great numbers. Zack began lowering his arm spreading relevance to the lower extremities. Below the head was a body heavy with hair, thick, coarse and very dark. Two limbs, thwart with the long brown hair, drooped at the animal's side. At the end of the limbs were long knife like fingers that could only be described as a kind of claws. Lowering the light yet further down on the dark creature more oddities became clear. Under the coat of hair the animal displayed a clearly defined set of muscles. By appearance alone one could tell the powerful strength the animal possessed. The stomach of the animal was ribbed like a washboard. At the mid section the animal revealed its sex; the beast was male.

Mark Fuson

The coldness that had enveloped the boy began to disperse. Warmness flowed down his left leg. His urination went unnoticed. Zack's eyes were lowering faster, leaving behind the towering animal and finding the source of the original sound that had drawn him into the woods in the first place. The wounded lay at the hind legs of the beast. His prey lay cumbersome, helpless and dying. It was not an animal. It should be, but it wasn't. Fear returned to the teen as his feet began pulling him towards the injured.

"You bastard. What have you done?" Zack muttered to the creature that stood still fixated on the approaching boy. "What the FUCK have you done!" His fear was turning into rage. The teen was furious at what he had seen. His blood was boiling, and his palms were dripping with sweat. Unsure what to do, Zack stopped and knelt down to the ground, keeping his right hand with the light on the carnivorous animal. Zack began clawing at the dirt trying to find or uproot a stone with his left hand. He dug in with great effort pushing through the dirt, leaves and moss. Scraping frantically until he hooked on to what felt like a palm sized rock. The boy began pulling, tugging and gripping on the object imbedded in the soil. And then it gave way, it a tearing motion a cold chill passed through his body as he fell over. Lying on his back with the torch unmoved from his target he glanced at his hand quickly. Blood had begun leaking from his knuckles and several of his fingernails were badly chipped and torn. His middle fingernail had been completely torn away, but in his palm lay one good size stone. Without standing, Zack took aim at the creature. With one swing the stone was released from his hand and shot forward moving upward towards the animal's head.

WACK!

The stone bounced harmlessly off a tree more than five feet away from the animal.

Zack began to whimper. "Go away!!! LEAVE! You!" A boy stumbled to his feet to emerge a man. Rushing toward the animal, Zack began shouting every obscenity he had ever heard his sister Marta proclaim. "I'll kill you, I will fucking kill you. Jesus fucking Christ I will end you!" Stopping just short of the animal, Zack released his last weapon, his torch. As the stone had, the light also began to fly at that the enormity of the creature. Different areas of the forest were lit from the light of the twirling torch on its path to the target.

Zack's eyes never actually saw it happen. The towering beast that hovered over its victim was now holding in its claws the flashlight that Zack had thrown. This brute now grasped firmly in his hand the torch and aimed it squarely at Zack. The light blinded him; all but the orbs were now masked by the white light. Zack looked on at the animal with hate. This was no animal, he knew what this *thing* was, but he was not ready to accept it.

The eyes had drawn him in; he was drifting into its control. Each stood motionless. Moments passed and the world around them had silenced. Zack stared blindly into the light of the torch, unable to say anything. The tunnel of light became mesmerizing; the world around him was disappearing. The longer he looked into the light the less he could see of the real world. And then the white light swathed him...

CHAPTER 3

I'd forgotten.

The flood of images in Darwin's mind began to subside. His heart rate began to slow. Never before had he experienced a psychic moment like this. His mind was back from that night so long ago. He had been there, and yet he had forgotten so much of what had transpired. Darwin cocked his head toward the sky to see the moon, which was now partially obstructed with clouds. Unsure of how long his flashback had lasted Darwin decided to check his watch, which now lay on top of his jeans near the rock. He knew it couldn't be much longer until he changed, but he was uncertain how long his flashback had actually gone on for. It was another part to his *gift* he had thought, a part of his supernatural gift that for the first time felt more like a curse than a gift. He was uncertain of everything he had witnessed in his vision. The entire vision was from his brother's point of view, and not everything he had seen in his vision was consistent with what he knew.

Looking at his watch Darwin could see it was just before seven-thirty. There are three moons a month that Darwin transformed for. On the second night of the full moon, when the moon was at its fullest, it was normal for him to change a little earlier than on other nights. This was the second night of the full moon and already he had maintained his human form almost ten minutes longer than the previous evening. His vision must have lasted nearly fifteen minutes, he thought. Could that have delayed it? Standing, holding his watch, Darwin became perplexed. He realized he was feeling different

24

than he had before. He knew what the change felt like, but that feeling had almost gone from him. Even his one physical warning of the change had withered away. Looking down at his groin, his saw his penis had once again returned to a flaccid state. More puzzled, and colder than ever, Darwin made a choice. After standing in the clearing a few minutes longer, he decided to dress once again.

What's happening? Darwin kept thinking to himself over and over. Would he sit here until morning, or should he return home? Would that be safe? He was able to exert some control while he was his alter ego, but only very basic commands. Go left. Go right. But he found his mind was easily distracted and in the morning his brain suffered from a haze that made him question even his ability to go right and left during his lunar activities. He had never killed, not a human at least. He had watched the news for reports of missing people, and there had been none. If he returned home tonight and the change came much later he was sure no one would get hurt. The first couple of times he had changed he was in town or at home, and nothing bad had happened. His only concern about returning home was being discovered for what he was. In the back of his mind a growing curiosity existed: What would killing a human be like? But more so, he simply wanted to try it.

WWHHHOOOOO, WHHHOOOOO! The owl had returned once again; perched clearly on the branch of a nearby tree looking north.

Darwin yelled up to the bird. "How's your night going?"

WWHHHOOOOOOOOOO! The owl squawked back.

"Yeah, me too." Darwin realizing he was talking to a bird began to chuckle to himself. "I guess neither of us is getting rodent for dinner tonight," chuckling a little more. "Damn, I was really looking forward to it too! Ah, the hell with this, you're on your own tonight Hootie! Maybe I'll see you tomorrow, but beware, I might feel like having owl for dinner!" The reality of his situation was too much; he began a deep belly laugh from the pit of his stomach as he headed up the path leading out of the clearing.

Hootie pushed off the branch and began its second attempt at Darwin, this time catching him off guard. Darwin, still chuckling to himself, raised his head to see a mound of feathers and claws flying down the path on an even glide plane with his head. The owl's claws grazed the side of Darwin's cheek opening a deep gash as the feathered object passed to Darwin's right. The power of the impact proved stunning, by the time Darwin had regained his balance, *Hootie* was perched on the maple, waiting.

"What the fuck was that for?!" He yelled at the owl that was now seated on a limb of the maple tree, continuing its provocative behavior. A stream of blood was now pouring down his cheek splattering the upper collar and breast area of his coat. Reflexive, he cupped his hand over the wound to slow the flow of blood. He held his cheek, staring at the owl with anger in his eye. Squeezing and pushing at his wound, drawing out the pain, he began to feel a fire burning in his stomach. With every contraction of his fist pushed more and more coagulated black fluid from his body. Each intrusion his finger made into his wound brought more pain, more anger and something else. He glared intently to the northern woods where the owl remained. The owl cocked its head, shifting from side to side, looking impatient.

Who, Whooooooo! Once again the bird departed the safety of its high perch, choosing a northerly course into the heart of the woods. Screaming and shrieking as it went until its sounds were absorbed by the growing wind.

Left to the solitude of the clearing Darwin could feel his anger running from him. He withdrew his fingers from his now closing wound. Glancing at his hand he could see he had lost a large amount of blood, and much of his clothing was now a lost cause. Blood rolled from his hand down the sleeve of his coat, even in the darkness of night he could tell his jeans had been stained too. He would have to hit a dry cleaner in the morning before the stain got too badly set.

Injuries did not take long to begin to heal since he had been marked. He could feel his cheek stretching and sealing itself; the blood that had been leaving his body in a torrent was now completely stopped. His face sounded like a rubber band being stretched to its threshold. Creaking, and pinging he could feel the severed skin reconnect itself. The sensation was almost a little ticklish. Both ends began to seal up like a zipper, meeting in the center of what was only seconds before a hospital worthy injury. Even the scar that remained on his cheek would itself be gone by morning.

In the distance, beyond the maple, Darwin's eyes began to present something. From within the woods, a light was growing; a cool colorless radiance was exploding outward in slow motion. It was expanding. With every blink of his eyes the anomaly seemed to grow infinitesimally larger. The light was consuming everything it touched, growing outward, drawing in all the surrounding dark matter. Fixated on the center of the light, Darwin could make out no details, no deviations in the color, and no features of any kind, the light was simply there. It pulled on him; he had to be in the light. The feeling consumed him; the hold of the light over him was even stronger than the pull of the moon. Darwin felt the weight from his feet disappear and the ground began to pass beneath his shoes, effortless. The light grew larger in his eyes until in one flash he was once again gone, to another time and place.

*   *   *

Through the haze, Zack could see blue and white. Blinding white light and something blue. His head ached worse than it ever had before and his eye's

Darwinism

inability to focus made the pain that much worse. He was cold, he couldn't feel most of his extremities, and even his ears seemed unable to work.

He was lying in the woods. Dawn had come and rain was falling heavy through the trees already having soaked the boy to the bone. What had happened, a fog blockaded his thoughts, nothing was clear. Pushing on the ground Zack propped himself up. More pain shot through his arm as he erected himself upwards. He was seeing blue and white, and now some green. Zack shut his eyes for a moment, giving them time to adjust. As he reopened them the second time images began to present themselves. A flashlight stuck in the wishbone of a tree branch, still shone brilliantly, it had been shining in his eyes all night. Scanning the area he saw a disturbed area of soil near him. He remembered digging; he had hurt his hand. Zack raised his hand to his face, his knuckles were badly scraped, bruised and were covered in dry blood. It was coming clear.

The forest looked as it always had, green and lush. He remembered having seen a creature, but had it been real? His hand seemed to verify at least that memory. He remembered he had wet himself while confronting whatever had been with him during the night. Ashamed, the boy began to tear-up. Then it started coming back to him, he remembered what had made him so angry, what he had seen. The creature had frightened him but what the creature had done had infuriated him. Zack again shut his eyes and began rotating his head into position where he was afraid he would again find his source of fury. Slowly he began opening his eyes, blue began to reveal as his eyelids rose. But as quickly as the blue had rushed in to fill his vision, it disappeared. In its wake nothing was there. Moss, leaves and some twigs, but nothing remained at all. The area seemed pristine and untouched.

Gasping, choking for air, young Zack had again cocooned into a child. Weeping, the boy covered his eyes; relieved, terrified, he sobbed openly.

"Zack, are you okay? Where did you go last night?" A small hand placed itself on the shoulder of the weeping boy. Young Darwin followed by Cornell Foster knelt down next to their brother. The children sat there in the rain while their older brother wept. Zack said nothing.

CHAPTER 4

Darwin found himself in a blank state, standing in the woods. It was familiar, even in the dark. He was no longer standing in the clearing; he found himself somewhere north of the maple tree. It was the same spot he had found his older brother on the morning after the camping trip.

His vision had brought a lot of questions into his mind. He was hesitant to accept everything he had seen. Had his brother seen another werewolf? Darwin only had a vague understanding of that night; his own memories were clouded and distant.

"FUCK ME!" Darwin in a fluster grabbed his wrist and looked at the face of his glow-faced watch. Eight-seventeen; nearly an hour had been lost and now the sensation had returned. "Fucking bizarre night!"

His jeans were ready to burst at the groin. His lunar erection was in full force; the change was coming, starting. Without a moment to react, it began.

The muscles throughout his body: head, arms, legs, ass, groin, came alive with a tingle in unison. A creak and pop in every cell, follicle, bone and tissue came with the stabbing moonlight. An erotic sweat erupted from his forehead, pooling down his cheeks and rolling off the stubbles of his chin. In and out, his chest rose and fell, hot clouds of steam exhaled from his panting mouth. The vapor propelled outwards from his mouth, further and further with each breath with the help of his expanding lungs.

A light-headedness and euphoric state swept over Darwin. He no

Darwinism

longer had the will to even try to save his clothing. His body was now being stimulated as though it had been injected with a lethal dose of adrenaline, he could not control or fight it; he did not want to. Within his jeans the first spasm began. Contained under the fabric only for the moment, his member began to erratically pulsate in an explosion causing the man to gasp and bawl at the top of his vocal capacity. Shouting in pleasure, shouting in desire, his orgasm began spreading. The climax spread to his left arm - a spasm followed causing another burst of energy to rush through his body. Next his calf muscle twitched, beginning another series of proclamations of pleasure and bliss that penetrated the heart of the woods. Each climatic outbreak that began did not cease, each new paroxysm spread, the stimulations made Darwin feel as though a thousand hands explored every inch of his body; and there was nothing he couldn't do. Hundreds of sultry evenings of self-exploration pushed into one sudden release of sexual joy would not near the feeling rushing through his muscles. Satisfaction, confidence, assuredness, and determination filled his mind. The world's greatest fuck was about to get a little bit better.

The epidemic of vibrations continued, now consuming him. Even his head felt masturbated. Darwin stood, with a gay expression washed over his eyes, ogling at nothing but seeing everything. The strength began to fill his muscles, he could feel it; it was like a drug he craved, he needed it. His entire mass quaked in unison causing his muscles to expand outward. Under the blood soaked coat a body began to sharpen, to form into something better. Moving outward: his pectoral muscles, breastplate, rigid shoulders, biceps, forearms, back and spinal ridges all began widening, growing, mounting their expansive assault, making way for their rebirth. The fabric covering his human body began to retreat away from the advancing muscles; the fabric grew taut and stiff all over. Every piece of available cloth began to fill with a growing weight behind it. Within the denim pants powerful hind muscles pushed their way flush with the material, being momentarily stopped by the stitch work – but only for a moment. Under the enclosure of his pants the metamorphosis also began to take hold in his erogenous zones. A once soft and round buttock had now grown solid pushing hard on the seams, a thickening fuzz extending outwards from his anus. His large throbbing member continued expelling his inhuman seed with tremendous force and pressure. Each expulsion enlarged the penis, longer, wider; it too sought release from the hold of the clothing.

Release was beginning.

Euphoria slowed for a moment, contained and held by fabric at every corner. Distracted, but conscious enough, Darwin managed to drop the last piece of loose clothing down to the ground, his jacket.

"Arg-AH, FUCK," the inhuman voice spoke, not quite beast but not quite man. "Shoes! The Shoes." Planted firmly to the ground the human feet also began to lengthen. Come morning, a human once again, Darwin could expect a long cold walk from out of the woods, and how far that may be, even he did not know.

The sound of fabric breaking and giving way began to echo in his ears. The closures around the arms and shoulders began to tear away; white-olive skin immediately pushed its way through. Small hairs bore through the skin in growing numbers. Buttons down the front of the shirt were being tugged left and right, threads holding for as long as they could, gave way, firing into the nearby night exposing a growing and defining chest. Hammer like arms ate through the remaining cloth of the shirt, shredding the fabric to the point it hung pathetically off the body it once housed. A mountainous torso with light brown hairs pushing through the surface now sat under the human head of Darwin Foster.

Shoelaces constricted the forming hind paws within the footwear but now even the solid leather casing and laced harness was giving way. Toes, heels, sides; all broke open, releasing feet with more animal characteristics than human. Small, sharp razor like toenails tore through the shoes and socks as though the footwear had been made of tissue paper. Fine hairs pushed their way to the surface of the lengthening paw-foot. A distinct hunch in the feet began to bend the forming hind paws. The heel and ankles distending upwards began increasing the height of the once average sized man.

Unmoved by his metamorphosis, Darwin continued to grin with pleasure as his humanity was consumed. Through his eyes the colors of the woods heightened, losing the darkness that had concealed it, trees, sleeping birds and watching pray all shifted into his visual spectrum. Crunching cartilage, a snapping in the jaw, and a shifting set of cheekbones, signalled the early beginnings of the coming canine snout. Opening his mouth wider his incisors began to elongate. New, radiant white, teeth pushed out from his upper and lower gum line shoving aside the inferior human teeth. Stubble on his face slowly forced outward from his skin creating an unshaven appearance. A man-monster grinned intently at the demonic possession consuming his soul; the devilish features growing from his face were a warning, a warning to all. Run. The innocence of Darwin Foster was changing. Every facial feature was broadening; his once youthful complexion was being taken away, replaced by another.

A rip formed down both thighs, the skin emerging was heavy in light brown hair. The bottom of the pant legs now hovered more than a foot off the ground exposing his now completely hair covered shins. Upward, his body grew, much taller than he had been before. Giving up, the remaining denim

Darwinism

came apart in one rapid tear, exposing his changing: calves, thighs, buttock and now softening but still sticky member.

Remains of the torn shirt drifted off the body revealing the completely nude and coming creature. Transformation persisted, the last human areas were assimilating fast; the monster would be stalking the woods soon.

A path of hairs that lead from his pubic line, up over his prized six-pack and continued on to the valley between his pectorals was rustling in fast. The hair slid through the skin to surface almost as though they had always been there. With ease they continued to spread across the ripped, massive body. Arms, legs, back, ass, genitals, feet; the onslaught of hair growth pushed across every inch of the body hiding and remaking the person he had been. Rapid puberty devoured the human, accelerating, growing, expanding, maturing, it was perfection.

Panting, it huffed in amusement, the laugh of the beast. A deep panting and growl was coming from an ever-extending snout. The sounds of pleasure that had begun with Darwin were continuing with the newly born creature. What stood in the woods now was not an animal, but a monster.

From the tips of the fingers one of the final traces of humankind were changed. Claws extended out from what had been fingertips, pushing overtop of the old human fingernails over two inches in length. The new digits that had poked out had but one use, to slice through living flesh. Soon they would have a whole forest to explore.

A head, now more than two feet across, rested on the towering muscular body. The fangs of the beast dripped with anticipation of the first meal of the night. Ears rose through the think mat of hair on the animal's head, cartilage still snapping and shattering. The sounds of blood filled creatures flowed into the brain, awakening the primal instincts within. Little independent thought of Darwin remained within the animal; the beast stood where Darwin had been only because the monster chose to. Glowing orbs now peered into the night. A werewolf was born.

A long howl filled the night air. Unlike anything a dog or a wolf might make, the sound was unique. A deep toned shriek consumed the night air flustering the sleeping birds. Trees and the neighboring wilderness stretched for hundreds of miles, this would be his playground until morning.

CHAPTER 5

It was a branch load of snow that hit Darwin Foster in the head that aroused him from his slumber. Startled, the young man bolted up from his cozy nest he had made under the tree. A bed of twigs and moss were piled under a large cedar tree where Darwin's alter ego had apparently decided to rest for the evening. The sub zero air of the morning bounced off his still hot skin; the reversion to his human form always left him burning up. The cold of this morning would strip away at his searing radiance in a matter of minutes.

About a foot of snow had fallen during the night, and it was still snowing, but only gently. Looking around he could see the track of large animal prints in the snow leading up to the tree. It occurred to him he had no idea how far into the woods he had traveled. He focused on his actions during his time as the wolf, but he could remember nothing. The taste of blood was still heavy in his mouth although he still felt oddly hungry. With no shoes, no clothes and no idea where he was, he realized he might be in for a long morning.

Without thinking or giving further contemplation to his situation, Darwin jumped up from his nest and began hurrying through the woods, backtracking his own wolf path. He felt great; as he always did when he reverted back to human form, but he could not help worry about how long it would take him to exit the woods. He wasn't even sure what time it was, the sun was up and it was bright, but snowy days often seemed brighter. Moving at a brisk speed through the snow he could already feel his bare feet going numb. He quickened his pace but he could not help but agonize at his

Darwinism

predicament. How far? How long? It all kept racing through his mind like a skipping record. As the cold found ways to enter his body Darwin focused all his strength of his mind. One thought only sat in his intellect. It repeated over and over like a computer program with an unfinished task.

Warning! Severe heat loss detected! Complete command process breakdown in progress. Reserve energy will be depleted in four minutes seventeen seconds.

The warnings repeated like a science fiction television show.

Must find an exit. Must find a way home. Distress signal. Home, home, failure.

The forest whipped by unnoticed to Darwin who, after only minutes on the trail, was struggling. The cold had eaten through his outer warmth and like locus was now after what inner warmth remained. With his eyes fixated solely on the trail, Darwin took no notice of nearby Mount Whitley, which made appearances every few hundred feet through the snow-clogged trees. The slender mountain peek was not the tallest in the area but the most noteworthy. Mount Whitley was a narrow jagged piece of granite that stretched high above the valley floor. Only a few trees adorned the sides of the rock, which set it apart from all other nearby mountains. It was the only mountain at some distance that could be seen from downtown New Haven. Moreover, had Darwin taken any notice to Mount Whitley he might have recalled the old rail line circumvented the base of the mountain, the very same railroad bed Darwin followed into the woods the previous evening. Something prevented Darwin from looking up that morning; it was as though he had become guided only by his instincts.

Ten minutes into his pursuit for warmth, the tracks were lost, swallowed by the swift rapids, frozen boulders and miniature icebergs of a strong moving river. Darwin was barricaded from the southern bank. It was 100 feet across, at least, and the depth remained unknown. On other side of the river in the snow was a clear outline of tracks that could be seen leading back into the woods. He had crossed here hours before, but it would be nearly impossible for the near mortal to attempt it.

"Well this is fucking great. I really got to work on controlling myself at night." He barked in annoyance. Dipping his toes into the water Darwin began to realize the gravity of his situation. Sharp penetrating icicles severed the feeling within his toes on contact. The sheer movement of the flowing water suggested his fragile little body, should it adapt to the immense cold, would likely be swept away by the current. Little bumps rippled across on his now stiffening skin. Holding himself in an attempt to slow the loss of heat, he weighed his situation.

"What river is this? The Thompson? The Thompson is way the fuck and gone...can't be: it can't be the Thompson. It doesn't matter, I crossed it; I have to cross it again."

Tap dancing back and forth, his concern grew.

"FUCK I'M COLD! Jesus Christ I can't feel my feet. Okay, It can't hurt me, it can pain me, but it can't hurt me. I just do it! The faster I get across it the sooner I will be home having a hot shower. Fuck what I wouldn't give for a hot shower right now."

With both feet forward Darwin leapt into the frigid water. The venom of the liquid ice withdrew every source of heat on contact. A body shudder developed and the clatter of dental work began. Wading deeper and deeper into the water Darwin focused on the southern bank, his goal. Fifteen feet out and river water had reached his upper shins, and at twenty feet his lower thighs were submerged. Darwin tried to lengthen his stride but the chill of the water had become a heavy drain on his energy. His legs pushed through the current, each stride becoming shorter than the last. At the center, the depth plunged. The crest of water now stabbing at his mid sections had severed Darwin's sexual organ making it retract to a pre-pubescent size. Holding his arms tightly to his body a feeling of exhaustion began to overtake him. His pace was slowing, every ounce of strength was now devoted to maintaining his position in the river. The oncoming water impelled upon Darwin's side, numbing and depleting his will. The southern bank was no closer: the tracks, the snow, and the woods, all remained stationary. Standing motionless in the river, hypothermia was setting in. Color in his skin was washing away to a ghostly bluish gray; around his mouth a frost had formed around the corners of his now bluing lips. He could feel none of his lower extremities, and his upper extremities were fading fast; he was dying.

In the near distance an image appeared. The familiar figure stood firmly in place on the stationary bank laughing.

"Steve! Fuck, help me, Steve!" Darwin shouted to the image that he recognized as his friend who continued to stand scornfully at the embankment of the river. His friend had followed him, Darwin was unsure how or why, but it did not matter. Throughout the years Steve and Darwin had been extremely close. Each always seemed to know what the other was thinking; maybe Steve had followed Darwin the night before? Did Steve know Darwin's dark secret? Did Steve share in Darwin's secret?

"You really fucked up this time didn't you D!" Steve guffawed at his friend. "Man, you are so fucking stupid. Just because you're immortal doesn't mean invulnerable! So what are you going to do to get yourself out of this situation?" Steve stood with one foot on a boulder, leaning forward smiling at his naked friend seeing the life draining with each lapping wave.

Darwin watched his friend stand at the bank continuing to do nothing.

Steve was standing within forty feet and yet he was making no motions or indications he would help. Annoyed, Darwin grumbled. "Never mind asshole, I'll get across on my own!" He had barely moved one step southward when he felt his balance shifting. Leaning downstream, Darwin shifted all his weight to his one stable leg trying to regain his fledgling balance. "Oh shit! STEVE!"

"That's it my boy, get angry, it's the only way." Steve's words floated across the raging river to a rapidly immersing Darwin. Unintentionally heeding his friend's suggestion, a fire began to burn within. Darwin glared at the southern bank, which now stood empty; Steve was gone.

Losing his footing, Darwin felt his foot lift from the gravel of the river and found himself drifting ever faster down stream. Floating on his back all Darwin could see was the treetops, water, sky and snowflakes. Everything twirled magically around his head. His mind grew cloudy, he couldn't concentrate; he could do nothing but let the river take him. .

STEVE! You're my friend, why, why, why? Oh Christ help me, why won't you help me! You're never there for me. I've always been there for you! You think I don't know about you! I know, I know too well. You. You. You. Warning, life, li-failing...

A cloud gripped around his thoughts. The fluency in his mind had become fragmented. The thoughts came to him in pieces, random thoughts and moments in time. Verbalizing his thoughts came out like the ravings of a lunatic. His vision had gone milky white; he could see nothing but fog with a blur of color to it. The sounds were changing from a roar, to a gurgle, to a splash, back to a compressed fluidic sound.

One thought came to him clearly. *Get angry, it's the only way.* Why had Steve told him to get angry? Feeling a warmness growing in his body, part of Darwin realized he was in the final moments of hypothermia. Another clear thought raced across his brain. *I'm immortal; I cannot die!* Darwin knew something was wrong, he could feel his life ebbing away from him. He sensed his heart rate slowing and his exhaustion had taken its toll. He wanted for nothing more than to go to sleep. Sleep. Just to sleep.

FUCK I AM DYING! Pulling his conscience back from the brink of oblivion, Darwin struggled futilely. Thrashing in the water, he was awakening, but he knew he didn't have long before death would again be pulling him back in. The water continued dragging him along. Growing deeper, rougher and stronger the river grabbed at Darwin's thrashing feet bringing him under completely. A powerful undertow pinned Darwin to the side of a boulder. Frantic, Darwin knew he was now trapped and his held breath was not enough to sustain him for long. Looking up through the crystal clear water he could see the surface, the air that he was in dire need of. The water felt as though it had wrapped restraints around him. He was frozen in place, unable to stir.

Anger. Frustration. Hatred. All grew within his dying body. Images of murder, death and carnage flowed freely through the remnants of his brain. He wanted nothing more than to make someone feel as he did. He wanted nothing more than to hurt the people of his youth. He wanted to eat them; drink their blood; taste their sumptuous flesh. He relished in the sounds they would scream, the pleading; the begging that would flow from their pathetic mouths as he tore into their muscles. Snapping through the brittle bones he would lick the marrow from them while he made his victim watch. He would do things, horrible things. Things that would make a serial killer turn away in disgust. His rage at his quandary rose to unimaginable levels. He could not die. He would not die! His gift had brought him here; his gift would release him from his underwater prison. His rage was peaking, glaring up at the surface, a wave a searing heat passed through his body. Focused on the surface Darwin imagined himself raising through the water. Nothing was in his way, the water would become air and the current would be his guide. He continued to struggle, pushing with his feet trying to gain elevation in the water. At first his rage changed nothing; he stayed planted squarely against the underwater rock. Again his feet dug into the gravel, pushing upwards, ever so slowly his body started to break free from the surge.

The river came back at Darwin, counteracting his movements at escape. Sinking back into the hold of the rock he began imagining the strength he felt when he changed. He imagined his muscles growing and filling with the primitive strength. He needed it; he wanted it. Pushing off from the floor of the river again, his body broke free of the current, and rose to the surface.

When he broke the surface of the water he greeted it with a large breath of air. Free from the depths, but still drifting further downstream, Darwin used his much stronger arms and legs to direct him self towards the southern shore. Moving across the remaining deep water with ease Darwin reached the shallows and marched out of the condemning river. On the shore, looking back he grinned maliciously at the conquered.

"RAAAHAAAHAAA," Darwin snickered to the defeated creek. Towering on the embankment he let out a long deep howl "OWWWWWWWWWHHH." Stopping for a moment he realized something about him was different. He had never growled or made animal noises before, not as a human, and yet he knew he just had. The sounds coming from his voice were also much deeper, hoarser than they had been before. He also thought the river seemed smaller, further away. Glancing down at a relatively calm pool of water a reflection bounced back at him. It was an image that seemed familiar but the image in the water was someone else. Broad, wide shouldered, powerful and hairy; he had partially changed. Staring back at him for the first time was his dark face. Long strands of fine brown hair draped off his face. A partial set of dripping canines protruded from his still human formed mouth. Behind the hair and teeth he could still recognize himself as the person he had been. He maintained awareness, he felt the strength and power flowing through his veins but he was now in control. The cold that had been eating away at his body had now disappeared, he felt warm and vigorous. The rest of his body had also undergone the metamorphosis, in height, muscle mass and hair growth. Under the light coating of fur that covered his body his human skin was still clearly visible. He was caught somewhere between human and monster and he loved this more than ever; raw untapped energy that he could feel and use. A new feeling passed through him as he stood admiring his beauty in the reflecting water, an intense cramping feeling in his stomach forcing him to hunch over to the ground. In waves, the pain hit, tightening its grip around Darwin's stomach. The pain was familiar, never had it been so strong, but he knew what it was.

It was hunger that was clamping down, incapacitating him. He was not sure how he knew, but the thought of raw meat in his mouth brought delight. He knew what he had to do. He was certain what he wanted to do. Rising from the ground he took a moment, smelling the air. An aroma was near and it was delicious. Running into the woods in search of the tantalizing taste, Darwin left behind the idea of escaping the forest, at least for now.

The wolf-man skipped and paraded from tree to tree, remaining upwind of his breakfast. The smell was near, he was uncertain what it was, but it was flesh. He wanted nothing more than to tear his teeth into the flesh and drain the creature of its blood. Darwin became aroused at the prospect of awareness while he killed; part of him had wondered what the feeling was like. A feeling had been growing in his mind in recent weeks that he would like to try eating a human. The curiosity had always existed within him and now suddenly he had been given the chance to go on the hunt. Darwin slinked through the bushes with speed. It was close; he could sense it. What was it?

I want it to be a man! Darwin thought to himself. This thought would later give him concern, but not now, not when the beast was influencing.

Darwin spotted a set of tracks in the snow. A single set of small hoof shaped tracks leading west. Feeling he was close Darwin slowed his advance, preparing for a surprise assault. His heightened instincts had been correct; he was only a few feet behind a young fawn that appeared to be unaware of Darwin's carnivorous approach. Crouching in the shadow of a nearby tree, Darwin scrutinized the creature. He sensed its weakness and inability to defend itself. He could smell where it had been, what it had done. The small animal weighed no more than fifty pounds; it would be a simple meal. The human side of Darwin wondered how he should do it, should he be merciful or should he indulge in his demonic urges. As he thought, the juice from his mouth dripped down his chin. Waiting no more, a decision within Darwin had been made.

On all fours, Darwin leaped over the foliage landing on top of the young deer. The small animal was confined between Darwin's legs before it had a moment to react. Holding the animal with his clawed fingers by the neck, his mouth dove in for the first major artery he could see. His sharp canines and dull human teeth bit into the animal, tugging and ripping his way through the hair into the flesh. Warm salted fluid began filling Darwin's mouth bringing with it contentment. Struggling inside with what he was doing, Darwin hesitated briefly while the animal squealed beneath his legs. Blood gushed across his face while his humanity paused but soon his lust took over and he began to swallow the blood in small gulping motions but it quickly evolved into a primal lapping and slurping movements. The animal slowed its resistance as it became drained of life. Darwin was excited by his actions, in primitive fashion; he ripped into the skin and started devouring the flesh in large moist chunks. Crouched over the now dead animal, Darwin rocked back and forth against the animal in pleasure. He had forever changed who he was.

*   *   *

Hours had passed in a few minutes it had seemed. He was deeper in the woods, he thought, though he wasn't certain. The woods were darkening and the sounds of night were nearing once again. The activities of the day seemed like a dream, he remembered the deer, and something else. He wasn't sure what was impressed upon his memory; it was close to his mind but every time he neared the memory, it dissolved.

At some point in the afternoon Darwin had stumbled across the smell of sulfur thick in the air. Even as the wolf he recognized it. A piece of his geology class had apparently stuck in his mind. The smell of sulfur indicated geological activity, usually a hot spring or geyser. Although he did not recall finding a hot spring, his other half apparently did. When Darwin had awoken in the late afternoon he was sitting in a very warm hot spring pool. The warmth of the water had warded off the re-onset of hypothermia. Sitting comfortably in the soothing water, Darwin realized he would not be leaving the woods today. The moon would again be rising, and by morning he may be even further into the forest than before. For the next few hours he would sit in the hot spring and ponder his actions and await the return of his power.

Although he was a young adult, he still received flack from his mother about calling home if he was going to be late. Darwin had been gone from the house for more than a day. He had left his home shortly after dinner the evening before telling his mother he would not be home until sometime the next day. Darwin wondered what his mother was thinking on this night; he worried that she might have search parties out looking for him. He had told her he was going into the city as part of his work with the cinema which would have normally been a fine lie, but without his return home today, she might begin to investigate, probably by first calling his boss. She would then learn that her son had booked three nights off in a row to go skiing in Arcadia. After comparing notes, his mother and his boss would begin to unravel his web of lies and upon Darwin's reappearance in town - he would face some tough questions.

He realized coming to the woods for his transformation had been a mistake. He should have known better. It had been three months since Darwin had turned and he had changed a total eight times, not including his half man half beast episode in the afternoon. Seven of his transformations occurred at home, work or in town and every morning he had managed to get home without anyone seeing him. On several of his post lunar mornings he had woke miles from his home, and yet he managed to get to his house safely. He wasn't sure why he chose to come to the forest now, after three months of his predatory lunar behavior in town

On the morning after his third night as a werewolf Darwin had woke on Main Street, lying in the middle of the intersection across from the Caprice Theater where he had worked the night before. He had transformed just as he was locking up for the evening. A Wednesday night in early October could never expect to be a busy one for a movie theater. Less than thirty people come all night, and every one of them had come for the early shows. It was Darwin's decision to shut down and cancel the late shows. Under normal circumstances he would have waited thirty minutes past the last scheduled movie start time before closing up shop. On this particular evening Darwin had been distracted and was more interested in getting outside than dealing with burnt popcorn and flat cola. In the back of his mind he had already begun to realize what he was, though he still wrestled with the numerous impossibilities.

The first two nights of the full moon in October he had remembered something happening to him. Darwin remembered the sensations and feelings that had shot through him; however he had also remembered smoking marijuana on both evenings. The morning after the first full moon he awoke on his bed, clothes from the night before lay at his sides in torn long and short strips of fabric. Lying nude on his bed he questioned how it had happened even though he had remembered having a wicked series of orgasms before losing consciousness. Images of his changing body remained in his head; of course he couldn't accept them as reality, especially after a night of doing drugs. On his second night, Darwin again decided to smoke some weed, this time going into the ravine behind his home but not giving much thought about what he had awoken to that morning. On the second morning Darwin again woke, nude but outdoors. Sometime during the night he had wandered several blocks away, following the course of the ravine, but he did not remember doing it. After two mornings of unexplained nakedness Darwin had begun to wonder if it was more than the drugs. He had remembered distinctly the feeling of tearing fabric running across his skin; he remembered the powerful orgasms that pulsated across his body. The drugs might have been laced, he had thought to himself. When he was fifteen Darwin began smoking weed as a release from everyday agonies. The feelings he got from weed were intense and he enjoyed how his body felt when he was stoned. Masturbation had become something extra special when he had smoked up. Never before, had he ever had such vivid hallucinations like the ones he had experienced on the first two nights. He knew the man who grew it and he trusted him implicitly which was why Darwin only smoked that one kind. Throughout the afternoon leading up to the third full moon he couldn't help but wonder if he had become a monster or if he had just become a raging drug addict. Never before had he considered marijuana a drug, never before had it caused him to lose control in such a radical way.

Darwin spent most of the afternoon thinking and wondering about what was to come that evening. He was in charge of the shift at the Caprice Theater, and although his sane mind told him nothing would happen, that nothing could happen, his other half told him to get ready for one hell of a night. The evening shift for a Wednesday consisted of two staff plus Darwin, one box office attendant and one concession person. Darwin would act as the manager in preparation for his promotion; he was in charge of the projector operation, complaints, assisting the other staff at their posts and completing the night's cash outs. Darwin had a good staff that evening. Cindy Holms was the best box office attendant the theater ever had, she was fast and accurate with her money and stunning to look at. The theater could account 10-20% of the ticket sales to horny teenage boys who would come down just to take a peek at her. Cindy had been with the theater for more than a year and Darwin had gotten to know her quite well professionally. Outside of work they hardly acknowledged each other's existence. Cindy was bright, blue eyed, blond haired, long legged and typically manipulative, especially with the boys. Darwin had suspected for a while that Cindy had been performing sexual favors to further her advancement in the theater. Cindy was especially warm and bubbly around the management and starting to warm up around Darwin, aware of his coming promotion. Darwin had not experienced any

Darwinism

sexual favors himself, but he could see it in the body language of others that it was happening. Cindy also made a solid $1.25 an hour more than the other box office attendants; the girl was good with her hands! In charge of the concession operation was sixteen year old, short and gangly, Tim Waters who looked like one large pimple that was ready to explode at any minute. Tim was quiet, distant and highly unpopular from the moment he set foot in Ridgemount High. He dressed with little fashion sense, cared little about his grooming and he listened to country music. The boy was destined to have a rough time in life but Darwin felt a certain kind of kinship for the awkward boy even though he didn't really know him. When Tim applied at the theater Darwin was given the chance to make the final decision whether Tim would be hired.

Theater management trusted Darwin's decision, though they disapproved of Tim's appearance saying, "As a concession worker he was not the best choice because to look at him one would make a person lose their appetite."

Darwin stood by his decision and Tim had made Darwin proud. Although his grooming still needed some work Tim Waters had proved to be one of the hardest working employees at the Caprice.

Darwin had developed a raging hard-on thirty minutes before the last movie had let out. He found himself standing behind counters, holding entertainment magazines, popcorn bags, anything to conceal his pulsating member. He watched the clock intently that evening, worried that it wasn't just the drugs. Inside his body he could feel a spirit rising, turning, coming alive. Darwin rationalized with himself but somewhere inside he knew his truth; he was not going to become a monster. His erection continued past nine o'clock after the early shows had let out; at nine-fifteen he made a decision to close the theater and send his staff home. Fortunately he had an efficient staff and most of the cleaning and closing duties were already done. Cindy and Tim left the theater around nine twenty five leaving Darwin in the office to finish the deposit slips before going home. The staff had only been gone for ten minutes and Darwin was relieved to be alone. Darwin sat in the theater office frantically filling out the evening's deposit slips. The money the theater had taken in during the evening matched perfectly to what the receipts said they should have. Relieved Darwin sealed the deposit in a bank envelope and tossed it into the house safe. Just before nine forty Darwin could feel his heart racing, his hard-on persisted even harder than before and he knew something was about to happen. Moving towards the rear exit his temple began running with perspiration, he was feeling warm and vigorous; he wanted to be outside more than anything. Just before the rear door, he stopped; his body was beginning to shake. *THE ALARM*! Darwin realized he needed to set the alarm that was just to the left of the rear door or he could forget any promotion. 4-7-3-5-6 into the keypad he pounded, the last number had been hit starting the count down to exit the building and the first explosion hit him. He had managed to stumble out of the theater into the darkness of the alley before losing complete control.

The next morning Darwin stood in the middle of town, naked and proud. In an almost voyeuristic fashion he calmly walked down the middle of the road, confident no one would see him, and no one did. He walked all the way down Baker Street, passed St Michael's Church and up Clairmount Boulevard to his home; not seeing another soul, not even a dog or cat. When he arrived home, bare-assed, he realized he had left his keys in his torn pants behind the theater, but he didn't really seem to mind. A strong confidence and residual lunar abilities still flourishing within him: an internal knowledge suggested how he could get into his home. Without giving it any further thought Darwin scaled the outside lattice of his home, passed his mother's bedroom window on the second floor where she remained in her slumber and continued onto the roof where he pulled himself atop the cedar-shakes. Casually and nonchalant he strolled across the roof to the other side of the house just above his bedroom window. It would have been a challenge to any normal man, but Darwin, with the grace of a gymnast swung off the edge of the roof through his open bedroom window landing softly on the bedroom floor.

He knew what he was. His mind still told him it was not possible, but he knew. The taste of blood was fresh in his mouth; he stared at himself in the long bedroom mirror on the back of his bedroom door. Grinning and moving his lips looking for fangs, flexing his muscles trying to see if they were any larger, inspecting himself for added hair growth, and he did look sharper and more refined with added muscle tone. The facial image that peered back seemed to be the same dashingly handsome young man he had always been, the only noticeable difference was in his eyes. The color remained the same; the whites of his eyes seemed to be unchanged but under them appeared to be a shine, added clarity that made them glisten. The glitter in his own eyes mesmerized him for quite awhile that morning as he stood in his bedroom focusing on the previous evening, with little conclusions. Whatever had happened to him he had gotten lucky, three nights in a row and no one had discovered him. It had been fun.

The first few days of his new power were a little scary in retrospect. He had been careless; he realized he needed to be more careful about flaunting himself in public. If someone found him walking down the road nude certainly they would not accuse him of being a shape shifter or a monster. But questions would be raised and his improving reputation would forever be tarnished, and there was the possibility of a criminal record for lewd behavior. Even in his new state of mind, he concerned himself with such trivial matters.

Darwinism

*　　　*　　　*

Soaking up the warmth from the spring, Darwin felt contentment. He was pleased with himself, he knew he would not return to these woods for a full moon, but he had learnt more about himself. Lying back in the warm muddy water he let his mind drift. Closing his eyes, his mind began to sink into another realm; it took him on a walk of exploration, through the past, present and future.

"My brother, my brother the werewolf!" Darwin bolted up from the water to find Zack hovering above the ground. Two feet above the water his brother floated, swaying with the gentle breeze that was accompanying the still falling snow. Zack wore a plain suit, shoes and tie, all in black the ensemble was not befitting for him. His face looked emaciated, withered, and tired. "You expected Steve, didn't you? You wanted it to be Steve, didn't you?"

"Zack? How..." Darwin stammered looking for the right words.

"I'm not real Dar, you should know that by now, neither was Steve. We're just part of your *gift,* as you refer to it. Your mind helps to communicate things to your polluted mortal mind, things the now immortal Darwin must know. Steve was an inner part of you; you were telling yourself to get angry. You already knew getting angry would make you change; you just needed to be told it was okay to use your power." Void of emotion the image of Zack continued to float above the water, hands clasped at his groin.

"What about my flashback last night, the images I saw, were they real?" Darwin questioned.

"Oh yes, very real. The images you saw were real, the other werewolf, your brother, everything was real." Zack stopped: not volunteering any more information.

"What I saw didn't happen." Darwin admitted to his brother. "You went into the woods..."

"Not me! Zack went into the woods that night, what he saw was real, what he did was real, what I am is nothing more than a representation of who he was." The stern stone face spoke. "What did you see in your vision?"

"I saw," Hesitating briefly, Darwin continued. "I saw Zack, in the woods. He saw something." Darwin looked into the bubbles of the spring; he did not want to face the truths that his mind was opening him up to. "Zack saw a monster."

"He saw a lycanthrope just like you. But that's not what bothers you is it." The hoarse voice barked. "What was it that he saw, baby Darwin?" Zack's veins bulged in his pale neck.

"I don't know what I saw." Darwin meekly replied.

"That's BULLSHIT and you know it, NOW WHAT DID HE SEE?" The hovering image shifted back and forth as it grew annoyed.

"I saw my DAD! I saw my DAD!" Becoming emotional, Darwin curled up in the water of the spring as though he was a small boy in a warm bath waiting for his mother to come and dry him off. He hated what his mind had shown him, his father, slowly dying at the hands of a creature that he had now become. He hated what his imaginary brother was doing, his mind was a cruel place that held many secrets and he wanted this image to stop. Sniffling, Darwin continued. "His throat had been torn out; the creature provoked my brother and drew him into the woods. Zack tried to fight back, but the creature... The creature killed them both!"

"You don't really mean that, do you? You are one of those creatures now, you love what you have become, don't you?" The floating specter asked in a cold dry voice.

Darwin rested for a moment, looking into the water. He didn't know how to answer himself. Stalled, Darwin looked to the image of his brother for solace.

"Tell me how the beast killed both your father and brother." Zack's image inquired, continuing to rock above the spring.

"After we found Zack in the forest we left for home, leaving behind all our supplies. We rode home as fast as we could. Zack wouldn't speak to us but we knew something was wrong." Pausing for a moment, he took a deep breath as he gathered the events in his mind. "We arrived home just after nine, drenched in sweat. None of us had ever ridden our bikes home that fast. When we got in the house Zack ran to our father who was in the kitchen having breakfast. I never heard what they said to each other, our mom escorted Cornell and myself directly upstairs. Zack and my father went into the garage; they were in there for hours, just talking. It had been a long night for Cornell and me so we both lied down and fell asleep for much of the day. When I woke up it was just after dinner and the house was real quiet, the only thing I could hear was the rain hitting the roof. Mom was downstairs in the living room reading, she told me my dinner was in the microwave. I asked her where Zack was and she said he had gone to bed. I asked where dad was and she said he had gone back up to the woods to get our camping supplies." Darwin became withdrawn from his memoirs, pulling his knees to his chest; he rocked gently in the mud of the spring. Turning his head upwards to see his brother, all Darwin found was the other edge of the spring and beyond that the blanketed white forest. Darwin mumbled to himself. "Thank fucking Christ!"

"I don't think you will find any salvation in Christ, though check out the local church if you think it might help, but I assure you Christ will turn his back on you as he always has." The voice spoke. Darwin rose from the

Darwinism

womb of the water to see where Zack had gone, but all around him there was nothing but solitude. He was alone. "I told you I'm in your mind, you don't need to see me to hear me, we are one mind, one voice. Now do I have your complete attention or do you want to quiver like the weak little pussy you've always been?"

GET OUT OF MY MIND! Darwin screamed within his head.

"Shouting at us will only hurt you *D*, you can't hurt us, we are a part of you whether you want it or not, and we were lead to believe that you had embraced us, were we misled?"

No longer speaking, Darwin answered only within his own mind. *No, I do love what I am.*

"Good! Then let us continue, let me guide you into the darkest reaches of your mind." The voice rang through Darwin's head as though it was a hollow room, but he felt more comforted by the familiar voice, more so than he had with the image of his brother. "Tell me what happened after your father left the house that evening."

He never came home. Mom waited up for hours that night, Cornell and myself as well. Zack stayed in his room, he didn't come downstairs at all. After the sun had gone down Mom began pacing by the front room window, but she didn't say anything. I don't know if Cornell was worried, we didn't say much to each other that evening. I remember Mom asked us what had happened out there. Neither of us was able to answer, not clearly anyway. Our memories had been blocked, but I don't think we realized it. I told my mother Zack had heard something in the woods and he went to check it out, but he never came back. Mom asked us if we had heard anything that night. I remember now; I said NO.

"Why do you think you told her that?" The questions echoed throughout his hollow chamber as though it was awaiting a response.

I don't know, until yesterday I had forgotten almost everything. I remembered the good parts, clear as day, but I didn't remember the sounds, I didn't remember Zack going into the woods, finding Zack in the woods, racing home, Dad returning to the camp site, Mom questioning Cornell and me; NOTHING, I REMEMBERED NOTHING! Why???

"What happened to your father, Darwin?" The voice spoke in a whisper.

They never found him. They searched the woods where our camp had been. They found nothing. They had found his truck right away, on the side of the road at the entrance to the woods but the camping gear, food, sleeping bags; none of it was found either. The police made Zack go back up to the woods a few days into the search, Cornell and I stayed home. The campsite appeared as though no one had been there for months; even the fire pit had looked unused. I think it was then people began to turn their back on Zack, his story was far-fetched and no evidence

45

existed to prove we had ever been there. For days searchers were in these woods, but they found nothing, he was just gone. After a week they called off the search. Months later my father's blue parka was found by a hunter, stained with blood, but no body was found. We were never sure what happened to him.

"But you do know, don't you?" A devilish little chuckle raced through his mind as he took in what was being suggested to him. "After they abandoned your father's memory, what happened?"

Zack killed himself. Darwin admitted.

Forcefully the voice demanded "When!? When did he do it?"

Darwin waited to respond. He knew when Zack had killed himself, but it was suddenly coming clear to him as to why. His brother had taken his own life a month later, after drifting away and becoming withdrawn and non-communicative. The whole family had fallen apart; his story of that night had been completely dismissed and so had his suffering. Darwin had always believed his brother had felt culpability towards his father's disappearance, mostly because his story wasn't believed and everyone thought he had made it up. Now Darwin could see, his brother suffered a far greater sense of guilt; he had taken blame for everything. Zack had seen his father's death; his own actions the next morning lead to the prophecy coming to light.

August 21, he did it on August 21. We were still coping with my father's disappearance, the search had been called off only a few weeks before and Mom, Cornell and I were still hopeful Dad might turn up. A lot of family and friends kept dropping by the house trying to comfort us; but they never tried to comfort Zack. He stayed in his room most days; the family had seemingly shunned him, for his version of events that night, I guess. I know now, my brother blamed himself for what happened. He saw Dad torn to pieces; he told Dad what he had seen at the camp. Dad ignored what Zack had to say and went up to the woods to get the camping gear we had left behind, it would have been the third night of the full moon. There was nothing in the woods with us that night, nothing at all. Imagined or real, we all had seen something but only Zack could remember. He had seen something that was going to happen, but he believed it had already happened. It had lured Zack away, and it showed him what it planned to do, but Zack believed what he had seen was real, he thought Dad was already dead. We raced home, Zack believing Dad was already dead, but in fact Zack was going home to send Dad to his death. Tears poured from his human eyes, an old wound had been torn open, and the pain reverberated within his mind. *My brother, Zack, I'm so sorry it made me forget what happened, please forgive me!*

"Why are you so emotional? Or have you forgotten what your brother use to do to you?" The cunning voice pushed through the fog bringing with it images from the forgotten and sealed reaches from within his brain.

Zack was perfect; he didn't deserve what happened to him! Darwin shot back.

"Oh, but didn't he?" Zack's voice brought a cold sweat throughout every corner of Darwin's body. The comfort of the hot spring could not even pull him from the discomfort the coming images were bringing.

The voice in Darwin's head was now changing; a much kinder voice began speaking quietly in an avoiding way. "Shhhh, it's okay, it's okay, just be quiet. You're a big boy now, aren't you, look at you! Dar doesn't that feel good? I like it, don't you? I think you will grow to love it, I did. Shhhhhhh! Mom's coming! If you tell anyone your big brother might have to spank you, and big brother doesn't want to hurt you because he loves you more than anyone else. Now go play, and I'll come up stairs in awhile and we'll have more *playtime*."

Lost for words, but it all had been true. He could not deny what the voice had said; word for word it had been his brother, and like a catalyst, he remembered what his brother use to do. Night after night when Darwin was very young, Zack would come into his bedroom and get into bed with him; his brother use to call it *playtime*. From the time Darwin was about three years old until he was six, Zack had pursued Darwin for after dark *playtime*. Darwin was a frightened child, but Zack was his older brother and he had never hurt Darwin, except once. Darwin had never told anyone about *playtime*, and he hadn't thought about it in years. He knew what his brother had done was wrong, but yet he remained conflicted in his feelings towards Zack.

"Didn't he deserve what happened to him?" The child like voice of his brother questioned.

Speaking out loud again Darwin rebutted. "I forgive my brother for what he did; I know he felt guilt for it, that's why he stopped."

"When did he stop?" A now intuitive little voice questioned.

Zack was thirteen. He tried... Darwin sunk back into the water, submerging his head, feeling the dirt clinging to his skin. Under the water he scrubbed himself, but the feeling would not leave him. The dirt was inside, under his skin. For the first time he began to hate his brother. *He shoved his dick in my ass. The MOTHER FUCKER, he tried FUCKING ME! He pushed so hard into me, I passed out from the pain; I was in and out of consciousness while he did it. He tried over and over putting himself inside me. I don't know how long he tried for; but he eventually gave up. I had a shower right away, I felt so dirty; I just couldn't get myself clean. I bled from my ass; the water in the shower was red. I think that's why he stopped; he knew he had hurt me. He never came to me again, it all stopped after that last time.*

"Do you remember how he took his own life, and how you felt?" A certainty rang with the tone of the voice, which had now reverted back to the older Zack.

Raising his head from the water, Darwin opened his eyes to find himself inside the garage at his home. His brother Zack sat solemnly at his father's workbench; in front of him was the carburetor of the lawn mower, and three cans of beer. His brother was slowly tinkering with the machine, spending more time drinking every beer that had been left behind in the fridge. No one had been in the garage since his father had disappeared, and Zack looked more like his father than ever before. He hadn't shaved since before the camping trip and was now sporting a short shaggy beard. Dark lines under his eyes highlighted his pain. Darwin watched his brother do as his dad had done, work and drink, drink and work. His brother sat at the cluttered bench, for what seemed like hours, Darwin saw little movement in his brother; only the mounting number of beer cans on the bench indicated the passage of time. Thirteen empty cans of beer stacked neatly into a pyramid, were all that remained when Zack rose from the bench. He had finished work on the lawn mower, even taking care and attention to sharpen the blades.

Zack wrenched on the mower cord to engage the motor, but it only sputtered and stalled. Again and again he furiously tugged at the cord and with a spark; it choked and spit until the motor finally began revving at full speed. His brother pulled a roll of black electrical tape from his pocket and ever so carefully, Zack wrapped the roll of tape around the lawn mower handle bar, taping the kill switch to it. The kill switch had to be held to keep the mower running, and now Zack was taping it up, preventing the mower from stopping. The depressed teen finished rigging the kill switch, and proceeded tipping the mower onto its side. Grass stained blades rotated at extreme speeds looking like one continuous green blur when Darwin stared into it. Knowing what was to come, Darwin found himself unable to turn away. His brother returned to the workbench where he placed the electrical tape in a drawer. Calmly, and emotionless the boy turned around to look at the lawn mower. A cloud of exhaust began filling the garage, but Zack stood there taking deep breaths. For several minutes Darwin watched the final moments of his brother's life. Zack emanated anguish that made Darwin connect with his pain, despite the previously forgotten atrocities. Zack had made amends, or had tried to. His brother had tried so hard to be better than Marta. Seeing the life begin to drain from his brother brought with it many emotions. Zack's eyes opened wide, wider than Darwin had ever seen them.

His eyes were glossed over with a building layer of water as he began moving forward. His brother stepped away from the workbench for the last time and started to run towards the lawn mower. Each leaping step signalled release in Zack's eyes; the running boy was smiling as his feet left the ground propelling his body headfirst into the spinning blades. Instantly, a room had been painted in red; speckled in the remains of Zack Foster's skull. The motor of turning the blades slowed briefly as it pureed through his flesh and bone, only his body remained on the floor of the garage. The largest piece of his face to survive was a two-inch fleck of his cheek, identifiable only by the teen's underdeveloped beard, which was the only bit to hit the workbench. The tissue from his face had been spewed throughout the room. Bone, skin, hair and teeth; every inch of the garage was now marked. The beer fridge had a small sprinkling of brain tissue scattered with some hair, but the garage door and ceiling took the brunt of the explosion. A mosaic of deep red protuberance flowed upwards along the garage door fanning outward up the door. The solid fragments slid through the blood to the bottom of the door, piling up in small amounts on the cold concrete floor. A steady flow of blood poured from his brother's neck, his heart still pumping for a short time after. The gray of the concrete disappeared with the advancing flow, and like the floor, so had Zack.

Shadows now lurked around the pool of steaming water, growing and dancing with each passing minute. Darkness was approaching fast and the crisp afternoon air was making way for the ice permeated night air. The clouds had parted revealing the purple hue of the December sky. The sound of the forest was muffled, quiet, as though with the coming of the snow, the forest had gone to sleep for the winter.

Waking from his time in the garage, Darwin was caught between emotions. A void of emptiness had been left in his head. Silence ruled his mind; the voice of his guide had now ceased. The day's events had worn Darwin out. He wanted nothing more than to toke up and go to sleep. Watching the sky, he knew it wasn't to be. For a time, the soft sound of simmering water kept his mind at ease, away from the cruel realities of his past. Darwin would try to ignore his growing anger for now.

Chapter 6

"Kill them, Darwin, Kill them all! You're better than they are and you know it. You haven't doubted it for a minute. What would be so wrong in killing everyone who has ever wronged you? They had no right, you know. Help us, help you." The voice echoed in the hollow cavern. Confused, Darwin rose from the stone altar he was laying on to look around.

"Hello!" He shouted. But he was only greeted with the recoil of his own voice. Unsure of where he was, Darwin looked around but found nothing recognizable. It looked like a cave, but it had no clear entrance or exit. Light pounced from the walls but no source was evident. Darwin moved around the room a little, examining the walls for anything that might tell him where he was. Despite his unknown surroundings, he was not frightened. Shouting, Darwin demanded to be recognized by his unknown companion. "ANSWER ME! You don't know what you're dealing with!"

"Temper, temper young one. You wouldn't want to lose control of yourself, would you? The familiar voice spoke snickered.

"I might, if I have to!" Darwin shouted back in rage.

"I think you will find your powers are not with you here. You may yell and scream to your heart's content, you can hit the rock if you think that will help, but I assure you, you will remain very much in your human form in this place." The certainty in the voice moved Darwin.

"Zack? Steve?" Darwin questioned the open air.

A mild chuckle floated through the chamber momentarily. "You have to

Darwinism

learn to think on a larger scale young one. What did your brother Zack tell you in the woods today? What did he tell you about himself?"

"Zack was only a representation from my mind, a way to communicate things I needed to know." Darwin said with some assuredness.

"Very good, we were worried you hadn't been listening." The voice replied.

"Who are you? What is this place?" A defensive Darwin sparred with the stone walls looking for an escape.

"You are at the inner most part of yourself. Deep within that part of you most humans are unable to fathom, but all have" The voice stopped for a moment. "You will find no exit from this place; you may as well have a seat and try to learn something. That is what you wanted wasn't it; to learn about your power?"

Frustrated but cooperative, Darwin took heed at the suggestion and returned to the stone altar. In this place deep within himself he continued to wear no clothes, but the atmosphere was comfortable, and the feel of the stone on his buttocks was not cold. Seated, Darwin waited for what his mind had to tell himself.

"You wanted to know more about your power, we are here to guide you. Lay back on the altar." The voice had barely finished instructing and the teen was already lying flat on the stone. "Do you know where you are?" His guide questioned.

Sarcastically Darwin responded. "The *inner most* part of myself."

A sound of evil penetrated the chamber in response. "Do not mock us boy!"

Darwin silenced. Answering only mentally, he apologized. *No I don't know where I am, I'm sorry."*

"There is no need to apologize in this place." A calmer voice responded. " Like Zack, this place is merely a representation, something tangible that your puny human mind can comprehend. Right now you are sitting in the hot spring, waiting for the beast to emerge. We thought we would take this opportunity to give you the knowledge you have been seeking."

Darwin interrupted. "How did this happen to me?"

"We do not concern ourselves with that information. How you were made is unimportant. You are and always will be a lycanthrope. Knowing how it began will not bring you any amity. Like all knowledge though, the answer may lie deep within you, however we are not the ones to guide you on that journey." The voice finished.

Darwin remained silent, disappointed at his soul's response, but he remained determined in his mind; he would discover how it had happened, and why.

Mark Fuson

"For three months we have watched you wander the streets of town and roam the nearby woods. For three months we have watched you avoid the one thing that you long for, why do you think that is?" The cold voice of his mind questioned.

"I don't know. When I think about killing, I get…" Embarrassed to say it, but remembering it was his own mind he was speaking to, he continued to admit his truths. "I get horny. I get hot and my mind begins to race. I want myself to be inside another person."

"You feel the need for sex?" The guide calmly questioned.

"No. Not sex. When I think about killing, the excitement that runs through me," Stuck for words Darwin raised his hands to the air as though he could grab the very word to describe his feelings. "I must consume them. I must devour their life force. Even in my human form I am thinking about killing people. The idea of gnawing on a heart or a lung gets me aroused, the taste of blood." Chuckling, Darwin stopped.

"What does the taste of blood do for you?" The cavern echoed.

"I've had orgasms while eating a rare steak. In the middle of a restaurant while with friends, the littlest amount of blood and I creamed myself." Darwin was beginning to enjoy sharing his experiences. For three months he had kept everything bottled up inside of him, and now he was able to tell everything to an interactive companion.

"The emotions you are feeling will continue to grow until you are no longer able to function within normal society. Your emotions manifest themselves in your human form as a way of telling you what your body needs. As the wolf you already exert a large amount of control over your actions, however, at this stage in your development you are still unable to retain much memory of your actions; this will change in time. The one constant thought in your mind right now is fear. Your fear of hurting a loved one is holding you back from your potential. We need to open that door, and bring forth your full abilities. If we succeed, and you can overcome your fear and gain the confidence that you are in control, you will be able to kill whomever you want. Succeed at this, and you will return to normal in your day-to-day activities." Finished, the sounds of the chamber drained away to silence. "If you could kill anyone, who would it be?"

"I don't know. There are too many people who have pissed me off over the years. Mike Dolker, Jason Vegsund, Mr. Hansen from gym class, that fuck-head who's banging my mother-RUMSFELD." Darwin gazed at the ceiling of the cavern as a wave of anger passed through him forcing his body to sweat a little. "A part of me thinks I don't care who I kill."

"You have no shortage of people you would like to see escorted off this world. If you had killed everyone that had ever wronged you, whom would you kill next? You might have to kill someone you don't know, could you do it still?" The sound of the voice had become almost playful, as though it was amused with the conversation.

"I think I would move to a city, there's no shortage of shit heads there. Drug addicts, thieves, gangs, hookers, I think there's always gonna be more food than I know what to do with. I can kill." Darwin announced with a smirk on his mouth.

"Our thoughts are as one on this young Darwin. The place you will be sending your victims requires that they have certain qualities. Killing a family of four does not serve our needs. So many people before you have been over zealous, killing whomever they came across. When you kill, it does not stop with the beat of your victim's heart. The afterlife, which you do not see, is an important part of what you are. When you select a person for termination their soul will go one of two possible ways. Up or down. Whether they are killed in an accident or by a demon does not matter, if they were destined for up then that is where they shall go, if it was down that had been chosen as their final destination – then let it be so. Your primary mission is to send us souls, souls that we already have a hand on. The essence of your victims helps us to grow stronger and to purify this world. You are more useful to us if you selectively target your prey." The voice knew its audience was agreeing with everything it was saying. An atmosphere had developed within the cavern, an atmosphere of presence. The cavern was not empty of souls.

"Where do they go when they die?" Darwin's humanity asked.

"You call it *Hell*." An image of Darwin now stood over Darwin looking into his own eyes. "Hell does not want you to kill the good people in this world; those people have already been selected to move onward after death. We need you to send us the, *sure things*, the people who are going to hell whether you kill them or not." The reflective image of Darwin soothingly spoke to his protégé.

Darwin looked at himself and asked another question. "What does hell do with them?"

"Your master does whatever he sees fit." Darwin's double responded. "You work for him in the waking world. That will never change; there is no release from what you are. You are what you are and you've loved it from the moment you achieved realization."

"Are you certain of that?" Darwin questioned himself. Staring his double in the eye he could see the blackness that extended into its soul. It was Darwin, but only in form. The essence of this messenger was from another realm, and Darwin wanted to test the messenger.

"We've always had a hold over you. You were always destined to be an apostle, Darwin Foster. Your being marked by the hand of Satan has only elevated you in a chain of command that you already were apart of. Your destiny has always been with us." The double stopped speaking and turned away, moving towards the cavern wall. Looking back his face was filled with emptiness. Sternness existed in his eyes, as though he had the gravest of news to share. "You are a good person. You want to do what is best, what is just, what is right. Now it pains you to know you are in essence a demon. Would it comfort you to know humanity's conception of Heaven and Hell has always been flawed? Do not agonize because you are on the so-called, *less preferred* team. A preacher, clergyman or monk does not automatically move on to Heaven because they devote their lives to God, the criteria to which people are judged in the afterlife is beyond the scope of the Ten Commandments. It is unfortunate, through the centuries much of our message has been lost."

A perplexed Darwin interjected. "I don't understand. Heaven and Hell exist, but neither is good or bad?"

"In so many words, yes." The messenger again moved toward the altar with a new life in his eye. "Heaven is where the snobbish of the world go. They have done nothing for the betterment of man, and although they have technically followed the rules on earth; are considered useless by those in hell. We like risk takers, those who are not afraid to stand up to the rules of the almighty when it is in humanity's best interest. For example, we watched you intently during your rough years in school, hoping you would carry out the executions you had so diligently considered. They deserved it - everyone knew it. Thou shall not kill, as far as Hell is concerned, should not be applicable in a purifying moment of a society such as that. Why did you not carry out your assault on the school?"

Darwin remained silent, unsure how to respond. This was the first time anyone had spoken to him about his plan. At the age of fourteen Darwin and Steve had decided they had enough of their school torture, but it was Darwin who had given the plans a lot of thought. The attack would have been a simple one. Eight targets, all in the same class, first period History. The plan was to walk into the rear of class with Darwin's father's shotgun he had now sawed off, taking out two students with each shot. Out of the eight he wanted dead, he would have been satisfied with the three ringleaders. His plan was not as elaborate as future school shootings but Darwin did not see himself as a murderer, only a boy who wanted justice for the years of ignorance and intolerance both he and Steve had faced alone. There were other plans, but this one seemed the simplest to Darwin. "I did not want to die."

"Death was not assured." Hell's correspondent replied.

"I would not go to jail for those mother fuckers which only left one option and I was not prepared to die for their crimes." Darwin admitted.

"That's why we like your kind, young Darwin. You have a sense of right and wrong and self-preservation. You will go far in this world." His image spoke. "Did you ever believe in God?

"No. I've never believed in God." Darwin replied, looking into his own eyes he noticed they were now green. Adjusting his eyes he looked at the whole image of himself the rest of his face and hair had now changed, in his place was Steve.

A much different voice than before, Steve began speaking. "God is very real, I assure you, he's just not very good. Can you remember the last time he was there for you?"

"Is Hell bad?" Darwin questioned.

"Humanity would have you believe it is, but Hell is just. Those who deserve torture, are, those who deserve an eternity of suffering, do, those who deserve damnation, are and those who understand our purpose are embraced" Steve announced with some enthusiasm.

"Am I damned?" A worried Darwin asked. Darwin remained flat to the altar but he cocked his head to keep a close eye on his friend's image.

Steve developed a hesitation, pacing the length of the room, not responding to the question. The cavern echoed with the footsteps of the pondering image. Steve held his fist to his teeth, lightly gnawing on his knuckle. After several minutes he stopped marching and returned to Darwin who continued waiting silently for his response. "You must try to look beyond biblical definitions. In your own understanding of damnation, you are damned. You are precluded from ever going to Heaven. At the same time damnation is in the eye of the beholder. For three months you did not see yourself as damned. You loved your *gift*. You loved your power. Does that sound like damnation? It is damnation for those who are never able to kill, those who cannot expand their minds and see things in a different way. A religious person brainwashed into their beliefs, unable to understand the relationships between Heaven and Hell, see it as damnation. You do not see it as damnation; you see it as a gift."

"What did you mean by Hell always had a hold over me? I always thought I was a good person?" Darwin, looking somewhat shaken, closed his eyes, trying to forget anything bad he had ever done.

"You don't honestly expect me to entertain that question, do you?" Steve grabbed Darwin by the shoulders giving him a violent shake, forcing the stubborn boy to listen to his crimes. Darwin slowly opened his reddening eyes, staring Steven in the eyes once again. "You have been destined for Hell from the beginning, if I have to tell you the violations you have committed, then you truly amaze me. You must accept your crimes, and make amends by exterminating the infestations of this world. You must come to terms with your actions on your own. Your brain is beginning the degradation. Part of your gift requires you eat human flesh, if you do not you begin to lose control, even when the moon is not full. Today when you got angry and transformed part way, your inability to quench your sadistic needs is a clear indication the degradation has begun. A werewolf can go for a month or two without human flesh and suffer little effect. After three months you begin to lose complete control, raping animals is the least of your problems. If a werewolf goes much longer than four months without killing a human, the damage their brain suffers is irreversible. You have little time left to save yourself from true damnation. If you do not prevent the collapse of your brain, you will live an eternity committing acts of unspeakable horror that you will choose not to control." Steve took hold of Darwin's hands that remained over his face.

In horror at the revelations Darwin pressed forward with the questions he needed answers to. How many more he could ask, how many more would be answered; this chance may never come his way again, no matter how much it hurt. "How do I control myself?" Red eyed and soggy, Darwin looked to his mentor, ready to accept what he had to do.

"Your clarity develops with each kill. Some achieve lucidity sooner than others; it depends on the individual. As your degradation gets worse however, the certainty of your actions may diminish. I urge you to select a target, soon. Because your degradation is advanced you may have some difficulties controlling your hidden desires, that is, if you wish to control them?"

"What do you mean?" Darwin worried.

"You could not control your urges with the deer, the same may also be true with a human. Chose your prey, and be prepared for things you might do." Steve released Darwin's hands and moved away. "There is another topic we need to discuss." Steve, standing facing the wall, paused; waiting for Darwin to question him, but no queries came. "The world is a large place, and although its size would make one feel a certain invulnerability, we must remain cautious."

"I'm not to make anyone into a werewolf, right?" Darwin spoke to his mentor's back.

"You must choose selectively who you bless with your bite. Not everyone serves the needs of Hell; not everyone accepts the power and gift that is bestowed upon them; not everyone is able to maintain a low profile. Kill the wicked, incorporate the kind. For a millennia the wolves have remained nothing more than a myth to society at large. Every now and again one of our members gets a little too confident, bringing a little too much attention to our cause. It is in our best interest that our numbers remain low, and that our members are selected wisely. We do not interfere in your assimilations; we do however intervene if you become careless. May I suggest you avoid creating new werewolves for the time being? But that decision is up to you. The number of werewolves in the world is low, and we would like to see more;

Darwinism

learn your power first; become intimate with it before you draw someone to our side." Steve finished.

Considering what he knew from movies Darwin suspected he should ask the big question. "How do I make another werewolf; a bite or scratch?" Darwin realized the stupidity of the question; common knowledge always said: if you were bitten by a werewolf, you yourself became a werewolf – but Darwin had not been bitten, what other way was there?

Steve was now gone, but his voice was still dominant throughout the chamber. "Most of what you know from movies on this subject is true. The bloodline is passed through an infection. A bite mark is effective but so is drinking the blood of an infected person. A scratch will also cause some people to turn, but not everyone. Some people are born werewolves and some men who pray to Lucifer are blessed with the gift. Several hundred years ago some mystics learned how to turn a man using oils and herbs, but the formula has since been forgotten. Making another into a werewolf is easy, just be wary of who you mark. Remember, eyes are watching you."

"Can I die?" Darwin shouted into the cavern.

"Everyone dies eventually." The cavern echoed.

A bright light enveloped the cavern, forcing Darwin to shut his eyes. The hollowness of the stone structure had disappeared and the hardness of the stone altar began to soften. In the distance Darwin could hear a bird, chirping happily. The sounds of a forest were coming alive in his mind. Driving his eyes to open the cavern had vanished, awaking in the hot spring pool. The sun was setting and the moon was beginning to rise. His lessons in his mind remained strong. He remembered his time was growing short, and he knew he had to devote his attention to killing someone soon, the question was, who? He felt mentally strong and he knew what he had to do. He would kill on this night, forever changing who he was; giving himself over completely to the power.

Chapter 7

Around two o'clock that afternoon the owner of the Twin Falls Ranch stumbled upon the clothing remains of Darwin Foster while searching for a wandering steer. The clothing was torn to shreds but the bloodied coat was intact. Darwin's name was written on the tag, a carry over habit from his mother. When Barry Dachauwitz came across the name in the coat he notified the local police at once. Two hours later, when it was confirmed that Darwin's whereabouts was unknown, Search and Rescue set up a base camp near the maple tree. A team of twenty men and women were scouring the woods for some kind of trace of Darwin.

A rescue of this kind would not normally happen at night fall, but the decision was made that time was critical, if he was alive, he wouldn't be for long. Even among the seasoned searchers it was widely felt that Darwin could not have survived any length of time in the woods without clothing; not in these conditions. The plan was to fan out in a semi-circular search grid away from the maple tree moving to the north looking for evidence.

At seven o'clock the moon shone brilliantly through the trees. The snow had stopped and the air was terse and hard. The search team had been on the move for nearly two hours and had found almost nothing. A barn owl was following team four, occasionally diving towards the duo. It was more amusing that anything.

"Listen up teams! We'll keep moving until the river, after that we're doing

Darwinism

an about face and heading back to base for the night." Fizzled across the radio of team four.

"Team one, roger that!"

"Team two, roger!"

"Team three!"

"Four"

Each team responded quickly. The coldness of the night was winning the battle to drive the search team from the woods, and the job at hand was not being taken seriously by some. Team four was comprised of Jason and Tina, colleagues at the fire hall. Jason was married with three children. Tina had recently graduated, was single and on the prowl. Jason had one big weakness, his infidelity and he could have been clinically diagnosed as a sex addict. Jason loved his wife with all his heart but his eyes always strayed when his conscience knew better. Add a few adult beverages and he would become a real player and he always had one or more interests on the go. A lot of people in town knew what Jason was about, but no one said anything. He was a likable guy overall, but so was his wife. Jason just couldn't keep it in his pants for more than a day or so. It made life for his friends socially awkward.

"It's cold out tonight, my nipples are getting hard." Tina said

"I'm hard too." Jason replied with a devilish grin. "My nipples, that is."

Tina smiled at Jason's blue eyes knowing full well what she wanted. She knew of Jason's situation and the hell it would cause, but she didn't care. From the moment she laid eyes on his boyish smile she knew she had to have him.

Jay was portly but had a way with words around the ladies that made him irresistible. Tina had attempted to resist him but she found an overwhelming attraction to his "in your face sexual advances." She had never thought of herself as a tramp, but that's what she was. Feeling daring she took her glove off and grabbed Jason's crotch and massaged it vigorously knowing the reaction it would receive. The two stopped in mid stride, saying nothing to each other. Jason smirked and moaned with pleasure. Tina moved in closer and began to unbutton his pants. Jason had lied, he was hard.

The two did not move another inch. Tina fell to her knees and swallowed his cock. Under the light of the moon the pheromones began to flow.

*   *   *

Still resting in the hot spring Darwin could feel the wolf coming. He was excited to get on with his night. He was committed to himself to killing someone. He would wait no more. The procrastination and delays would not allow him to lose his mind. He was bigger than they were, he was better than they were. For the first time Darwin knew it was about being comfortable in what he was. He was comfortable, but for him to reach full acceptance he could no longer avoid what he was intended for. Killing the deer had felt right, but he still longed for the flesh of a man. It was an addiction to something he'd never tried before. He was eager to give in. His first kill would be whoever crossed his path, there would be no control.

A sweet aroma cut through the sulphur. Darwin knew this smell, and it was close. He had found his prey.

*   *   *

Team four was less than a mile from the hot spring. Jason was close to climaxing and Tina was working his plumbing like a pro. They both moaned in pleasure and deceit.

"Oh God, fuck me lord!" Jason uttered in bliss. "I'm gonna cum!"

Tina worked like a machine until her mouth began to fill with his salty seed. A real tramp, she swallowed every drop and kept on sucking moving right on to the next session of fellatio.

Jason looked at the moon with a *shit eating grin* on his face. He had, once again, cheated on his lovely wife. His indiscretions had now become a matter of routine with him and he no longer cared. Deep in his own mind he had already decided his marriage was a lost cause. Tina was just another notch on his belt. She was attractive, but just another whore.

Off in the distance Jason's ears heard something. Only for a moment; it had sounded like screaming. As quickly as his ears picked up on the sound it went away and then it was gone.

*   *   *

Darwin's wolf raced through the woods moving in on the smell of the semen. It was getting closer and so was he. He could smell a man and a woman. The anticipation of breaking flesh was too much for him to stand. He raced towards the two taking no care for the noise he was making. If they ran it would be even more thrilling. He was on his first hunt.

Through his wolf eyes Darwin fixated on a heat signature not too far away. He had control over what he wanted. He would eat these people.

Could I stop if I wanted to?

The beast barrelled through the trees like an avalanche. Jason and Tina had no chance to get off a shout before they had been silenced. The animal bit in to Jason's throat severing his head from his body. The animal lapped up the blood in tissue in its mouth with delight. Tina released Jason's cock to a rainfall of blood pouring from above. She looked up to the collapsing body of Jason to find the werewolf moving towards her. She quickly rose to her feet in a vain effort to bolt. Darwin, the beast, grabbed her shoulder and lifted her up to his face. She was pretty, even as the wolf he knew that; but his appetite remained and she had to die. Without thought he rammed his razor claws through her pants and into her moist vagina. Tina didn't scream, she only mumbled and cried. Darwin tore out her uterus and dropped her sad body to the ground. He swallowed it whole and then he went back for seconds. The girl squirmed and tried to crawl, but the wolf was too strong. The animal grabbed her legs and spread them revealing the bloody gaping hole. The monster dove in and ate his way to her heart. She let out a few deathly screams for the first few moments before trauma took her from this world.

The scream had been heard by the other teams.

Darwin was still hungry after his two kills. The essence of his victims flowed through his veins enhancing his high and making him feel more powerful and confident than he ever had before. He felt no guilt in what he had done; in fact, he wanted to take it further. His senses had intensified and he could hear more food closing in on his location. He would wait until they reached him and then he would kill again.

It was team three that reached Darwin first. Darwin allowed them to find the bodies of Jason and Tina first before revealing himself to the newcomers. When the two fat men came upon the bodies they both hollered to the other teams.

"HEY, oh God, they're dead!!!" One yelled into the night.

The search teams were near but Darwin knew there was nothing they could do to stop him. From the shadows he emerged behind the two *roly poly* searchers who were bent over the hollowed out remains of Tina. Darwin grabbed a head with each paw and crushed their skulls together to form one mass. As he watched the skulls collide, crack and combine Darwin found himself becoming aroused at what he was doing. Even as the wolf his sexual urges were coming on fast and strong. Holding the glob of flesh and bone in front of his teeth, he took a large bite, swallowing the material without chewing. He still wasn't satisfied.

Darwin charged into the trees towards the flashlights he could see. They were near. This time he would fuck his victim and then kill them. He wasn't sure why he wanted to do it, all he knew was he was on the best high of his life. The flesh had satisfied a portion of his craving, but he longed for more.

He raced up towards them; he sensed that they knew their fate. Like deer caught in the headlights, so were his prey. All around Darwin he could hear the other search teams evacuating the forest. He would catch them all one at a time if need be.

Darwin hit the pair knocking them down. He turned and went back to the closest person who was on the ground but trying to get up. Instinctively

Mark Fuson

Darwin hopped onto the back of his victim, slicing a hole with his claw through the butt crack, revealing a tender sphincter. Darwin pushed in and began humping his victim like a bitch.

From behind the monster came the search partner armed with a large boulder. It flew through the air and hit Darwin in the side of the head. It hurt and garnered Darwin's full attention. The animal rose to its feet and towered over the brave soul. Darwin looked down at the young man who he recognized as being a year older than him. His wolf brain had a hard time remembering his name.

Dan? Kill him? Turn Him?

Indecision got the better of him. The young searcher held his ground and did not appear to be frightened by the monster. The young man was furious and Darwin could almost read his thoughts. Darwin opted to stroll away to greener pastures.

Darwin charged through the trees towards the south. Along the way he encountered four more searchers who he killed on the spot. The last kill of the night was a searcher from team one; Darwin ate almost the entire body, leaving only the feet behind. After his final kill of the night he felt fulfilled.

Darwin sauntered back to town having been granted more control over his creature than ever before. He could still feel his wild tendencies inside, but for the moment he was in control. Darwin would be able to change back near home. He would face his new reality in the morning.

Chapter 8

Darwin had returned to his human form behind the garage around five in the morning. No one went into the garage after Zack had killed himself and now it had become Darwin's safe haven. Darwin had decided the previous month to put a house key under a loose brick in the walkway leading out to the garage. Using his hidden key, Darwin snuck into the house, stark naked, but feeling alive and stimulated. His hands and mouth were stained from the blood of the people he had killed. Even in his human form running his tongue across the dried blood gave him pleasure. He felt strong and sure of what he had done; no regrets. What he had done seemed surreal and he wasn't entirely sure that he had done any of it. The dried blood was all he had to prove it.

In the early morning hours Darwin showered up and went to bed; he knew it would only be a matter of time before someone showed up demanding answers of where he had been. He wasn't sure what story he would give them or who might be asking.

*   *   *

The smells floating up through the stairwell would normally have woken Darwin out of a sound sleep. But it was a light tapping on his bedroom door and his mother's urging to come downstairs that got him up. As Darwin rose from his bed the aroma of frying bacon sunk deep into his nose. In the background beyond the bacon he could smell toast. A wrenching feeling clamped down on his stomach as his hunger made itself known. The human was as hungry as the wolf. He paused briefly at the window before rushing to put on clothes and heading downstairs. Outside Darwin could see the neighborhood streets had not been cleared and the snow drifts sloped upwards to the roofs. Towards the south end of Clairmount Boulevard Darwin could see several downed trees, branches mostly, but the large cedar at the end of the street appeared to be suffering a significant list; now hovering just over the side walk. He could see a dark sedan parked in front of his house. *The Police.* He buttoned his shirt up and prepared himself for the lies he was about to tell.

Darwin edged his way down the spiral staircase to the living area poking his head around to see if his mother was anywhere to be seen. The television continued to blare throughout the living area but his mom appeared to be nowhere. The news was on, and he recognized the scenes that were being shown.

"I hope you've got a damn good explanation of where you've been the last two nights!?" His mother shouted.

Darwin spun around and found his mother, her boyfriend and a man in a suit sitting in the breakfast nook. It was game time.

"Mrs. Foster try to remain calm, just be happy that's he's alright. Son, I'm Frank Newman with the New Haven Police Department, come with me to the living room, I have a few questions I need to ask you. Mrs. Foster if you don't mind I'd rather do this privately, he is an adult after all." Newman said to Marie not waiting for her response.

Darwin said nothing and escorted Newman into the 1970's era living room. The officer seated himself on the mustard yellow couch across from Darwin who opted to sit in his father's pleather recliner. Waiting for the interrogation to begin Darwin found a numbing sensation from the faux brick and family pictures that littered the wall. He hated this room.

"I'm not sure if you've heard but we had a tragedy last night so I'm looking for some answers – and it starts with you. Can you explain why your clothing was found in the woods north of town?" Newman demanded.

Grabbing the remote Darwin muted the television before beginning his web of lies. "I was jumped. They stripped me and took everything, before I left for Arcadia; I was never in the woods. They must have dumped it there." Darwin replied, knowing that was not a stretch. "I'm not sure who did it so I can't press charges."

"Is that a fact? Did you ever think it might be a good idea to call for help, let your mom know that you're ok…something!" Newman raised his voice. "What did you do after they stripped you? You were naked? Where did this happen?" Newman queried with his black note book in hand.

"I was behind Steve Cardwen's house. After they left me in the alley I went to Steve's house, no one was home but I knew where they kept a spare key. I got inside and borrowed some of Steve's clothes. After that I came home and packed my bag for Arcadia." Darwin offered as a well rounded lie.

"Why were you behind the Cardwen residence in the first place?" Newman asked in true police fashion.

"I often take the lane as a short cut to their house. I was just stopping in to hang out. The guys just jumped out of the alley and surrounded me." Darwin replied.

"So you think these perpetrators knew you were coming?" Newman asked to clarify.

"I don't know, but they knew who I was." Darwin offered.

"What makes you say that?"

"They made comments about me visiting my "fag" friend. They stole my clothes to "get me ready for my visit" with Steve." Darwin lied to Newman but somewhere in the lie it was grounded in truth. "It's happened before; it doesn't really shock me anymore."

"Did you fight back?" Newman asked like a disapproving macho father.

"Of course, but I lost." Darwin replied.

"This happened two days ago, you seem to be in really good health. No bruises or marks on you anywhere?" Newman asked smugly.

"I heal fast and rarely bruise." Darwin stated knowing his house of cards was beginning to implode.

"Whereabouts in Arcadia did you stay?"

"At a friend's condo, it belongs to Clint Littleford. Excuse me, how the hell is this a police matter? I said I'm not pressing charges." Darwin said.

"Eight people were killed looking for you last night in those woods." Newman said bluntly. "I've got one more in hospital."

"What happened?" Darwin asked for his own sadistic reasons.

Newman huffed a little and then responded. "Some kind of animal got a hold of them. We're not sure what at this point. Honestly I've never seen anything like it. Our one eyewitness described an animal that was bear like in size, but fast. He couldn't say what it was, and he was damn close to it. All I'm asking you is, tell me this isn't a goddamn hoax, because God help you if it was!"

"No sir, no hoax." Darwin stated with as much intensity as possible. "I was jumped, probably by the same guys who have hated me my whole life. They had masks on so I didn't get a good look, but there were four of them."

"Do you have any receipts to prove you were in Arcadia, just so I can tie up this end of the investigation?" Newman asked with his public relations grin.

"I'm not sure, I didn't buy much. I'll have a look through my things and see if I kept something. Am I a suspect or something?" Darwin asked now concerned.

"Darwin, I've got nothing on you right now. But if I find out this was a hoax, and you're lying to me, your ass is mine!" Newman stated as he got up and made his way to the door. "Oh one more question...how did these attackers take your clothes off?"

"Two held me down and the other two pulled the clothes off. Why?" Darwin asked.

"I'm not sure why they would tear the clothes into shreds and leave them deep in the woods after the fact...everything from your underwear to your shoes; your coat was the only thing which was intact but it had blood on it. Do you have any idea where the blood came from?" Newman asked inquisitively.

My blood, from the owl...fuck!

"Maybe I injured one of the attackers, I really don't remember." Darwin told hoping it was enough to satisfy the inquisition.

"Hmmm, maybe." Newman replied, annoyed. "Would you be willing to provide a DNA sample, to eliminate you as a source of the blood?"

"I'm not injured, so it can't be mine." Darwin laughed nervously.

"It's voluntary at this point, but I can get a warrant if need be." Newman threatened as he turned to make his way to the door. "I'll let you think about it, you let me know."

"Sir." Darwin barked. "Who was the survivor?"

"We're still attempting to notify his immediate family, I'm sorry I can't tell you his name until that's happened." Newman bowed his head and made a dash for the exit. "I'll be in touch if I need anything from you, glad you are ok." Frank Newman ran off quickly like a child who had just found the prize Easter egg.

Darwin wondered to himself if he had infected someone during his attacks. There was a survivor, implying they were hurt. Darwin wondered if he had passed his gift on. He knew it was a male, but nothing more. The attacks from the previous night were like a blur of excitement to him and he couldn't be sure of what he had done.

"Did you hear that wind last night Darwin, that was something else, wasn't it?" The boyfriend said making a point not to comment on Darwin's well being or police visit.

Looking up from his newspaper and breakfast it was Darwin's worst way to start the day – even worse than a police visit. Rumsfeld. Ronald "J" (just call me jackass) Rumsfeld, an insurance salesman who believed he was God's greatest gift to women. The puny little man wore brown rimmed glasses, too large for his head, sported a mustache too grand for a man of his stature and was in the early experimental stages of 'comb-overs". The stench of the cheap aftershaves made eyes water if one stood too close to him. Out of humor, Darwin had tried to identify the smell and had concluded the aftershave was a combination of Walmart specials that had been carefully handcrafted by none other than Ronald J Rumsfeld.

Another element to this man that made Darwin hate him was his red hair, he never trusted anyone with red hair, and this man had an abundance of curly red hairs, thinning on his head but pushing through the collar of his polo shirt in great amounts. Ronald Rumsfeld had been "seeing" Marie Foster for more time than Darwin cared to remember. His mother had remained single for years after his father had been killed, but in recent years, had been spending more and more time with this deplorable man. Ironically Marie had met Ronald in the liquor store, day after day, week after week they would run into each other stocking up on their favorite escapes. They had one thing in common from the get go and it had been their bond ever since. On this morning Darwin could see they were indulging in the tried and true beer/clamato hangover cure.

"Well I'm glad you're okay honey. That's just awful what happened to those people. I told you there are bears up there but you didn't want to believe me." Marie Foster said in a vindicated manner. "Why did you lie to me about going to the city?" Marie Foster hated confrontation, and Darwin knew she'd drop the matter quickly.

"Is there any food left?" Darwin questioned, making a point to not look at the inexcusable man and to change the subject.

"No sorry, honestly we thought you'd have left for the theater already." The head of red curls returned to the remaining bacon. In a teasing fashion Ronald twirled his tongue over and around the bacon only nibbling ever so lightly on the piece of meat, making his point to the starving killer.

I would kill you now and feel damn good about it, but I will not give you the satisfaction of a fast death. "I only work this evening. What time is it, by the way?"

"Where's that beautiful watch your mother gave you for your birthday?" Rumsfeld took pleasure in evading the questions of the boy who he knew had a strong hate-on for him.

That's not what I fucking asked; now tell me before I lose my cool! "It was stolen along with my clothes; I really need to know what time it is; none of the clocks are working." Darwin s continued staring at his nemesis but he sensed he was only to be ignored.

"Yeah the power was out last night, bitch of a wind storm. I'm sure your mom can tell you what time it is." Rumsfeld smirked at the heated boy.

Darwin could see clearly, poking through the matting of red arm hairs, a watch on Rumsfeld. Growing warmer Darwin realized in his present state of mind he could tear into Ronald before the first fang or hair protruded from the teen's body. Attempting to remain calm, Darwin decided to inflame the situation a little. "I guess the power went out to your watch too?"

Rumsfeld dropped his bacon to his plate and slid out from the breakfast nook. The small little man strutted toward the sink maintaining his eye contact. Casually he flipped a switch bringing with it a scrapping-gargling sound of the garborator. Pushing the remaining food into the churning hole, the sound of the garborator changed as it chewed through the heavy food offerings. Leaving his plate, the scantily dressed man walked passed Darwin into the living room without uttering a word.

Darwin grabbed the phone that hung near the door to the kitchen and began to dial. Frustrated and angered he could feel his cool slipping. His lessons from the night before were becoming very clear to him. Looking at Rumsfeld, all Darwin could think about was ripping into his jugular. He wanted to and at that point he knew his fear of murder had left him. For the moment he tried to hold back his urges and go about his day while he considered the events of the full moon. Unaware he had already dialed the phone began ringing in his ear.

"Hello" The female voice pleasantly answered.

Still distracted by his fledgling instincts he managed to get out some words. "Ah, hi, Mrs. Cardwen, is Steve around?"

"Darwin Foster, when are you coming over to hook up our new surround sound, you promised me almost a week ago that you would do it?" The woman gleefully asked.

He had forgotten. Working at the movie theater, Darwin was considered to be one of the most knowledgeable entertainment sound system operators in town. He had often been asked how he calibrated the bass and amps so perfectly. For Darwin it was simple logistics, play with it until it sounds perfect. Many people in the stereo business considered it to be a sort of science, but to Darwin it was nothing more than part of his job, a job he knew how to do well.

"I can come over now if you feed me some breakfast." Darwin saw this as the perfect opportunity to get some human grub and still look like the perfect angel that the majority of local parents saw him as.

"You be over here in twenty minutes and I'll have a whole-wack of flapjacks waiting for you and Steve should be home by the time you finish." Mrs. Cardwen sounded thrilled at the prospect of having company with her. The Cardwen home had been dysfunctional for years. Mr. Cardwen had been running around with girls Darwin's age for more than ten years. Mrs. Cardwen had always stuck by her man, being a staunch Mormon and all, but

Darwinism

inside her loneliness was spilling out into her daily behavior. Numerous times Darwin and Steve had been on the way out of the house only to be cornered with small talk by Steve's mother. The lady was kind hearted on the surface and Darwin felt for her, but he still dreaded the idea of spending more than an hour listening to her church stories.

"Where is Steve?" Darwin asked.

"I don't know, I think the devil's getting a hold of my boy, Darwin. Maybe he was out with that no good Clint, I honestly don't know Darwin, I can't keep track of him despite my best efforts. You'll keep him straight for me won't you sweetie?" The question was meant as a reassurance of her slipping family values that no one in her household shared.

Steve wasn't a bad guy, but if you critiqued him using the Mormon values Adolf Hitler might have looked like a saint compared to Steve. Steve enjoyed promiscuous sex, he enjoyed drugs – mostly weed and shrooms though he had tried *E*. Alcohol had been his constant companion since Darwin had first introduced him to it more than four years ago, but Steve introduced Darwin to marijuana so there was no animosity for developed habits that each other had suffered.

Steve was anti-religious, which had been a source of tension between him and his mother. He had also gone as far as urinating and defecating on the temple steps in protest. One of his greatest moments was when he brought a ladder to the temple one night and painted a pentagram above the main entrance. Under the insignia he wrote "Only lies dwell within". When several of the bible bangers arrived the next morning a few passed out at the sight, though Steve and Darwin were nowhere near the temple when it was discovered so they could only laugh at the stories they heard.

Steve had a few problems, but he always kept them in check. His anger had run off on him a few times, but that came mostly from his anger towards his father. Steve and Darwin had grown up together; they cared for each other in a way only best friends could ever understand. They looked out for each other.

"I'll try his cell, but I'll be over in a bit to help you out." Calmly he hung up the receiver and went upstairs to grab a jacket and cell phone. Darwin called Steve but was greeted by an automated message. Steve was notorious for letting his battery die. Darwin's concern for his friend persisted knowing how unstable his home life was. He really needed to see him now.

On his way back downstairs Darwin passed Ronald who sat on the couch watching WWF wrestling. He heard his mother in the shower, but decided he was in no mood to talk to her further today. With no shoes left he had little choice but to take the old dusty rubber gum boots his father use to wear at the plant. Today, Darwin's sense of fashion was extremely lacking with only a

69

coat from his youth that did not fit and hand-me-down shoes. If he had time, he would need to hit the thrift store.

Leaving the Foster home brought Darwin some comfort. In his current state of mind he was uncertain what he might do. He would have loved nothing more than to carry out his thought in the kitchen with Ronald, but a murder in his own home would draw too much attention. He understood the consequences of that. Darwin found peace of mind in the quiet cold streets of New Haven. The walk to Steve's house allowed him time to reflect, to premeditate his next victim.

CHAPTER 9

Mike Dolker, I could do him first. But I think he moved, but I know his little henchman still lives here, Jason Vegsund still works at the Me-So-FatSo Burger. I could catch him as he leaves for the night. Now that I know how I could change right in front of him; that would scare the shit out of him! Oh wait! Better idea, I could off one of Tim Waters tormentors, that way if I fuck up and there's an investigation they won't point the finger at me. Christ Darwin what the hell are you thinking, I doubt they will think you ate the guy! You're a goddamn monster! You can do anything you want; I need to just do it. Trust the beast. Everything I have been told, everything, my entire conscience can feel the truth behind it. What do I fear, what??? I'm still a GODDAMN PUSSY! THOSE BASTARDS MADE ME WEAK! I've never been able to stand up for myself, and even now I worry. They won't hurt me anymore!!

"Darwin Foster!" An elderly voice shouted from across the street. "Where you off to in such a rush?"

Darwin stopped in his tracks, scanning the other side of Baker Street for the voice that had pulled him from his contemplations. Within seconds Darwin realized he was a solid five blocks in the wrong direction. In his daze he had blocked out all other stimuli only to awaken in the center from downtown, across from the Caprice Theater. Regaining his bearings Darwin could see an old man with silvery white hair waving frantically in Darwin's direction. Ray Silverdale, perhaps one of the last movie theater pioneers, was outside clearing the walk in front of the theater. "Shit!" Darwin uttered

Mark Fuson

under his breath before giving a proper response. "Hey Ray! I'm just headed to the thrift store for a few minutes then I'm expected at the Cardwen house for breakfast."

"Breakfast! It's kind a late son, damn you must have had a good ski trip!" The medium height but heavyset man let out let out a deep-hearted belly laugh. The roundness of his belly swayed with his breathing; if Ray Silverdale had a beard and mustache he could have easily put the drunken excuse of a Santa Claus out of business at the Mid-Way Shopping Center.

Darwin crossed Baker Street without paying any attention to the possibility of oncoming cars. Somewhere inside, his fear of death and injury was beginning to take a back burner, and he wasn't even realizing it.

"I need you in by four thirty tonight if you don't mind, you and Tim are gonna get all the prep work started early tonight, Cindy's called in sick so the girl I hired is starting tonight but I'm going to be busy training her myself, is that alright by you?" Silverdale questioned, his cheeks bright red from the cool of the afternoon air creating an undeniably joyful appearance in the man.

Darwin began answering as he walked away, remembering he had told Ray he was going to the thrift store and then on to the Cardwen's. "Sure thing Ray, I'll see you this afternoon."

"Aren't you gonna tell me about your ski trip?" Ray shouted, as Darwin was already part way back across the street on a direct path to the thrift store.

"I'll tell you all about it tonight Ray, promise." Darwin quickened his trek through the snow knowing Ray would keep him at the theater starting now if he could. The thrift store was only a few doors down opposite the Caprice, and Darwin knew he could be in and out within a few minutes. Several pairs of shoes, a couple of pairs of jeans and some shirts, nothing elaborate, just enough to augment his dwindling wardrobe. If he had to transform again in the coming days he might also need some cheap clothing to rip through. He did not mind shopping at a thrift store. He felt no shame in buying clothes that were less than top quality. Darwin's beliefs made him feel old but he always considered a dollar in his pocket better than a dollar in someone else's pocket. Entering the store Darwin really didn't care what kind of finds he made, he had some items he needed and he would buy whatever best suited him.

Ding, Ding, Ding: the charms announced as Darwin strutted through the door into the shop. The store was a typical second hand shop; it was a first hand mess. Much of the new inventory was scattered about the aisles and floor of the store as the elderly staff sorted through it over the days and weeks. The sound of the Christmas carols echoed in the virtually empty store, Wayne Newton's version of Jingle Bells was playing accompanied by someone humming the traditional Las Vegas tune.

Darwinism

"Merry Christmas!" Darwin celebrated making the humming stop.

And a little head popped up from one of the racks. The little woman was Terri Bailey, widow of more than fifteen years who decided to devote her life to clothing the less fortunate. Darwin happened to be fortunate compared to other locals but Terri Bailey loved him just the same. "Lord have mercy! Darwin Foster, I was just thinking about you."

"Good morning, Mrs. Bailey, oh I guess I should say afternoon." Darwin towered over the little woman who was no more than four foot nine. Behind her thick black-rimmed glasses dating from the 1960's her eyes magnified to look like they were as large as golf balls. Dressed in her standard issue *Sally Anne* apron tiny Terri Bailey looked as though she belonged in her surroundings. Only one other place Darwin could imagine this tiny little woman, Friday night Bingo.

"I have some new clothing I put aside for ya, it just came in yesterday!" The excited woman shouted as though Darwin was still standing at the door to the shop. Now standing next to the little lady Darwin squinted at the force of her voice.

"That's great Mrs. Bailey, I also need some shoes if you have any." Darwin shouted back at the little midget as she ran through the store colliding with some of the overcrowded racks and shelves as she went, causing some more unwanted items to hit the floor.

"Shoes! Nobody ever looks at our shoes, and this past while it seems we've had a run on them. I guess since the mine closed its doors people have to think more economically. I don't care, it's good to see, it's a damn shame most of those shoes are never used again, ain't nothing wrong with them either. What size you need honey?" The voice shot over the racks to Darwin's ears, but he still couldn't see the woman behind all the clutter. One little push on the racks and she might be buried and lost forever, Darwin considered.

"Size eleven if you've got some." Darwin poked around the shirt racks as he waited patiently. In the back of the store he could hear the proverbial cusses of a dedicated woman.

"Oh Jesus and Mary, Lord what on earth did I do with them. I swear my mind is as sharp as an Indian's some days." The sound of more clutter could be heard collapsing to the floor. The entire back end of the store appeared to be ready to implode on itself. The racks and shelves all seemed to shake and rock with her curses.

Darwin snickered to himself at the racial comments from this little lady whom he adored so much. Terri Bailey would never hurt a fly but she was about as tolerant as a Nazi with a bad hang over. Her demeanor seemed to be good humored although not politically correct, and Darwin admired that quality in her. "Hey Mrs. Bailey, nice work on the decorations, it's got a real

New Haven charm to it." Looking around the store Darwin could see every ornament was used, every strand of tinsel had garnished more than its share of trees and the artificial tree in the far corner of the store that was cornered by clothing racks on three of four sides looked like it had no good side to display. The store personified what poverty in New Haven was. Happiness was only within the peoples' devotion to their town, no matter how sad their efforts may seem.

"You're a sweet heart! You got yourself a little lady yet, you should be thinking about settling down and starting a family." The rocking of the shelves seemed to be intensifying as more items rocked and fell to the ground.

"It's not really something I'm interested in, not at this point in my life. I'm too young to devote my life to one person." Stopping at the shoe rack Darwin could see a glut of golf shoes, bowling shoes but no ordinary everyday use shoe. Fumbling through the unorganized mound he began looking for the sizes, any shoe would do for a full moon, although a golf shoe might be a little impractical, it could do.

"I met my Frank when I was thirteen and he asked me to marry him when I was fourteen, it was a love that so few people have the fortunate pleasure of experiencing these days. I knew he was the right one for me the moment I laid eyes on him. I knew I had found my soul mate and my feelings for anyone else could never compare to what I had. One day I will be with my Frank again. I think there's nothing wrong with a boy marrying the girl he loves, as long as it isn't lustful. Lustful love is destined for failure. When you find her Darwin, you'll know, and you'll understand what I mean." The rocking of the shelves began to slow and the little woman emerged with a stack of clothing more than half her own height. The little figure wobbled from side to side at the weight she was carrying, releasing the load at Darwin's feet. "There you go hun, I hope you can find everything you need."

"I'm sure I will." Darwin replied.

"Oh mercy, I almost forgot, I got this dilly of a tie. When I saw it I thought of you right away. You start with this and I'll go grab it." The excited woman again disappeared into the abyss of the store, shelves and racks resuming their musical dance to the Christmas carols that continued to flood the store, now performing, Bing Crosby and White Christmas.

Darwin began searching the clothing, which he could see right out was a mother load. Everything was in his size, and not overly tacky. Darwin did try to maintain some sense of coolness in his dressing habits; just because he had started shopping second hand didn't mean he couldn't still keep an eye out for a brand name label. The pile in front of him contained khaki colorings, dulled plaid shirts, plain white and black t-shirts, a few sweaters and several pairs of jeans in excellent condition. On the shoe mound Darwin had only

Darwinism

found two pair of sneakers in a size eleven and he now added it to his hoard of clothing that he had all but decided to take.

"Son of a Bitch!" Bellowed from the back room of the store. "Oh Lord!"

"Mrs. Bailey, are you okay?" Darwin shouted with concern.

Moments later Terri Bailey emerged grasping a tie, and clenching her other hand tightly. "I've gone a sliced my hand open hun, I sure hope I didn't get any blood on this gorgeous tie, it's a motion picture themed tie. When I saw it I just knew you had to have it, especially if you're going to be a big wig manager over at the Caprice. Terri Bailey carefully handed the silk tie to Darwin who remained crouched on the floor.

Darwin only briefly noticed the tie, which he could see was quite beautiful and very appropriate for his work, but something else had begun to distract him. His nose began identifying an aroma in the air. It was heavy in metals, iron or some other form of metallic substance. The smell was also warm, very warm like a fresh roast out of the oven or a streaming carcass in the snow. A saltiness developed in the air that gnawed on Darwin's hunger. It reminded him of the fun from the previous evening. Darwin gazed up at Terri Bailey who was now applying a handkerchief to her bleeding hand. The blood was only slowing running from her wound, the white of the handkerchief was soaking through with the red, but the wound itself was nothing more than a one-inch gash.

Darwin became mesmerized on the motion of the blood oozing outwards from the cut, no longer able to concentrate on the clothing, shoes or Terri Bailey. He became fixated on a droplet of blood that had escaped the handkerchief and was now slowly rolling away from Terri Bailey's index finger. The tear of blood crossed her knuckle and quickened its speed to the end of her weathered finger nail before being released to the air and dropping to the floor below. Darwin's eyes hunted the blood drop, stalking its every movement making sure not to lose focus on the spot of carpet it had impacted on. Terri Bailey moved off to the back of the store uttering a few more biblical curses, but Darwin had no conception of anything around him that was happening. Once again alone in the front of the store Darwin instinctively crawled across the floor to the rapidly absorbing bloodstain. The saliva trickled from the corners of his mouth as he moved in towards the dirt of the carpet, to the shiny red dot that called to him. Tongue extended, he moved in to kiss the carpet. In one pass of his tongue the blood had been reabsorbed into Darwin's body creating a momentary sense of euphoria, bringing with it a sudden sweat and convulsion. The energy of the blood acted as a powerful endorphin. Darwin now completely collapsed to the floor, eyes glazed over, small canines now visible in his grinning mouth.

Ding, Ding, Ding: The chimes of his orgasm rang out. Darwin felt the

Mark Fuson

powers rushing through is body, his muscles had begun to partially fill with his primal strength and the nubs that his tongue now rolled against told him he was only seconds away from losing complete control. Darwin now flushed, but partially consciousness, scrambled to hide the evidence. He needed to eat more; he was still losing his control.

"Mrs. Bailey, got a delivery for you, it's from your Aunt Helen." The postman stopped at the edge of the counter near the front door of the store. Darwin remained silent in his collection of clothing, cowering, wishing he had not allowed himself to give in to his sudden desire. It was too late now, his actions had been done, and Terri Bailey's blood rushed through his veins making him want more. He couldn't kill these people, Terri Bailey or the Postman, it would take whatever will he had but he knew it was imperative he salvage his civility and get out of that store. Even as his rational thoughts returned, images of Terri Bailey's headless body decorated with the remains of the Postman in place of the dilapidated Christmas tree continued to fuel his raging hormones.

Darwin, feeling a coolness return to his body, and the sharp points in his mouth retracting, stood up making himself known. In his arms, he held a mass of clothing, not really caring what he held, this clothing brought him back to the days of elementary school and junior high when a textbook was his best friend. Darwin, looking as human as he did before, with the exception of the bulge in his pants, stood up. He smirked at the postman making an effort to keep his teeth concealed even though he was more or less sure they were human in appearance again.

"God bless Aunt Helen. She may be ninety-three but her Christmas cake would knock the thorns right of Jesus' head. Sorry to keep you waiting, I just nicked myself on one of the racks, I've been meaning to fix it too; I guess it's my own fault. I've just been too busy getting things ready for our big Christmas rush." Terri Bailey had returned to the front of the store this time her hand had a cotton bating taped around her cut. Darwin could not help but stare at the bandage; his attention was refocusing on his emerging desires.

"You alright Darwin? You looked a little flushed, like you're in love, I must warn you, I'm already spoken for!" Little Terri Bailey chuckled with delight at her humorous observation. To look at Darwin one might have thought he was in love, surely his expressions indicated he was infatuated with the object of his desire.

Removed from his lustful thoughts Darwin raised his head, leaving behind the sumptuous wound of her soft and frail flesh. "I was wondering the same thing about you, I hope your cut wasn't too bad." Darwin spoke in an alluring manner.

"Such the gentleman you are." Terri Bailey exclaimed. Are you intending

Darwinism

to take all of those clothes hun? If I had children you'd be putting them through college for me!" Again chuckling, Mrs. Bailey motioned to Darwin to put the clothing of the counter top at the cashier. Red faced and uneasy Darwin did so, keeping his groin flush to the countertop.

"I love the tie Mrs. Bailey, I think it will look great for my first day as manager." Darwin fumbled with his back pocket attempting to remove his wallet to pay his bill, finding it he began blundering through the stack of old receipts it contained looking for some cash.

The postman, who looked somewhat annoyed with Darwin, left Terri Bailey's package now partially obstructed under the mass of clothing and shuffled back towards the door. "You have yourself a good day Terri, I can see you've got your hands full. I'll check back later, maybe if your aunt made you Christmas cake, maybe you might let a tired old postman have a piece.

Shrilling with laughter Mrs. Bailey scoffed at the unnamed postman. "Go deliver your mail and maybe we'll talk!" Continuing her heckle, the postman departed the thrift store without uttering another word. Looking up to Darwin she found him in another world. "Darwin, are you sure you're alright?"

"I've never been so perfect Mrs. Bailey. In fact I can't remember a time I felt so good." Darwin smiled, showing off his human teeth to the tiny woman. With his erection subsiding Darwin realized he had left the shoes he wanted next to the unsorted pile of bowling and golf shoes. Dropping his wallet on the counter, Darwin went to retrieve his shoes while Terri began ringing up his sale.

Running back to the counter Darwin caught Mrs. Bailey staring at him, only for a brief second. At the cash register the once energetic woman now seemed quiet and removed. She typed into the register the numbers just as fast as Darwin had ever seen and she was making a point to avoid eye contact. "The postman is quite friendly with you." Darwin withdrew a fifty, two twenties and a ten from his wallet and dropped them to the counter. "I think you like him, don't you?" Darwin prodded with a sort of sexual intuition.

"Darwin Foster, I love my Frank! I always will. Don't you be saying stuff like that to me; I am a faithful wife." Visually upset by Darwin's comment her speed on the cash register increased becoming more and more erratic.

"I don't doubt that Terri, but it's okay for you to accept your feelings for another man. Frank would have wanted you to." Darwin took hold of her bandaged hand with the loving touch only felt from people who truly cared or understood. "It's time for you to let go Little Berry, release your pain." Darwin held firmly onto the bandage. Terry Bailey ceased her work on the cash register, sobbing openly but remaining tight lipped. Darwin looked on at the timid child, understanding fully her pain, her desires and her wishes. Nothing

77

she could say to him would deny what he felt from her. He was convinced that Terri Bailey had split apart like a Russian Matrioshka doll, each figure smaller than the last leaving only a tiny child like figure where there once stood a proud and strong woman. Examining her innocence Darwin felt pity on this lonely creature; her sadness filled the air like smoke, making Darwin feel poignant. Releasing her hand the woman remained motionless. Darwin bagged the entire garment selection on the counter himself, leaving the money on the counter not caring about the possible change he would get. Terri Bailey paid no attention to the clairvoyant's departure. Her eyes peered ahead, water logged, into a different dominion. She remained motionless in her store for many hours, undisturbed in her thoughts.

Moving as fast as he could through the snow clogged streets and walks Darwin again headed towards the Cardwen home, where he was expected some time ago. The incidents at the thrift store continued to be considered in his mind, but only in a passing sense. He had not become worried at his sudden impulsive actions with the blood; even his sexual reactions and partial metamorphosis did not play a large roll in his thoughts. Terri Bailey was a very sad and lonely woman and her pain was most of what he now thought about. The emotions of the woman were of guilt, love and dedication. Everything he sensed from her was more clear and detailed; an inventory of her past.

His own feelings were disrupted; the idea of slaughter and feeding had taken a back seat to what he now saw. Terri Bailey was a simple woman as were her needs. She had truly fallen in love with her husband Frank at a very young age. The romantic boat rides out on Lake Lonetain with the wine and cheese. The peaceful car rides into the mountains where they would make passionate love for hours in the grassy alpine meadows; movies and dinners night after night; her history with Frank had been long and revered. One afternoon on one of their alpine frolics Frank coined the nickname, Little Berry, which he reserved for his continuing description of his wife over the years. He called her his Little Berry for her small, and sometimes sweet, but mostly tart personality. Terri Bailey devoted her every day of existence to her husband, despite his later fraternizing and courting of other woman, openly and knowingly. Frank did it to hurt Terri, even though her feelings for him were strong and dedicated to the day he passed on. What she felt now was failure. By admitting her love had fallen on denying ears for so many years, she was conceding that there was no future with Frank in the afterlife.

Darwin knew they would never reunite in death; Frank had gone in another direction; one his loving wife would not follow in. He wasn't sure how he knew, the perceptions he had were only impressions, but it left him understanding more of Terri Bailey than he ever thought possible.

CHAPTER 10

727 Cadmore Avenue was a one-story home that was developing the neglected look. The neighborhood was not all that far from Clairmont Boulevard, but the class of people living here was quite different. The vast majority of people living on and near Cadmore Avenue were hardworking laborers, primarily uneducated and all with their problems. The Cardwen house was smack dab in the middle of this neighborhood, and the Cardwen family themselves could have been the ruling imperial family of the slums.

Theodore and Sally Cardwen were exceptionally tough parents. Theodore was old school in his discipline though he never hit his children out of anger, only for punishment, but what he deemed punishable made one question his motives. Steve Cardwen had his share of broken bones and black eyes throughout his youth, though he seldom spoke of how he won the honor displaying his medals. Steve's ability to survive his father's torment was only surpassed by his ability to survive his mother's. She never hit Steve; though she had a natural ability to mock, belittle and crush what remaining self-esteem he had. With Jesus at her side Sally Cardwen labored at molding her son into the good Lord's image, in her efforts to save her son, she had only pushed him further away, transforming him into the unknown rebellious teen.

Steve kept much of his family problems to himself; Darwin had learned most of what he knew about the Cardwen's through his observations in the house and rumors on the street. The bruises on Steve were an obvious sign of what was happening. It was the way Sally spoke to her son that always made Darwin feel a little gratefully for his own mother, despite her alcoholism.

Steven that's filthy, it's a sin to play with yourself, no boy should ever play with himself. What girl is going to want a little faggot who can't stop touching his penis? You're pathetic, you'll never have anyone love you like I do. Jesus will pray for your sins, though I doubt it will help. You've been touched by the hands of evil; the heavens will smite you in your sleep if your father and I can't get you cleansed.

The religious jargon had done more to wear down Steve than any amount of physical punishment that could have been dolled out by his father. Maybe it was the sincerity of his mother's words, or maybe it was how she said them. Sally Cardwen seldom raised her voice and her tone was always belittling. One of the most common tactics the woman had was embarrassment. All of New Haven knew about Steve's chronic masturbation problem, although he had actually indulged in the activity no less than any other young man. The entire congregation of the New Haven Church of Later Day Saints prayed upon every sinful action Steve had ever committed in his mother's eyes. Most churchgoers, though believing that their spirits are good, can't help but gossip about other people's private lives. The gossip created from the prayers had no hope in being kept within the temple community; everything Sally Cardwen accused her son of in the temple became fact and ammunition for torment in the public school system. Darwin just laughed at how ridiculous Sally Cardwen really was. She was a hypocrite through and through who wouldn't know true faith if it punched her in the face. Darwin wasn't familiar with the Mormon teachings, but it seemed counter productive to outcast a family member through embarrassment. It wasn't in keeping with what he knew of spirituality.

The front door to the Cardwen house opened before Darwin had even reached the porch steps. "There you are! I was wondering if you were ever coming, your flapjacks were starting to get cold." Standing in the doorway was an abnormally happy woman. A grin stretched ear-to-ear exposing her over painted lips and yellowing teeth and the redness of her hair clashed with the whiteness of the outdoors. Her hair with full body and lots of volume, made the woman look ready for a night on the town, which Darwin knew to be unlikely, she never went anywhere. Sally Cardwen was wearing a tropical fruit pattern blouse and tight white jeans; clearly a thrift store window bargain she was unable to say no to. "Ah! What have I turned you into?"

What, oh fuck she knows! Flashed into Darwin's mind, but only briefly, before realizing she was pointing at the three large bags that she recognized to be thrift store standards. "Sorry I'm late, but Mrs. Bailey had some things

Darwinism

set aside for me that I needed to take a look at before she went and sold them on me."

"Don't you worry about that Darwin, the thrift store always comes first. Looks like you made a pretty good haul too." Mrs. Cardwen retreated into the warmth of the house, which tinged of sweet stale cigarettes. Both Theo and Sally smoked, and so did Steve, but that was one secret that Sally had not found out about yet.

Darwin placed his bags next to the shoe rack and kicked off his clunky boots. He had barely undone the first button of his coat when Mrs. Cardwen began with his interrogative nature. "That's an awful coat Darwin, couldn't Mrs. Bailey have found something a little better for you?"

Darwin, still a little off balance from Mrs. Cardwen's candor, politely responded. "This coat is a few years old, from when I was a kid, mine was stolen while I was out of town. I don't like it either, it doesn't fit, but it's the only warm coat I have for right now. Mrs. Bailey had some nice looking jackets, but nothing in my size today." The stench of his lie masked the cigarette smell for a moment. Mrs. Cardwen was a quick study and she usually could tell when a person was lying, but today, she seemed more thrilled to have the company.

"I'm so excited about our new entertainment system, Theo and I both agreed straight out you should be the one to set it up, no body knows more about this kind of thing than Darwin Foster. I can't wait to watch the Ten Commandments with full surround sound!" The carefree woman pranced through the living room into the kitchen continuing to talk as she went.

Darwin had lost interest in this woman already. Her overpowering personality could only be tolerated in small doses, and although he had only just arrived and he was already scheming of ways to leave. Looking into the living room Darwin only saw a handful of unopened boxes near the wall unit. BLUE RAY-DVD and SONY were the only clear words he could see from his vantage point, but immediately he knew the job shouldn't take long.

Without delaying Darwin dove into the boxes, deciding to forgo his pancakes until after he had finished his work. Mrs. Cardwen returned from the kitchen a few moments later with one cup of coffee and a pack of Marlboro Lights, not stopping to offer Darwin any coffee. Her caffeine in hand she sat on the sofa and chatted Darwin's ear off while he worked, keeping him mildly distracted. Every topic flew threw the living room: the thrift store, Darwin's mom, the temple, Christmas and then Steve.

"Have you heard what Steve's latest plan is?" Mrs. Cardwen asked Darwin whose head was buried behind the wall unit.

"Ah, no. I haven't seen much of him lately, what's he up to?" Darwin's question echoed off the walls and through the wall unit itself, while he continued to connect the red-to-red, yellow-to-yellow.

"My son, I swear if he hadn't popped out of me I'd assume he was someone else's. Last week he tells me that God has warped my mind and if I had any sense I'd pull my head out of my *A*—" Sally Cardwen avoided swearing at all costs, even at the risk of sounding ridiculous. A-hole and Poo-head were about as much of a cuss as this woman could produce, though she had no problem with other slurs: faggot, nigger, chug, retard.

"He said he was leaving, as soon as he had enough money. He also said he was never returning and it was because of me!" Mrs. Cardwen's voice resonated in a dumbfounded way.

"He hasn't mentioned anything to me about it, but I haven't seen him since last week. I'm sure he doesn't really mean he'll never return. But in all honesty Mrs. Cardwen, you and Steve have always butted heads, maybe him leaving wouldn't be so bad." Darwin knew his statement might cause some animosity, but he didn't care.

Out to in, out to in. The process was very repetitive.

"Do you think I have a warped mind?" Mrs. Cardwen casually asked.

Darwin considered his response. Truthfully, yes, he did think she had a warped mind, but then he thought most religious people did. He also questioned her motivations for pushing Steve so hard. His grades had always been good, he had never been arrested and he had never had sex at home. Darwin felt maybe she had pushed harder on Steve over the years in a futile attempt to wane his rejection of her values, or maybe she sensed something in Steve that was not conducive with Mormon life.

"I think everyone has a warped mind, including you Mrs. Cardwen. Steve's a good guy; you and Steve just have different values; that doesn't make him bad, or you. He's your son, the love you feel should be unconditional, and if it's not, then I guess you have a warped mind." Darwin pulled himself out from behind the wall unit. Every box was opened and room was littered with Styrofoam and plastic, but it was finished.

"Okay let's take it for a test drive." Hitting all the power buttons on each of the new pieces of equipment they came to life with a low hum. Darwin asked Mrs. Cardwen if she had any DVD's, of course she had the Ten Commandments in hand, ready to go. A few seconds later the blare of the studio logo came through on the screen and Darwin was satisfied he had succeeded in his work. Before allowing the opening credits of the movie to begin, Darwin promptly shut down all the equipment.

"Thank you Darwin, you're very efficient." There was sharpness in her voice, and the excitement had seemed to have passed. Sally rose from the

Darwinism

sofa and disappeared down the hall towards the bedrooms without saying anything more.

Darwin knew she had been offended by his comment but he didn't care. His comments were truthful and he didn't believe in sugar coating the truth, especially when talking about family or friends. Poking his head around the corner from the living room Darwin found a heaping stack of pancakes just waiting for his watering mouth. A pound of butter, a new bottle of maple syrup and a jug of orange juice had all been laid out nicely on the linoleum of the dinning room table. Darwin decided he had earned his keep, and seated himself at the head of the table and began devouring the carbohydrate feast.

From the kitchen a comment forced Darwin to slow down his bingeing. "Are you going to say hi or has my mother converted you too?"

Darwin, with his mouth full of the last pieces of his brunch, immediately replied. "Fsht, I ddn't ear yu." His words came out garbled, but clear enough to be understood. Grabbing the jug of orange juice that was now nearly empty, Darwin cleared his throat. "Steve! Man, what's up? I haven't seen you around much lately."

"You'd stay away from your home too if you had parents like I did." Steve came into the dining room and pulled up a chair next Darwin. "So I see you got suckered into installing the ultimate in religious entertainment. Was this your payment?" Steve pointed to the pound of butter that was now only about half a pound's worth and the heavily depleted syrup bottle.

"I was hungry. Besides your mother does make awesome pancakes." Using his knife Darwin cut another chunk of butter and placed it on his empty plate. Instinctively he grabbed the syrup and poured it over the lone butter.

"I think you're out of pancakes." Steve said teasingly to Darwin as the fork was pushing into the sweet butter chunk.

"So your mom said you were with Clint?" Closing his mouth around the dripping butter, he retracted the now empty fork and returned it to his plate. Slumping back in his chair he now seemed satisfied.

Steve grinned at his friend who looked like it had been his first experience eating food. "I just told my mother I was with Clint, but I wasn't."

"Where did you go then?" Darwin asked as he took the last of the orange juice to wash down his stick of butter.

"I've got a secret. I'll tell you, but you have to promise you'll keep it between us." Steve looked as though he had the weight of the world behind his eyes. Eager and excited, Steve didn't give Darwin the chance to confirm his willingness to secrecy. "I'm leaving New Haven, and I'm not coming back."

The pit of Darwin's stomach dropped and the blood in his veins had ceased to flow. Darwin was not excited to hear the news. Steve had severed their bond in one fell swoop. "When?" Darwin questioned, quietly.

"Soon, maybe tonight, but I want you to come with me?" Steve was alive, blanketed with a joy that Darwin had not seen in years. The dimples in his cheeks were deeper than they had ever been before. A smile, a true genuine smile was accenting his boyish good looks. Steve looked at his friend who said nothing in return to his news. Grabbing Darwin's forearm, Steve appealed to Darwin and their friendship. "I can't stay here anymore D, you see what happens here - in this house, the worst of it you've never seen. I have to take this chance and leave now. I don't want to leave you behind, we've been friends since grammar school, we understand each other better than anyone else, but understand me, and if I stay here any longer I'm going to go postal."

Darwin looked to his friend who he knew was being sincere, but Darwin had his own problems he had to deal with, his own secrets to reveal. Darwin wanted nothing more than to accept Steve's offer, but he knew he couldn't, not now at least. "Where will you go?

"I think I'll head to the south west, maybe Los Angeles. I don't know. Right now I just want to hit the open road, I'll figure out where I'm going when I get there." Steve squeezed his friends' arm tightly. The firm touch of his hand told a thousand words and a million feelings. Steve didn't want Darwin to go, he needed him to go.

"Steve, I really want to." Stopping, his eyes turned to the still empty plate of food in an effort to shield his tearing orbs. "I'm going through some shit right now that I need to sort out first." Choking up, Darwin stopped.

"D, whatever it is, we can sort it out together. You can't tell me you're happy in *New Hell*. It will be good for both of us to leave; this town has done nothing for either of us." Steve let go of Darwin only to watch his friend collapse into an emotional wreck. "If we leave now maybe we can start being who we really are and be honest with each other."

One tear rolled down Darwin's cheek, and then another. His nose was clogging with his internal emotional goo. Darwin had experienced so much in recent days, and now he was losing his best friend, his only true friend. It was the first time in a long time Darwin did not know what he should do. He wanted to go with Steve. Steve was right about *New Hell*; it had done nothing for either of them. Leaving now could be dangerous, traveling with his best friend on the open road without him knowing about his gift. Darwin considered admitting to his friend his own secret and for a moment taking a chance and passing the gift on to Steve. "Steve, there's something about me you don't know." Darwin stopped. Steve continued peering at his friend, emotions unchanged, still vigorous and happy. Darwin took comfort in his friend's appearance, but at the last moment he backed away from his admission.

"There's nothing I don't already know about you but whatever you have to tell, whatever it is you are so worried about, I'll be there for you, no matter what." A sparkling flash from within Steve's eye brought Darwin security, but still he knew he could not risk his friend, he had to work through his evolution before risking his friend's safety.

Darwin knew he had to stay behind, telling his friend was going to be the hardest thing he would have to do. "Steve, when you get to where you're going, please write me. I will come to wherever you are; I just can't go now. I know you would accept anything I have to tell you, and I will tell you, I just can't yet. You have no idea how much I want to go with you." Darwin rolled his head back and looked into the cheap chandelier while he battled his words. "FUCK! This hurts so much." Wiping away the steady flow of tears Darwin got up from his chair and walked into the living room to get ready to leave his emotional nightmare. Inside his body his emotions were beginning to fight with themselves, Darwin knew his hypersensitivity and emotional instability could push him further than he wanted to go. He had to leave, even though it gave him more grief than staying.

"D, where are you going?" Steve chased his friend into the living room trying to continue their conversation.

"I have to go, Steve. Please don't leave without seeing me first. I'll be at the theater tonight." Darwin already had his boots and jacket partially on when he opened the door to the house in an effort to leave. "I can't have you seeing me like this, I'm sorry."

"Hey man we've gone through a lot of shit together, we've both seen each other cry, don't been ashamed. Please don't leave Darwin, I need you!" Steve pleaded to his friend.

Darwin ran over to Steve and embraced him, kissing him on his cheek as he pressed his body against his friend. It was the closest the two had ever been together and Steve reciprocated.

Crying openly, Darwin grabbed his thrift store bags and left the Cardwen home, leaving Steve standing on the cold of the porch. Darwin didn't turn back as he moved through the snow to Cadmore Avenue. Sulking and sobbing he had turned his back on his friend in an effort to save him. Darwin moved down the road wishing, for the first time, that he had not been given the gift. The emotional bond with Steve was strong, stronger than even the two of them realized. Every step towards Baker Street felt like a step in the wrong direction in the pit of Darwin's stomach. He would have given anything to turn around, but he could feel his will sliding. His desire to kill was again resurfacing. It wasn't going to be long until he had to choose a victim again, and no matter what, it could not be Steve.

CHAPTER 11

Darwin arrived at the Caprice Theater just before four o'clock. He had decided against going home though he did not feel like going to work either. Inside the theater Darwin stored several clean uniforms, and there was a shower that he could use if he needed to. With all the emotional baggage he had carried on his shoulders today a shower was exactly what he felt like having. The killings from the night before really weren't bothering him, they were part of him. His frustrations came from his normal life, and the people around him. In his past life Darwin would endure the tribulations, but as the wolf, he was realizing that did not have to be the case.

The small changing area was seldom used by any of the staff. Usually it was only the male staff who used the changing area, but occasionally Cindy or one of the other females would venture into the small musty room. It was each staff's responsibility to put a sign on the doorknob indicating privacy was needed, and in the many years Ray Silverdale had been using that changing room policy, there had been only a handful of accidental peep shows.

With the water on nearly full, Darwin was not cleaning himself in the shower, just defusing. As in recent days, his mind began a journey. His eyes fixated on the cracked white tile of the shower wall. Within each crack Darwin found a piece of himself. The cracks in the wall were a portrait of his crumbling and reshaping life.

God not Steve! Please keep him here with me I can't live without him. With each passing second the crack in the tiles grew, showing more and more what was hidden behind the wall.

A world had opened up to Darwin that he never knew existed. Behind the cracks of the wall were the hidden secrets of New Haven. Every lie, crime, act of violence, it was all clearly displayed within the wall. The themes of the cracks were torment, suffering and anguish. Every citizen of New Haven was accounted for in the fractures, and Darwin could see all the pain they had ever caused.

You fat fucking cunt, you're lucky to have me, no one would ever sleep with a big ugly ass like you.

I'll kill her fucking dog! She'll just think it ran away. That'll teach her for not learning to keep her dog quiet at night.

You call this dinner! Better stuff comes out of my ass.

You're having an abortion!

You tramp, you expect me to believe that I got you pregnant! You fucking whore, I should have known a little whore like you would try to pull something like this.

What did I tell you about wearing your shoes on this carpet? Is it time for another lesson?

The bitch asked for it! You can't rape the willing!

My son masturbates to gay pornography. He masturbates to the images of small boys; he's a pedophile I tell you! God help him! I caught him sodomizing himself with produce, can you believe that, the filthy little bastard. My husband disciplines the boy until he's unconscious but nothing seems to help. Pray for him.

Shhhh, it's okay, it's okay, just be quiet. You're a big boy now, aren't you, look at you! Dar doesn't that feel good? I like it, don't you? I think you will grow to love it, I did. Shhhhhhh! Mom's coming! If you tell anyone your big brother might have to spank you, and big brother doesn't want to hurt you because he loves you more than anyone else. Now go play, and I'll come up stairs in awhile and we'll have more playtime.

They all deserve to die!

Everything the town had ever witnessed seemed to be flowing into his eyes. He could see things in himself he didn't want to see. He could see things in others he didn't want to know. The universe of New Haven had tapped into his emotional distress fueling his pain with the pain of others. Verbal abuse, physical abuse and sexual abuse: New Haven was crawling with people who deserved to die. Was his mind showing him what he needed to do? Every image, every sound from the past and present made Darwin yearn for more blood, a taste of the power that had rushed through him with Terri Bailey, and the others. The town had an ample supply of food, almost anyone would do, he was certain now. Mesmerized by his apprehension, Darwin began to feel good in what he was about to do. The pain and triumphs of his day started to empty away into the drain. A idea was forming, forbidden, but intriguing.

"Hey Darwin! I thought I'd shower here today; better than showering at school." Short and gangly Tim Waters strolled into the change room as though he hadn't a care in the world.

Darwin pulled the curtain back to see the piece of meat that had strolled in the door. Small and bony, Tim sat with his back to the shower and was beginning to remove his shirt. From behind, Darwin could only see the pasty white of his skin, a long bumpy spine stretching from his waist up into his sumptuous neck. The tiny arms of this boy showed his inferiority to Darwin, hardly any muscle. Darwin couldn't respond to Tim's question, he was trapped, fixated at the image of Tim Waters. Darwin had been thinking of killing, and Tim had arrived at the wrong moment.

"So do you think we'll be busy tonight?" Tim politely asked.

Darwin wanted to be closer to Tim; he could feel himself being pulled closer by the smell of the boy. A raging appetite was developing and Darwin knew that pancakes were not what he needed. He was going to kill Tim Waters, he was going to tear out his throat and maybe chew on his eyeballs. The thoughts of ripping into his flesh became all consuming. The boy deserved to die, what purpose did he serve? Turning off the shower Darwin stepped out and moved closer to Tim not taking a moment to dry off.

"By the way, thanks for your advice about my problems at school. It's really helped. I still get teased but not as much as before. I still wish they were dead though, I can't ever forgive them for what they did to me." Tim, now only wearing tight white briefs stood up to find a naked Darwin hovering overtop of him.

Darwin looked down on the small boy, his white flesh still looked more satisfying than anything that he could imagine, but the boy's last comment had brought Darwin down a notch. "You wish they were dead?"

Tim was unsure of what to say as his mentor, friend and colleague who was now standing well inside his personal space. "I'd kill'em all if I could." Tim hesitated.

All of a sudden Darwin knew that Tim should not die. Tim was a good person, just like Darwin, and Darwin would have to remain in control a little while longer while he found someone else to pay for his urges. "You're a good kid, something good will happen to you soon." Darwin decided he would help little Tim, he knew the tormentors, and Darwin would just have to seek them out and eliminate them.

Tim stepped around Darwin to get into the shower. Darwin's consciousness was returning to him slowly. Aware he had nearly lost control Darwin put on his uniform and headed onto the floor of the theater, trying to remain focused on the work for the evening. Tim had a long shower before he entered the theater floor, uncertain what had just transpired with his co-worker and unsure what he should do.

The halls of the Caprice Theater remained void of discussion between Darwin and Tim for much of the afternoon. The two young men worked together behind the concession checking the CO2 and syrup for the pop machine, priming the popcorn machine, counting the evening's float money, restacking the free entertainment magazine rack, and replenishing the condiment stand, but neither looked one another in the eye. Darwin spoke only what needed to be communicated to Tim who had remained distant and cold since the incident in the change room. Ray Silverdale had emerged only briefly to introduce the new box office attendant, but neither Tim nor Darwin could recall after the introduction the person's name.

At six thirty the box office opened and the first customers began trickling through the door. Darwin left Tim to man the concession alone while he went to collect tickets and greet the incoming customers. Still a little dazed, Darwin had enough consciousness to recognize two of the first customers to enter the theater. Terri Bailey and the postman came through the doors of the theater as though they were teenagers on their first date. Terri Bailey greeted Darwin with a giant smile and when she was close enough she gave him a warm hug.

"Thank you Darwin Foster, I don't know what you did, but thank you!" Terri whispered into Darwin's ear only loud enough for him to hear.

Darwin smirked but didn't respond. He felt happiness in what he had seen. Little Berry was out enjoying herself with another man. Darwin knew he was responsible, but he wasn't sure how he had done it. His spirit lifted, Darwin was able to function normally for the rest of the evening. When Terri Bailey and the postman left the theater two hours later Darwin had overheard Terri suggesting they stop by the Me-So-Fatso Burger for a late snack. It was vindication, and it was recognition that good could come from his power, even if he didn't fully understand how it all worked. As the happy couple left the theater that night Darwin felt a greater sense of purpose.

"The new box office attendant is damn good, not as pretty as Cindy mind you but a hell of a lot faster." Jolly Ray Silverdale stood next to Darwin just inside the door of the theater. The last customers were on their way in to the final showing of the night; an over rated sci-fi film. "I think she can look after the last few customers on her own. So tell me about Arcadia!" Ray gave Darwin a light punch on the shoulder as a sign of his excitement.

A lie. What would be a good lie? He thought quickly to himself. "The weather was good for the first day but the snow started falling on the second day and the wind made things a little difficult to see." That should do, he thought.

"What do you take me for Darwin, come on! You must have gotten some action!" Ray Silverdale was a jolly old pervert. Ever since Darwin had started work at the Caprice Ray had always been poking around into his sex life.

Was Ray one of the bad elements of New Haven? Darwin thought back to the cracks in the wall. There were vague impressions of Ray Silverdale, but nothing concrete. Darwin relaxed his mind and tried to look beyond the web of deceit and misgivings that kept deluging his mind. "No Ray, the action was kinda lacking, just a whole lot of guys drinking beer." *Leave me alone you perv; I was getting along fine until you started talking to me.*

"Damn boy, not even a circle-jerk?" Ray continued probing quietly but not in a joking manner. His questions were serious. His interest was genuine.

Get off my back would you! I didn't go skiing; I had eight search and rescue members for dinner and I raped a fucking deer when I turned into a half man half wolf thing after I got angry!

Darwin turned to his voluptuous boss who was beginning to look like a well-rounded blabbering meal. "You got me, Ray; I slapped my monkey on the chair lift with my buddy Clint. It was great! I showered my load on some ski class we passed over, you would have loved it, Ray!" Darwin chuckled to himself at his erroneous lie. Walking away Darwin saw little Tim Waters behind the concession counter, his line was beginning to back up and Darwin decided he needed yet another distraction to keep him focused. His shift was almost over, only a few more hours to endure and he could begin his hunt.

Ray Silverdale remained near the front door to continue collecting the last few entrance tickets. The old man seemed to be thinking of other things now, maybe images of showering globs of semen. The forbidden images kept Ray very much amused and to himself.

"What's with the service in this place? I think it's because they hired one too many fags." Two obnoxious teenage customers stood at the concession, taking their time forcing Tim Waters to endure their comments. A growing line of impatient people was stacking in behind.

Darwin interjected into the situation, recognizing the customers as Tim's own high school bullies. Moving rapidly behind the counter Darwin knew he would want to kill these people even before hearing their pleas. He sensed their malevolence radiating off them like the cold from an open freezer. "Move along!" Darwin said sternly.

The two perfect complexioned teens snickered to one another. "Oh look, his boy friend has come to his rescue once again!"

Darwin hated them. Both boys were everything he ever hated in his own tormentors. The two teens stood bold and confident in their superiority. The thought of growing claws and pushing through their beady eyeballs grew some arousal in Darwin. "If I have to tell you again you'll be asked to leave entirely." Darwin explained as calmly as he could, still envisioning the feel of the corneas between his fingers. "You wouldn't happen to be seeing *Strikers Back* now would you?"

"What's it to you?" One of the pompous teen exclaimed.

"You have to be at least eighteen years of age or accompanied by an adult to see that movie. And since I know you're both only sixteen I suggest you go to the box office, they'll refund your money." A blackness filled Darwin's eyes, evil designed to terrify the arrogance of the boys.

With revenge in their eyes one of the henchman looked at Tim. "You're dead Waters!"

Both teens moved away slowly keeping their eyes on Darwin. Even as they exited the theater, the boys glared back at Darwin. Tim said nothing to his boss, continuing to work and lessening the line of waiting customers. Darwin knew these boys would retaliate against Tim. Darwin watched his small defenseless friend working hard, trying to be a good and honest person. Much of what Darwin saw in Tim he had also seen in himself. Darwin knew Tim would kill his oppressors, in hail of gunfire, a homemade bomb, dismemberment, or maybe a good old torching. Every consideration would be given at repaying the worst at Ridgemount High for their years of unwarranted hatred. Watching Tim, Darwin felt pity, the road ahead for him was long and arduous, and he wasn't convinced Tim had enough friends to help him through the difficult times. Steve had been there for Darwin and Darwin for Steve. Neither Darwin nor Steve could have survived school without each other; they would not make it through life without each other.

Continuing to help Tim at the concession Darwin could not help but wonder if and when Steve would come to see him. Would his friend leave New Haven? Darwin kept his eye on the doors, but as the time passed fewer people came through, and the street beyond the doors was almost deserted. The cast of light from the street lamps and town Christmas decorations illuminated the lightly falling snow.

The hours passed in silence for Darwin, Tim and Ray, the calm of deliberations filled the halls of the Caprice Theater. Ray had allowed the box office attendant to go home after the last show had started. The Caprice Theater only had six cinemas and four of the six cinemas had let out by eleven thirty when Ray Silverdale emerged from the office having completed the night's cash out.

"Darwin, can you lock up tonight?" Ray questioned Darwin who still remained behind the concession, still consumed by the outside world. "Darwin?"

"Yeah, sure." Darwin meekly replied.

"Hey, I'm sorry if you were offended about my questions earlier. I won't bug you about that anymore." Ray gave Darwin a little wink and turned making his way to the exit. Turning around one last time Ray Silverdale shouted back. "Oh, Tim can you stay with Darwin until after the last theater lets out, shouldn't be much past midnight? Just make a note on your timecard."

"Sure, Ray!" Tim shouted back happily. Young Tim was so excited to have his job and he always said yes to anything Ray had ever asked of him.

Retiring to the snow of the street, Ray left the theater, leaving the tense boys in command. Darwin was feeling all right, though his urges were still in the back of his head. He was more concerned that he had not heard from Steve and not knowing what his friend was thinking or doing was taking its toll.

The Caprice Theater was spotless; Tim had worked hard to avoid making eye contact with Darwin he had finished all of the evening's work and much of the prep work for the following day. Even the emptied theaters had been cleaned leaving only cinemas two and six to be tidied after the movies had ended. With Ray out of the building Tim concentrated his cleaning to the public washrooms, away from Darwin. In the lobby the puppy dog eyes of a saddening Darwin still had not moved from view of the front doors, and still no one had come. No one had even walked by. The silence was thick throughout the halls of the Caprice that words from the still playing movies could be clearly heard by both Tim and Darwin.

Just before midnight the last movie let out and Tim, wanting to leave as soon as possible, quickly rushed in to begin cleaning. Awkwardness had been the theme for the evening in the theater and going home was first and foremost on Tim's mind. Tim was startled when he saw Darwin standing at the top of the cinema six, watching the boy work at cleaning the theater. Darwin had said nothing, and Tim couldn't be sure how long Darwin had been present, but the awkwardness was greater than ever before.

"About earlier today, I'm sorry if I freaked you out. It was my fault; I should have put the privacy sign on the door." Darwin confessed to his mechanical maid.

"That's okay, Darwin. I wasn't freaked out." Little Tim continued sweeping the discarded pop and popcorn containers down to the front of the theater.

"So are we still friends?" Darwin asked as though he was regaining the confidence of a child.

"Of course we are!" Tim shouted up to the top of the theater. "It was just a little weird."

"What do you mean?" Darwin threw out into the emptiness of the theater.

Darwinism

"I just, I mean." Tim stumbled with his words, unable to clear up his comment. Tim stopped with his broom in hand and looked back up to Darwin who had advanced a little further into the theater. "I just thought for a moment you liked me more than just a friend, I wasn't really ready for it."

Laughing in a giant outburst Darwin was relieved to hear this boy thought Darwin had a boyhood crush on him. "Tim, well fuck, I'm lost for words!" Darwin grabbed a garbage bag Tim had left midway down the theater and began helping his friend finish the evenings work.

"What should I do about Rick and Bill?" Tim asked after the laughter in the theater had subsided.

Darwin knew immediately that Tim was referring to the pompous assholes at the concession. *Kill them; kill the fucking bastards, and their families too – to make a point. They deserve to die!* "Do you really consider killing them?"

Tim Responded quickly. "Everyday. All I think about is ending it. I hurt so much Darwin," The boy paused for a moment as his emotions exploded "Why won't they just stop!?" The boy exclaimed as the waterworks poured from his face. "Why can't people like us control the town? Why is it the assholes that get all breaks?"

Darwin was pained by this pathetic image. Darwin knew all too well that Tim Waters was fighting a futile battle. If the boy had the will and the means to end his suffering, he would. Tim had a quality that Darwin lacked, a sense of duty – the ability to see the greater good even if it meant ending his own life in the process. Tim would kill everybody on his way down and feel just in his actions. History would judge him as a monster, even though that was the one thing he was not, and never could be. Darwin went to console the weeping child, giving him a hug of friendship. Holding onto Tim tightly the claws tearing through the boys heart were clearer than they had ever been before. Darwin too began to weep with the boy, the similarities of their pasts were too much to ignore.

Darwin pressed his face against the boy, absorbing his emotions, seeing the pain first hand. The stories the boy held were even worse than Darwin's own.

A shower room incident; Darwin could see a gang of boys standing over the frail and naked body of little Tim. The others were pissing on him, urinating in his face. One of the boys, Rick, held the limp and bruised face of Tim Waters up forcing his mouth open. Bill began urinating in Tim's open mouth. Another, much older boy came at the defenseless child with a golf club. The gang spread Tim's legs exposing his anus. The older boy, the familiar older boy, forced the golf club handle inside small Tim's body. Only a whimper could be heard for the barely conscious child. The older boy pushed and shoved the club into the small ass; the onlookers laughed and cheered as he went. "Take that you faggot! We're doing you a favor, enjoy it bitch." The words echoed in a familiar way, Darwin knew the voice that had spoken those awful words, Mike Dolker. The vision from inside Tim Waters ended, Darwin found himself weeping with young Tim in his arms, Disturbed and furious by what he had seen, Darwin knew the suffering Tim had endured at the hands of one of his own high school tormentors. Letting himself go, Darwin knew what he had to do, a plan was coming together.

"This will hurt Tim, but don't be afraid." Darwin whispered into Tim's ears.

Tim hadn't even responded to what Darwin had said when Darwin began to change. The strong arms of Darwin Foster tightened their hold on Tim Waters, rapidly growing in size. Tim struggled a little; looking up at Darwin's darkening face and eyes.

"DARWIN!" Tim shouted in disbelief.

Canines extending from his gums, Darwin looked at the cowering boy. In a roughening voice he comforted the child one more time. "Relax, I'm bringing you over, no one will ever hurt you again." The sound of Darwin's shirt ripping and shoes buckling were not enough to take Tim's widening eyes off of Darwin's metamorphosis. Darwin's fingers stretched across Tim's tiny back growing and sharpening claws as they went. Digging into Tim's back, Darwin tore through the boy's shirt cutting the soft and supple skin underneath. Tim didn't scream at the pain, the pain of his youth was more than enough pain to last him a lifetime. Watching Darwin transform, Tim began to understand what was about to happen to him, and at that moment he embraced what Darwin was doing, trusting his every action. Long strands of hair pushed through the skin of Darwin's reforming face, reshaping human ears pushed upwards and the buttons down the front of his shirt broke open one at a time.

Darwin discerned the boy's willingness at first glance. Fully aware of what he was doing, Darwin dove into Tim's neck and bit into the boy's shoulder. The warm saltiness of the blood began flowing past his canines causing a reverberation within his body. The taste was blissful; the taste was sinful; the taste was joy. Life from the boy leaked from his wound into Darwin who could now see everything about Tim Waters.

Control it. Stop.

CHAPTER 12

The cold of the night air swept across his hot body in waves like ocean water slamming against the rocks. Looking up at the street lamps he could see puffy white balls of cotton falling in increasing numbers. The sounds around town were padded, and muffled; creating closeness that was comforting. Christmas lights strung across the street still blazed at their full intensity casting red, green, yellow and blue colors on the new fallen snow. Large clouds of steam rose from his mouth dispersing in the night air. Feeling the weight of his chest rise and fall like a pendulum, comfort tingled in every pore of his body.

Lifting his head from the snow it was clear he was still downtown, several blocks from the Caprice. The fog in his brain was parting but the images from the past several hours were dreamlike. He remembered attacking Tim Waters in the theater; he recalled how good his flesh had tasted. A raw steak with sauce smothered over it. It was meat better than the butcher had, more tender, livelier with a thousand and one flavors and emotions. He had lost control and torn into his little friend, even though he intended to pass the gift on to Tim, but now he couldn't be sure he had stopped in time. He could remember nothing! The deer was vivid and so were the search and rescue dinner guests, but Tim was hazy.

Standing up, he could see the sign at the Regal Drugstore, the pink neon cast could be heard humming clearly through the deaden town. He was still clothed, his pants and shirt hung off of him like rags, but he had remained partially dressed. The shoes had not faired as well, no longer shielding his feet from the snow; they were nowhere to be seen.

As the seconds passed the fog lifted higher and higher and Darwin was feeling fantastic. He felt like a very strong and healthy human. Shoving his hands into what was left of his pants Darwin found the keys to the theater.

TIM! My god Tim! In a sprint Darwin began running back to the theater still unaware of what time it was. The snow on the streets was nearly a foot thick and had been unplowed, no tracks of any kind could be seen on the road or sidewalks; New Haven was deserted.

Arriving moments later at the theater Darwin went directly to the front door. With keys in hand, Darwin pushed, wiggled and forced that key into the hole. The lock had never been as difficult as it was now; shoving and banging caused the door no ill effect. Slowing for a moment he looked at the keys in his hand. *Wrong god damn key!* Switching one key to the left on his key ring the key slipped into the door and the bolt lock slid aside giving the teen access to the warmth of the theater.

The lights behind the concession still glowed as though they were still open for business, but silence was the master of this domain. The stench of blood was in the lobby area of the theater and as Darwin moved towards the hall with the cinemas. Darwin didn't want to know what he had done; the thought of killing Tim Waters sickened him. The boy deserved better, he had tried to help him, but had he killed him instead?

What was I thinking? I knew I couldn't control myself. Fuck what if he's dead, in the theater? I'll have to leave New Haven tonight!

Darwin entertained his worst dreams while edging his way down the hall to cinema six where he knew he had his last encounter with Tim. Stepping barefooted as lightly as he could on the soft carpet of the theater Darwin slid past theater one, two, three, and four. Every theater door remained open and the ghostly white screen within the empty cinemas dominated the view from the hallway. Darwin could hear nothing from the theater as he approached the entrance to theater six. Before the door, Darwin paused, taking a deep breath preparing himself for what he did. Moving into view of the giant white screen; he saw...

NOTHING!

There was nothing. The theater looked as all the others had, giant, empty and clean. Blood once again rushed into his heart.

I imagined it? I did change though. What the fuck did I do?

Running to the bottom of the theater where he had last seen Tim, Darwin continued to find nothing. The floor, the seats, the carpets, everything appeared to be in perfect condition. Worried he had made a mistake Darwin ran back up to the top of theater six across the hall into five, and again there was nothing. Theatres four, three two and one were all the same, nothing was wrong. Even the smell of blood seemed to be gone. Moving from room to room Darwin checked everything, behind the concession, the public washroom, the office, the projection booth and finally the staff changing area. The Caprice Theater was as it should be, with the exception of the lights; Darwin could find no evidence that he had done anything inside the theater.

In the staff changing area Darwin showered but was not mesmerized by the cracks of the wall. His senses appeared to be in his full control and still heightened, but the visions did not return. Darwin stayed in the hot water for a long time, washing away his deeds. The blood came off easily revealing an innocent man – underneath the coating of darkness.

In the humid change room of the Caprice Theater, Darwin Foster re-clothed his human body, choosing to try on some of his thrift store purchases. A pair of fitted jeans that conformed nicely to his bubble shaped buttocks and a forest green cotton/polyester shirt with a white muscle shirt underneath brought out his human side. Realizing he had no socks Darwin chose to wear the old clunky boots of his deceased father, barefooted. Darwin headed towards the back door of the theater; killing the lights and bringing rest to the secrets that the theater held.

Alarm set, bags of clothing in hand, Darwin went home. The chill in the air was worse than before and the flakes of snow had doubled in size. Walking to the front of the building the tracks he had made coming back to the theater were long since covered, only small depressions in the snow remained. Had anyone else looked at the street they probably would have overlooked the disappearing footprints. Darwin walked home, the night absolved in his mind but his curiosity stronger than before. The silence of the winter's night again brought him solace.

DONG! DONG! DONG! The town hall bells tolled.

3:00 a.m.

In the distance Darwin could hear the sounds of sirens, somewhere nearby.

CHAPTER 13

"Darwin, do you ever think about sex?" Steve had asked Darwin with the curiosity of a child when he was only thirteen. The question had been asked and wondered by every boy, everywhere in the world. The Friday night sleepovers and the truth or dare games always brought out the question of sex. The childhood curiosities of Steve Cardwen had created much of his trouble with his mother and with the school – though his mother could be owed much of the credit for the trouble at school. Darwin was curious too but until he had met Steve he had never been bold enough to talk to anyone about his feelings and desires.

The childhood duo had played together for years before puberty, even during Darwin's rough years at home. Their early history was simple and pure. Bike rides around town, playing video games at the store, breaking windows at an old abandoned factory; getting into boy trouble had been their bond.

"Hey Darwin! Check this out."

I'll show you mine if you show me yours.

Darwin had started puberty much earlier than Steve, but Steve always seemed to know more. Darwin's voice changed when he was ten and a half, and he had discovered masturbation by the time he had turned eleven. Steve had been a late bloomer compared to the other boys in New Haven, who all seemed to sprout young. It had been a blessing for Darwin to begin to grow. Much of his own school harassment came from his puny size, but in a matter of months Darwin had changed, shedding his small and weak image. He

Darwinism

hadn't become popular but he wasn't physically picked on to the extent he had been. Puberty had been great for Darwin, transforming him into something better and relieving some of his pain.

It was Steve who had brought back the hell of grammar school. Darwin wasn't sure why he had stayed at Steve's side throughout the torment. Deep inside Darwin knew if he abandoned his friend his own torment might cease, but he couldn't leave Steve to fend for himself.

Darwin hadn't seen it happen himself, but he had heard about it. Every student in Ridgemount High had heard about it, even schools in the next county had heard about it. It was every boy's worst nightmare, the sort of event that brands you for life, and it had happened to Steve. *Poor Steve.* It was the first week of high school, the first year Steve and Darwin had not been in grammar school. Before graduating to the big school they had been told all sorts of stories of what to expect.

"You will have your own lockers, and expect four hours of homework every night, maybe even five or six hours. Some of the older students smoke and some do *other things,* stay away from them boys and girls – they're horrible people – the kind of people that get tattoos. You will also be expected to shower after gym class with the other students." Ms. Fletcher had listed off with joy all the differences between high school and grammar school. Everything she had said had been forgotten when the word *shower* had been uttered. Some boys were proud, some boys didn't care, some boys were ashamed and others –Steve – were afraid.

He hadn't said anything throughout the whole summer leading up to that shameful day in September when he became labeled. Darwin and Steve had played a lot of games, games their parents would not approve of, but it was harmless fun and Darwin felt no shame in what he did with his friend. What started at night ended in the morning and was forgotten about until the next time.

Shit, you're still bigger than me!

Yep, always will be too!

It was harmless fun that most boys have during their coming of age. The thoughts that must have been racing through Steve's head that summer must have been overwhelming. He had never mentioned to Darwin specifics, but in later years the writing was clearly written on the wall.

The Ridgemount High boy's shower room was small but it could accommodate twelve boys at a time, four boys on each side of three walls in the square room. When the room was full with twelve boys it did not leave much room for people to avoid colliding with each other. The shower room was more like riding an inner city subway, with a steamy hot smell, odd sights and a nervous atmosphere for the undersized riders. All one could do was get

Mark Fuson

in, do their job, and get out, and hope you didn't have an unfortunate fanny-tap. Steve had been in line waiting to go into the shower room, a large white terrycloth robe wrapped around his tiny waist. The stress of the first time must have been immense on him; other boys from higher grades, more developed, and more muscular all flaunting their bodies in front of Steve who had only ever seen Darwin naked until that moment.

Barely five feet tall tried to keep his eyes focused on other things, tried to keep his mind distracted with other things. Everywhere he looked it was the same story: a strong torso, a bare ass, a well-hung piece of meat, hairy armpits. Even the smells in the shower room were purely masculine. The pressures on the boy were too much and when it was his turn to enter the shower the tapestry of his future came undone. Removing his towel and placing it on the hook before entering the room, he could already tell his penis was much larger than it usually was in its flaccid state, but he couldn't turn back, he tried desperately to think of un-arousing things: His mother naked, his grand mother masturbating, anything that would defuse his growing pressures. It was the naked body of the star member of the wrestling team that set Steve off. Grade ten student Teddy Holmes, brother to Cindy Holmes, backed out of the shower shouting back a sexist comment to one of his buddies. Before the wrestler had a chance to watch where he was walking, his bare muscular body collided with Steve, setting him off.

Instantly Steve had changed from soft to hard and erupted spontaneously over the backside of Teddy Holmes.

Steve's chances at a life at Ridgemount High ended on that day. At only thirteen he was knowledgeable about sex, but what happened to him in the shower had amazed, shocked and destroyed him. The counselors of the school tried to reassure Steve what had happened was normal and that in time people would forget, but no one did. Even the snickering of the schoolteachers and secretaries could be heard throughout the school wherever Steve went. Steve had probably wanted to kill himself after the incident and through some miracle he didn't. Darwin had chose to remain with his friend throughout those days, though he was never sure why.

Steve was unable to attend school for several weeks after his steamy encounter with Teddy Holmes and it hadn't been the black eye that Teddy had awarded Steve for his sudden and pronounced admiration of the wrestler that had kept Steve out of school. What kept Steve at home was the internal bleeding and concussion Theodore Cardwen had inflicted on his son.

"Mr and Mrs Cardwen, we're sorry but Steven had an accident this morning in the shower with the other boys." The Principle had told his parents at an impromptu meeting that afternoon.

"What kind of accident?" The concerned parents had asked in unison.

Darwinism

The principle had to bite his tongue when he told the Cardwen's of their son, their pride and joy, their flaming Nelly. "Young Steven ejaculated all over our star wrestler and now poor Steve has a black eye."

"That ain't all he's gonna have either!" Theodore Cardwen exclaimed has he stormed from the office shouting obscenities of the worst kind. Steve had honestly expected understanding and caring from his parents. He had been a little naïve.

"It was an accident mom! I don't know what happened dad! Please don't hurt me; I didn't want it to happen, it just did."

The screaming and terrified child would have endured one of the longest car rides home he had ever experienced. Riding in the back of the old Buick Steve wished and prayed that the car would break down, or better yet they would get into an accident that would kill his parents. His pleas would fall on the deaf ears of his praying mother and his disgusted father. Rolling up the drive to the slum manor on Cadmore Avenue Steve would have considered bolting from the car, if he honestly thought he could have outrun his father.

Sally and Theodore Cardwen made Steve walk ahead of them up the uneven brick walkway to the house. Each step felt like a step towards the gas chamber, pending doom was around the corner; it was a certainty. They even made Steve unlock the door to the house with his trembling hands and enter first. Sobbing convulsively, the boy knew his black eye would soon be his least worrisome injury. And he was right.

Sally had closed the front door behind the dysfunctional family and Theodore began immediately his corrective assault on his son who was trying to remove his shoes. The first dead blow was to Steve's center back – near his spine. Steve vocalized none of the pain that was spreading through his body, not a weep or a whimper, but he collapsed from his injury, becoming vulnerable to the full assault.

"You God damn little faggot!" Theodore blared in rage at his child. "Your shit stops here and now! Or by god you'll never leave this house with your filth again!" The steel-toed footwear of Theodore Cardwen swung into his son's stomach creating a hollow thump throughout the living area of the Cardwen home. Steve's fluidic gasping and choking followed; the boy lost his breath as what food he had inside him regurgitated all over the linoleum of the entrance way.

"What will it take? What in God's name will it take?" A few more blows to the child at the mid section causing bruising to most of the major organs. Theodore was ready to go several more rounds, but his son was already conceding defeat. "Get up God damn little fairy! You can puke all you like in your room! GET UP!"

The child tried to squirm but the air was not there to allow him to obey

101

Mark Fuson

his father's commands. Blood had begun leaking from his nose and mouth only adding to the filth of the entryway floor. The cowering child looked to his father for mercy but only found a man consumed with hate and bigotry. His mother was in the background, hands clasped and eyes upturned to her god. Steve had known his fate was sealed and his punishment would be severe for his *sins*. His *accident*.

Theodore Cardwen knelt down and picked up his limp son grasping his frail arms and legs tightly as to create more pain. The brutal man dug his overgrown dirt imbedded fingernails deep into Steve's flesh leaving ten white indentations in the skin. Theodore was intent on hurting his son; there was no lesson he was teaching. He took pleasure in abusing his son whom he had always considered a massive disappointment. Raising the small body of his son to head level Theodore Cardwen walked to Steve's bedroom door and propelled Steve into his bedroom like a stuffed animal. Steve collided with the wall adjacent to his bed, his head impacted with the drywall leaving a sizable hole, larger than any previous holes in the room.

Steve had bounced limply onto his bed where he remained unconscious for two days. The blood from his face drained unhindered into his bed sheets for the next several hours forever staining them. He needed to be in the hospital, but that was not an option in the Cardwen home. Cardwen problems were dealt with in the Cardwen way, harsh, privately and cheaply.

Darwin didn't see Steve for three weeks. It was several years before Steve had even told Darwin what had happened, but Darwin had known it was something cruel. After three weeks Steve's black eye still was not healed and he walked like the elderly. Slow and hunched and he winced at the pain in his back when he sat. Darwin secretly cried for Steve, unsure of what he could do for his friend. Maybe it was the torture in the Cardwen home that made Darwin feel compelled to remain by Steve's side. Maybe Darwin understood pain and losses in a different way, and he could see something in Steve that others couldn't. Maybe his decision to remain as Steve's only solid confirmed friend was a testament of his soul. Maybe he felt something for Steve he couldn't understand, but something he couldn't ignore. Maybe Darwin couldn't walk a new road alone.

Maybe

Steve's persecution began on his first day back, the girls snickering as he passed by, the boys shouting the obscenities and threats of *kicking his faggoty ass!* He took it in stride, keeping quiet and to himself, walking the long way to class avoiding the crowded hallways, and skipping his physical education class whenever he could. Even in his attempts at becoming a loner, the harassment over his ten-second orgasm with Teddy Holmes never ceased, never died down; was never forgotten.

On a good week he would be teased and bullied only twenty to thirty times a day. That included every innuendo, every sarcastic comment, every hidden joke about geysers and premature arrivals, every comment about a career in fudge packing, every horrible nickname: the little gun, the creamed filled squirt, the load blowing fairy. The French students had their own nicknames for Steve: Le petite Éclair was the favored among les François, but Steve not understanding French, tried to block out the rest. Of course then there was non verbal abuse, the blocking of the hallways as Steve went about his day, the intentional (accidental) tripping –which would be sarcastically apologized for after the fact. His economic status was also attacked, Steve's clothes were less than department store quality and it was just one more thing he could do nothing about. The sound of the girls making an *ewwww* sound as he passed was usually directed at his poverty-wear name brands.

In class Steve was subjected to the diminishment of his personal worth. Group projects were big in Ridgemount High and seldom were students allowed to choose their own groups, and Steve always seemed to get placed with the jocks, snobs, preppies and all round tough guys. Steve never was given a say, never assigned any of the work, not even allowed to sit with the group as they worked, and when the assignment was complete the group would band together and complain Steve had done nothing. Whether he chose to do nothing or the choice was imposed upon him, it didn't matter, he knew he wasn't welcome. Even amongst the *geeks, dweebs* and *losers* Steve was considered an undesirable, a person who might draw too much attention to their already nerdy ways.

Steve was a homosexual, a fag, a faggot, a Nelly, a fudge packer, a queen, a queer, a homo, a meat eater, sausage lover, pervert, pedo, pedophile, a bitch, a cream eater, an anal probe-er, fairy, poofta, pansy, Oscar Meyer in search of a bun, a 175, and a deviant.

Steve was greeted almost daily, but never with a, *Hi, Hello, How are you doing, Good to see you* or *Hey Steve, what's new?*

"What are you looking at faggot?" Was common.

"You should do everyone a favor, slit your wrists you useless pansy!" Was suggested every other day.

"Hey look, he still hasn't killed himself! Hey Steve do you need some help? I have lots of ways you can give everyone what they want. How about rat poison, that's what they use to kill vermin isn't it?"

"175! Before we gas you, you're going to suck all of our cocks, consider it your last request fulfilled!"

Few people understood how verbal abuse could tear away at the human spirit. Steve was ready for the physical abuse; his father had prepared him for that. No one could prepare themselves to the effect of being belittled, decried

Mark Fuson

and condemned daily. Every hall, every corner, every private location within the school that Steve could hide in for a brief while was eventually discovered; and the raiding parties would drive him back into the thick of the school halls to endure his sentence.

Darwin could not be there every moment. Class schedules prevented him from spending more time with his dangerous friend, but when the bell would ring, Darwin would search the halls looking for Steve, whom never seemed to be hard to find.

Steve hid in the library for the first few weeks whenever he could, but soon the ravenous pack of wolves discovered the quiet sanctuary and began spending their time there. Whipping tightly bound balls of papers at Steve's head with suggestions of his future written on the inside.

Kill yourself! You're only going to die from AIDS anyway!

When the students of Ridgemount felt particularly artistic they would add colorful drawings of knots and nooses with specific directions on how to make sure the knot held for someone who weighed 130 pounds – or someone roughly Steve's size. Other notes suggested lethal drug combinations. One note had read:

Vodka and Aspirin aren't sure enough. To make sure you do it right, we suggest something with codeine – but if you have access to any prescription sleeping pills they would be your best bet! Hope that helps FAG!

Steve had probably considered what the school counselors had told him. *In time they will forget.* October and November that year were long, very long. Steve endured the dehumanizing nature of his peers only to go home and receive similar verbal treatment from his parents.

In late November a rumor began to circulate around the school that Steve and Darwin were in fact lovers, and that they had been so for a long time. It started like a landslide starting from the top down, gaining speed and destructive force as it went. Darwin spent much of his spare time with Steve, and it had not gone unnoticed by the rest of Ridgemount High. Darwin had fielded questions about his relationship with Steve and his answers had always been cryptic and evasive. In the long run his ambiguous nature had only worked to fuel the abusive nature of the students. Steve and Darwin were not lovers, it was true they had experimented a little prior to entering High School, but nothing more had ever occurred. Darwin and Steve never discussed it with each other; the rest of school had already labeled them and the need for discussion seemed irrelevant. Had Steve had any other friends he might have told Darwin to get lost, in many ways Darwin's presence confirmed what the students believed, and it gave them the drive to pursue and conquer Steve Cardwen. Despite some tense feelings that Steve may have felt on occasion at Darwin's presence, he was mostly thankful to have someone to stand by him in thick and thin.

"Only 189 more days to go until summer." He would tell himself. "Every day done is one day closer to being rid of these bastards."

His mental pep talks helped for the first few months, and Darwin being nearby also helped, but as January, February and March rolled around Steve became less and less optimistic.

Throughout the winter that year Darwin began taking the abuse and assaults right along side Steve. When Darwin would arrive at school in the morning he too was also greeted the same way Steve was. Every pain and torment that had been solely Steve's became a shared event. Darwin may not have showered another boy in sperm but by hanging out with Steve he had become "guilty by association", a term his history teacher had mentioned when lecturing on Nazi Germany. And although Darwin was from a better neighborhood his clothing was about as good as Steve's. Since his father's passing and his mother's alcoholism had started to rage on, money had been much tighter forcing Darwin to wear clothing with alligator logos on the pockets and pants that bore names no one had ever heard of before. He was a geek and a fag, just like his friend, and the abuse should therefore be shared. The notes addressed to Steve now also bore the name Darwin on it.

> Dear Nellies,
> Dear Queens,
> Dear Pedophiles,
> *Please note: Your presence in this school can no longer be accepted. If you continue coming to school you will suffer perpetual agony. Be poetic like all fags; pull a Romeo and Juliet!*
> *Signed*
> *Gods Warriors*

"FUCK I HATE THEM!" Reading the note over and over again only made him more enraged. Crumpling the pink piece of paper he flung it at the wall, bouncing harmlessly a few feet from both boys.

Steve had begun to cave around his fourteenth birthday. More than six months of constant verbal assaults and beatings had finally pushed him to the brink.

Darwin had experienced bullies throughout much of his youth, this was nothing new except the level and intensity was far greater than anything he had ever experienced. The short lull in bullying between puberty and the

Mark Fuson

Ridgemount Days had been a nice reprieve for Darwin. Getting back into the habit of worrying about his safety was hard, but it came a little easier for him than it did Steve. "I know man, let's try to think about the future. We won't be in Hell forever."

"We can never escape New Hell!" Steve had exclaimed one afternoon as they sat quietly in the bowels of the school near the old metal shop that had long since been shut down. "Why can't we just leave?"

Darwin being the voice of reason kept reminding Steve. "And go where? We're not old enough to work, and we have no money."

"Other kids do it." Steve sulkily responded. He needed a way out; he couldn't wait for time to release him from Hell. "What if we just killed them Darwin, you and me? We come to school one day and just fucking waste them, all of them!"

"Steve, I have no issues pulling the trigger while looking them in the eye. Those bastards deserve what they've got coming. But we'd get caught, we'd go to prison, maybe we'd even die." Darwin had trouble rationalizing reasons to not do it. His mind hovered on the line of being dedicated and motivated to carry out Steve's suggestion. Darwin had considered several plans himself, in the back of his mind over and over.

It played out much more like a fantasy more than a plan. Running into history class swinging an axe, decapitating as many of the beasts as they could. Several Molotov Cocktails smashed at the entrances to the classroom incinerating every student, condemning those who sat back idly allowing the atrocities to continue. A mixture of ammonia and bleach creating a toxic blend of chemicals similar to mustard gas, the plan sounded fun, but it wasn't sure enough. A sawed off shotgun point blank at the ring leader's head would have brought joy and satisfaction but the method was slow and cumbersome – he might be able to take out two or three people but undoubtedly he would be overpowered by the time he moved on to fourth. On a much larger scale he had considered an accident with the school boiler; a gas leak, a steam explosion – it would be spectacular but the death and mayhem would be too random. Then there was the Muslim extremist way, a homemade explosive vest with jars of nails and screws attached to his body – the ensuing explosions would mangle and wound many and even kill a few including himself – but again, too random. He had also considered the less entertaining way of poison, but two problems existed with this idea: one - he had no poison, and two - he could never get close enough to anything they ate to plant the poison. His final solution was more dramatic though it would leave him dead and the criminals alive – however they would at the very least be mentally disturbed for the remainder of their days. Darwin would enter the class with a sawed off shotgun and after a short speech condemning the unwarranted evil he would

Darwinism

turn around, stick the gun in his mouth and blow his brains across the room and into the faces of his enemy.

"I can't live this way Darwin." Steve confessed.

I know —

Both boys sat quietly on the floor. Neither boy said another word. If either had the means necessary to carry out their blood lust thoughts, the school would have been painted with the blood of every sinner that had ever committed a crime against them. With nothing more than the will there was little else they could do.

This was the time their lives began to change.

After what seemed to be more than thirty minutes of silence Darwin came up with a thought. "Steve, I have an idea." It wasn't so much an idea as an escape. It wasn't so much a solution as a band-aid to their problems. Darwin suggested to his friend they skip school for the remainder of the day and go to Darwin's house. Darwin had seen his mother do it for the past several years, - stay home and drink - and it seemed to work for her.

Steve followed willingly without saying a word. They left school that afternoon charting a course through desperate waters. Darwin didn't know what he was doing; all he knew was escape seemed to be available in liquor. Steve didn't care; escape in any form was a welcomed distraction from his miserable life. They didn't run or even try to move quickly. Their efforts to remain secretive seemed almost effortless. Twice on the way out of the school Steve and Darwin passed two different teachers and aside from a scowl and a disapproving brow, they did nothing to stop the two from leaving. Several police officers passed the boys on their way to Clairemount Boulevard, but even they did not seem to care that duo was wandering away from the school during school hours. All through the town the boys walked towards Darwin's home without interference or any degrading comments. Had anyone known why Darwin or Steve were skipping school and had tried to stop them – they would have only been delaying the inevitable. Darwin was determined it was the right thing to do. It was their destiny.

Darwin took Steve up to his room with a bottle of dark rum he had swiped from his mother's liquor cabinet. Steve looked ready to drink until he died. Death and depression consumed him. He had no emotion, no feeling, no desires left; he had reached the lowest feeling achievable by the human spirit. If Darwin had left him alone that day, he would surely have taken his own life.

"Bottom's up!" Darwin raised his half full mug of straight dark Jamaican Rum. Steve followed suit, still remaining elsewhere, but following the actions of his friend. The coffee mugs they were drinking from seemed almost appropriate although Darwin probably didn't realize it when he grabbed them from the cupboard. The mugs were originally a gift for Marie Foster from her sister, a way of bringing laughter into the dreary home – but it never did. Each mug had its own comical saying on it that suited the underage owner.

I have one nerve left and you're getting on it!

And –

Fuck the world!

Darwin took a large swig before the taste and power of the liquid forced him to slow his pace, coughing and choking from the intense burning flavor in his mouth. Steve on the other hand took one gulp, and a second gulp, and a third, swallowing in long controlled bursts to his stomach. Unfazed by the taste he finished his "Fuck the World" mug and slammed it down awaiting his refill.

"Shit!" Darwin looked at Steve in shock. The effect on Darwin had been like molten lava and his throat felt like it was swelling shut from the heat. His friend had finished nearly four ounces of alcohol in less than twenty seconds and Darwin had barely swallowed one ounce. Feeling the pressure he kicked it up a notch and consumed the rest of his rum despite the burning in his throat. "Another?" He rasped at his friend who still sat without emotion on the floor of Darwin's bedroom. Darwin didn't wait for a response, filling the mug nearly to the rim this time, as well as his own. Raising the mug again Darwin waited for Steve to join the toast.

Steve sneered at Darwin. A redness was filling into his Scandinavian cheeks; life was slowly returning to the battered boy. Raising the "Fuck the World" mug, Steve toasted along with Darwin. "Fuck the World, fuck the good looking, fuck the rich, fuck the religious, fuck the athletes; fuck everyone!"

"Here, here!" Darwin clanked his mug against Steve's and then proceeded to consume the contents.

Stopping partway through his drink Steve asked Darwin. "So do you want to be the wife or should I?" A wide smile stretched across his rosy cheeks as the alcohol was already relaxing the overwrought brain of Steve Cardwen.

Darwin belted out in laughter partway through his drink, spitting the rum in his mouth all over Steve. Panting for air and holding his chest Darwin keeled over guffawing at the suggestion. Unable to respond both boys went into hysterics, the first real laugh that either boy had shared in months. The alcohol continued penetrating deeper into their gated spirits, crushing wall after wall of protection they had built around their fragile minds.

This first afternoon of firewater indulgence was only the beginning of a continuous event. In the first few weeks that spring they had nursed their first hangovers together, learned that with alcohol limits needed to be adhered

Darwinism

to, certain combinations of mix and alcohol did not work and alcohol could be used at school in thermoses, bottles and fountain drinks without anyone noticing. Drinking at school became common. Coke bottles filled with one part rum and three parts Coke would allow Steve and Darwin to walk casually though the halls with their medicine in hand. Strong breath mints could cloak any residual alcohol smell and keep their secret hidden from those who might judge their coping ways. Drinking at school became as normal as attending class, and for the remaining few months of that school year, it actually helped to make going to school tolerable. What became a problem for the two boys was a matter of supply and demand. For the first few weeks Darwin had skimmed various alcohols from his mother's liquor cabinet, but he knew that would soon become too obvious. Even Steve had ventured into his father's stash, but both boys knew that would be suicidal if Steve got caught. Going without liquor at school was not an option.

The teasing, bullying and occasional beating was less noticeable when the senses were dulled. They needed enough alcohol to get them through to the end of the school year and they were running out of ideas. Every suggestion was considered.

Maybe we can pay someone to buy us a bottle?

Could we make our own? It can't be that hard…

What about Chinese cooking wine, we can buy that without ID?

None of the ideas were very good which only left one alternative. *Thou shall not steal,* unless it's necessary. Darwin and Steve decided they could steal a bottle or two from the grocery store. A pair of baggy pants could conceal one or maybe even two twenty-six-ounce bottles, assuming the belt around their tiny waists was synched to the last hole to keep them from falling down. A few snack purchases of potato chips, cupcakes and sodas would be the necessary diversion from their thievery.

In their first attempt Darwin and Steve entered the KMG Supermarket, walked directly to the snack section and selected one bag of black licorice before hastily proceeding to the cashier. Back in the parking lot the boys chewed on their unwanted candy frustrated at their nervous behavior. This scenario was repeated over and over throughout that first week, sometimes the boys got brave enough to walk by the alcohol and maybe even be bold enough to take a glance at the bottles. It was the beginning of the second week that some headway was made, when the boys met an interesting character.

"You'll never get anywhere the way you're going about it." The gentle voice spoke with a knowledge and assuredness. Standing over Darwin and Steve who were sitting on the curb was an extremely tall and poorly dressed man who looked to be in his early twenties. He wore blue jeans that were blackened at the knees with soil, dry mud coated boots, a white t-shirt stained yellow under the arms and a red baseball cap that bore no distinguishable team symbols. His face was weathered as though he spent much of his day outside and it appeared he seldom shaved but wasn't quite able to grow a proper beard. The man was dirty and a strange odor wafted from him in waves, a sweet-pungent smell that neither Darwin nor Steve was familiar with.

Darwin remembered his first impression of this stranger. *He has dirt under his fingernails!* His mother had always warned him to stay away from people with dirt under their fingernails. A person that didn't take care of their fingernails had no self-respect. Dirt under their nails indicated there was dirt in their soul. Looking at this man, Darwin thought about what his mother had told him, but he didn't feel that way about this stranger. Aside from his blood shot eyes, the man seemed quite approachable.

"I've been watching you for days. I see you come down here wearing your baggy pants, wandering around the store for a few minutes and never walking out with more than a bag of candy, so I says to myself – Clint, I think those boys need your help." The tall thin man looked down at the two boys as they continued to chew on their candy. "So am I right?"

Steve spoke first to the new stranger. "I don't know what you're talking about, we just wanted some candy." Chewing in large sloppy chomps not looking at the man.

"Oh, I guess I was wrong then. I thought you might need someone to boot for ya, but I guess I made a mistake. Sorry." The tall man retreated towards the store not looking back. The mysterious person entered the store and Darwin and Steve remained outside sulking at their predicament, not realizing they had turned their back on the assistance they needed.

A few minutes later the tall man reemerged from the KMG holding two large plastic bags in his hands walking in the direction of the boys. Neither Darwin nor Steve noticed the clanking sound of the man as he approached. The sound of bottles banging into each other rang louder and louder but it did not arouse awareness in the boys, only random thoughts.

Fuck I wish I could have a drink!

Just one quick one; just one to loosen me up.

The clanking bags stopped in front of the two boys drawing their eyes upwards to the familiar dirt ridden face. "I don't care what you say. It was booze you were after and rather than seeing your sad asses thrown in jail for stealing – well here." Clint extended his arm with one of the bags until Darwin reached up to accept the gift.

"Thanks, but why?" Steve asked in disbelief.

"Lets just say I sympathize with guys like you. I've heard about you, I don't believe a word of what I'm hearing but that doesn't change the fact I know you're in pain. I eat lunch over at the diner most everyday and I've seen

Darwinism

you two here for the past week, wandering the store and never buying much. So the other day I follow you two into the store and I see you looking at the liquor, not once but twice. The candy is nowhere near the liquor, so I figure you two aimed to steal yourself some of the hooch. So am I right, or should I take my liquor back?"

Darwin was thumbing through the bag of bottles in awe: Two twenty six ounce bottles of vodka, one Mickey of rum and several miniature bottles of tequila. *Pay dirt!* "NO! You were dead on right, but mister I don't think we can accept this, we have no way to pay for it."

"You're Darwin right?" Clint asked.

"Yes, sir."

"First, if you call me mister or sir one more time I'm taking the booze back. My name is Clint and I expect you to be calling me by my name. And as for paying for it, if you believe in paying your debts I have a way you can pay me back. Do you know Old Clayburn Road, it's about three miles west of the town limits?" Clint asked to both boys who now seemed more attentive than before. Darwin and Steve shook their heads in affirmation. "Come out to 169 Old Clayburn Road tomorrow afternoon, around two o'clock. You know anything about gardening?"

Both boys frowned mentally at the idea, but they also tried keeping an open mind, after all alcohol was at stake. In unison they shook their heads, knowing nothing about gardening accept bullshit seemed to help flowers grow.

"Well that's all right then. I can teach you everything you need to know, but mostly I just need a couple of extra hands to haul around some dirt and what not. For your help, if you like the work, I will continue buying your liquor for you, how does two twenty-six-ounce bottles of your choosing each week sound?" Clint threw it out expecting acceptance on the first round of negotiations but he quickly saw the hamster wheels turning in the little minds in front of him.

Darwin was first to counter the proposal. "Geeze, that sounds great Clint. But I think we could use some extra spending money too if we're gonna work for you. Our parents might start to wonder why we go to work but never make any money."

True. Clint thought.

Steve interjected second. "Yeah, I think if were going to be hauling dirt around your yard that should be worth at least…"Pausing for a moment, eyes rolled to the back of his head, Steve conjured a number that would not be offensive to Clint. "…Twenty bucks a week, each." Steve looked upwards to Clint who looked impressed that the boys had the guts to ask for more.

"Okay, two bottles and twenty bucks' each." Smiling at the boys Clint turned away and walked to his old pick up truck with the tattered sign, *Clayburn Nurseries*, hanging from the side panel of the door. Shouting back Clint reminded his hired help. "And don't show up drunk tomorrow, I expect strong backs and sober minds. And be prepared to get dirty!"

With a new source of liquor at their disposal and money in their pockets, Darwin and Steve could also boast to their families they had jobs. Elevated to the working class would give them some prestige, and allow them to spend some of the money in an attempt to fit in a little better at school. New clothes and maybe even a girlfriend could do wonders to help stop the torment they suffered at school. Things were looking up. Summer was around the corner, and for the first time they both had something to look forward to.

The following afternoon was a Saturday and both Darwin and Steve had a heavy weight sitting on their brain. The first bottle of liquor was gone and the events from the previous evening were a blur. They had celebrated with each other at their newfound wealth. Steve had spent the night at Darwin's, drinking vodka and watching horror movies on the hand-me down DVD player Darwin had in his room. Staying up until four in the morning had played havoc on their abilities. Slowly they rolled their bikes west out of town toward Old Clayburn Road, across the Brookmere Stream and past the remnants of the old train station that had been empty for nearly forty years. The road leading west out of New Haven was used very little; most cars went east towards the main highway, which was fifteen miles in the other direction. The westerly road linked several small communities over a hundred and fifty miles, it was considered a national scenic route and was driven mostly by tourists during the summer months. In early May few cars passed the boys, it was a calm and clear day and the fresh afternoon air helped to cure their pounding headaches.

Rolling up the drive at 169 Old Clayburn Road the place looked more like a derelict industrial site rather than a nursery. Head level grass and shrubs surrounded the gravel driveway leading into the property. Rolling through the tunnel of grass and weeds they might have turned back if not for the big sign at the entrance to the driveway.

Clayburn Nurseries
Wholesale shrubbery, flower and exotic plant dealer.
By appointment only!
Call: Clint Littleford
345-2845

The wall of grass and weeds began to thin as they continued up the drive when the first building came into view. A three-story office building with

Darwinism

broken windows on every floor and rusted metal exterior wall panels stood at the head of the drive. In front of the ugly building was Clint's battered pickup truck with two small maple trees propped on the back with several bags of nitrogen rich fertilizer. Above the entry to the office building was the weather worn sign that read: Haven Industrials and Excavations - Since 1896.

"Hey boys! Ready for a hard day?" Clint Littleford looked even more rugged than he did at the supermarket. His long hair appeared to have a severe case of bed head and the clothing he wore was remarkably familiar. "Leave your bikes here and come around back and I'll show you the operations."

Darwin and Steve dropped their bikes as ordered and followed in behind Clint who was emitting a foul odor.

"So this here place used to be the Haven Industrials and Excavations Company back in the 1960's. Before New Haven Coal started operations this was the primary mining company in the valley. She operated form 1896 up until 62', and then this spot was pretty well used up. They shut her down throwing most of New Haven out of work but then in 63' they started up operations south of town at another location. So anyway my family picked up the old mine site for a song, and my dad started a nursery business here on the grounds back in 69'. Many of the old mine buildings are still standing but not it the best condition, so if you wander around at all you best stay out of any building you might come across. Here at the front of the operations is the old administration building, it's in good shape, but I don't really use it for anything. Behind the old office building leads into the heart of our current operations." A vast ground of small trees, shrubs and flowers extended deep into the property behind the administration building. The colors and bouquets danced and illuminated the old mining remnants that were dotted throughout the floral garden.

Clint continued. "So back here is where you'll be doing most of your work, trees and shrubs are over there on the left and they extend westward for nearly a quarter of a mile, in the center here is the perennials and they continue west as well and branch off into three separate fields about 2500 feet from here. And here on the right I have the annuals, I don't carry much in the way of annuals, not much demand for them in New Haven so I only have this small 500x500 plot. The exotics are in the greenhouses and the greenhouses are beyond those tall maple trees just beyond the annuals. My house is also over there; I live in the house that use to belong to the mine foreman. It's quaint, but it's nothing I'd want to bring a date home to if you know what I mean."

Steve and Darwin looked at each other and shrugged at the comment.

Clint continued with his tour. "Now near my house is the central mine shaft, I do use part of the old mine tunnels for storage but I'd ask you stay

113

out of the tunnels for the most part. The first one hundred feet is fairly safe but beyond that there's a fair amount of water and the ceilings are prone to cave in from time to time. So stay out of there. As for the greenhouses I have five altogether and I grow various Lilies and Orchids, and a few other exotic gems, which I doubt you'd know. During the late summer and early fall I grow poinsettias for Christmas which I do a fairly good business with. I also have a selection of herbs I grow for the Twin Rivers Resort. Me and the chef of Twin Rivers got a little friendly one night after a Fourth of July event, I guess we got into the grass a little heavy..." Clint chuckled and backed up from where he was going. "Well to make a long story short the Twin Rivers chef contracted me to grow all the herbs they use in their cooking for the resort. They only use the freshest ingredients and since I'm the best damn horticulturalist around, well it only seemed fitting they hire me to grow their herbs. And as for anything else I haven't mentioned, I can grow anything anybody wants, they just need to tell me what, and give me time to grow it. Any questions?"

Darwin and Steve smiled and shook their heads politely.

Hort-o-cul-tralist?

Perennial?

Herbs?

Moving beyond the maple trees a series of greenhouse emerged. Inside, even at a distance, large green plants could be seen through the condensation of the windows. A large dirty white three story house was before the greenhouses. It looked old and run down, the kind of building you might expect a shadowy figure to glare at you from behind the dusty glass. The house appeared lonely, an old broken and falling down picket fence surrounded the front of the home and what garden there had been was now completely overrun and ivy was eating the entire front of the house. The sweet pungent smell returned as the tour passed by the entrance to the mine. Darwin and Steve both looked down into the throat of the mine but they could see nothing of interest, only a strong unidentifiable odor.

"So things are pretty rough for you at school?" Clint asked as the group continued moving toward the greenhouses.

Steve and Darwin remained silent at the question.

"I hear stuff. People in this goddamn town talk too much. I don't listen to it; well I don't believe it - I should say. When I was a kid I had a rough time in school, maybe not for the same reasons, but I know it's tough having everyone hate you for things you had no control over. I just want you to know, I don't care what you two do. I'm cool with whatever you are and whatever you want to be. I heard about some of the things that goes on, and frankly it makes me sick that kids are treated this way and nobody does a fucking

Darwinism

thing about it. I saw you two and I thought maybe you might need a friend, I know I needed one when I was your age. So anyway, when you're with me, feel free to swear and talk about whatever you like, just as long as the work gets done I don't much care about the rest of your behavior. I will treat you as my equal, age means nothing to me." Clint stopped at the entrance to the green houses and picked up two forty-pound bags of nitrogen rich fertilizer and flung them onto his shoulders. "One thing's for sure, you'll put on muscle doing this work, looks like you two could use some too. Grab a bag and follow me, most of my big money work happens in the greenhouses."

Working at the nursery had been a saving grace for the boys. Throughout the late spring Darwin and Steve worked side by side in the greenhouses and in the fields learning all there was to know about horticulture. The flow of alcohol continued in the halls at Ridgemount High along with the abuse but with newfound hope, the negative comments began to bounce harmlessly off their broadening backs. The arrangement with Clint expanded through the summer months to a nearly fulltime job. Along with the extra hours of work came extra alcohol and more cash as well as another benefit. By the fall of that year Steve had finished his growth spurt and the laborious work at the nursery had helped both Steve and Darwin to develop a nurturing set of muscles. Life in New Haven would never be good, but life would also never hit the lows it had during that first year in high school. Clint would become an important figure in both Steve and Darwin's life and most importantly Clint would become a source of guidance they both lacked in parental figures.

At fourteen years old, Darwin and Steve had been given an escape, a distraction; they had been given someone who cared. They had been given salvation.

CHAPTER 14

The sweet pungent smell cleared from his mind. The sultry air of the greenhouse cooled and now Darwin once again found himself in his bed, rising from the dead of his sleep.

"Goddamn hydrangeas, fucking things always did grow too fast." Darwin uttered to himself with his eyes pushing open. His reverie faded into history where it belonged. Swinging his legs over the side of his bed Darwin felt a pressure within his bladder making him realize his first order of business. Leaving the warmth of his bed it was clear he should have come to expect one thing, over a thousand mornings should have taught one thing, his morning erection made going pee impossible for at least five minutes. Standing over the toilet, penis pointed in the wrong direction, Darwin waited for his unknown nocturnal sexual urges to die away. "Fuck, I'll never understand the morning boner. Always with the Hitler salute" He jokingly told his penis as he grasped it tightly as though strangling the life out of it would help.

A joint and a quick beat would be nice.

He thought while continuing to wait for the floodgates to spring open. Softening in his hands, the morning erection began to falter. Waiting patiently, Darwin rotated his head cracking the cartilage and bones in his neck in an attempt to further wake himself. Yawning repeatedly one after another he struggled to shed his weariness and begin the day.

This will hurt Tim, but don't be afraid.

The explosion of blood in his mouth was as fresh as biting into a raw steak. The essence of the boy had been so real – had been such a dream. The images of Tim's limp body faded into focus. The black polyester slacks soaked in his blood, the purple Caprice Theater golf shirt, torn open revealing countless large gaping wounds in the boys' shoulder. He remembered taking a large mouthful of supple and tender flesh into his animal-human mouth and chewing on the uncooked meat with joy. He drank the blood like it was the sweetest soda, a forbidden beverage never before indulged in. The power had consumed him in seconds, the spirit of Tim Waters had rushed in his veins and he had learned everything about the boy, his darkest secrets, and his hidden desires. It was too real, the vivid images flashed in his mind, the smells and tastes still vibrated through his soul. He had done it again.

The deer. The Searchers.

"That didn't fucking happen, did it?" Darwin mumbled to himself as he thought about work the previous evening. He remembered his dream, meeting Clint, his first days working at the nursery, but he didn't remember dreaming about killing Tim. He didn't remember finishing work and he didn't remember going home to bed. It wasn't there, and yet there were images in his mind that seemed familiar and clear, but too unimaginable to believe. Darwin now able to release the flow of warm yellow fluid into the bowl decided he needed to call Tim sometime in the morning, to put his mind at ease.

One shake. Two shakes. Three shakes: anymore than that and you're playing with yourself.

Who had come up with that silly phrase? Every man in the world shook his member after relieving himself, and it was certainly more than three times. Shaking the remaining drops was a necessity, shaking it more than three times - why was that a crime? Every boy, teenager and man has a fascination with their penis, and virtually every card carrying member of the male species shook his penis an extra couple of times just to spite the ridiculous phrase. Darwin considered the saying to be something a mothers' group had come up with. *It's not proper to play with yourself. You filthy little bastard, that's a sin!*

Stepping into the shower that morning Darwin felt normal, aside from his conflicting dreams, visions and memories that he was unable to sort through. He had slept like the dead. His appetite was healthy for a hearty breakfast of eggs, toast and hash. He was excited at getting outside and doing something with his day. He wanted to call Steve – *why?* He felt like going for lunch, he felt like going shopping, he even felt like going to work. Darwin felt excellent.

Tim Waters was not a homosexual. In fact the oddly shaped boy was something of a stalking pervert with extremely kinky fantasies. His young innocent face and hard working demeanor was only a cover for his secretive desires. Tim relished in the idea of someone showering him in human waste.

He craved the taste and wondered what the sensation of his tongue penetrating an anus would be like. On many occasions he had pushed his own finger inside himself to get some taste of what it was that he wanted to try. His own taste was less satisfying; he knew he wanted to try someone else's. Caroline Buckheart, Rebecca Travis, Cynthia Clevard; these were people Tim watched, followed – stalked. Tim masturbated at the park, on the bus, on the roof of his house, in his friend's bedroom and even in class at school.

Darwin had seen Tim, quietly sliding his hand into his pants through the zipper and gently rubbing himself to climax while other students worked quietly, unaware of his actions. Darwin didn't know how he knew; it came to him like facts from the page of a book. He wasn't disgusted by the knowledge, quite the opposite. Darwin found a little arousal in knowing about someone else's sexual fantasies. Still, he was uncertain how he would know that for sure; only his instincts told him it was true.

Toweling off in his room Darwin turned on his television while he dressed. The small 13-inch television only received a handful of channels but it was color and Darwin usually only watched movies on it using his old and crippling DVD player. Darwin flicked on the set for some background sound as he dressed. The TV came alive with a buzz and hum as the glow of the picture began to brighten. Flipping from channel three up to the best available channel, twelve, Darwin walked away. Listening to whatever program was on. Instinctively and stark naked he grabbed his phone and dialed Steve, but again he was told the cellular customer was unavailable. He would have to keep trying and he knew it was important that he did.

Black jeans and a charcoal sweater were now in each hand as Darwin moved back his bed with his conclusive decision of what he would wear. Laying out the clothing on the bed Darwin cheerfully hummed random tunes as he began to dress. Again standing in front of his window he was unaware of Mr. and Mrs. Abbott who were now gawking from the sidewalk into his room at his still naked body. Taking their dog "Killer" for his morning walk they had come across the image of Darwin parading around in his birthday suit proudly. The Abbott's, who had been married for more than forty years, seemed captivated by the youthful sight. Even "Killer" sat idly at Mrs. Abbott's feet wagging his tail diligently in honor of his human god.

"KLTV breaking news, special report." Blazed across the television grabbing Darwin's subconscious attention.

Wiping his underarms in a clean sweep with some deodorant Darwin took a moment to marvel at his smell. A soft blend of soothing lavender accompanied by crisp, clean fragrant smell of his underarms pleased him in how he would please others. Slipping his sweater over his head Darwin noticed

Darwinism

the images on the TV were strangely familiar, in a déjà vu way. Sitting on the end of his bed he started to absorb the news.

"This is Kate Stoneway reporting to you live for the second day in New Haven, a small mining community of 15,000 just off of Highway 15 in Brookmere County. After the carnage the night before the town of New Haven thought it could begin to heal. But again this quaint community has come under assault by an unknown person or thing. With a death toll of seventeen, and possibly more fatalities yet to be uncovered, local authorities are scrambling to reassure this frightened community" The reporter continued on in her false caring way attempting to evoke a feeling of compassion and sympathy to the viewing audience.

"I did this. I ate nine more people, no wonder I feel so fucking great!"

Kate Stoneway continued her Emmy efforts. "It all started around midnight when neighbors' notified police of what was first thought to be a domestic disturbance. Upon arriving at this home..."

The shot switched to a pre-taped interview of Officer Newman. "We're not sure what we have here. The murders were gruesome, done in an insane manner. To view the bodies one would almost believe an animal killed the victims, but we'll have to wait for the coroner to make his final judgment. Based on the randomness of the killings and the times they occurred I would venture to guess there was more than one killer, but we have no solid proof of that. New Haven citizens will adhere to a curfew until further notice until we can find the answers we are looking for. What we do know is there is a killer on the loose, whether it was an animal or a crazed lunatic doesn't really matter – it's out there, citizens beware of your surroundings. I think from the attacks the previous night, we can conclude it is probably a large animal. That's all for now, thank you." Officer Newman was harassed for answers as he walked away returning to the crime scene. The mass of reporters continued to shout their unimportant questions from beyond the yellow, police line – do not cross, tape.

"A total of nine murders occurred throughout New Haven between midnight and 4:00am. The exact time of death is unknown in every case at this time but Police do know that two of the murders occurred at almost the same time in completely separate ends of the town leaving them to believe there was more than one person or thing at work." Kate Stoneway continued to recount Darwin's evening

Tim, did you change already?

"Fifteen year olds Rebecca Travis and Cynthia Clevard were found slaughtered in the Travis home. The girls had been having a sleepover," The Stoneway sympathetic pause was added for posterity. "...and by all accounts everything had been quite normal. It was a mother's intuition that discovered the brutality in the bedroom. Just before 4:00am the bodies of both girls were discovered, and police indicate that the scene while gruesome was also inhuman in nature. One officer was quoted as saying:

"Pieces of the girls were missing, *it* tore into them removing pieces, organs, bones, and it looked like some of the sexual organs too. Whoever did this also defecated on the girls; they had no soul whoever they were."

"– But the mayhem continued. Three teenage boys were found savagely beaten near the drugstore on Baker Street early this morning. Police say these killings were far different than the other murders. One boy had his skull crushed in; the other two were severally beaten. Police are uncertain how the boys officially died; officials say it was possible the boys survived the beating only to freeze to death in the snow. Covered by the evening snow dump it was the morning plow truck that unearthed the grizzly discovery. The boys, who have not been named yet pending notification of next of kin, were between the ages of 15 and 16. With all the atrocities in New Haven it saddens this reporter to have to continue. Another two bodies were discovered in New Haven within the past little while, police have not announced any information about the latest two discoveries, ah, I'm told the bodies were only discovered a short time ago." Kate Stoneway paused and held her hand to her ear holding her earpiece as information came through the airwaves. I'm told the police will be holding another press conference in the next half hour; we'll join that press conference as soon as it begins. We'll bring you more from New Haven, as it comes in, back you." Kate disappeared in a flash, replaced with a gray haired studio anchor that seemed un-amused to be on television so early on a Saturday morning.

The door bell chimed summoning Darwin to the front door.

Tim. Steve. The Police?

Three police officers greeted Darwin when he opened the front door. Rigid and serious, the two male and one female officers were without humor or character. Their faces were painted over by their job and the task they were there to conduct was a mystery.

THE POLICE! Am I under arrest?

"Are you Darwin Foster?" The female officer queried holding a plain black notebook in her hand with some scribbling on the pages she was reading from.

Without hesitation or delay Darwin answered the stern woman's question. "Yes I am." Simply put.

Am I under arrest?

"May we come in and have a word with you, Mr. Foster?" The woman looked blankly towards Darwin, her eyes almost looking past Darwin into the house and into the backyard.

Mister!

"Please." Darwin tried to keep himself centered emotionally, expecting the handcuffs to come out at any moment to formally charge him with several of the New Haven murders. He led the officers into the living room and had them sit on the couch. Darwin chose to sit in the pleather recliner across from them, waiting for the twenty questions to begin. One of the male officers, *Moose,* Darwin had arbitrarily labeled him, didn't sit, but instead chose to stand and keep an eye fixed on Darwin.

"Mr. Foster I don't know if you're aware but some horrible things happened last evening in New Haven. There were several murders around town, by our count at least nine that we know of, and eight the night before. The department has had its hands full trying to get the massive investigation together. It has also been a challenge for us to identify some of the bodies as they were pretty badly mauled." The female officer paused in her comments and again referred to her black notebook. Moose remained motionless, eyes continuing to examine Darwin. *Just try and run! We got your faggoty ass!*

"I'm sorry to have to report to you Mr. Foster, your mother, Marie Ann Foster, was found dead this morning..."

The bullet from the officer's mouth penetrated Darwin directly in his temple. A swelling in his brain followed instantly bringing on a four-alarm headache. Darwin's breaths became short and labored as his emotions let loose. Water streamed down his face where her words had penetrated, his nose became clogged and a series of convulsive choking coughs riveted through his body. He hadn't loved his mother in a long time, but it still hurt.

"...at the home of one Ronald Rumsfeld – age 52. Mr. Foster I am very sorry to have to be the one to tell you this. I've brought along Officers Parker and Holt, they are trained crisis counselors from the Burkwood detachment, on loan to us for today. If you would like someone to talk to they are here to assist you."

Darwin attempted at containing his brief episode of bawling to regain some composure. His eyes puffy with disbelief, his head swelling and pounding within his skull Darwin looked at the officer for answers. "How did she die?"

Officer Holt spoke up beginning his crisis intervention. "Son, I don't think you really want to know that. Do you have any friends or family we could contact for you?" Officer Holt was moving the conversation along so they could move to the next crisis.

"There's no one, no one nearby. My friend Steve is all I have in this town." Darwin pushed the water in his eyes back into the corners. Continuing to inhale through his clogged nose he was gaining control over his brief outburst,

Mark Fuson

though his brain functions were shutting down one by one leaving him vulnerable.

"Do you mean Steve Cardwen; he is a friend of yours?" The unknown female officer again spoke. If she had a name, Darwin had lost it; even the male officers were again nameless, except for Moose.

"Yes." The timid Darwin spoke.

"We're looking to speak with Steve Cardwen, have you seen or heard from him in the last twelve hours?" Her pen in hand, the interrogation had begun.

"I saw him yesterday afternoon, around three I guess. I haven't heard from him since." Darwin wiped his nose with the sleeve of his sweater leaving a long snot trail behind. Officer Parker, being a trained crisis counselor, pulled a packet of tissue from his multi-pocket paramilitary jacket and gave them to Darwin. "Why are you looking for Steve?

"Have you heard from Steve within the past twelve hours?" The stern female again questioned, probing the validity of his answer.

Not knowing why he was doing it, Darwin began answering the officer. "Steve told me yesterday he was leaving New Haven for good. He's been saying it for years though. Steve wouldn't have left without seeing me first; I don't think he's actually gone – he didn't say goodbye – maybe he's been killed too and you haven't found him yet?" Darwin only half believed everything he had said and he had known that the minute he had spoken the words.

"We need to account for everyone's whereabouts." The pen began to scribble notes down on the pad, emotions, feelings and observations. (- An officer's intuition, keep an eye on this one. The murders, although random in appearance, have too many connections even in such a small town as New Haven. Yes, there are clues here.)

"It is well known around New Haven that Steve Cardwen and you have had a rough time. I'm told both he and you were bullied on a regular basis at Ridgemount High School. I'm also told Steve was abused extensively by his father, Do you think it's possible that this could have been a form of reprisal against the town?" The question hung in the air, an affirmation of what they were really after.

Calmly, with a partially clogged nose, Darwin responded. "No, Steve hated this place, I won't lie to you. But Steve lacked the balls to do something like this. I thought it was an animal that did this?"

"It may have been an animal, we're not sure yet. I have to ask Mr. Foster, about your whereabouts last night." She spoke sternly; pen clenched tightly waiting for her breadcrumb trail to lead her somewhere.

Darwin answered immediately. Too quickly he thought, but the damage was done. "I was at work, at the Caprice Theater, until sometime after one, I didn't see what time it was I left."

"Can anyone else verify this?" Officer pen and paper replied.

Darwin responded again without thought. His nerves were showing. "My boss, Ray Silverdale left the theater at 11:30. I was alone with Tim Waters after that. We left the theater around one-thirty." *Stupid! Don't volunteer information.*

"You were with Tim Waters last night, all night?"

"No, only until closing." Darwin said. *Stupid!*

"And then where did you go?" The emotionally devoid officer looked like she was winning the lottery behind her cold dark eyes.

"I went home and went to sleep." Darwin stated.

"Anyone see you, or can verify this?" Ms. Dragnet asked.

"I sleep alone, so no." Darwin answered. "I am suspect!"

Dragnet responded curtly. "Two nights in a row we have deaths, and both nights have a connection to you. I think it's safe to say you are a person of interest."

"But. I. This is bullshit! I've just lost my mother, and now you're accusing me of being involved! They know it was a Goddamn animal, they had a witness!" Darwin began to sweat and cry.

"New Haven Police would like you to remain in town, I'm certain Officer Newman will want to question further. In the meantime Mr. Foster, I am very sorry about your loss, would you like Officers Parker or Holt to remain with you for a while? Placing her pen and paper in her vest pocket, Officer of the Gestapo stood not waiting for Darwin's answer.

Darwin contemplated, but he really wanted them out of his house. "No thank you. But if you have a number I could call later in the week when things start to absorb, I might like to talk to someone then." *Nice touch!* He thought.

Officer Moose pulled a business card from his vest pocket and handed it to Darwin. Darwin paid little attention to what was written on the card, only choosing to hold it in his hand instead.

"If you think of anything we might want to know, give us a call." Ms. Dragnet-Gestapo shot at Darwin.

The police left the house whispering little secrets and codes between themselves. Darwin left the comfort of the quiet living room leaving to lock the door behind the police as they left. Officer Moose turned his head one last time to look at Darwin, but he said nothing.

Closing the front door behind the officers Darwin quietly spoke parting words to the officers. "Good bye." But they seemed uninterested in his civil efforts.

Darwin dead bolted and chained the front door quickly, immediately returning to his bedroom where he was greeted by Tim Waters.

"Tim!" Darwin shouted with excitement. "How'd you get in?"

"Through the window." Tim was still wearing his black slacks and purple Caprice Theater golf shirt; blood stained much of his shirt that now hung pitiably from his body. The black polyester slacks also looked distinctive on the boy. The fabric was shredded all the way to his upper thighs and on his feet there was nothing at all. Darwin knew by his appearance alone that Tim had been his accomplice last night. Tim moved to the bed and sat on the edge. "I need a drink Darwin!"

Darwin didn't hesitate, not asking Tim what he wanted; Darwin ran to his private liquor stash and grabbed a bottle of Jack Daniels whiskey and a one-ounce shot glass. Returning to the bedroom Darwin placed the bottle in front of Tim who no longer looked much like a small boy. He had changed and now he was muscular looking, not huge, but definitely bigger. Tim had a perplexed look on his face with a certain level of disbelief. Hidden under the shroud that now consumed the young man, Darwin sensed pleasure from him.

Tim poured himself a shot, and downed it, and another, and another. The gaping wounds on his neck were no more. Scars remained, but even they were becoming quite faint, and they certainly did not tell the story from the night before. Darwin realized everything his mind had been showing him throughout the brief morning had happened. Darwin now wondered whom he had killed.

Tim began to speak. "So about last night. I would never have thought it was possible. I never believed in that kind of crap before, but it happened. You bit into me and I knew what was happening right away. My mind was on speed! You were right - it hurt like hell, but it also felt good. When I felt your claws break my skin," Tim paused with a smirk and then continued. "I got turned on! I don't much remember what happened after that; I woke up maybe thirty or forty minutes later feeling really sore and stiff. Everything ached. I was still lying at the bottom of theater six and you were gone. The blood was everywhere, around me, and on me; I was in a lake of it. I'm not sure why but I got up from the floor after a few minutes, and I was starting a feel better, I wasn't really hurt that bad. I decided to clean up the theater and go home." Chuckling to himself. "It's almost amusing now. I finished cleaning up just after one fifteen and by then I was feeling great. I had tons of energy and even my wounds were healing nice, I knew what was happening to me, but I went about my cleaning without really thinking about it. The blood cleaned up real good too by the way; we didn't get any on the carpet so I think no one will know."

Darwinism

"I know. I saw it later that night. That took me for a mind fuck." Darwin admitted now grabbing the bottle of JD for a few swigs himself.

Tim continued recounting his evening. "So I left the theater, I didn't set the alarm and I think I left the lights on, but my mind was racing with all these weird ass ideas. I started walking up Baker Street toward home. I guess I had made it to the drugstore and those mother fuckers from school stopped me, you know Rick and Bill, only this time they had Jason Every with them. He's a year younger than Rick and Bill but they still hung out together, probably for the drugs Jason could get. The streets were so quiet, and there wasn't a soul around. As soon as I saw them I knew I was screwed, especially for what happened at the theater earlier that night."

"Sorry about that." Darwin uttered under his alcohol filled breath.

"No worries man. I took care of them. I don't know how, I didn't even understand how this power worked. I was pretty sure you had made me a *werewolf*?" Tim looked to Darwin for confirmation. For the first time little Tim Waters uttered the word of the mythical creature he had become. His voice was still filled with disbelief.

"That's right." Darwin confirmed.

"I had no idea how to change though. So all three of them start wailing on me. Jason and Bill grab me and Rick starts slugging me in the stomach and face. I remember they were saying stuff too, about you. They laughed as they were beating me; it was about you I think. They said - they said: Faggety Foster rides again!"

"While they're hitting me I just feel this rage pooling inside my gut. I'm angry, furious, ready to explode, but I know from experience I can't over power them. But this time it was different, as he hit me I started to feel myself pulling away from Jason and Bill. I don't know how I did it, I just did. I remember I had broken free and instead of running away, I was confronting them. I felt so powerful; I could do anything; so I did. I grabbed that fuck-nut Jason Every by his tiny head and I began to push. He screamed in pain but I kept pushing harder and harder. It felt terrific to finally inflict pain to one of them. His eyes bulged from his head and I think some brain began to leak from his nose. I couldn't believe what I was doing, but I didn't want to stop, I felt great!" Tim held his hands out; his fingers mimicked claws as he started pushing at the empty space between his palms.

Tim was reliving his first murder, and clearly by his expressions, he felt no remorse for his actions. "Rick and Bill were on me, trying to stop me but they felt so small against my body that I knew they couldn't do anything. When I released Jason, my hands, my clawed hairy hands were covered in blood. I was unstoppable and turned to Rick and Bill. The fear in their eyes fueled my urges. I wanted them dead, and I wanted them to suffer. It gets sortta fuzzy

Mark Fuson

after that, but I know I killed them." Tim finished recounting his evening and resumed with the JD.

"That's all you remember doing?" Darwin questioned.

Swallowing another shot of booze Tim cleared his throat to respond. "Yeah, for the most part. I have some other images that flash in and out of my mind, but I can't make sense of them. What did you do last night?"

Darwin looked at Tim and debated his response. Truth. Denial. What should he tell Tim? Tim was a monster now; Darwin knew he had a responsibility to teach Tim what little he knew about the power. "After I made you, I really don't know." Darwin paused to select his words. How could he tell Tim how little he understood his power? "Tim, what do you think so far? Do you like it, do you hate it?"

"It's the most fantastic thing that has ever happened to me! No one will ever hurt me again! You have no idea how thankful I am to you." Tim smiled, partially alcohol induced. "How long have you been this way?" Tim wondered.

"About three months, a little more than that I guess." Darwin replied.

"WOW! Only three months!" Tim enthralled with the news throughout his next obvious question that even Darwin could foresee. "Who made you?"

"I don't know how I was made, Tim. I just changed one full moon. I was never attacked, bit or scratched. I don't recall ever drinking any blood and I never wished for it, I really don't know Tim. It just happened and I have been trying to learn more about the power ever since. I love being a werewolf too but you must understand we have to be careful. Last night we got careless and now we need to protect each other." Darwin finished as he regrouped his thoughts once more. He was afraid to scare Tim away and they needed to have this talk now.

"What do you mean, nobody can hurt us. They can't touch us! We can do whatever we want Darwin." Tim's naïve nature surprised even Darwin.

Darwin realized Tim was probably still on a high from his transformation and unable to grasp certain simple truths that even as a supernatural monster they needed to understand. "Last night we killed a lot of people in New Haven. We did it. I think you killed at least five people. Rick, Bill and Jason are dead but you didn't tear them apart like an animal, you beat them to death with your fists which means you could still be a suspect in their murder."

"That isn't possible! And you know it! Who would suspect me?" Tim returned to the JD for another round.

"What's more improbable Tim, a werewolf killed them or a tormented boy who worked down the street at the theater who would have been on his way home from work around the time they died. Yes it's unlikely Tim Waters

Darwinism

could crush a skull but the police will be looking for answers, and I think they will be looking for you. They've already been here. I'm a suspect. My mom is dead." Darwin said solemnly.

"You killed your mom?" Tim exclaimed.

"They think I did, I don't know if I did." Darwin stated. "We've got to do something quick."

"We could leave town?" Tim suggested.

Darwin considered the possibility for a moment but discounted it. "If we left it would make us look guiltier. We've gotta take the heat off of us, here."

"Okay, but what makes you so sure we even need to do that?" Tim questioned, his eyes filled with human fear hiding his true evils.

"You killed Rebecca Travis and Cynthia Clevard too." Darwin reported to Tim who seemed to be in denial right away.

"You can't be sure of that." He uttered.

"Part of your power is gaining a sense of a person's spirit when you drink their blood. When I bit into you last night your essence flowed into me. I understand everything about you now, even your darkest secrets. I know about your hidden wishes. I know Rebecca and Cynthia were a big part of those desires Tim. They were torn apart in Rebecca's bedroom, the things that were done to them, and what I know about your fantasies tells me it was you that did it."

"I woke up at the school this morning. I don't know how long I had been there but I was up against a door out of the snow. When I came to I couldn't think of where else to go, but I thought of you." Tim stated out of the blue, attempting to turn the conversation elsewhere before giving in. "So you know everything about me..."

"Yeah, everything. It's really weird too. I only discovered that power yesterday. I was with Terri Bailey at the thrift store and she cut herself. A drop of blood hit the floor and I was compelled to eat it, it seemed gross but I couldn't help it. When I licked the blood I was given an infusion of knowledge. I understood the woman much better and I knew what she wanted, what she needed. I told her to let go of her dead husband and move on. Last night she showed up to the theater with the guy who delivers her mail – I don't know his name. I thought that was so cool, with a sample of a person's blood I could know everything about them. When I bit into you I had forgotten that I would also gain all of your experiences and because I drank so much of your blood I gained an extremely clear view of who you are. Don't worry though, the things I saw, yeah they are a little kinky and kinda weird, but I didn't care. I just feel like I know you on a much deeper level now." Darwin raised his hand sticking his index finger into his mouth.

127

Clamping down as hard as he could in attempt to break his skin and draw blood with his teeth, Darwin winced a little at his self-inflicted pain. A second later he withdrew his bleeding finger and extended it towards Tim. "Drink my blood, it seems only fair."

Tim didn't hesitate. Grabbing his supervisor's hand and sticking the finger directly into his mouth, Tim sucked on the finger as though it was a baby soother. Joy and pleasure could be seen rushing through Tim's body as he partially transformed. When Tim opened his eyes they were full of colors and life. As Darwin retracted his finger from Tim's mouth he could see that Tim and grown a small set of canines. The boy panted in satisfaction at what Darwin had given him. The blood and essence of Darwin raced through Tim's body as his orgasm leveled off. Small hairs pushed to just below the surface of Tim's darkening face.

"Fuck me!" Tim exclaimed. "What a rush, but I don't sense anything from you!"

"Maybe it's something that comes to you later as you've been the wolf longer. But you should go look at yourself in the mirror, it's pretty cool."

"Why, what's wrong?" Tim exclaimed.

"You started to wolf it up." Darwin had barely finished his sentence and Tim rushed from the room to the nearest mirror.

"Jesus! Ain't that the fucking limit?" Tim returned to the bedroom only a minute later, nearly human again, still uttering amazement under his breath but also showing a new wet spot on his pup-tent groin.

"So you had an orgasm too." Darwin stated with pleasure. "I get them every time I change, except once when I got angry. I changed out of anger once and I don't think I had an orgasm. When the full moon comes out my change is always singled by a raging hard-on and then a series of the most intense orgasms. Even when I drank Terri Bailey's blood, just as you did mine, I had an orgasm. Pretty fucking cool! It's what makes being the wolf so addictive, it feels good!" Darwin returned to the JD, topping off Tim's shot glass before taking a large mouthful from the bottle himself.

"Who did you kill last night?" Tim asked with curiosity under his breath.

"I don't know for sure. I can't remember. We will be able to control the animal, but we must give in to its needs. I didn't at first and I developed a problem with control. It's called degradation; I'm recovering from it now. It's where your mind kinda falls apart. As a werewolf you need to eat human flesh, if you go too long without it your mind starts to deteriorate. I had not killed anyone since becoming a werewolf until two nights ago, I had to; my degradation was advanced. I'm feeling great now, but my memory still isn't what it should be, but it's improving." Darwin educated his little pup.

Darwinism

"Why don't I remember much?" Tim asked.

"Probably because your body is still changing. By full moon I bet you're gonna be a wicked werewolf. Have you noticed your new body yet?" Darwin asked with delight.

Tim flexed his bicep, which was small, but noticeable. "Shit, look at that!"

"You should get bigger in the next few months. A cool perk of the gift." Darwin stated proudly.

"What else is there?" Tim asked still massaging his larger bicep.

"I guess our actions as the wolf are dictated in part as to the persons we are in life. What you did to Rebecca and Cynthia was odd, but it was something that you as a person fantasize about." Darwin stopped.

"What did I do to them?" Tim wondered.

"The short answer. You ate them. That's normal – for a werewolf. But you apparently shit on them, which is not so normal. From what I know from you, that's something you're into, so I think our personalities impart dictate our actions as the wolf." Darwin took another swig of JD to let Tim digest.

Tim looked down at the bed covers. His eyes glazed over with hate and frustration. "I hated those fucking cunts! They got what they deserved."

Darwin knew why Tim hated them, but he hadn't until he sampled Tim's blood. Rebecca and Cynthia were the worst kind of bully, they found ways to demoralize, dehumanize and reduce Tim's self worth by using sexual public humiliation. The first occasion had been with Rebecca. She had lead Tim on, arousing him, giving him an erection and then announcing to everyone within an earshot to check out his *little woody*. Cynthia had been equally as cruel following the lead of Rebecca claiming that she had seen Tim masturbating outside her window as she dressed. This hadn't been true, not until later, but Cynthia never knew that Tim really had started doing it. Tim only decided to start masturbating outside her bedroom window since everyone believed he already did it. Much of Rebecca and Cynthia's accusations were teenage bullying. Tim had never done anything to them; he had never really talked with them. Somewhere, sometime they just decided to make up rumors and stories about Tim, which lead to no girl ever wanting anything to do with him and the jock population constantly giving Tim attitude adjustments in the locker rooms and dark corridors of the school. Rebecca and Cynthia took pride in their work on Tim, and they never wavered, not even for a day. Caroline Buckheart also took part in the attacks on Tim, but for now she had avoided Tim's purging of New Haven evils.

"I think I remember their screams." Tim said quietly.

"Really? What did they sound like?" Darwin wondering what murder sounded like, his own mind still preventing him from experiencing the full spectrum of feelings he could experience as his alter ego.

"It's still vague. I remember pieces. I was next to the bedroom window looking in. They were sleeping but the lamp on the bed stand was still turned on. I slid the window open and crawled through. They didn't hear me. I stood over top of Cynthia; she looked so small and helpless. I bit into her throat waking her up; her scream was muffled and full of blood. The sounds she made were enough to wake Rebecca. The look on their faces, they knew it was me, but they knew I was something else too. Cynthia with the blood gushing from her throat could barely utter a word. Rebecca was so funny. Her mouth opened and she forced air out to get off a sound out, but nothing came. It's so jumbled, maybe it will clear up in time." Tim stared blindly towards the television paying no attention to what was on the screen.

"We've got a bigger problem Tim, what do we do now?" Darwin asked with a new seriousness.

"You mean about the police?" Tim asked, now with his now rosy JD cheeks.

"Yeah." Darwin stated as he looked out the window, noticing a parked car with two men up the block, watching his house. "They're coming for us, you know that?"

"Too bad we can't make them all werewolves." Tim laughed to himself.

Darwin stopped and grinned. The idea was crazy, but simple. It was the old adage, the best way to vanquish an enemy, is to make them an ally.

CHAPTER 15

The plan, in its raw form, was to call Officer Newman to the house. Darwin would tell him that Tim was there and they both had new information they wanted to share with him. It wasn't a well thought out plan.

Darwin had assumed by biting Officer Newman, the heat would be taken off the duo. The call had already been made, and he was on his way. The question was would he be alone? Tim and Darwin would have to hold him down, bite him, and wait for the new metabolism to assert itself. If Officer Newman arrived with back up, or got off a shot with his side arm, things could get messy. The plan was to not kill anyone. Killing Officer Newman would make the situation far worse, he was needed alive, and on side. It was a huge risk, but it was the best option with the walls closing in rapidly. With the lead investigator out of the picture they would then have to turn their attention to the coroner, but that could wait until later.

Even if they managed to turn Officer Newman, there was no guarantee that he'd help them. Darwin was holding out hope that inflicting the gift on Newman would force him to play ball. If he failed to comply, Darwin and Tim could scuttle his existence. That still left the possibility that all three would wind up in a secret military research facility. If he had any sense of self preservation, he'd play along.

Both Darwin and Tim sat fidgeting in the living room. Officer Newman said he'd be over within the hour. An hour was almost up and the anticipation was eating away at both Tim and Darwin. The sedan with the two men inside

131

was still sitting down the street ensuring Darwin and Tim did not attempt to flee. Darwin could see them through the curtain, one talking on a cell phone; he suspected the conversation was with Officer Newman reassuring his watchman that he would be safe. Newman had asked the boys to come to the police station to make their statement, but Darwin convinced him that Tim was too traumatized. Darwin's lie consisted of Tim witnessing the murders of Rick, Bill and Jason, and that he had a decent description of the culprit. Tim had taken several hours to calm down to the point he could talk, he was frightened and was in borderline shock. Darwin thought Tim could help, but that it best to do it somewhere where he felt comfortable. Newman argued the point a little, but eventually agreed to come to the house.

Tread lightly young Darwin...

Looking though the peephole of the front door, Darwin could see another unmarked sedan pull into the driveway. Through the peep hole he fell through the tunnel into the darkness.

"It is a big responsibility you are taking on yourself little one." His mother spoke.

Darwin found himself again, in the inner most part of himself, the cavern with no exit. "Mom, what do you mean?"

"We are not your mother. We are your keeper, we are you." The image spoke.

Darwin wrinkled his forehead in confusion but said nothing.

"The path you travel is a burdensome one. The Eyes of Night watch intently. Proceed with caution. The responsibility is yours and yours alone." The fading image whispered.

I don't understand. He thought.

Purification begins today.

Darwin found a large head staring back at him through the tunnel of light. The door bell chimed and he once again found himself in the living room, as though he had never left. He was left with an odd feeling behind him. He was being watched, and something pivotal was about to happen. In the next few minutes he would forge a path that had never been attempted before. He was more than just a new werewolf; he was something much more.

"Hi Darwin, thanks for getting in touch! I'm very sorry about your mother." Officer Newman said with sincerity as he stepped into the Foster home. He was alone and relief swept across the plotting boys.

"Thanks for coming so fast. It's been a rough morning. When Tim showed up and told me what he saw, I knew you needed to know. The kid was a wreck when he got here. He's actually been a great distraction from my own grief." Darwin sobbed just a little, but it was all for show. The plan was working, it would work. "Can I get you some coffee?"

Officer Newman nodded, with a slight hesitation, before cracking a smile. He turned his attention to Tim Waters who was rocking back in forth on the love seat, putting on his best performance. "Hi Tim, I'm Officer Newman. I've informed your parents that you're ok. They're waiting patiently to hear from you. I told them I would have you call as soon as you felt up to it. Darwin said you didn't want to be around anyone right now...can you tell me what happened?"

Tim continued rocking back and forth on the love seat, wiping his nose from time to time. The anticipation of carrying out the plan was killing him. Darwin had pre-warned him that Officer Newman would need to feel comfortable enough for them to restrain him and do their work. Tim would play along. Darwin would make coffee and Tim Waters would tell the story of his nocturnal exploits, from a third person point of view. Both boys could sense the apprehension in Newman; they would wait until it had subsided.

Tim and Darwin were the prime suspects; Newman would deal with them delicately with the intention of convincing both Darwin and Tim to come to the police station for a better conversation. Once the pups were at the police station, it would be game over. Newman would have his confession.

Both teams were setting up their cards for the game.

"Take your time Tim. Anything you can tell me would help. Do you mind if I record this?" Taking his recorder from his suit pocket, Newman didn't wait for Tim's answer "You want to help me stop this don't you? You don't want anyone else to die do you?" Newman applied the remorse card to get Tim to crack open a bit.

Actually I have a whole list of people I need to visit still...

"It was big; really big." Tim sobbed openly.

"Where did you first see it?" Newman plied.

Tim continued rocking in rhythm with a ticking clock in the hallway. The house was quiet with the exception of the clock, and the sputtering coffee maker in the kitchen. "I was walking home. Rick yelled at me from a block away. The three of them were in front of the drug store. They were coming towards me."

"Do you know what they wanted, Tim?" Newman asked with softness.

"To hurt me." Tim said, now raising his head to look Newman in the eye. "They wanted to hurt me; like they always do."

"Tim, do you know what self defence is?" Newman conspired with the hopes of an early confession.

Tim shook his head and returned his eyes to his clasped hands in his crotch. "Yes." He replied.

Mark Fuson

"Sometimes we do things to protect ourselves, horrible things, but the law doesn't see it as a crime, because it was *in self defence*. Are you telling me the truth Tim, was there something else, something big?" Newman was going for the jugular.

He's just a fucking kid; I can break him, then the other one.

"There was something big. They were beating me, kicking me. I don't remember where it came from or where it went, but it..." Tim stopped, knowing he was beginning to excite himself at the recollection of his vengeance. "It went very fast. It was very strong...I crushed his head." Tim said in a lustful daze.

"What was that Tim?" Newman shot back.

Got him!

"Sorry?" Tim replied knowing full well what he said.

"You said I." Newman smirked, tipping his hand.

"It was a werewolf you know, what I saw." Tim stared with contempt at Newman knowing the officer could care less if it had been in self defence. Newman wanted to wrap it up quickly to make himself look good.

Newman chuckled. "Tim, enough with the lies; It wasn't even a full moon last night. We found your name tag at the scene of the crime. I know you had motive, my only question is how you did it. Then it occurred to me...you had help. Besides, your story has one inescapable hole, they never beat you, there's not even a mark on you!"

The glass bulb swung through the air impacting Newman in the temple. Black searing fluid splashed throughout the living room propelling Newman off the sofa colliding with the glass coffee table, but not breaking the top. He was out cold.

"Darwin, what do we do now?" Tim asked in shock.

Darwin already had a set of canines out and a fuzzy face. Without replying to Tim, Darwin grabbed hold off Newman's hand, and bit down bringing out the think globs of plasma. Darwin huffed and snorted as he tore away at the flesh. Tim ran over and found Newman's side arm and disarmed him. He was theirs now.

Twenty minutes later Newman awoke lying on the floor, with his legs duct taped together. Darwin and Tim had used his own hand cuffs to restrain his wrists. At first his eyes fluttered but then consciousness returned. He looked at Darwin and Tim in disbelief but made no attempt to move. He was their hostage, and his training told him to remain calm and try to talk some sense into them, without pissing them off.

"Why?" Newman asked.

Darwin sat on the love seat and smiled at him. "Frank, we need your cooperation!"

Darwinism

"I'm not sure I can help you, there are officers outside, they're going to check on me sooner or later…what were you thinking?" Newman pleaded with the duo in the hopes of getting them to see the situation logically.

"Tim was telling you the truth, everything except the werewolf that is." Darwin toyed.

"No shit." Newman said in annoyance.

"Oh sorry, you misunderstood. I'm kinda new to this. "Darwin paused for a moment smiling at Tim who was also enjoying himself. "Tim's a werewolf." Darwin smiled with joy at the squirming officer.

"You expect me, or anyone else for that matter, to believe that?" Newman replied.

"You will soon enough." Darwin stated looking at the partially healed wound on Frank's hand.

"Untie me, before this gets any worse for you!" Newman hollered louder, hoping his voice would reach the street. He began struggling trying to break his restraints.

"Should I tape his mouth?" Tim asked already moving towards Newman.

Darwin smirked at Newman and asked "Is that going to be necessary Frank, or can you behave like a big boy for just a little bit longer?"

Frank Newman stopped and looked at Darwin with abhorrence. "What do you want?"

"Frank. Frankie boy. You were going to arrest us. You weren't here to listen to poor Tim, and you could give two shits about my mom. You wanted a promotion, and a quick arrest was going to give it to you. Maybe even some book deals, possibly a movie too. The worst thing is you were never in pursuit of the truth, you just wanted the arrest. You even planted evidence! My question to you is how many others have you sewered in your pathetic career?" Darwin gazed into Newman's awed eyes. Darwin had sampled Frank Newman's soul, and he knew it to be true.

Frank lay on the floor, with nothing more to say. The young man had reached in and tore out his balls and fed them to him on an e-coli infested dinner plate. Frank was feeling different now; submissive.

"The wolf did it. No evidence! It was an animal, yet you're coming after us anyway! Why mother fucker, why!?!" Tim shouted in anger kicking Newman in the face.

Frank moaned in discomfort briefly but again returned his eyes to Darwin. The young man had a presence to him that Frank was becoming mesmerized with. It was an unusual feeling and danger seemed to no longer be present. Frank was becoming receptive; his resolve was dissipating. "I'm sorry." Frank cried.

Mark Fuson

"Stop crying you pussy. You can make it up to us. I'm thinking you're almost ready to try on your new skin...how do you feel Frankie?" Darwin asked.

"Strange. What did you do to me?" Frank asked.

"We're fucking werewolves and you've got a bite mark on your hand...put it together Frank!" Darwin shouted at Frank with a huge smile on his face and then suddenly Darwin realized. "Oh I forgot you're a shitty cop who has to plant evidence to get his arrest!"

Frank knew the answer. His mortal mind was dying and his new immortal one was taking form. Reality was warping and fading. All that he knew was changing, and this amazing young man before him exuded a radiance that he couldn't take his eyes off of. Darwin was his master. He could do nothing but comply and he wanted to do so, without resistance. The remnants of his mortality questioned his situation, but like a sedative, he was losing to the stronger power. "I'm a werewolf?"

"Like you had to ask!" Tim exclaimed. "I knew while Darwin was biting me what I was becoming. Fucking moron."

Darwin knelt down next to his new pup and rubbed his head. Tears were rolling down Frank Newman's cheeks, but they were tears of joy. Being so close to his maker was like touching God. "Frank I chose you because we have important work to do. I need you to make this investigation go away."

Frank remained attentive to Darwin's question. "It won't be easy. The coroner will find hair samples from the Baker Street bodies; they'll be linked to both you and Tim."

Darwin looked at Tim for solace. "Can you believe this guy; I was getting pinned for your fun." Darwin shook his head and returned his full attention to his new worshiper. "How'd you get hair samples from us?"

"One of my men, he works with me on...sensitive cases. Robert Fletcher, he broke into Tim's house this morning. Your sample came from the Caprice change room." Frank replied now fully cooperating and willing to volunteer more.

"So we need to pay a visit to Rob and the coroner. Anyone else I should know about that would help make this situation disappear?" Darwin asked.

"We'll need to find some kind of animal in the woods, we need an animal corpse. We need a cover story for this to stick. We've got a lot of families screaming for answers. And the media, the media is having a field day with this." Frank informed. "If you want this to go away quickly we need the coroner and Fletcher to back us up. We need to find a cougar, mountain lion or a bear; something to shut up the grieving families and the media. The media must be onside. And then there are the survivors."

Darwin had forgotten. He had been seen by one search and rescue person during his lunar attack. Another had survived his attack, and was now probably a werewolf too. Darwin sighed realizing that turning Frank Newman was only the tip of a much larger problem. Darwin would have to turn Robert Fletcher, the coroner and possibly more. He'd have to find the survivor too. "Ok, we'll start there. How are you feeling?"

"Better. You can untie me, I won't run." Newman responded.

"Not yet, we gotta make sure." Darwin bit down on his hand drawing out a stream of blood. He shoved his fingers through the lips of Frank Newman who initially resisted but then began to slurp of the essence of his God. As Frank began drinking the juice his metamorphosis began. Darwin backed off knowing he had achieved his goal. Frank Newman was one, he would help them now.

Frank effortlessly ripped apart his hand cuffs and tore through the duct tape releasing himself. He stood in front of Darwin, panting in joy, with a new wet spot on his pants. He was bigger, and his clothes were taut, but nothing ripped. The new born werewolf stood in front of Tim and Darwin awaiting his instructions.

Darwin and Tim talked for awhile longer with Frank Newman, but Darwin had a lingering idea in his mind. He was very much aware his power seemed to flow outwards to the others around him. Darwin wondered if he could reshape his town into a new haven for himself. To make the police situation go away he would need to infect many people, so why stop there? Darwin wondered if it was possible for him to take control of the entire town, creating a place where he and his followers would never have to be afraid of being discovered or persecuted. It was an exciting prospect. Darwin could select who was turned and who was food. He could single handedly create a utopia, and dispose of those who were undesirable to him, those who had wronged him and those who had wronged others.

His heart raced in excitement.

CHAPTER 16

It was a coup d'etat. Darwin had read about them in school. As he understood it, it was the removal of a governing body by force and the replacement of that body with a new one. There had been many coup d'etat's throughout history. Darwin knew that the success of the coup was based entirely on who you involved in the overthrow. It was essential to have your "ducks in a line", so to speak. The one thing that Darwin did not have on his side was time to contemplate his plan. The wheels of mortal justice were toiling and even with Frank Newman on side, concluding the cover-up and taking control of New Haven would be a challenge. The second concern he had was - what would he do once he had achieved control? The possibilities were overwhelming. Power was not about the government, it was about taking command of the population.

How far should he extend that control? The path ahead of him was both certain and uncertain. Certainty existed that the criminal investigation would have to be dealt with for Darwin and Tim's survival; he was certain he could fix this. The solution to that problem created a new problem. Making new werewolves to participate in a cover up solved the criminal investigation but soon these new beasts would also become hungry. What then? Within a few months New Haven could once again come on the radar with national, perhaps even international authorities as more missing persons and murders were reported. The Foster coup d'etat would need a long term plan to deal with these issues for its success and survival.

138

Darwinism

Unsure how far to extend his influence, Darwin also wondered if he could maintain control over the populous. Frank Newman was co operating without resistance; Tim also seemed willing to do as he was told. Would others infected by Darwin fall to the same fate. Only time could answer that question. New and unwilling members of the family would need to be identified, and dealt with, if Darwin could not manage them.

Should I risk making more? What if they lose control? What if they don't cooperate?

New Haven Memorial was a very small hospital. In the days after the mine closed it dealt mostly with an older retired population. For years there had been talk of closing the hospital, but local outcry always managed to secure funding for just one more year. It was a care center that could handle immediate triage and emergency surgery, but the serious problems had to be shipped elsewhere. There were a total of forty beds over two wards, and there was an attached extended care facility with three hundred beds for the elderly. The place was dead most of the time. When Darwin strolled through the doors there were ten possible patients he could visit but only one that really interested him.

Dave Cronin was twenty two and had been in hospital since he was attacked two nights prior during a search for Darwin Foster. He had been attacked by an animal and had suffered deep lacerations on his back and trauma to his anus. His recovery had been going well, most of his wounds healed much faster than the doctors had expected. He was still in hospital but mostly for observation. Frank Newman dropped Darwin and Tim off so they could meet this brave search and rescue member, and pay their respects. Frank would meet up with Robert Fletcher and venture back on over to the hospital, once Darwin gave him the signal.

Dave Cronin was a local boy who was trying to make good. His family had lived in the slums on Cadmore Avenue a few doors down from the Cardwen's. Darwin never really knew Dave or his parents but he knew of them. Dave was working hard to leave New Haven. From what Frank Newman was able to tell him, Dave Cronin wanted to be more than the typical townie. He was trying to be more than what Cadmore Avenue would allow him to be. Apparently his work in search and rescue was opening up work opportunities in the national parks and he was very close to leaving. With Darwin's arrival at his bed, this was no longer a possibility.

Darwin and Tim set foot in the single occupancy room to find Dave Cronin awake and cheery. He was sitting up right in his bed watching a reality TV show, Prison Row. Darwin recognized the intro music upon entering the room; he himself had caught a few episodes. The show was unique; putting normal everyday citizens behind bars and subjecting them to prison law.

Mark Fuson

Contestants could quit whenever they wanted, but the last man standing took the gold. Strip searches, the shower room, the dinning hall; the producers had it all in the show. The spin was a couple of the contestants were actual former inmates. In addition the contestants were encouraged to drive other contestants to quit. Civility was rapidly diminishing on the show and the once law abiding citizens were squaring off into gangs. Overall the show was very funny to watch, at least Darwin thought so.

"Dave! You're looking better than I thought!" Darwin shouted.

Dave looked at Darwin and cracked a devilish grin. "You ass raped me the other night, didn't you?"

Tim and Darwin burst out laughing. "Holy shit!" Tim exclaimed.

"So much for being subtle!" Darwin replied. "Yeah, I tapped that tight little ass of yours. Sorry, I was a little worked up at the time. I'm surprised you remember me."

Dave smiled and giggled a bit. He turned his TV off and pushed it to the side. Dave had been waiting for this moment. He had played the attack over and over in his head and he knew that something was different about him. His wounds had all but healed, he felt good – really good. It was a large animal and it had been on a full moon. With Darwin in front of him he knew he was right. Dave wanted to be mad at Darwin for the rape, but with Darwin in front of him the anger just slipped away. "I think you were a little more hairy too."

"You will be too, now; you already knew that though." Tim said.

Dave's smile was ear to ear. The young man was at attention, but he didn't want to be overbearing. He would wait for the education that was given to him. He would respect his maker. "What now?"

Darwin plopped his butt down on the edge of Dave's bed and grabbed his thigh. Darwin was growing more confident in his control, and he could see even in Dave that the obedience existed. "That depends on you." Darwin said in a sly way.

"Ok."

"What have you noticed so far?" Darwin asked.

Dave smiled again. "I feel different…like something is nagging at my insides. It's sorta like wanting a smoke."

"Smoking wouldn't help." Tim shot back.

"You want to eat some flesh, don't you?" Darwin asked with a huge smile on his face.

Dave blushed and looked down at the bed sheets, ashamed to admit it was true. "A little. I don't think I'd do it, but I'm curious."

Darwin squeezed Dave's thigh with a firm grip. "You must eat flesh; and sooner or later you are going to. So why not start now?"

Darwinism

"How" Dave asked.

Darwin raised his eyebrows and moved his head in closer to Dave. In a whisper Darwin told him. "I want you to change, right now. I want you to kill someone. Pick whoever you want. Eat them."

"I don't know how." He replied.

"Concentrate. Feel the fire in your gut. The fire heats your blood which begins pushing through your heart. Soon you begin to pant, slow at first, but then faster. Visualize your body, growing, changing and expanding. Close your eyes and imagine blood pouring over your body merging with your soul." Darwin spoke softly to Dave who complied.

In silence, Dave began to breath stronger and deeper. His body took on an unusual shutter and his skin glistened with sweat. He began grunting and his body went into spasms. For almost a minute Dave struggled with his eyes closed. Darwin was about to give up and let Dave feed from him instead, but then it happened. Dave's eyes bolted open full of color and light. The change had come and Darwin watched like a proud father as his latest creation began to take form.

*   *   *

Frank had told Fletcher that it was urgent they meet; new information had come forward that needed to be investigated. Fletcher had worked along with Frank for three years. Together they had both edged their way into a form of policing that was unethical. Neither Frank nor Robert had ever intended on conducting themselves the way they had; it just happened over time.

It began with a suspected pedophile. Police had their suspicions who the man was. He had been abducting young girls, raping them and then letting them go; they had a suspect in mind; just no evidence to tie him to the crimes. There was no DNA evidence and the girls said the man wore a mask. Months had gone by with no new leads or evidence. Finally, after a long night of beer drinking, Fletcher and Newman decided that they would create the evidence tying their prime suspect to the crimes. They kept it simple. Newman acquired DNA from one of the victims from hospital samples, and Fletcher placed it at the suspect's home, in his car and in the bathroom. Combined with a well coached victim to identify the suspect's car there was now enough evidence for a search warrant. Both men knew it would mean their jobs and possibly jail time if they got caught, but in their hearts they knew it was the right thing to do.

Their plan worked. Their suspect was arrested, and eventually convicted. He served only four months before he was murdered in prison. Looking from the outside in one wondered if they felt any guilt or responsibility for how it had ended. Both men felt it could not have ended better. With the convicted

141

Mark Fuson

pedophile now deceased, the appeal, and accusations of police corruption went away. It was almost perfection.

The arrest brought both Newman and Fletcher great notoriety. The taste of fame was a hard to walk away from. Their peers, the courts and other law enforcement agencies now expected the duo to continue their fine police work. The pressure must have been too much to bear because their modified police work continued and expanded. They always got a man, not necessarily the right man, but a man just the same. They both became capable of convincing themselves they were arresting the right person, or a least a bad person, who was guilty of something.

Robert Fletcher was working to wrap up the Foster-Waters case. He expected they could go to a judge within a day for a search warrant. Both Darwin Foster and Tim Waters would be finished in both the legal and public sense by week's end. Fletcher believed in the use of propaganda to vilify the suspects and he always made sure his contacts in the media were given damning evidence to convict his suspects in the court of public opinion. Frank would be satisfied with what Fletcher had to show him. The case was open and shut. Frank had even devised a nice little drug problem for Darwin that made him lose control in the woods with the search and rescue. He had gone wild, and the drugs gave him, what appeared to the rescuers, to be super human strength. Drug addicts often had incredible strength during a high; it wasn't a stretch. All that needed to be done now was ensure Darwin would have drugs in his system, and drugs found at his home. The same would be done for Tim Waters. A cover story for Tim would still need to be worked on; something to the effect that Darwin manipulated Tim into getting involved in the rampage. It really didn't matter what the story was. The real evidence Fletcher had - the stuff that real policing came from, told him that Tim Waters had motive and no alibi. This case was large, but Fletcher still had it taken care of.

"You don't trust me, I told you we'd have this wrapped up in a day or so." Fletcher said through the open window of his cruiser. "How'd the meeting go?"

Frank Newman approached the vehicle and got in the passenger side. "Something's come up."

"I told you I've got this." Fletcher said, now annoyed.

"I met with Waters and Foster this afternoon. The plan has changed. We're not pursuing them further." Newman said knowing full well that Fletcher would not accept that answer.

"Frankie! Stick to the plan, stick to the formula. We've got these little shits, let's just wrap this fucker up and get on with things. You think these guys are genuinely innocent?" Fletcher shouted dumbfounded.

Darwinism

"Remember our first – special - case? The skinner?" Newman said with a furtive tone.

Fletcher sat back, with a shudder. He hadn't thought of that time in a long while. "What about it?"

"They know. I'm not sure how, but they know. They knew more than anyone should. They knew you were involved, and what you did. Little bastards are blackmailing us; our freedom for theirs. We've got to take care of them. Arrest is no longer an option." Newman stated as a matter of fact.

"They're just kids, what could they possibly know?" Fletcher asked in disbelief.

"I wouldn't ask this of you unless I thought it was necessary. Do you want to continue coming home to your kids or do you want to wind up in protective custody in prison? If we don't take care of this tonight, we might both be royally fucked." Newman instilled.

"You're sure?"

"As shit!" Newman said frankly.

"Ok! What's the plan?" Fletcher asked, now on board.

"Foster is going to call me in a little while and tell us where to meet them. He said once we're both in front of him he'll give us further instructions. But that meeting is going to go a little differently than what he thinks. They're going to disappear tonight. It will look like they fled town. We'll dispose of them, and cremate the bodies down at the mortuary. We can dump the ash into the river. It will look like they fled town except they'll never be heard from again. The whole thing will be done by morning. No glory for us, but it's necessary" Newman implored.

"Something stinks about this, Frankie." Fletcher stated attempting to rouse his policing instincts.

"Getting fucked up the ass stinks Bobby." Newman replied.

*   *   *

Darwin and Tim sat outside the morgue waiting for Dave to return. Darwin had left it to Dave to decide who he killed. It was an experiment to see how others would choose their kills without direction. Darwin was settling rapidly into his new roll and he wondered how quickly others like him would adapt. Darwin tried to control himself early on in his new life, but for what purpose? Giving in to the lust of his beast had been the best thing he could have done. His mind was clear and his direction was obvious. Darwin wasn't a monster. Darwin couldn't even be described as an animal that stalked in the night, killing at random anything that crossed his path. He was a sentient being who exercised rational thought and logic; as long as he didn't ignore the beast. He was part of a supernatural underworld that could be defined as evil by the church, but another part of society could see it as nothing more than the ultimate good. What Darwin was and what he was creating was an evolved species of mankind with a strong sense of ethics. As his order established itself a sense of justice and commandment would assert itself. He knew in the early part of his transition some innocence would be squashed. Darwin believed this phenomenon would be short lived and that soon his followers would become part of his societal sanitizing. Darwin's utopia would be the bliss of the blessed.

"Suck my cock." Darwin blurted out to Tim.

"What?" Tim asked in amazement.

"Get to it!" Darwin barked.

Tim rolled his eyes for a moment but slowly got up from his chair immediately falling to his knees in front of Darwin's crotch. He said nothing.

"Just fucking with ya Tim!" Darwin said while grinning at his little pup.

Tim got off his knees and sat back in the chair next to Darwin. "I would do it only because I feel I owe ya big time! That's how thankful I am!"

Darwin laughed. He loved the obedience.

Dong. The elevator chimed, and the doors slide open. Out from the carriage wheeled a gurney pushed by Dave Cronin still wearing his hospital gown. He was now in human form but with drying blood around his mouth and hands. Lying on the gurney was a corpse covered with a white blood stained bed sheet. Dave had made his selection.

Her name had been Brenda Millar. She was 82 when her rib cage had been torn open by Dave Cronin. The woman was a long term resident of the Palliative Care Unit and was well into her twilight years. She was old and frail and her eyes were as good as looking through wax paper. She never saw Dave coming. Dave Cronin selected her out of pity. As the creature, he wandered the beds drifting in and out of the shadows, looking for the best choice. The large beast crept along the corridors coming close to discovery several times, but his unlikely existence seemed to protect him from detection. One old body after another; each looked just as appetizing as the previous. Dave finally selected his first, not by sex, size, smell or anything else that had to do with appetite. On all the other residents' bed stands were pictures of family and pets. Cards and trinkets adorned others. Brenda Millar had no pictures, cards or knick-knack's; her bed space was void of life much like her little body. Dave Cronin ate her out of mercy.

Outside the morgue Darwin and Tim inspected the deceased Brenda Millar. The old woman almost looked happy with her heart ripped from her body. It was probably symbolic of her life.

"That was amazing!" Dave exclaimed. "I felt so alive; it was erotic!"

"What now?" Tim looked to Darwin for guidance.

"We'll put her in the morgue. Newman should be here soon, and then we can get on with our other business." Darwin said professionally. "Dave, roll her in through those doors, find an empty fridge and slide her in. Was there any mess upstairs?"

Dave began wheeling Brenda Millar away. He responded nonchalantly "A little blood, nothing serious."

Darwin sighed and wondered how much cover up was needed. Eventually nurses or residents would find the blood. It could become more unwanted attention, he thought. "Tim, when Newman gets here, I want you to turn Fletcher."

Tim looked at Darwin with his big eyes. Joy had filled them and Tim Waters seemed humbled by the request. "Awesome! I'm gonna be a daddy, and at the age of sixteen! Should we toy with him first, or just get on with it?"

Darwin shook his head agreeing with the question, but he had no answer to the question. Darwin remained silent; his mind was only thinking about the big picture. He had three werewolves at his disposal, and a forth on the way. It appeared to him that his plan was coming together quickly and soon the operation would become a logistical nightmare. As he thought back to his history lessons Darwin knew that a coup d'etat wasn't just about taking control, it was about keeping it. No one man controlled everything; objectives would need to be delegated. Depending on how Fletcher's initiation went, Darwin considered turning integration of the New Haven Police department over to Newman. Newman could then turn and dispose of anyone in the department he wanted. With the New Haven Police Department part of the family, any illegal activities could easily be covered up.

"We should do the hospital too." Tim suggested without thought.

Darwin wrinkled his nose, confused at first, but then he realized what Tim had meant. "Turn the staff?"

"A lot of food here, not that we need a lot right now, but when we do this place has plenty that won't be missed. If the doctors and nurses don't care about the patients, we can farm this place. It might help take some heat off of us while we take control." Tim offered.

"Tim, you might just be brilliant!" Darwin hollered in the cold cement corridor of the basement.

"He's a kid, how smart can he be?" Frank Newman stated as he rounded the corer with Bobby Fletcher in tow.

The two cops stopped in front of Darwin and Tim. Newman, knowing what would happen, and Fletcher living in his little cop and robbers world was still plotting the boys' murder. Fletcher had never directly killed anyone, not by his own hands anyways. Standing in front of the boys he was now preparing himself for snapping Tim's neck while Newman choked out Darwin. That was the plan anyways. Newman had asked Fletcher to - play along - and to just - follow his lead.

"Let's see your hand Fletcher." Tim demanded.

Fletcher looked to Newman who gave his head a simple shake. Fletcher extended his left arm towards the boy revealing his hand palm up. Tim Waters sliced through his palm with his canines before Fletcher was even able to blink. The burning pain of the wound came as a shock. In a reflexive motion Fletcher pushed Tim hard causing him to fly down the hall. With Tim in mid air Fletcher drew his side arm and fired a shot directly into Tim's chest. The bullet bore a hole deep into Tim's body. Dark red fluid bubbled through his shirt almost immediately and he gasped in awe. On the floor Tim looked back at Fletcher who kept the gun pointed in Tim's direction. Blood leaked from his gift wound, down the stalk of his gun, and dripped to the floor into a puddle. The two looked at each other, not knowing what would come next.

"Stay where you are! If you move, I'll shoot again." Fletcher shouted at Tim who was poking his wound.

"I liked that shirt, dick!" Tim stated sarcastically.

"Chill, it's all over. Put the gun away, you won't need it here." Newman told Fletcher as he placed his hand onto the drawn pistol. Slowly Fletcher began to lower his weapon.

"One more!" Fletcher announced before quickly turning the gun towards Darwin and firing two rounds into his chest.

Darwin wheezed with discomfort only for a moment, but he remained standing. "Enough already!" Darwin demanded.

"Bobby, enough." Newman said. "You could shoot us a hundred times and it wouldn't make a difference."

Fletcher looked to Newman in confusion. Had he just said that? He said "US". The two boys had bullet holes in their chest and yet the looked perfectly fine other than the blood. Fletcher knew something was terribly wrong and for a moment he became frightened. "Frankie?"

"We've stumbled into something huge my friend. They bit me earlier today. You have no idea, the power, the feeling of ecstasy that you are going to have." Newman comforted.

"What the fuck is this shit!?!" Fletcher coughed out.

Newman bit into his own hand drawing some blood. Newman then grabbed his partner and scuffled as he tried to get the blood into Fletcher's mouth. Fletcher resisted but he was powerless to fight against Newman, who was stronger and more agile. Fletcher begged, coughed and winced but the bloody finger came closer and closer to his mouth. Only one drop of blood fell onto Fletchers lips, but it was enough.

The gift had only flowed through his veins for a few moments but the drop of blood had an impact. He stopped tussling as he quivered. A vibration rolled through his body as he seized. His eyes puffed and bulged as though his insides were being pureed and then his ocular organs began to fill with light. He smiled in elation and his crotch began to fill out. He didn't change, but the wolf was in him, and his resistance vanished.

Darwin approached the latest inductee. "Welcome to the club. Hope you enjoyed your first taste. There will be plenty more."

"What am I?" Fletcher asked in amazement.

"Beware of the moon my friend! Ahhhhwwooooooo!!!" Darwin howled which started as a fake sounding human-wolf howl, but it quickly morphed into the real thing.

*   *   *

An hour later the five men were inside the morgue sitting around the slab. What remained of Brenda Millar's corpse lay on the stainless steel table; her body, now dinner. The men had feasted on her remains over the last hour. Dave Cronin had tried unsuccessfully to place her corpse into a fridge, but because of all the recent tragedies in New Haven, the morgue was well over capacity. Darwin, Tim, Newman and Dave all tore off pieces and consumed them in carnivore fashion. Darwin sampled a few parts but found he really enjoyed the eyes; he chewed on them like bubble gum. Tim was a breast man but he also had a side of brain. Dave and Newman found themselves into organ meat and bone. Fletcher sat quietly at the table, refusing to eat at first, but as his new personality took hold the others could see him licking his chops. Temptation finally gave way and Fletcher discovered he was an ass man who also enjoyed a glass of bile on the side. All five men wolfed it up and it wasn't long before Brenda Millar was put to rest.

The wolves of the steel table discussed their future, and what that might look like. The New Wolf Order, as Darwin suggested, would have to control all aspects of New Haven. It had already been agreed upon the police and hospital staff would have to be converted. Infiltration of these facilities would have to be done at lightening speed and covertly. Next on the list was the media. In this area both Newman and Fletcher admitted TV and print needed to be dealt with. The first was The Haven Chronicle, the group decided the entire staff would have to be brought on board but the Editor and Chief Sam Thomasen could be disposed of. This decision was more of a personal vendetta between Fletcher and Thomasen; Darwin didn't press the issue, he could relate to vendettas. The TV news was less of an issue. The group felt that only one reporter from the city would need to be converted. Vivian Yee of channel six covered Fletcher and Newman frequently and other media outlets followed her leads. With Vivian part of the group, New Haven should drift from attention. City Hall was more complicated, the fact was the politicians weren't needed, and Darwin would control the town. A new council would be formed from members of Darwin's choice, however the community would still need to function, and contacts with the outside world would need to be maintained simply to keep prying eyes away. The City Hall question was a conundrum.

Newman attempted to educate Darwin on the inside politics of New Haven. "Mayor Bollen controls every aspect of this town. She can't simply disappear. She has powerful supporters; if she disappeared someone would start asking questions. And then there's the issue of her family, and the council's families for that matter."

"Frank's right. You're right back to square one if we're not careful. Are you sure turning the council isn't an option?" Fletcher asked.

"Bob, I'm not prepared to turn everyone. Those with purpose, those who can contribute will be turned. Once we have the essential people, then we will select the ones we want from the community at large to join us, the good ones, the rest, the undesirables, will be…consumed." Darwin vowed.

"How will we choose who lives and who…goes?" Dave asked.

"I will have the ultimate say in who is brought in, you may turn your families if you wish, but anyone else will not be without my explicit permission. Failure to abide by this will result in termination, let's consider that law one. We must control the population; if we can't control our own numbers we may infect people who could pollute our kind. There are people who are good in this world, I want them. Drug addicts, abusive husbands, the local whore, the thief, the liar, the priest and bible banging followers, the person who took advantage of their fellow man, the pedophile the ex-con, all will be purged. Let me say it another way, you will not turn these people under any circumstance. Bluntly, I have no use for them. Are we clear?" Darwin looked around the table to find he had the attention and admiration of his followers. The longer Darwin spoke, and was around his kind the more he felt like he was a dictator. His power was growing and it was all consuming.

"YES SIR!" The group yelled in unison with out prompting from Darwin.

"Tim has suggested, until we can establish ourselves that we use the senior population of this hospital as a source of food. I think it's a great idea. We shouldn't require large amounts of food; I lived for three months without eating human. I must admit, I feel a hell of a lot more powerful when I do eat human, but we can live without it. I think in the short term we will eat the seniors, most won't be missed. We can hide their deaths under a veil of

Darwinism

natural causes. With the help of the coroner – oh that reminds me – Fletcher can you look after her?"

"Turn her?" He responded quickly.

"Yep, she'll need to keep family members and outsiders assured that nothing out of the ordinary is going on in New Haven, plus I need her to make my own problems go away." Darwin said.

"Sorry about that Darwin, I'd have joined you long ago had I known what you were." Newman interjected jokingly.

Darwin looked around the table to his interim council. His plan was coming fast and steady. Soon he would be in command of something big, and he wondered how his overseers would judge him. He had not been drawn into the inner part of himself; if his mentors had a concern they should have intervened. Darwin knew the path he was on was precarious, but it was the chosen one.

"Darwin, shouldn't we take control of the communications network, phone, radio, and internet?" Fletcher asked.

"Is that even possible?" Darwin responded.

"It would be a challenge, but we should have the ability to disconnect from the network should someone try to get a message out alerting the outside world. I think we could set up a monitoring system; identify our troublemakers; tap their phones and monitor their internet, if they step out of line; we unplug them and then deal with them accordingly." Fletcher answered.

"What's to stop them from leaving town and telling someone in person? There wouldn't be anything to monitor then." Tim offered.

"Tim's got a point...what's the solution?" Darwin put to the group.

"Check points." Newman suggested.

"What would that entail?" Darwin asked.

"It would be the same principle of the telecommunications monitoring. We identify our problematic citizens, and watch for them specifically. If we see one headed out of town, we intercept them. It would require manning the routes in and out of town, but I think it could work, at least until the threat no longer exists." Newman sold.

"This town has roughly 15000 people living in it; I can see us taking on maybe half that number. The rest will need to be dealt with. Unless we are planning a pig out, what do we do with the people until we need them? Sooner or later someone will notice the town's dwindling numbers. There's a chance one of our citizens could escape before the town has been completely purged. We might need to consider a detention center." Darwin suggested.

"We don't have a jail in this town large enough to accommodate those kinds of numbers." Newman responded.

"The gulags, concentration camps, re-education centers; throughout

149

history large numbers of people of been rounded up for the common good. Why can't we do the same?" Darwin asked.

"We're taking over a town, not a country. This is the modern world. A camp would be seen by satellites, airplanes or even drones. Someone in the outside world would find it." Fletcher answered.

"Only if it was above ground!" Darwin smiled, knowing the ideal spot to put a concentration camp. It would require some exploration and a little work, but it could work. "We'll use the mine. It's Clayburn Nurseries right now... but there's a huge underground network of caverns and tunnels. I think we could convert them into underground housing that the outside world would never see. I've been down there a few times, I know the owner. I think it could work with some upgrades."

"Does it have more than one access point?" Dave Cronin asked to get in on the discussion.

"It's something we'll have to look into. I'll assimilate Clint Littleford – the owner, he can tell us about the mine in detail once he's one of us."

"Who the hell are you guys? Frank? Who are these people?" Jane Wannsee demanded as she stepped into the morgue unexpectedly.

Robert Fletcher hadn't let the others even respond when he jumped on top of Jane and bit into her shoulder. Darwin had, after all, ordered Fletcher to turn the coroner. Fletcher simply couldn't see a reason to wait. Jane screamed and fought as the once crooked cop now brought her into the fold as the first female of the group. The other four sat back and watched, wanting in on the action, but this was for Fletcher.

"I'm kinda hungry, anyone else want anything?" Dave Cronin asked as he went over to the fridge to retrieve a corpse.

Tim spoke up right away. "Yeah, I'm down with that!"

A moment later Dave returned with a large male body hung over his shoulder. He flung it down on the slab splashing some of Brenda Millar's remains onto Darwin. Darwin recognized the man, his first kill. It took him back a moment, to the last time he could consider himself human.

Tim tore into the thigh and began chewing on a hunk of flesh but quickly spat it out. "YUCK, tastes like chemicals!"

"Probably embalming fluid." Newman said with a chuckle. "Guess you'll have to go out to eat!"

Fletcher returned to the group partially wolfed. Jane Wannsee lay on the floor slowly rolling in her own blood. She moaned in pain and held the gaping hole in her shoulder. She would turn before bleeding out; her wound was already partially healed.

"You get a nip on the hand but she gets her shoulder ripped apart, how's that fair?" Tim asked.

Darwinism

Fletcher looked back to the woman in rebirth only to come back with "I was hungry."

"Bobby, give her some blood." Darwin ordered before refocusing the group. "Frank, I want you to head up the Police Department. You're in command of security. Your first order of business is to take control of the department. You and Fletcher get down to the station, and start bringing some of your colleagues over. I want that wrapped up by noon. Tim and Dave, you stay here at the hospital. Get the head nurse and the on duty doctor first and work your way from there. Don't forget about the paramedics too. I want status reports by noon, but earlier if you get finished. We'll need to have a meeting with our new members as soon as possible, to keep everyone on page. Agree?"

"YES SIR!" They shouted in unity.

"What should we do with Wannsee?" Newman asked.

"How are you feeling lady?" Darwin asked looking over his shoulder to the groggy but waking woman.

"What have you done to me?" Jane Wannsee asked.

"That's a shit attitude to have lady!" Dave accused.

Darwin hopped off his stool and crouched down next to his newest member. She was three times removed from his bloodline, but he thought he'd test his methods of persuasion on her. "I'm Darwin, you're, Jane?"

The woman looked at him with a guard and a lack of trust, but she answered. "Yes."

"I want you to go with Frank and Bobby. You know them; they can explain things to you. You have nothing to be afraid of. OK?" Darwin said softly.

"Sure." She responded.

"Get to it, people! We've got a town to take." Darwin announced.

His team exited without further discussion. Newman and Fletcher helped Jane off the floor and soon Darwin was in the morgue by himself. The marching orders had been given and soon there would be no turning back from the plan. He was giddy with anticipation and he actually jumped up and down like a little boy for a moment. The town was soon to pay for all the misdeeds of his past. New Haven would be reshaped into his own kingdom and the possibilities were endless.

The silence of the morgue awoke Darwin with a chill. He looked to the bank of fridges along the wall. They were all closed and none was more remarkable than the next. But Darwin found himself drawn to the unit at the end of the bank. He slowly walked down the corridor and found himself standing in front of the unit. On the door was a small paper card that read: Foster, Marie. Darwin stood looking at the door knowing that his own mother

Mark Fuson

was behind the steel. Had he put her in this place? Darwin remembered his mom, the woman before the tragedies, he had loved that woman. Darwin was sorry that he had been so cold to her in the remaining years of her life. She had been hurting as much as he had and he had resented her for trying to cope with her loss. Darwin knew he had been a hypocrite; he had needed to cope as much as his mother had. In front of the fridge, Darwin apologized to her openly as he cried.

The decision to open his mother's cold tomb came after his mourning. Darwin had to know what he had done to her. Had he mutilated her; had she suffered?

Darwin rolled out the sliding metal stretcher to find his mother, intact, and without a scratch on her. Relief washed through him. He looked down at his mother's pale ghost covered face, her life force long since expired. He hardly recognized her with a now slightly sunken in face. As he examined his mother, he could see nothing that suggested to him a werewolf had attacked her. Her death remained a mystery.

He stood over her looking at her face trying to remember what her voice sounded like, but it eluded him. Marie Foster's eyes bolted open bleached with red and she spoke. "STEVE" Hissed from her lungs.

Darwin shot back, startled. He looked to find his mother rising from her cold sepulchre place. The nude grey body of Marie Foster jumped onto the floor and began trundling her feet along the tile floor. She reached towards her son with one arm, the other reached deep inside her cunt. The zombie of Marie Foster kept advancing. Darwin could do nothing except slide along the other mortuary units in a feeble attempt to get away. He was paralyzed. Marie flung her vaginal hand at Darwin sending a stream of sticky congealed blood at him hitting him square in the mouth. Darwin shut his eyes to make his vision disappear but he could still feel his mother's vaginal fluids on his lips squirming its way into his mouth. Even with his eyes closed he could hear his mother's feet scrapping across the floor.

And then silence returned to the morgue; the sound of the feet was gone. Darwin's mouth was still heavy with the taste of iron, but he braved the real world and opened his eyes again only to find Marie Foster two inches from his nose. The cold grey skinned woman glared at him with contempt. She moved in and shoved her tongue down her son's throat. Darwin choked and threw up inside his corpse mother's mouth, but she persisted.

And then it was over. Darwin looked around only to find his mother back on the stretcher in her fridge as though she had never left. Darwin was backed into a corner, covered in vomit and vaginal fluid. Darwin gagged and threw up more Brenda Millar to the floor.

His mother lay in satisfaction.

CHAPTER 17

New Haven on a crisp December morning was a scene right out of a Frank Capra film. The streets glistened with a light coating of frost that sparkled in the frigid sunlight. The garland that hung from the lampposts had been dusted ever so lightly with a breath of snow. Christmas was in the air and a festive feel was growing on the streets. The merriment of the citizens was a fraud. The mothers wishing each other a merry Christmas was disingenuous. The rivalry and jealousy felt among many of the townsfolk was overwhelming. The peaceful atmosphere was nothing more than a façade of what small town life should be. Many of the townsfolk simply didn't know what the true meaning of the holiday season was. Consumption and greed had taken many of New Haven's citizens; and it was spreading like a cancer.

Darwin could feel this now. The town emanated a vibration that he could sense. New Haven was attempting to live up to an idea but it had no understanding of how to achieve it. The town didn't comprehend the idea. Small towns should be a quiet and safe place where you can leave your door unlocked, not worry about where your children are and everyone knows everyone. New Haven citizens locked their doors because they had no idea where their kids were – probably because they're breaking into a house somewhere, and everyone knew who was fucking who. That was the real New Haven. Having said that, New Haven was good at making appearances.

Darwin could smell Cindy Holmes. She had a distinctive sweet odour that was hypnotic to him. Her smell reminded him of a bakery and the fresh bread that came from the oven. Fresh bread was a favourite of his and when he was around Cindy Holmes he had the same feeling he did when he was at the bakery. Darwin could eat a whole loaf with butter; it was that good. Cindy Holmes aroused those feelings in Darwin, even before Darwin was blessed he felt warm around her. His new personality, his new senses made Cindy simply too tempting to resist. He had sought her out, an urge he wanted to fill while his troops were out doing his bidding.

It was just before nine in the morning and Darwin had found Cindy at the Bakerberry Coffee House. She was sitting at a window reading Dickens. It was such a cute scene he could barely stand himself. Darwin strolled across the street over to the shop keeping his eye on his sweet jewel. When Darwin hit the sidewalk Cindy looked up from her book. She looked not at his face, but gave his body a once over; she appeared to like what she saw. Darwin was wearing a tight fitting shirt that showed his muscular chest and arms. The weather was cold but Darwin purposely left the coat behind. He wanted to show off; he was feeling cocky.

Inside the Bakerberry Darwin pulled up the stool next to Cindy who was still fixated on his bulging biceps. Darwin grinned at her knowing he was going to get laid.

"What's up chicky?" Darwin asked mischievously.

"Darwin, you sure got…big!" Cindy spit out exasperated.

Darwin smiled trying to be modest. "I'm nothing compared to your beauty!"

"I heard your mom was in the hospital, is she ok?" Cindy asked with sincerity as she placed her gentle cold hands on Darwin's firm and hot forearm.

The cold grey woman flashed into his mind. Darwin felt the vomit backing up into his throat forcing him to look away from Cindy for a moment.

"What's wrong?" she asked.

Darwin forced the image of his mother from his mind. He opened his eyes and looked at Cindy with tears streaming down his face. "Ah, she's dead." He cried.

Cindy leapt from her stool and embraced Darwin, pressing her breasts against his chest. Her sweet aroma became overpowering as he buried his face toward the nape of her neck. Darwin wept openly in joy and horror. The image of his dead mother still frightened him, but he felt safe in Cindy's arms.

"I'm so sorry, is there anything I can do for you?" Cindy asked.

Ride my cock.

"Can you come over to my house right now? I have something I need to show you." Darwin asked with an ulterior motive.

Darwinism

Cindy thought about it for a moment, but eventually she shook her head. She had never been to Darwin's house. She had never spent anytime with him socially. She truly liked Darwin but until this day she had never considered spending time with him. Cindy was now having new thoughts of her co-worker. She was becoming wet, and she wasn't sure why. She felt guilt in her lust; in Darwin's pain she was finding a growing sexual urge that she knew to be wrong, but unavoidable.

Darwin drove Cindy to his home only exchanging small talk for the short drive. Cindy made an effort to avoid asking about Darwin's mother but she was curious.

What's in his pants???

"I hope you don't mind; what I want to show you is in my bedroom?" Darwin asked as they pulled into his driveway.

"How long have we known each other? It's not like you're the big bad wolf or anything." She replied on the sly.

Darwin took Cindy into the house and up the stairs into his room. The house was dead and all the lights were off. Darwin swung his bedroom door open to expose his untidy room. He stepped in and went to his desk. A moment later he looked back to find Cindy standing in the doorway. She seemed shy.

"You can cum in here you know." Darwin said with meaning. "I won't bite."

Liar!

"I'm not sure if I should." Cindy said meekly, now moving into the bedroom.

"Why not?" Darwin asked as he still shuffled through his desk drawer.

"Everything that's happened to you, is my being here the right thing?" She asked.

Darwin pulled a photograph from his drawer walked over to the young woman who was now sitting on his bed. Darwin sat down next to her and handed her the photo. Two children were in the picture, a very young Cindy and Darwin. The picture was of them at the MacCarran Park playing together. Cindy had forgotten about that day. It was a birthday party for a mutual friend but Darwin and Cindy spent most of the day together. When Cindy took the photo in her hands she was touched that Darwin had remembered that day.

"Do you remember?" Darwin asked.

"I didn't, it was so long ago. I can't believe you have this." She said in happiness.

"I've always liked you. That's why I kept this picture" Darwin admitted.

Cindy looked to him and smiled. "Why are telling me this?"

155

Mark Fuson

"If not now, when?" Darwin asked in endearment.

Cindy gave in and planted her lips on his. She slowly and softly opened her mouth to allow her tongue to toil with his. Darwin did not push the situation choosing to allow Cindy the privilege of dictating their speed. Darwin found himself in immediate arousal, pulsating to the beat of his heart. He placed his hand on her breast and lightly caressed it, rubbing the nipple through her blouse. Cindy wasn't wearing a bra; her breasts were a good size but not too large. Darwin could tell that Cindy was his and he felt fantastic.

"You're a great kisser, Cindy." Darwin said as they paused to look at each other.

"It's not all I'm good at!" She announced, ripping off his shirt and exposing his hairy chest. She pushed him down forcefully onto the bed and tore open his pants only pulling them down to the knees. His cock bobbed up and down through his underwear like an animal poking through the trash. Cindy threw her top off showing Darwin for the first time her young opulent breasts. She began grinding her ass on his throbbing cock and he moaned with pleasure. Darwin put his hands behind his head and smiled in delight. Cindy leaned down and licked his lips before moving southwards towards his nether regions. Her tongue forged a path through his fur until she was face to face with his eager tool. Cindy pulled down his underwear and swallowed his cock all the way down to the base; only something a real pro knew how to do. Darwin sighed in relief as his sexual tension was sucked from his bone. Laying on the bed he looked down to this beautiful woman through his chest wondering if she was only doing this because she felt bad for him, or if she truly wanted to do it. Darwin dropped his head back to the bed and allowed himself to flow into the sexual abyss. He felt warm and his balls were bubbling. He would cum soon.

My chest is hairy...

Darwin looked down at his chest again and realized he was much hairier that normal. He looked human still, but his chest was not normally as hairy as it was at this moment. Darwin looked at his arms too, but found only his chest to be partially transformed. He lay back on the bed allowing himself to go. He didn't care.

Cindy stopped and jumped off the bed. Darwin was taken aback for a moment until he realized she was removing her jeans and panties. The girl jumped on top of Darwin straddling his body. His cock disappeared inside of her. She was fast; faster than Darwin could have ever had hoped for. Cindy Holmes began bouncing up and down drawing him closer and closer to explosion. He wanted to wait but his urges were moving too quick and his balls were fully loaded. Cindy was a screamer. With her body now dripping in sweat Darwin could see that young Cindy herself might climax before him. She began quivering and panting as she bounced. Each violent collapse on Darwin's cock seemed to release her and bring her that much closer to the big "O". Darwin watched in awe as she rode his cock like a bull. She moved, twisted and slid along the shaft contracting and squeezing as she went. Then it happened. She began to orgasm. Her body shuddered in delight. While in full sexual quake Cindy slid off Darwin and once again dove head first onto his member. She squeezed his penis with extreme pressure using her lips which triggered Darwin's own orgasm. Cindy's gratefully swallowed the gift of Darwin's seed.

It took them both several minutes to recoup from their short but intense sexual adventure. Cindy lay on top of Darwin's hairless chest listening to her man's heart. Darwin said nothing, only petting her head.

Darwin's phone rang forcing him to lift Cindy off his chest. Darwin apologized but he threw her off to the side. Cindy actually enjoyed the strength in his throw. Darwin jumped off the bed, pulled his pants up and grabbed his phone from his coat pocket.

"Newman here. We've finished the ones on duty. I've got them locked up in cells until they come around." Came across Darwin's phone.

"Excellent! That was faster than I expected. Any problems?" Darwin asked.

"I've got some detainees in cells that know something's up. We had to put our new inductees somewhere to make sure the change took. Cells was the only place we had. Anyway we've got two guys down there arrested in the last day for property crime and public drunkenness. They know something is wrong because they're watching me put officers into cells, some covered in blood."

"So get rid of them, feed them to the pups." Darwin suggested.

"I was going to suggest that." Newman said relieved.

"Good, get it done. How many others do you need to do?" Darwin asked.

"I've got two other crews on rest days, twelve guys in total. I'll need to visit them at home to bring them around." Newman replied.

"Maybe you should call them at home and ask them to come to the station…it would help us avoid anyone from seeing what you're doing." Darwin offered.

"That's actually a good idea. We'll do that." Newman affirmed.

"Keep me posted." Darwin hung up without saying another word. He turned around to find young Cindy Holmes lying on her belly ogling him.

"That sounded really strange from here." She laughed. "What was it really about?"

"Just a little project I'm working on." Darwin quickly changed the subject. "You want to do it again, I'm ready for seconds!"

"Sure!" Cindy shouted.

"Steve's never gonna believe this!" Darwin said smiling ear to ear as he again took his pants off exposing his growing member.

"I always thought you and Steve were together. I never thought you would want me! Shit, that reminds me. What's this about Steve Cardwen and you leaving town together? I ran into him the other night, and he said you and him were leaving town." Cindy asked as she assumed the doggie position.

Darwin slid in behind her pushing his member against her rectum. "I have to talk to him about that. I have a better plan for Steve." Darwin pushed his meat inside of Cindy who once again seemed accustomed to the sensation. Darwin began violently ramming his cock inside her. His balls slapped against her butt creating a giant red mark on her. She still moaned in pleasure. The two fucked for hours; Darwin's chest fuzzed up repeatedly, but for some reason Cindy failed to notice. She consumed his seed over and over again that afternoon, she was consumed by him.

Chapter 18

It was late in the afternoon. Darwin had infused Cindy Holmes multiple times with his seed; he was feeling at peace. Darwin had never had sex as many times in one afternoon as he had on this day. His power of persuasion seemed to influence even the non-blessed. Cindy Holmes devoured him as though he was a forbidden chocolate but he had done little to get it. Was it his power or was it his self confidence that his power gave him? He was unsure, but he was sure he would indulge in more.

Darwin had business to attend to. As leader he still had responsibilities and he had already committed himself to investigating Clayburn Nurseries as a potential holding facility for the unwanted citizens of New Haven. Darwin had to speak to Clint alone because of what knew to be in those mine tunnels. Clint Littleford had converted a vast underground space into a drug operation. He primarily grew marijuana, but he also ventured into mushrooms. Darwin wanted to keep this aspect of Clint a secret. It had already been decreed by Darwin that no drug addicts would be turned, or anyone from the criminal element for that matter. Clint was a drug producer, supplier and all-round undesirable. Darwin had enjoyed the benefits of Clint's operation for several years. Darwin, himself, had indulged in marijuana and other drugs throughout the years. In his dealings with Clint, Darwin could see he detested that element of society, even though Darwin treaded the line between the two lives. To keep himself appearing as genuine to his cause, the Clint Littleford connection would have to be suppressed.

Darwin rolled up to the main house at Clayburn Nurseries and found the old pick up truck parked off to the side. Darwin hadn't been up to Clint's house in months. He had been getting his marijuana directly from Steve who still worked for Clint. Steve never charged Darwin which made it that much easier to avoid Clint. Darwin didn't hate Clint; he just loathed what he stood for. Clint was making money, but Darwin could see how the illegal activity had affected so many youth in town. The youth of New Haven often didn't stop with alcohol and weed, the high they sought could only be found in better drugs. Clint may not have sold those drugs, but he pointed the young in the right direction. Darwin had managed to avoid that fate. He loved his weed, but knew better than to venture into anything harder. Clint was the man Darwin loved to hate. He supplied a substance Darwin loved, but he also turned people into useless sloths which Darwin had a deep hatred for. It was a conflict within him; and he wanted it both ways.

Darwin marched up the steps to the house; he tapped on the door a few times and waited. Inside he could hear the TV and Clint speaking. After a moment Darwin knew that Clint was not coming to the door, so he rapped it again. This time Darwin could see through the single pane glass that Clint was coming to the door talking on the phone. When he saw it was Darwin his face lit up.

The door swung open and Clint waved Darwin in. "I gotta fly man, I've got company. I'll call you later. Yep...no worries. Bye!" Clint hung up the phone and turned his attention to Darwin who was now sitting on the old paisley sofa. "Darwin! Dude, where have you been? It's been too long my friend! You're looking big these days, roids?"

Darwin extended his hand and shook Clint's firmly. "It has been too long; but no roids. What have you been up to?"

Clint seated himself across from Darwin in a 1980's recliner that had been patched with duct tape on the arms. "Same shit my friend. I'd love to get out of this business, but the money is too good."

"Ever thought of doing just the nursery, you've gotta have enough money saved from the underground stuff." Darwin asked.

"Shit dude, once you're into this stuff, it ain't that easy to quit. If I closed up shop my silent partners would come knocking in short order. This business is fucked! Once you're in, you're in! Hey you want a beer?" Clint asked attempting to be a good host.

Darwin nodded and Clint ran off to the kitchen. "Have you seen Steve lately?" Darwin asked raising his voice to carry it to the kitchen.

"Not much. He's been having a tough go at home I think." Clint said as he re-entered the living room now holding two local pale ales.

Darwinism

"What's going on?" Darwin asked, now concerned.

"His fucking dad has been kicking the shit out of him again. I saw him last week with another black eye. I tried talking to him about it, but he didn't want to." Clint told Darwin in a sombre tone.

"That fucking dick. I'm gonna kill him!" Darwin said with truth in his voice. "I talked to Steve the other day. He wanted me to leave town with him. I couldn't, I wanted to, but I couldn't"

"You two have been bum buddies for as long as I have known you! You should have gone with him!" Clint proclaimed while opening his beer.

"That's not funny Clint! You know we were picked on in school for that very reason." Darwin said in vain.

"Dude, let it go. I know you two love each other. I've seen how you two carry on. There's nothing wrong with it. You're out of school; you can leave this shit hole. You should!" Clint said, as though it was that simple.

Darwin thought for a moment. He never considered himself to be gay, but his feelings for Steve were strong and it was love. The one downfall of his gift was his distraction. The last few months he had kept his distance from Steve, mostly from the fear of what he might do to Steve. In the last few days those worries had left him and he could now see Steve in safety, and he wanted to. The takeover plan was getting in the way of his personal priorities and he knew he had to make time to find Steve before he left New Haven. Darwin knew that it was a distinct possibility that Steve may have already left. "You might be right." Darwin told Clint.

"Fucking rights!" Clint shouted.

"Clint, I've got something I want to ask you." Darwin said.

"Shoot."

"Would you be interested in joining a movement, something big? It would allow you to leave behind your criminal ties, and work for the good guys" Darwin stated.

Clint laughed openly at the suggestion. "Dude, it would never happen. Like I said I can't just up and quit. My financers would come looking; they'd expect compensation –and that doesn't mean money per sae. Besides, what could you possibly offer that compares to what I have now?

"Immortality." Darwin stated with ease.

"Dar, don't fucking come here and waste my time. I do want out, but the only way I can see that happening is if I up and leave town...I could never come back." Clint restated his position.

"There's a group of us. Our numbers are small right now, but I'm recruiting. The plan is to take New Haven – we've already started. I have the police force, and soon the hospital will be ours as well. I will make this town pay! All the sick fucks in this town will wish they had never crossed my

Mark Fuson

path!" Darwin told his plan with commitment like a crazed politician who could see no flaws.

"Take the town? Are your on meth now?!? Get the fuck out of here Darwin and take your fairytales with you!" Clint got up from his seat and moved to the door.

"My plan needs you. I need the mine for a detention center. I want you to join willingly, but if I have no choice…" Darwin threatened.

"Shit dude, you just don't give it up. You could never take the town, and if you did, then what? You think the people in this town would tolerate you as their dictator? Eventually the feds would show up and depose of you and your followers. And on top of that what reason would anyone have to follow you? Why are you wasting my time with BS Darwin?" Clint asked with the front door now ajar.

"I'm a werewolf; A new breed of man. This plan will work." Darwin said with intent as he rose to move towards the door.

Clint began whistling a traditional circus tune and dancing in a circle. Darwin was playing a joke or was completely bonkers. Clint wasn't sure what the answer was but he knew Darwin Foster was definitely not right in the head. "I think you heard about those animal attacks the other night and decided to play a really stupid and sick joke. It's fucking juvenile, Darwin!"

Darwin stood in front of Clint, raising his heart rate to bring about the change. "I killed them Clint. The search and rescue guys, I killed them. I ate them. Tim Waters killed some of his old friends in town the other night. This is very real." Darwin sternly told Clint as his eyes began to fill with color.

Clint wasn't looking at Darwin to see his eyes. Clint was now watching the perfectly polished black SUV rolling down the drive. "Darwin, go hide. These guys are bad news." Clint left Darwin at the doorway and went outside to confront the intruders.

Darwin stopped his transformation and stayed within sight of the SUV. He watched Clint go out onto the drive, waiting for the SUV to pull up. Clint put himself out in the open; there was no hiding from them and he knew it. The vehicle stopped near Clint and two black men and one Hispanic looking male exited. They approached Clint acting as though they were friends but Darwin could see the two black males were packing. From within the house Darwin could hear the conversation more clearly than he expected; another perk of his gift.

"We expected shipment two days ago, what's hold up?" The Hispanic male asked.

"This crop isn't looking so hot; I don't even think it's salvageable. I think some contaminants got into the water supply, most of the plants began withering a few weeks ago, and the buds we did get were a fraction of the size they should have been. I did call last week to report the issue, didn't you get the message?" Clint smiled nervously knowing full well what these men were there to do. They would collect the money owed to them, one way or another.

"They said you were one of the best. I trusted you with my money, up front. And now you tell me this lie to my face!" The male shouted at Clint.

"It's no lie, have a look for yourself!" Clint demanded.

"Word on the street was you were planning on leaving with my money." The man stated calmly. "My friends here look out for my interests. Why don't I leave you guys to talk it over? Maybe in an hour or so you'll have a different perspective on the situation."

"Clint, these guys bugging you?" Darwin exclaimed as he made his way towards the group.

"Darwin this doesn't involve you, get in the house." Clint begged.

"My friend come on over!" The leading male requested with open arms.

"I intend to, you piece of shit. You see Clint's my buddy, so if you've got a problem with him, you've got one with me!" Darwin yelled with confidence.

"Not bright kid!" The man looked to one of his henchmen who smiled and moved towards Darwin.

The towering man grabbed Darwin by the scruff of the neck and dragged him forcibly behind the house. Clint began shouting and protesting to leave Darwin out of it, but soon he had his own bill collector to worry about. Darwin remained tight lipped but he grinned in delight as he could feel himself about to rage. Soon the man pulling him by the hair would be dead. Darwin wanted the man to know he would be dead, and that he couldn't stop it from happening. He wanted this man to experience fear in his last moment of life.

Darwin was picked up by his hair and tossed against the house buckling some of the old siding. Darwin crashed into the wall but remained standing. He raised his head and watched as the large black hands came towards him again. Darwin let himself go and began to change. The attacker threw a full force punch into his gut which Darwin merely grunted in pleasure to. Another hand on his head thrust Darwin's face into a quickly rising knee. The impact cracked Darwin's nose and opened a torrent of blood which only lasted a few seconds before the wound healed. Now Darwin began to fill out, and the strength was with him. Darwin stood up against the pressure of the hand in his neck. His attacker resisted without success and now Darwin looked eye to eye with this man, who was no longer towering over Darwin. The attacker froze at the sight of the changing and contorting body. His mouth opened to scream but he was unable to exhale. He found himself flying through the air rapidly towards the other debt collectors. He hit the ground and rolled a few feet before coming to rest near the feet of Mr Hispanic. The world faded to black with the gates of hell opening up for him.

The severed head looked blankly up at Mr Hispanic who could not believe what he was seeing. "Jerome! Jerome!" He shouted frantically.

Jerome came running out from behind a green house with his gun drawn. "What is?"

"He's fucking dead! Willy's dead!" Mr. Hispanic stated as he shuffled towards the SUV.

Darwin emerged from behind the house, fully changed and looking nothing like his former self. The towering beast charged towards Jerome who fired off five shots without success. Darwin's massive claws grabbed the undesirable's head and squeezed with all his supernatural strength lifting the muscle bound man off the ground. He screamed in agony only for a moment. Blood began leaking from his eyes and nose until his skull collapsed under the pressure. Grey matter shot from the cracks in his head, seeping through Darwin's claws. As the monster, Darwin found himself completely aware of his actions. It was the most control he had ever experienced as the wolf. With Jerome finished he now turned his attention to Mr Hispanic who was locking himself inside the SUV.

"Holy Mary, Mother of God, pray for us sinners, now at the hour of our death." He repeated it over and over, holding his rosary.

Darwin hopped onto the roof of the vehicle laughing inside his mind. This evil man was seeking solace from God, but soon he would be meeting a very different God. Darwin wanted to taste this man, to see if he could sense his sins. Darwin saw him as nothing more than the typical religious hypocrite and he took delight it what he was about to do.

Darwin punched through the roof with as much strength as he could muster. He found his arm went through the metal without much trouble and he was next to his prey. Darwin latched on to Mr. Hispanic's head and pulled him through the hole in the roof. The opening was not large enough for a man to pass through but Darwin forced the body up and out of the hole. The still praying man pleaded and begged for his life even as half of his face hooked up on the jagged metal opening and peeled off. Darwin found the skeletal face weeping in front of his snout. The wolf looked into his eyes but found nothing worthy. His canines pierced the front of his chest and his back with Darwin's massive bite. The blood flowed into Darwin's mouth with a story.

This man was named Jesus Esparente. He was a very evil man who had personally killed hundreds. Darwin sensed nothing good from him as the blood washed down his throat. There was too much evil to discern and the imagery all compacted into one hellish nightmare. The psychic connection

Darwinism

broke and Darwin bit down completely snapping Jesus Esparente's spine. Darwin flung his body across the driveway discarding the shit that he was.

Heated and infused, Darwin jumped from the vehicle. The animal was out and he wanted to run. The blood of Jesus was rushing through his veins and he contemplated eating the rest of his body.

"My God, it's true." Clint said as he slowly walked over to the hulking beast. Clint looked on at Darwin in awe. Clint had just been saved by Darwin and he knew it, but his mind could not accept what he could see standing before him. "That is you…isn't it?" Clint asked, now cautious with his proximity to the carnivore.

Darwin wasn't able to speak. As the half man-wolf creature he could speak partially. In his full transformation speaking just wasn't possible. Darwin wanted to change back, but he was still too worked up. He was in control and now he thought about just biting Clint without his permission. Darwin slowly moved towards Clint.

"Bite me, please! I join willingly. Oh Darwin, turn me, please!" Clint proclaimed as he fell humbly to his knees extending his hands towards the animal.

Darwin bent over and sniffed Clint. The apprehension that had been there was no more. Clint was now ready to commit himself over to the gift. He could force the gift onto people, but there was something more satisfying having someone beg for it. Darwin would have turned Clint either way, but now he would do it with Clint's permission. Darwin licked Clint's face softly who in turned smiled and closed his eyes. Darwin placed his mouth around Clint's forearm and gently bit down until the skin broke. Clint winced in pain but said nothing with a huge smile on his face. Darwin quickly let go and ran over to Jesus for a quick meal.

Clint watched as his friend, the werewolf, ate another human being. Soon he would want to as well. Clint looked down at his delicately made wound knowing his life was about to change drastically.

*   *   *

Darwin changed back in front of Clint inside the living room after Jesus was completely gone. Darwin smiled as his human face returned and Clint watched on in delight. The muscles deflated and hair fizzled away. His bones popped and snapped a little and soon the human Darwin Foster stood naked in Clint's living room.

"Got some clothes I can borrow? I wrecked mine." Darwin said with a chuckle.

"Dude! This is some fucked up shit! You're a werewolf, dude!" Clint said with a permanent grin stuck to his face.

Mark Fuson

"You're one too." Darwin stated as though Clint had already forgotten. "Clothes?"

Clint kept smiling but said nothing. He ran off to his bedroom and returned a moment later with some clothes. He handed them to Darwin who began dressing right away.

"So who were those guys?" Darwin asked.

"Organized crime at it's finest. They heard about me and wanted to buy and expand my operation. I don't know why I agreed to it. Long story short, I made a deal with the devil. They wanted more production than I could deliver and they didn't want excuses why I wasn't delivering. It was their money, plain and simple. The only problem with what you did was others will come looking for them, and they'll still want their money." Clint informed.

"Don't worry about it; they won't want to mess with us." Darwin said.

"So what's this plan for my mine you have?" Clint asked.

"It's tough being a werewolf on your own. You've gotta eat, you know?" Darwin looked to Clint who had no idea. "I got myself into some trouble, with the police. The whole werewolf thing got out of control on me and the only way I could think to make my problems go away, was to make more werewolves. If New Haven became a werewolf town, then I wouldn't have to hide, or anyone else for that matter. The mine is where we want to store the food, out of sight, but easily accessible."

"What kind of food?" Clint asked stupidly.

"Dude! Seriously!" Darwin stated in amazement. "Humans! You are a creature of the night; we eat humans…that's just how it is! The mine will be a detention center for our food. We don't need to eat humans exclusively, but we do need to eat them on a regular basis. If we don't we go insane."

"The mine will be a prison?" Clint asked.

"Yes, I've been down there, I think it could work. You know it better than anyone. Is there more than one exit? What do you think we'd need to do down there to house and contain – several thousand people?" Darwin asked, reassuming his leadership roll.

"Several Thousand!" Clint shouted slumping back into his chair. "Where are they coming from?

"Most from New Haven initially, but once that supply is gone we'll look at other options. For now we're looking at detaining roughly seven thousand New Haven residents. It won't be all at once, but when it happens, it will be fast." Darwin stated calmly.

"And the rest of New Haven?" Clint asked referring to the other half of the population.

"The plan is to turn them. I will hand pick the ones worthy enough for the gift, but I will accept recommendations from my close friends. Once we

Darwinism

have the town I think the new routine will settle in nicely. My chief concern right now is getting the detention functioning. Would you be interested in running it?" Darwin asked with a sadistic grin focusing his influence.

"This is really happening, isn't it?" Clint asked, but only received a bigger smile from Darwin. "There's one exit from the mine, about seven miles from here. You would need to seal it off. The mine has multiple layers in three distinct sectors. I think you could probably contain those kinds of numbers in sector A, from 1000 feet to 4000 feet below grade. That part of the mine is in good shape, I have electricity running at those depths and seepage isn't an issue. If you can figure away to get security down there, and basic necessities to house them, it could probably work."

"How long do you think it would take to upgrade it?"

"That's beyond me. I guess depending on the size of the labour force, you might be able to get some of it up and running within a week." Clint stated looking at the ground shaking his head in disbelief.

"We're not worried about comfort; these people as being disposed of. I'm not interested in being humane and giving them dignity. I want to make sure they don't escape…that could cause us some issues if one got away." Darwin responded. "Get it done. I'll get you some help up here to start work on it. The first batch will be in a few days, our trouble makers will be sent first."

"How are we moving the rest up here?" Clint asked.

"We'll cross that bridge later. I guess it depends on how quickly we move and how much grief the unworthy give us. I'm just glad to have you onside man!" Darwin stated in genuine friendship. "You won't have to work as a criminal ever again…actually I would ask that you never speak of your former life. You ran a nursery, nothing more."

"Sure. I can do that. Any reason why?" Clint asked.

"Never question your master!" Darwin replied sternly. "Because you were a good friend in my human life I'll answer you. Bluntly, I have no use for criminals. I like weed and alcohol. It got me through some tough times and that was thanks to you. My platform now is the eradication of the criminal element. If my followers knew about your past I myself would look like a hypocrite, I want to avoid that. You sold drugs, those drugs were harmless – in my opinion, but it started lots of people down a path which they never came back from – too busy chasing the dragon. My brother Cornell was one of them. He leapt from weed into much harder drugs; we never got him back. Just don't mention what you did, understand?"

Clint shook his head in agreement. The request of him wasn't a big deal and Clint had never known that Darwin felt the way he did, even though he was fully aware of Cornell. "How did Steve take it?" Clint asked.

"He doesn't know yet." Darwin got up from the couch and made his way

167

to the door. "I'll be in touch, I have to go." He had to find Steve, it was the only thing left that continued to nag at him. "Don't forget to get rid of those bodies in your yard and that SUV."

"Yeah, I'm on it." Clint replied.

"You might try eating them. They're pretty cold by now, but it's still good eating." Darwin stated casually as he walked to his own vehicle.

Clint said nothing more, discounting what his master had suggested. As Darwin left his house Clint found himself looking at the bodies and beginning to fantasize. His tongue rolled across his lips wetting them.

CHAPTER 19

It was Steve who made first contact with Darwin. Steve had sent a quick text asking if Darwin could meet at the Me-So-Fatso burger right away. With the request in hand Darwin sent word back to Steve he would be there in ten minutes. The takeover plan for New Haven took a back seat and Steve was now at the forefront of his mind. Keeping Steve as a priority would be the challenge.

At that moment a dream entered his mind that Darwin had experienced many times before; a very distinctive feeling. He felt like he was in a dream where he needed to get somewhere very important, but no matter how hard he tried he kept getting diverted from where he really wanted to be.

I need to do this, I need to get there. Fuck I forgot something, I need to go back. I must go faster, the plane is leaving, where is the plane, where am I going, where was I going? AHHHHH – something is holding me back!!!

He knew in the recess of his remaining humanity Steve mattered. Clint had given it to him straight, so to speak. Darwin wondered if he was in love with Steve, in the homosexual ass pounding sense. His feelings were strong for Steve, but were they romantic? Darwin was confused, but the wolf allowed him the willingness to at least explore the possibility. The one thing Darwin had never been able to do was explore his sexuality. He was straight and all other possibilities were simply impossible. The wolf had made him sexual and he knew it. Sex with Cindy Holmes was fantastic, and he looked forward to another session with her. Raping Dave Cronin as the wolf had been invigorating. Even his sexual encounter with the deer was something worth cherishing. In his heart Darwin knew it was about the sensation, nothing more. There had been no emotional connection. The only time in his life he had experienced a connection with another person was with Steve. They had never been physical, other than some innocent truth or dare when they were younger, but nothing more than that.

Darwin could remember only one time when he came close to kissing Steve. Steve had showed up at Darwin's house with a fat lip and two black eyes after his father had beaten him. Darwin brought him into the house and up to his room to console his friend. To break through the emotional bullshit they both had begun drinking heavily. Steve described how his father had yelled at him for more than an hour for being a worthless faggot. Steve had taken the verbal abuse like a wall for the majority of the time; he was use to it. His father's tactics changed to physical when Steve began to cry at the suggestion of his father that he do the world a favour and remove himself from it. Steve told his father in tears that he did not mean it, but Steve was shown physically that his father did mean it.

Darwin was speechless. How could any parent tell their kid to kill themselves; the world would be a better place without you in it. Darwin cried at the suggestion, Steve was too important to him. Sally and Theodore Cardwen may have hated their son, but Darwin loved him. Darwin held his friend, crying openly as Steve told Darwin he would end it and give his father what he wanted. It was the only thing he could do right for his father. As a friend there was nothing that Darwin could say that would change the situation at home for Steve. Darwin created a picture of freedom in the outside world that, if they both worked towards it, would allow them to leave New Haven once and for all. It wasn't that simple of course, and it took a lot of coercion on Darwin's part. Steve finally repented and agreed to leave New Haven, as long as Darwin came with him. Darwin, of course, agreed without question and added that he loved him too much not to go. It would take awhile to save enough money to be able to leave, which could give Darwin enough time to talk Steve into other ideas, more reasonable ones.

Steve moved in very close to Darwin and the two held the position for more than a minute, with their eyes closed and nothing to listen to but their breath. All that existed between them was their unspoken love and the feeling of heat from their lips. They never actually kissed. They both ended up falling asleep a short time later and Darwin had kept his arms around Steve for a long while. It was extremely erotic.

If Steve had kissed him he was sure he would have reciprocated. Knowing that, was he gay? The question was one he never gave much thought. He was sure he could spend his life with Steve and be very happy. Immortality would allow them to spend as much time together as they could bear. It would allow them to explore their feelings without fear of reprisals from others. They could simply be what they wanted.

Darwin was approaching the Me-So-Fatso Burger with vigour in his stomach. The next hour could reshape his life. Darwin would be honest with Steve and share the plan with him, and finally induct Steve into the family. In celebration, the two might pay a visit to Sally and Theodore for a feast. Darwin could not help but think of the different scenarios. What would Steve's reaction be? In his heart Darwin knew it would be well received, all of it.

A block from the restaurant Darwin passed the New Haven Police Department. He saw two men in civilian clothing walking into the precinct. Darwin recognized them as off duty officers, soon to be werewolves in his army. The winds of conquest were around him and his attention wasn't needed, at least not at this moment.

As Darwin rolled by the front windows of the restaurant he could see Steve sitting alone in the corner almost trance like. Even from the lot he could feel the waves of grief radiating from Steve. The man was in complete pain and despair. Darwin stopped the car abruptly and ran inside.

"Steve! Where have you been?" Darwin bellowed from across the restaurant.

Steve kept his head down and his eyes glued to the straw of his drink. It was clear, even from a distance that he had been crying. On the floor under the table Darwin could see he had a duffle bag with him; he was leaving, with or without Darwin.

"You had me worried man! I thought you were going to leave town without me!" Darwin said cheerfully but his words weren't penetrating Steve, the grief coming from him was almost toxic. Darwin threw his arms around Steve and gave him a hug.

Smells good!!!

"I had to see you before I left." Steve quietly spoke.

"I'm glad you did! I was starting to think you weren't going to call. I have some amazing shit to share with you." Darwin said in excitement.

Steve raised his head and looked Darwin in the eyes. His puppy dog eyes looked as though they were ready to burst open. The young man trembled in his seat, occasionally looking to the street. "I did some shit Darwin, the other night. I'm really fucked."

Darwin grabbed Steve's hand and held it tightly. "Hey man, you can tell me. We've been through a lot; there ain't nothing we can't tackle. Not now!"

"I killed them." Steve began to cry.

Mark Fuson

You're a werewolf too?

"Who?" Darwin asked with a genuine curiosity.

"My parents."

"What!?! Holy shit dude. Seriously???" Darwin stated, completely stunned and dumbfounded and partially proud.

Steve looked Darwin in the eye and shook his head softly while showing a light smile. "I know we said we'd leave town together. I know we were trying to save money to make it happen. I really wanted to do it that way. I really felt things were beginning to happen for us. I did, but I overheard my parents. They were sending me to a special hospital, to fix me. I confronted my mom about it, but it didn't go well. We fought. She told me I was no son of hers and until the devil had been washed from my soul I never would be. I wanted to argue more, but I thought I'd be the bigger person, so I began to walk away. But that bitch hit me with a rolling pin across my back."

Darwin spoke up. "There's nothing wrong with you!"

"I know." Steve blew his nose into a coarse cheap napkin and continued. "I just snapped. I didn't mean to do it, it just happened. I hit my mom in the face and she flew across the room. She crashed into the counter, hard, and sort of collapsed into the sink. It was full of dishwater. It was an accident; she knocked the blender into the sink too. It was plugged in."

"She electrocuted herself? It was an accident." Darwin stated, knowing the situation was no big deal.

"I slit my dad's throat with a carving knife while he slept. I figured I was fucked so I might as well make it worth my while. He woke up as I finished the cut. I've never felt as satisfied as I did while he bled out. I yelled at him as he died. I told him to enjoy hell. You have no idea how I felt." Steve said.

"I have a pretty good idea." Darwin replied with slight grin. His friend had been busy and the crimes that he had committed were no longer an issue. Steve believed he was in trouble but Darwin would bring him in to the fold and all of these mortal troubles would disappear. Darwin had already assumed the Cardwens would be on the list for disposal, and that Steve would want to take care of them personally. It gave Darwin a level of delight knowing that Steve could break through his shell and allow his emotions to handle his real world problems even without the wolf. Darwin knew that this would be his only chance to hear the story from Steve with his corporeal concerns. Time was not a concern and neither was Steve's safety; Darwin decided to let Steve continue telling his story. "What did you do with the bodies?"

"I left them where they were for awhile. I kept checking in on my dad to make sure he was still dead. That's crazy, isn't it?" Steve asked truly expecting an answer. "I even made a sandwich with my mom still head first in the sink. I just worked around her. I thought about what I should do. I thought about

Darwinism

calling the police. I thought about calling you. I decided to get rid of the bodies. I cut them up and put them into garbage bags, then I froze them. I'm not sure what I should do now. The police already found them I think; they've been at my house all day. I've been hiding out. I didn't even want to use my phone to call you in case they traced it. But I needed you."

"I wouldn't worry about it man, I think I can help make this go away." Darwin said getting ready to tell his secret.

"That's not all I did that night Darwin. I went down to the Caprice after hours; I was going to tell you what I had done. I got into the booze while I was cutting up the bodies, so I was a little drunk. I don't know what time it was, there was a lot of snow on the ground. The lights were on inside, I knocked and banged on the door, but you never came. That's when I got a crazy idea. I got it in my head that you would never come with me; you'd never leave New Haven. But you might. You might if you had no reason to stay, or a reason to run. I don't know what made me do it...I really fucked up."

"You can tell me." Darwin squeezed his hand a little tighter.

"I went to Rumsfeld's house. I don't know why I did it. I killed him too." Steve paused for a moment as he relived the moment in his mind. "I went right to the front door. I could see the light in the living room was still on. I just knocked. He came to the door and opened it. He said to me: *You're Darwin's little faggot friend right?* I agreed with him and I told him I really needed to speak with him. It was almost easy. He invited me in and that was it. Once the door was closed I pushed him down. He fell easier than I thought. When he was on the ground he started cursing at me. I jumped on him to hold him down. The phone was nearby; I just wrapped the cord around his neck until his face went blue and he stopped talking. That's when your mom came in. She came downstairs and saw me on top of Rumsfeld. I grabbed a pillow from the couch at the same time I asked her to stop shouting. She wouldn't, she just kept screaming and shouting at me. I pushed her down and begged her to be quiet, but she wouldn't, I intended to kill her, but I kept talking to her like I wouldn't. I don't know why. I just pushed the pillow over her face until she stopped breathing. It was quick."

"You killed my mom!" Darwin said making a point to not alert the entire restaurant while his stomach leaked through his legs to the floor. "Why!?!"

"You hated her, but you would never leave her. You hated Rumsfeld more. I thought if Rumsfeld was out of the way you'd feel better about your mom. Then I thought you'd feel better if she was with your Dad. I know; I fucked up bad. Do the police think it was you?" Steve asked.

"Yes." Darwin replied. It saddened him to know how his mom had died and why. Darwin had definitely had unpleasant thoughts about his mother in recent years. He was mad only that Steve would make such a poor decision. Had he remained mortal Steve's situation would have been dire.

"I'll tell the police the truth. I don't want you to go to prison over what I did. I love you Darwin, I have for a long time. You saved me; several times. I'll leave a note explaining what happened. I'm going to make a run for it, if I can live in freedom I will. If they arrest you I'll turn myself in and set everything right. It's that simple. Are you mad at me?" Steve asked.

"I'll miss my mother. But you are right, she will be better off now she's with my dad. I think if things were different I'd be furious. We're lucky, we get a pass go on this one." Darwin said with a tear streaming down his cheek.

Steve's attention turned to a police car he could see coming down the road with its emergency lights on. His heart sank because he knew that he was out of time with Darwin. Instinctively Steve got up from the table and moved around to Darwin planting a light kiss on his lips. It was enough to disturb the butterflies in Darwin's stomach and momentarily distract him. All Steve said was "I'm sorry."

Darwin was alone at the table and Steve was gone. Darwin sat with a smirk on his face and a warmth inside of him he had never felt before.

Could this be love?

"Darwin!" Frank Newman hollered as he approached.

Darwin opened his eyes to see Frank Newman and two other uniformed members standing at his table. Darwin looked to Frank, surprised to see him. "What is it Newman?"

"NHPD is yours. We dealt with the two inmates too. I brought Officers Kuntz and Lanter over to meet you. They wished to express their gratitude personally."

Each officer approached and shook Darwin's hand thanking him for the gift. Darwin could see the wounds on their hands were almost healed. Darwin had little to say to his new subordinates, he was more concerned where Steve had gone. "I was just talking to Steve Cardwen."

"Cardwen?" Newman interrupted. "Was that the guy we saw running out the back when we pulled in?" Newman asked.

Darwin bolted out of his seat. He had lost Steve, again. "Shit!!! Get your men out there, find him Newman. Don't harm him, do you understand? When you find him, bring him to me. He's being turned, but he doesn't know that or anything about us." Darwin demanded.

Newman looked at Kuntz and Lanter and gave the direction. "You heard him let's get to it." Newman fled to the cruiser in the parking lot and sped off with the lights flashing. Darwin went to his own car, texting Steve as he went.

His text read: Steve come back! Police not 4 u! All is ok!

Darwinism

Darwin sped out of the lot waiting patiently for a response. His phone remained silent.

*   *   *

Two hours had gone by since Darwin had last seen Steve. The town of New Haven was now falling under the darkness of night. Every officer of the New Haven Police Department was on the streets looking for Steve Cardwen. Roughly one hour into the search his cell phone had been located in a snow bank but Steve was no where to be found. Steve had left behind his duffle bag at the restaurant; inside the bag was some money, clothes and personal items. Darwin looked through the bag and found a few pictures of him and Steve from the previous summer. Darwin remembered the day they had been taken.

Darwin and Steve had gone to the lake one afternoon. They smoked some weed and ate some hot dogs they roasted on a campfire. It was their own private beach and for the day they saw no one. Steve had brought a camera with them and snapped three pictures that afternoon. Darwin enjoyed the one of Steve and him with their faces next to each other smiling in absolute enjoyment with the lake in the background. Their hair was wet and their eyes were wide; they were happy. They hadn't had much pleasure in their lives, but when they were together they were reborn into freedom.

Darwin placed the pictures into his pocket. They were dear to him. With the pictures close to his heart, perhaps, the wolf would help Darwin find his love.

The town had been sealed off but there was no sign of Steve. Every vehicle leaving New Haven was being inspected; even neighbouring communities had been requested to stay on the lookout. The Cardwen family home had been checked and was under constant surveillance and so was the Foster residence but the NHPD was stretched to the maximum. Newman had considered asking search and rescue to get involved, but their members were still in shock due to a recent tragedy. Darwin knew locating Steve would be up to him. In their brief conversation Darwin had the distinct impression there was more to what Steve was saying. He had ordered Newman to check all obvious locations but in his gut Darwin had begun to worry.

Darwin closed his eyes and lightly inhaled bringing about the intoxicating smell that Steve had over him. The sweet lavender smell mixed with his sweat was unique and Darwin could taste it; could he track it? The odour was strong throughout town; it was almost visible in the night sky like an aurora. Darwin could visualize in his mind the scent and it was concentrating to the south.

"Young Darwin, you trouble us with mortal feelings." The dark image of his mother spoke.

Darwin was again in the cavern within his mind. He was surrounded by his mother, Zack and Steve. The trio were ghostly white with sunken eye cavities and long silvery hair. Their image was disturbing to Darwin who knew they were only representations. The form they had chosen to appear to him as created a sense of unease.

"You have been warned." Zack said.

"Your plan was given permission, yet you persist on pursuing mortal feelings. Why?" His mother asked.

"Feelings are not mortal or immortal. They exist in both worlds." Darwin insisted.

"You have become distracted by unimportant matters. This will only continue, and ultimately destroy you." Steve assured. "You must abandon the one you call Steve."

"I WILL NOT!" Darwin screamed in hatred. "He can be like me. I have asked for nothing and I submit to your will! I am embarking on a great plan of conquest that will only help to make us stronger, but I need this for me!"

"This is impossible young Darwin." His mother lectured.

"Focus on the path. You are the one." Zack said ominously.

"It has been decided. The one you call Steve will be expunged. Darwin will focus on the task at hand." Steve informed coldly.

"And if I refuse?" Darwin asked in anger.

"This is impossible young Darwin." His mother repeated.

"Then let Steve leave! I will let him go!" Darwin suggested in frustration.

The three said in unison. "This is impossible"

"Darwin must purge Steve." Zack said calmly.

"Your remaining humanity can only be sluiced with his end. The one you call Steve should die by your hands." Steve insisted.

"Not a chance! I will never kill him. I'd sooner die than allow him to!" Darwin hollered as he began pacing the room.

The three images floated across the floor as one, hovering just off the ground. They again surrounded Darwin.

"Your death is impossible." Zack assured.

"Steve is my chosen partner! He would rule along side me. He has already killed and he has not even been marked!" Darwin debated.

"Young Darwin, it has been written, so it shall be done. Steve will cause your destruction. This time line must cease to exist. A leader in Darwin Foster is only possible through his death. His life force will infuse you for all time." Darwin's mother said as she began to crumble into dust.

"No! I refuse." Darwin said in tears.

"Compliance is irrelevant." Zack said in a hollow tone as he too crumbled into dust.

"The decision has been made." Steve said as he disappeared into a plume of flames leaving Darwin alone in the cavern.

"I will not. You have my soul, but you do not have my will! YOU DO NOT! I know you can hear me. I will follow my heart and I will deliver you unbelievable wickedness! But I will have Steve!!!" Darwin roared in defiance.

The cavern remained void and silent. The walls began to slide away like sand into a sink hole. It did so in taciturn. Beyond the cavern walls Darwin found himself once again in New Haven, behind the wheel of his mother's car. The glow of the aurora surrounded the Church of Latter Day Saints, on the hill. Darwin was looking directly at it and he knew he could find Steve there.

He turned the key to the ignition but not even a spark was heard. He tried it again and again but the same story was repeated. In frustration he exited the vehicle and began running towards the hue on foot. He considered changing but thought better of it; he didn't need the hassle of witnesses. Even as a human on foot Darwin knew he should be able to reach the temple within ten minutes. He considered calling Newman, but he did not want to spook Steve. Darwin would intercept and comfort his friend and explain the situation as calmly as possible.

For some reason Steve was in the one place in town Darwin would never have thought to look. Why had he gone there? Steve had no use for the teachings of the Mormon faith. In that place was the pain of his family life. In their teachings was the intolerance he had experienced. Sally and Theodore Cardwen had been brainwashed into believing their faith over their required and unwavering adoration for their son. Darwin thought he knew Steve better than anyone and was certain that Steve could have no feelings or connections to the temple. He hated everything about it. His rage ran deep for the people and the ideals of the faith. They taught hatred and intolerance for anyone who wasn't one of them. Of course the followers would deny it, in actuality they were incredibly nice people, to your face – if you were an outsider. Inside the faith Steve painted a much darker picture; to him love was conditional on your complete and utter acceptance of God and the teachings as the temple knew them. The possibility of Steve being a homosexual was simply not compatible for the temple and the Cardwen's.

As Darwin began the climb to the temple his heightened senses detected smoke, light, but present. He knew at that point what Steve had gone there to do. Darwin rushed up the hill using the ice covered steps through the woods to reach the temple. He slipped only once but quickly recovered. Steve had lit the temple a blaze.

Darwin rounded the last few steps at full speed; he could hear screaming from within. Flames surrounded the entire building and had begun inching their ways up the walls. Darwin could hear the screams of the followers who had already begun coughing and choking. The front doors of the temple were closed but he could see them vibrating with the kicking and punching of the trapped congregation inside; they were sealed in. The screams of panic quickly turned to pains of dying. Through the windows it was clear the flames were also inside and people were beginning to burn. The entire building would be a candle in the night and the NHFD would soon be en route.

Darwin walked up towards the steps that led to the doors of the temple. Resting on the first step was a plain white envelope that he knew was from Steve. With people dying in the Mormon crematorium only feet away, Darwin grabbed the letter and opened it.

It read:

> I'm sorry for what I have done. You made me the evil that
> I am because you didn't love the good that I was.
> I murdered my parents, Marie Foster and Ronald
> Rumsfeld.
> I have nothing left. Nothing in me.
> I love you Darwin.
> Steve Cardwen

The note echoed that of a suicide note; Short on details and very hopeless. Darwin stood in the snow in front of the temple reading the note over and over; the screams had all but ceased and the only sounds that remained were the cackling timbers and occasional coughs. Darwin sank into tunnel vision, unable to move or think. He stood there for what seemed like an hour. His dream about needing to be somewhere took hold again, and like the dream he just wasn't able to get there. Steve was moving further and further away from him and it seemed as though Darwin might never see him again. His overseers were succeeding and Darwin boiled at the thought of losing to yet another bully.

"HEY, is there anyone inside?" A man shouted as he approached with a large group in tow.

Darwin stood in stupor blankly looking at the note. He didn't notice the crowd of on lookers that were gathering around him.

"Are you OK?" The man asked.

"They're all dead." Darwin plainly replied not removing his eyes from the note.

"What are you looking at?" The man grabbed the note from Darwin's hands. And quickly read it. "PEOPLE! STEVE CARDWEN DID THIS!" He shouted to the group.

Darwin snapped from his daze attempted to grab the note back. The man, who was taller than Darwin held the note higher the Darwin could reach. Darwin was growing angry and wanted to tear into the man, but Darwin could see the crowd was too large, and they were all on their phones informing the town of what Steve had done. Soon every set of eyes in New Haven would be hunting for Steve Cardwen.

Darwin grabbed his own phone and advised Newman of the situation. With a little luck NHPD could pick up Steve before the town found him. Darwin looked to the sky once again to attempt to find the image of Steve's scent. The glow of the fire washed out the blackness of night and the radiance of his scent wasn't visible.

He's raging. He's raging. He's raging! The school!

It was only a hunch. What better way to tell the world who you were pissed at it than to eliminate the symbols of the groups that had caused you pain. The temple was first and Darwin knew how Steve felt about the school. Darwin began his trek through town as the streets began to fill with curious on lookers who watched the Mormon temple burn to the ground. As Darwin marched past different groups he could already hear Steve's name being tossed around. Another perk of a small town was the inability to keep a secret or the ability to spread a rumour (information) quickly. The streets of New Haven came alive as the show began to unfold. It was almost like an impromptu parade with families lining the roadway, fire trucks blasting up the road with the siren bellowing and pickup trucks with people loaded into the box. The pickup trucks were what some would call an angry mob.

Darwin knew, in the mortal sense, that Steve had crossed a line. He felt for his friend; no blame could be assigned to him for what he had done. Darwin understood fully what the burning of the temple meant. Steve may have very well killed twenty, thirty maybe even forty people at the temple. He was a mass murderer. That thought brought happiness to Darwin; Steve was living out his mortal fantasy. They had thought about shooting up the school as kids, they had thought about doing a lot of things that might have been considered evil. The only thing that prevented them from acting out on their true feelings was the threat of prison. Steve had let go of that fear.

"He's gonna kill himself." Darwin uttered privately as urgency flashed before him.

The hue, as Darwin had thought, led right towards the school. The trail was not as bright as before, but it was visible. There was no smoke yet but he knew that time was running out. Darwin had to find Steve first. He had to turn him as quick as possible. His overseers would be made to see that keeping

Steve was the right choice. The overseers would be thankful to Darwin for forcing the issue.

"Darwin! Get in. We got a lead on Cardwen. We think he's at the school." Newman shouted from a cruiser that had pulled along side.

Darwin said nothing but jumped into the vehicle immediately. Newman hit the gas and sped off towards the school. Neither man spoke to one another. Newman could feel that Darwin was focussed on one thing only. The blocks went by quickly and soon the school came into view, still free from flames and smoke. Newman pulled into the staff lot and bolted from the vehicle heading around to the backside of the school.

As he ran away he shouted to Darwin "If I find him what do you want me to do?"

"Bring him to me. I want to turn him." Darwin said firmly.

Darwin stood before his prison looking at the front entrance to his own personal hell. The halls and lockers snickered at his return. The sinister building held the secrets of thousands of abused students. The school had harboured and nourished an impious veil of school yard bullying, assaults and dehumanizing behaviour. Instead of building character and instilling values this place taught the young the chain of command and the class system. Old world views were maintained through life lessons in social etiquette. You were reminded of what you were and what value you held. Sometimes you were told what you were, and you had to live with it. Fighting the system was impossible. The evil in the hallways, pep rallies, home rooms, lockers, library, gym and shower room made the presence of good an unlikely sight. The eyes of the halls watched as the innocence of youth was quickly beaten from the new arrivals. Your choice was to either become heartless and dole out the punches, or you would be sentenced to indefinite torture for standing up in defiance.

Steve had returned to the place where it had all started. Darwin was beginning to understand what was going through his mind. The moment in time where he ceased being human. Steve would return to the shower room where he sprayed his pubescent seed all over Teddy Holmes. In that brief unenjoyable orgasm Steve ceased being human. In that moment he became the piece of shit that he was. In that moment he became a faggot. If he could go back and undo the time line Steve would return to the shower room and destroy it. He would take steps to ensure he didn't become aroused in the locker room, even if that meant masturbating five times that morning. He would have done anything to avoid the torment of his peers and inevitably his parents.

Darwin smashed a window into the teacher's lounge next to the front door to get inside the dark school. Ridgemount High was a labyrinth of

Darwinism

hallways but Darwin knew every secluded spot and un-travelled corridor. The hallways glistened with a perfect sheen. Darwin ran as fast as he could down the main hall passed the snickering lockers to the central stairwell. He flew down a flight of stairs and rounded a corner. The gymnasium loomed in the distance; the smell of gasoline was now becoming apparent. Darwin sprinted as fast as he could and burst through the gym doors to find a gas coated hardwood surface which he briefly slipped on. He continued towards the boy's change room at breakneck speed crashing into the door as he slid to a stop. Darwin's motor skills were failing him; his panic was too great to work within. The door was heavy and refusing to open; Darwin slipped pushing the door shut again. Inside the change area Darwin could hear sounds that were not obvious in distinction. Slowly Darwin regained his balance and moved the overly heavy door.

"STEVE!" Darwin shouted as he wrestled the door.

The change room was now silent and threatening. Darwin entered the chamber where he found the air thick and humid. The smell of young men permeated the walls. Even the smell of gasoline was not enough to hide decades of testosterone. In the main locker room Darwin could see a dim light in the direction of the shower. His heart sank. Steve had not answered him and now there were no sounds coming from this room. Darwin walked slowly over to the narrow corridor that led to the shower. The light was coming from the other side of the doorway. Darwin ebbed his way closer to the passage; in the low light he could see the outline of the torture chamber room he knew so well from his own years at Ridgemount. Darwin crossed the threshold of the doorway and tripped two booby trapped candles causing the room to come a light. As the flames engulfed the shower area the scene became clear. He was too late. Steve hung naked by the neck from a shower head. A towel was wrapped around his neck. Where his penis should be was only a red gaping hole and blood streamed down his legs. On the tile floor of the shower Steve's genitals lay discarded with a knife nearby. He had severed his own privates from his body. The room began to fill with flames and Darwin looked on in horror realizing his only true love, the one he never experienced, was now gone forever. Darwin watched as his lover began to burn, searing his tender skin and blistering it into redness. A path of fire began to stream away from the shower room along the walls, leading the way out. Darwin knew his time was short. He looked back to Steve one last time as his hair engulfed and disappeared for eternity.

"I love you Steve, and I always will." Darwin said as his eyes burst with light and water.

CHAPTER 20

It was the week before Christmas and Fairhaven Cemetery had been working around the clock to accommodate the mourners. It was a community cemetery, not bound by any one faith. Catholics, Mormons and even the occasional Jew laid their loved ones to rest. Fairhaven attempted to keep the faiths reasonably separated, but of course space was limited. The Mormons preferred the knoll that had the view of their blackened shell temple. The Catholics had particular interest in the large oak tree, but there were several other smaller trees that appealed to them. The Jews, for the most part, kept to the cremation plots. Other faiths that buried their dead were scattered around the edges and in the less prime areas.

The Cardwen family plot held no stature in the community. Cadmore Avenue residents were not wealthy enough to buy the prime spots on the knoll. Theodore Cardwen had selected, years prior, the best plot they could afford. The plain patch of grass was as low on the knoll you could go before you were on the flats that was considered to be Catholic territory. The view from the Cardwen plot was nothing special. On a clear day, when the temple existed, you could have seen the very top of the temple steeple. The plot now only gazed towards a barren hill and an opening in the trees. Theodore Cardwen was a failure even in death.

The service for Sally and Theodore had been held the previous day. The funeral for Steve was to be held at one o'clock the following day. Many of the town residents had developed an intense hatred of Steve Cardwen. Darwin

Darwinism

was spared the agony of association only because Steve had killed Marie Foster. In the eyes of many it had appeared that Steve had even betrayed his only friend. Instead of a backlash, Darwin had been given a wide berth. Few approached him, few asked how he was doing; they knew he was hurting but were unsure as to the real reason.

Standing next to Steve's plain casket that now hovered over the hole, Darwin felt comforted that Steve's service was well attended. Darwin had not expected anyone to show up; he actually had expected an angry mob. He wasn't sure if Newman or Tim had done it, but Steve's service was attended by every new family member, now numbering over one hundred. The large turn out helped to keep the protesters back, they were near by but they decided to keep their distance when they realized they were outnumbered. Even a couple of non family showed up, Terri Bailey and her postman friend as well as Ray Silverdale.

The sky was brilliant blue, but stark and cold. The cemetery was a sea of white with the occasional bouquet of flowers strewn across the graveyard. Silence blew across the landscape like a roving death squad; the hunted lay in silence hoping to be passed over. Darwin looked on at his friend, bitter that he had to leave him in this cold place next to those who had help to drive him here. Darwin had tried to have Steve placed elsewhere, but the last will and testament of Sally and Theodore Cardwen was clear in its instructions. Steve was to be placed in the family plot. Steve, having no will of his own, fell under their jurisdiction; despite the fact he was eighteen, he resided under their roof making him fall victim yet again to the values of his family. Darwin had pledged to himself, once he controlled the town, he would have Steve exhumed from this place. For now, the mortal ritual would be followed.

Darwin's eulogy:

"Steve was my friend. He was a man that I loved. I'm not good with my emotions, but I think I could even call him my soul mate. We had both protected each other in the rough times, and we brought joy to each other when times were unbearable, even if those times were few and far between.

He was a good person, living in a world of hate. He was surrounded by it; we were surrounded by it. Steve tried to keep his head to the ground, I helped him the best I could. His church, the kids in school, all demonised him for something they only suspected, and never actually knew to be fact – as if it really mattered. Steve Cardwen, had anyone bothered to get to know him, or to try to be his friend, would have found a soft and caring person who only hoped to better the world in which he lived. It seemed for every good deed he did, he was rewarded with only punishment. His father beat him mercilessly for things that just didn't seem important. Steve wasn't a drug dealer, rapist or child molester. He was nothing evil. His father beat him, his mother belittled him, and they insisted he was useless.

Here we are today, saying good bye to this wonderful person, who left our world on horrific terms. The world will record Steve Cardwen's existence as only the events of his last few days. History will ignore how we got to where we are; history will paint a picture of a troubled youth who did unspeakable horrors because he was unable to cope with a little personal drama. History will say Steve Cardwen experienced some bullying as a child, that he couldn't tolerate the rules of his parents; all of this he used to justify actions.

Let history show that Steve Cardwen was the best kind of person – he became the monster he was because of us. We are all capable of acts of unspeakable horror. If you poke a bear hard enough, you might just get bit. We all played a role in what has happened. We all knew some piece of this puzzle. We all condoned the teasing, the black eyes, the crying in the corner; we all knew more than we cared to know.

I am guilty. Steve is dead because of me. I lost sight of what was truly important, and in one brief moment I lost my chance to save him. Some have asked me if I am angry with Steve for killing my own mother. My response to you is, I will miss her, but she is in a better place. My mother had been suffering for years and although it pains me to know that Steve did it, I am happy to know her suffering in this world is at an end. That may be hard for some of you to understand – sometimes I don't understand it.

There was a time, not long ago, that Steve and I planned to leave New Haven and start a new life. We had dreamed of that time for many years. I don't know that either of us knew where we would go or what we would do. For some reason we knew it didn't matter where we went; being together would have been enough. If only I hadn't been so self centered in the last few months, I might have been able to stop this. I am guilty; guilty for becoming too absorbed in my own self interests to save what mattered in this world. I will carry that guilt for all time. I allowed a truly beautiful part of this world to be destroyed. It is my shame, it is my burden.

Our purpose in this world is to improve upon it; to leave it for future generations better than how we inherited it. From where I stand here today, we have a long ways to go. People should not be persecuted because of who they are or because of some Goddamn religious belief. True evil in this world is only to chastise those who are different. That evil is our own fear. We fear the abuse we exercise on others, that is why we do it; to prevent the abuse from happening to us. That is pure evil, to sell out our fellow man for no reason other than our own protection. It is cowardice.

The events that have occurred in this town because of Steve Cardwen are not acts of evil but a consequence of evil. We must understand that we can not continue to treat others as we have Steve for there are inherent consequences of those actions. We cannot blame Steve for what he has done. Place yourself in his shoes and imagine life living in constant fear and terror. When would the next attack come, from whom, for what? Would you be terrorized for something real, or made up, would you be beaten when you got home for being a faggot or just ridiculed? Being verbally abused by his parents was a good day for him; sort of like a day off. The congregation at the temple would hear Sally Cardwen's stories of her son and this would filter through the religious cult like a drug. The best way to help him was to make him want to change. The only way to make him want that change was to make his life a living hell. The rumours of the congregation would reach the high school and there the sentence would be carried out in earnest. There was no reprieve for Steve, school, temple, home – it was all the same. We cannot change the skin we wear, no matter what religion tells you. This was Steve's reality.

I challenge anyone of you to say you could have done better than Steve. I know I couldn't. I suffered abuse too, but not to his extent. Even I wanted to run a murderous rampage at times to take my revenge on all the juvenile bullshit. How Steve held it together for as long as he did, I'll never know. I applaud him for holding it together for as long as he did.

I offer my heartfelt apology to my friend. I am so fucking sorry…"

Darwin broke down in tears and was unable to continue. He walked away from the service, briefly placing his hand on the casket before moving on down the hill. His followers stood silently as Darwin walked away into the graveyard alone. No one attempted to follow him. Each person offered their regrets to Steve before leaving the casket to be lowered into its temporary purgatory.

Darwin replayed over and over in his mind the last hours of Steve. Could he have moved faster, was there something he could have done differently? If he had only run a little faster, if only he hadn't stayed outside the temple for as long as he had. If only he had cut Steve off at the restaurant and told him the truth about what was happening. Darwin should have bit Steve right in the restaurant. Almost any scenario his mind contemplated was better than the situation he now found himself in. His heart was still coming to terms with his loss. The idea that he could no longer call on his friend to make him laugh, share his feelings and talk about their pains; it all caused his chest to have extreme pressure placed upon it. Darwin tried not to sob, but every time he thought to a moment in time where he was happy with Steve he began to ache.

Darwin walked through the cemetery with no particular destination in mind. He had experienced loss before and he knew the road to recovery would be a long one. When his dad went missing Darwin was told his father would return, but over time this became unlikely. It was a gradual separation. When Zack took his own life it was both a blessing and a loss, but the pain was different. The loss of Steve, seeing him burn, smelling his flesh char and knowing it could have been stopped tore through Darwin like an icicle. His pain was regret, remorse, anger and rage. His soul was tugged in one direction and then in another. One minute he felt like letting the wolf out the next Darwin was considering taking his own life to reunite with his love. He was confused; he was hollow. The leader that he was to be in Steve's absence seemed to be impossible.

Clear on the east side of the cemetery Darwin found himself beside a marble statue with an angel releasing a dove from her palm. Darwin looked at the beautiful woman and wondered what the artist had hoped an admirer would get from the image. Darwin found it intriguing. The dove symbolised peace and yet the angel was releasing it. Did she mean to let go of peace? Or was the message that peace could only be found in release? Darwin found no comfort in the image, only distraction for a brief moment before his mind returned to his grief.

A bench in front of the angel was calling to Darwin. He seated himself down and looked at the world around him. The cemetery was void of activity; he was far enough away from the funeral that he couldn't see a soul. Darwin, for a time, sat and listened to the wind in the tree tops. One of the smaller oak trees was nearby and one branch in particular that groaned with the push of the breeze. The light creaking was soothing to Darwin who sat and listened to it for as long as Mother Nature would allow him to. His mind went blank and he thought of nothing. He stared off into the distance looking at nothing, and looking at everything. He wanted to eat but nothing appealed. He wanted to sleep, but he was not tired. He wanted to change, but he had forgotten how. The world continued to move around him and he sank into his own self wallowing.

What would a world with Steve Cardwen have looked like, Darwin thought. No matter how hard he attempted to imagine Steve along side of him, the image was always blank. Steve could not be envisioned in any meaningful way. Even with his eyes closed the image of Steve became hard to draw on. In a quick moment of panic Darwin began to forget what he sounded like. Dawrin focused as hard as he could but then he began to second guess himself. Was that really what he sounded like?

The smell of lavender and sweat returned to Darwin's nose. He closed his eyes and could plainly remember what his friend smelt like in the hours before his death. Darwin lightly inhaled through his nose and the smell was present plain as day. He began to feel a soft pressure on his lips. Darwin found himself kissing the air and imagining it was Steve. For a moment he recreated the feeling of joy he had during that brief moment. He knew that he would never again come as close to love as he had in that moment. His remaining humanity was officially dead and his overseers had carried out their promise to achieve the desired effect. A battle for Steve's memory was now being fought and Darwin was losing.

"Make'em pay D!" Steve said with a grin.

Darwin broke from his trance to find Steve standing in front of him dressed as he was the night he died. Darwin looked in disbelief but said nothing. He was momentarily convinced he was hallucinating. He was happy to see him for any reason that Steve had chosen to appear.

"Chin up! You've got a plan to carry out! Make me proud. I wish I could be there with you, but we weren't meant for this life." Steve said in a positive timbre which Darwin had not seen before. "I'll be ok D. I love you." And as quick as it started, Steve was gone.

"I love you too." Darwin said to the now empty graveyard.

He understood what Steve had come to do. It was Steve, the Steve that would have existed without all the emotional baggage of his life. He had appeared to Darwin to relay a message, and he understood it, fully. His pain was alleviated slightly, but he had a renewed sense of purpose in Steve's blessing.

Darwin wiped his raw nose and got up from the bench and made his way out of the graveyard. The grief in his stomach was pushed aside for a more important task. Darwin's war was about to begin.

CHAPTER 21

Mayor Bollen's office had been inundated with calls from the media and various agencies ever since the tragedies. With the funerals over and interest dissipating her office was finally returning to normal. In two days city hall would close for the year and not reopen until the first week in January. It had been a long year, but an absolutely abysmal month. Basic issues surrounding unemployment, crime prevention and downtown improvement had all taken a back seat throughout the year for various reasons. Mayor Bollen had campaigned on bringing back big industry to the area, but her critics questioned what industry that might be.

The most likely idea to be considered by the New Haven council was a university. For this plan to succeed all New Haven needed to do was to donate the land and offer a sizable tax break. In exchange the university would be built, bringing with it grants, notoriety, exposure and thousands of students who would need to eat, sleep and be entertained. The university plan had been well received as it was seen to be the idea with the least risk. It had already been suggested the university be a medical school to tie in with the already large senior population.

Mayor Bollen was in her office looking over the latest proposal from Harland & Associates; the board of trustees for the proposed school. The group was hoping to break ground in the spring, and construction would take three years at a cost of two hundred and fifty million dollars.

A knock came to the large mahogany door which swung open at the same time. "I'm sorry to disturb you. Suzan Petroff from bylaw enforcement was hoping to speak with you?"

Mayor Bollen didn't even look up from her dossier. "What's it regarding?"

"Clayburn Nurseries." The young secretary responded.

"Alright, send her in." The mayor responded irritated.

A moment later a rough looking woman wearing dirty coveralls entered the office. Suzan Petroff looked to be in her forties and you could tell by looking at her she had been around the block a time or two. She had dirt under her finger nails which was a good sign for someone in her position; she wasn't afraid to get dirty. The gruff woman came in and proceeded to the chair across from the mayor, not taking notice to the plush white fabric. Mayor Bollen watched in horror as Suzan planted herself in the chair with no regard to what she had just done. "Thanks for seeing me Ma'am! I hate to bother you with this but I'm not getting any help from the police, and the proprietor won't let me on the land to do an inspection."

"I don't follow you..." The mayor said.

"So I get this call from Polytron Metals. They ask me if I knew what the building code for fencing height around construction sites in New Haven was. I said of course I know, I ain't retarded. So I ask them why they needed to know. They said they were commissioned to make fencing, gates and barbed wire for Clayburn Nurseries, they just wanted to make sure it met our code. I'm like, wait a second, I don't have a permit order for them."

"What's the fencing for, Susan?" The mayor asked.

"That's the bitch of it. Polytron didn't know - all they could tell me was it was high grade stuff, the kind they use in the prisons. So I head on out to Clayburn on my own. I tried getting access to the property but this guy Littleford refused me entry. I told him he'd be cited for building violations, and I would be back with the police...he didn't care." Susan said frustrated.

"What did the police say?" Mayor Bollen asked as though she was following a check list.

"The dickheads said they wouldn't go with me, that they had more important matters. They've never done that to me. So I said, fuck it, I went back out to Clayburn and did my own special ops. There's something strange going on out there, really strange. You see Polytron drops off the fencing at the front gate, and this crew of men come out with their own vehicles and bring it into the compound. Then they take most of it underground. And they're building a really big fence around the property. I'm certain this is a police matter, but I need you to pull some strings to get them to go out there, they aren't listening to me." The uncouth concluded.

"As it happens, I have a meeting with Frank Newman in ten minutes. You're welcome to stay and ask him yourself. You have to understand that they've had a lot going on in the past few weeks, a bylaw infraction doesn't rank high on their list right now." Mayor Bollen attempted to rationalize.

"Ma'am, have you ever heard the saying – don't pee on my leg and tell me it's raining. I already spoke to Frank Newman, he's the one that bluffed me off in the first place. I'm telling you this is beyond bylaw enforcement, we might even consider calling in the feds if Frank refuses to do anything." Susan begged.

"We have proper channels and a chain of command in this town. If Newman wasn't concerned it can't be anything illegal. I'm not prepared to go above him and call the feds because some hippie gardener is bringing in some security fencing." Mayor Bollen again rationalised.

"It ain't some fencing, they brought in! The flow of trucks from Polytron is constant. Whatever they are building underground, it must be huge. Besides, why the hell would you need security fencing underground?" Susan said.

A rap hit the door and the secretary popped her head in again. "Frank Newman is here."

"Send him in." Mayor Bollen replied.

Newman entered the mayor's office wearing a suit all in black, including the dress shirt. The only element of color on him was the plain bright red tie. Newman cracked a smug grin to Susan before extending his hand to Mayor Bollen. "Tara, how lovely to see you."

"Cut the sexist bullshit Frank." She replied.

"You know I only do it because it drives you crazy!" Frank laughed to himself without his audience joining in.

"You know Susan Petroff I presume?" Tara Bollen asked.

"Of course! She's our handy bylaw enforcement officer. Where there's an infraction she'll be there!" Newman again joked to a cold crowd.

"Susan was just telling me of her concerns about activity at the Clayburn Nurseries. What can you tell me?" The mayor asked once again asserting her authority.

"Madame Mayor, I have already told Ms. Petroff that we are unable to spare any officers at this time. It simply isn't that important." Frank insisted talking down to his female master.

"That's not what I asked you Frank. What is going on at the Clayburn Nurseries?" The Mayor responded more curtly.

Newman sat looking blankly at the Mayor waiting for the response to come to him. "NHPD cannot drop everything just because the bylaw officer can't get access to see how high a fence is. The fence isn't going anywhere; it can be checked in the New Year." Frank said dismissively.

"You got your head up your ass or something? I told you it was in the

Darwinism

mine! Who the hell builds security fences underground?" Susan barked back like a little pit-bull.

"I'm sure it's nothing." Newman assured with his little grin.

"Frank, if you are unwilling to go out there and check it out I might have to call in a different agency and with your repertoire it might not look very good for you. I will do it if I'm forced to, but I think this is something that you are more than capable of looking into. Will you please take Susan out there?" The Mayor asked with coercion.

"I know Littleford, he'll demand a warrant. At this late hour of the day, I wouldn't be able to get one. Besides I don't have much to go on for a judge to even issue a warrant." Frank deflected.

"Why do I get the feeling you're not being up front with me Frank?" Tara asked.

"Do you want your update on Waters, or should I come back when you're focused?" Newman asked with coldness.

"Yes, Frank, you can tell me about the Waters case, while you take me and Susan up to Clayburn Nurseries. That's an order; and I remind you as Mayor, I am technically your superior!" The Mayor asserted.

"Of course." Frank said with yet another little grin.

*　　　　　*　　　　　*

Frank drove slowly out of town towards the nursery with the mayor. Susan Petroff followed behind him in her city truck. Frank drove past the proposed site of the university and the potential subdivision for student housing. The land was barren for the most part but it had a few poplar trees scattered about. Mayor Bollen pointed out where the proposed buildings were to be built and where the grand entrance to the grounds would be. The Mayor envisioned a two road entry through iron gates like an old east coast university with immaculate gardens between the two roads leading up to the main building. That was what she envisioned, but of course the board of trustees had something far less elegant in mind.

The Mayor had asked Newman to her office for an update on the Waters case. Steve Cardwen had been assigned blame for most of the tragedies in town but five outstanding murders could not be tied to Cardwen. Darwin Foster had been eliminated as a suspect in any of the murders and it was now believed that a rouge timber wolf had killed the search and rescue. The lone survivor who had seen the animal could only describe it as a wolf of some kind. The five remaining murders seemed to have a link to Tim Waters, and the families of the deceased were pressing for an arrest.

"We won't be able to arrest Waters." Newman stated as he drove even slower up the hill past a rusted sign that said: New Haven Coal 2 miles.

Mark Fuson

"Damn it, Newman, we need an arrest in those cases. The families are pacing furiously. They can't understand why Waters hasn't been picked up yet." The Mayor said.

"I can't arrest someone who didn't do it." Newman plainly stated.

"Frank, everyone in town knows the kid did it. It's another Cardwen all over again. Foster probably had a hand in it too." The Mayor retorted.

"Well why don't you be Miss Policewoman and solve it yourself?" Newman shot back sarcastically.

"Watch your mouth!" Mayor Bollen sat stewing in her seat. "Frank I don't appreciate the belittling attitude you have towards me. I'm a woman, get over it!"

"Of course, I meant no disrespect." Frank lied openly. "Waters can't be arrested due to lack of evidence. What we assume and what we can prove are two different things. Fact, Waters was in the area of Main Street at the time of the first three murders. Fact, he did have an axe to grind with the victims. Fact, his name tag was found at the scene of the crimes. Fact, the DNA all came back canine. FACT!" Newman said bluntly as he lusted over the Mayor's neck and was no longer watching the road.

"Newman, the road!!!" Tara yelled as the cruiser swerved to make a sharp corner. She became unnerved when she realized Frank had made the turn without looking at the road. His eyes remained fixated on her. She was just about to comment when he returned his attention to the drive. After a brief moment in silence she asked for clarification. "The DNA was contaminated?"

"Every last sample, even the murdered girls had canine DNA." Newman stated now solely focused on the road. "Of course there is the other possibility."

Tara Bollen looked at Newman, waiting but she realized she had to coax it out of him. "Well?"

"The animal that took out the search and rescue, it came to New Haven and had a feast." Newman smiled at her as though it was that simple.

"You're blaming the murders on a wolf. Newman how did it get into a second floor bedroom window? The Mayor asked seeking simple logic.

"Who says it did? It's possible it slipped in through a partially opened door. Who can say? The fact is we have no evidence to go to a judge with. But we do have a witness who will go on record saying he saw a large wolf like animal kill his search and rescue partner. This witness was attacked too, he just happened to live. It seems unlikely that a wolf would come to New Haven, but that's sure what looks like what happened. I'm sorry Tara, the Waters case is done. I think it's time to put the misery of this town to rest, move on." Newman insisted.

"The families of the victims won't be pleased. Waters was already convicted in the court of public opinion." The Mayor said looking at the mine which was now fast approaching. She left an uneasy silence between the two.

Frank quickly changed the subject as he pulled up to the new gate at Clayburn Nurseries. "Got any plans for Christmas, Tara?

She looked at him in disgust. "Frank, I'm Jewish."

"You're a Jew?" Newman asked as though it was a genuine shock.

"Wow, you really are dense some days." Tara jiggled her Star of David pendant away from her chest for Newman to see.

"You don't look Jewish." Frank said, digging himself a little deeper.

"Wow! Thank you Adolf Newman." She said nothing more.

Frank stopped the car at the gate and began honking his horn repeatedly. A few moments later Clint Littleford could be seen driving up to the gate in an ATV. He stepped of his quad and unlocked the big gate allowing the city to come onto the grounds without question. Newman drove through the gate not stopping to talk to Clint. Mayor Bollen inspected the grounds and in her own mind agreed that work being done was unusual. From her vantage point she could see a new fence being built around the perimeter of the property. The fence was at least 20 feet high and it had razor wire along the top. Her instincts told her it looked very much like a prison, but she kept her opinion to herself. There were a lot of workers at the mine site with lots of building materials. The work being done was both extensive and unusual; the Mayor now realized how right Susan Petroff had been.

"So how come he let you onto the grounds without issue?" The Mayor asked.

"If I were a small business owner, doing work that might be considered illegal, and I saw the mayor coming to my business, would I really want to have a fit and refuse her entry. Wouldn't it be better to cooperate; that way I don't get dinged with fines." Frank answered in complete rationale.

"Then why didn't you tell him why we were here, you just drove passed him." She wondered openly.

"Geeze Tara, it's like you don't trust me." Frank stopped the vehicle near where Jesus had died a few weeks earlier. "We'll ask him nicely for a little tour. You can even sweeten the deal and offer to buy some poinsettias for the staff at city hall. I'm sure after a few minutes it will be very clear what's going on here, then you can make him buy a permit and Susan can do her inspection. If we're reasonable I'm sure he'll be too."

"I told you I'd be back!" Susan yelled at Clint as he pulled up in his ATV.

"You sure showed me, lady." Clint retorted with heavy sarcasm.

Tara Bollen approached Clint and extended her hand. "Hi, Mr. Littleford, I'm Mayor Bollen, sorry to intrude on you like this."

Mark Fuson

Clint shook the Mayor's hand graciously. "Please call me Clint. I'm sorry that you've been dragged into this. I just didn't want the hassle with Susan. I hear her inspections are like a prostate exam administered by the KGB."

The group chuckled with the exception of Susan who seemed unsure if she was offended or not. "You're right; she is the best damn inspector around. So do you mind telling us what you're up to?"

"Well, the truth is I'm growing marijuana and I need to protect it." Clint said bluntly.

"Excuse me?" The Mayor asked politely.

"Oh sorry. I know that sounded bad. I've been commissioned by the government to grow medical marijuana. I was actually trying to keep it hush-hush, the less who know about it the less I'll need the security. I was given a grant to build the fences and create a large secure growing area underground. You can see it if you'd like?" Clint offered.

"You have permits for the marijuana, I presume?" The Mayor asked.

"Oh, there's no weed here, not yet. I'm not required to have the permits until we're ready to begin growing." Clint said.

"What do you say Susan, feel like going for a walk underground?" Mayor Bollen asked as she began walking towards the mine entrance. "How far of a walk is it Clint?"

"What kind of operation do you take us for, we're full scale. We've reopened the old mine train, we can ride into the mine in style. You should put a hard hat on though." Clint ran over to a shed and emerged a second later with four hard hats.

The group put them on and proceeded to the train which was sitting on a side track outside the mine entrance. The train had seven cars in total including the engine. Two cars were carriages with a safety cage designed to transport workers and the remaining cars were flat deck loaded with more fencing and razor wire. Clint fired up the motor, hit the horn, and began rolling the train into the depths of the mine. As the engine rolled onto the mainline both Susan and Tara noted a spur line that ran off behind a building they had not previously seen. Another kind of mine car, similar to a box car lined the tracks. What struck the woman most was they appeared to be brand new. As the rocky old mine train entered the cold shaft daylight disappeared. The shaft was lighted with incandescent bubs strung along the rock face that barely cast enough light to see more than ten feet. Pushing deeper into the mine the train rocked and shuttered violently as Clint put it to full speed.

Tara looked back to the end of the train and could feel the distinct sensation of descending. A sign came into view only for a moment that said: Sector A, and an arrow pointing left. They rolled along faster; corridors briefly came into view which appeared to have large growing lights and plants in

Darwinism

them. It was cold, damp and smelt of skunk in the mine and something began to feel very wrong to the woman.

"How much farther is it?" Tara hollered to Clint, but she was ignored. She assumed he was unable to hear her through the rumble of the train. She pulled her phone from her purse to call her husband only realizing with the phone in hand that there would be no signal underground.

Clint slowed the vehicle as they passed a series of large security gates that lined the track. Finally the train came to a complete stop in a large rectangular chamber. Everything right of the train was bright and well lit and a chamber stretched on farther than was visible from the train. Security fencing ran wall to wall and floor to ceiling in three layers and appeared to be drilled directly into bedrock. Razor wire was intertwined into the fencing which was also adorned with signs indicating the fences were electrified. On the left side of the chamber was a gate that appeared to be for people that passed through the security fences in three stages. There was also an identical system on the right side of the chamber. Looking beyond the three barriers it was clear the chamber was also divided down the middle with another floor to ceiling fence.

Both Susan and Tara knew what they were looking at was not what they had been told. The sign that hung in plain view telling the men to go left and woman and children to the right told them a very different story.

"Isn't it fantastic?" Clint shouted as he leapt from the engine. "I never thought it would have been possible, but yet here it is."

With her heart racing and fear closing in Tara decided her only card to play was to act dumb if she and Susan had any chance of getting out of there. Her sixth sense was ringing loud and clear. "It is fantastic, quite the operation. When will you be online?" She asked attempting to hide the spasms in his voice.

"Today, as a matter of fact; it's a bit of a dry run rehearsal, we're not quite ready, but the agenda is advancing, so what choice do I have? Anyway, if you'll follow the sign to the right we can begin the tour." Clint marched over to the man-gate looking back to find the woman reluctant to follow. "This way ladies."

Newman stood behind Tara and Susan driving them like cattle towards the gate. Tara kept looking at the sign "Women and Children" knowing something was desperately wrong but they held their wits realizing it was their only defence. The group passed through all three gates which were in the open position. They found themselves in a long rectangular room with a security barrier running down the left creating a partition from the men.

"Why is the room separated into two parts?" Susan asked calmly.

Clint looked at her in disbelief but decided to play along. "Different varieties; if they co-mingle it's possible that problems could arise. It's best to keep them one hundred percent separated. So if you'll come this way, I've got some really cool shit to show you."

The group moved farther from the entrance and Susan's unease became more obvious as she continued to look over her shoulder for the train every few seconds. The train and man-gates were long gone within a few minutes and the group was now deep in the cavern. Clint stopped at a large ramp that descended deeper, to another level. He looked at the woman and smiled.

"Take your clothes off please!" Clint asked smugly.

"I beg your pardon." Mayor Bollen responded.

"You should beg everyone's pardon, do what he says." Newman said with a scowl of hate in his eyes. When he realized she had no intention of following his direction he wound up his fist and punched her in the stomach.

The mayor collapsed on the ground with the loss of her breath. Susan jumped on Newman's back in retaliation only to be thrown off with a force she did not anticipate. She fell to the ground like a child's toy.

"I wish you'd take this more seriously. You can either take your clothes off, or I'll do it for you." Clint said with lust in his voice as his tongue massaged his small but eager canine nubs.

"Why are you doing this?" Tara said as her voice began to collapse.

"Frank, I guess we're gonna have to do it." Clint said.

Frank went over to Susan who was still on the ground and kicked her in the side as hard as he could. He began tearing her coveralls off only to find she was wearing nothing underneath except what some would call granny panties. Newman tore her panties off with his teeth leaving Susan Petroff completely nude. He even took away her work boots.

Clint approached Tara who was now more willing to comply. He did not have to ask her again and she began to disrobe. Within a few moments both woman were nude and shivering.

"Are you going to rape us?" Tara asked as though she knew the answer.

"Don't flatter yourself lady. I can get better sex from a willing participant. You are going to your new home!" Clint announced with pride.

"We'll freeze to death down here!" Susan shouted.

"We're not barbarians! We've got bedding, clothes and food for you ladies in the living quarters. Come!" Clint demanded while beginning to descend to the lower level. The group remained silent other than the sobs of the women and the occasional scream as they stepped on a sharp rock.

"Sector A, level 2." Clint announced. "This is your new home. As the first inductees, and on behalf of our leader, I wish to welcome you. You have been selected to be the representatives for the female population. Let me restate that, Mayor Bollen you have been selected. Susan, you really are of no

Darwinism

importance, but if you wish to aid the Mayor, who are we to interfere." Clint laughed along with Newman. The nude women just stood there quaking.

"What is this place?" The Mayor asked.

"Our leader, and saviour I might add, has a plan for New Haven. Unfortunately the plan isn't for everyone. Soon others will be here to join you, it will be your job to educate them in the rules. The rules are very important. I will explain the rules to you, and you will explain them to the new arrivals. Failure to abide by this first rule will result in your family's death, are we clear?" Clint asked with authority.

Tara shook her held slightly and waited for direction; her gut still ached.

"New arrivals will be wearing the institutional dress when they arrive at A2. That area on the surface you saw with the strange box car looking things - that building is the intake unit where we get everyone ready for the decent to A2. You, of course, are the exception to the rule. Once the new arrivals get to A2 they must not go up to A1, ever, if they are caught on A1 they will executed on site. That goes for you too. Once a month a food delivery will occur on A1, when it arrives a bell will ring here on A2. You may select ten of your citizens to go to A1 to retrieve it, no more, excess people will be shot. From time to time a siren will go off on all three levels, A2, A3 and A4. When you hear this siren you, and you alone, must come to A1 for information. You must arrive on A1 within ten minutes, failure to do so will be cause for punishment for your entire population. Contact with the men is prohibited; this is also cause for punishment. Don't bother attempting to escape; unless you can dig through a mile of rock and earth, you're stuck here. If you encounter a fence you'll want to steer clear of it, they are all electrified and they will kill you if you touch them. You are free to move about on all three levels, I think you will find your accommodations quite spacious. Everything you'll need is somewhere down here, just look around and you're bound to find it."

"Why are you doing this?" Tara asked meekly.

"For the same reason you chose to raise old lady Beatrice's property taxes to the point she couldn't afford it so she'd lose her property to the town. Then you move in and – donate-it to the new proposed university. But you don't stand to benefit from that transaction, do you? You did it in the name of progress for New Haven, didn't you? You ask why we do this; the same reason you do? Because I can. A month ago I was just a horticulturalist who grew marijuana on the side. Now I run a detention facility. I'm not a bad person, actually that's one of the reasons I'm really drawn to this movement. Our leader is about unifying and improving our people. New Haven will be an exceptional place to live once the dark work is complete."

"What the fuck happens to us then?" Susan bellowed.

197

Mark Fuson

"You're our treat!" Newman said playfully. "See you soon!" Newman reversed direction back up the ramp.

"The rest of the council should be here later tonight. You'll want to get yourself settled in. I'll also make a personal point to have your family join you as well." Clint turned and began walking away.

"You'll never get away with what you're doing!" Susan shouted.

"We have gotten away with it. Darwin killed the search and rescue. Waters killed the three boys and two girls. We own the police, hospital and I think we got the fire department too. While you've been talking to the media promising action against the heinous crimes in New Haven we've been recruiting. The town is ours, you've lost. It was way too easy!" Clint chuckled and headed up the hill. "Oh, one more thing. Don't try to make any fires down here; old coal mine! The coal dust and fire don't mix well."

The two nude women were standing at the entrance to A2, all alone and in shock. The ramp continued down to A3, but they could see boxes on A2. Frozen to the core and in disbelief at their situation, they shuffled over to the supplies holding each other in comfort. It was the beginning of their nightmare and the birth of another hardened community.

*   *   *

Frank and Clint emerged from the mine awhile later to find Darwin at the entrance dressed in a fine new suit. The young man looked like he was prepared to do battle in the world of politics. The train came to a grinding halt and Darwin approached.

"Thought I'd come out to see the operation." Darwin said, offering to shake Clint's hand, which was accepted.

"Wish you were here an hour ago. We just admitted our first two residents. We got Mayor Bollen and a woman from bylaw enforcement."

"Excellent! Newman, make sure you round up their families, get them up here tonight, but quietly." Darwin executed. "The rally is tonight at eight at the Caprice. I expect both of you to be in attendance!"

In tandem they replied "Yes sir!"

"If you'll excuse me, I also have to round up the council members. We want to get them at the council meeting at seven." Newman said.

"Don't let me stop you." Darwin replied giving a nod of approval. Newman returned to his cruiser and sped off. Darwin and Clint remained at the mine entrance with an awkward silence.

"Darwin, how are you?" Clint asked placing his hand on Darwin's shoulder.

"Fantastic, how should I be?" He replied sternly.

"It hasn't been that long since Steve…"

Darwin cut Clint off harshly. "You are never to speak that name to me again, are we clear on that! I'll fucking gut you if you do!" Darwin looked through Clint's soul like death. Clint merely shook his head, and nothing more was said.

Chapter 22

The marquee read: Theatre closed for private function. The movie posters had been removed from the street display and now the Caprice looked like it had gone out of business. Around seven forty five that evening a flood of people were arriving at the theatre all with big smiles and an uplifting attitude. The family had grown to over two hundred members. The meeting would be the first of many, but this would be the most important.

Ray Silverdale ran around excitedly greeting the patrons as they entered the cinema. Ray had only been inducted into the family the previous week but he was already enthusiastic about the prospects. He had been asked by the leader to personally see to any needs the attending guests may have. The family was flipping the bill for the event, and money was no object.

Darwin now controlled the town treasury and any capital he required could easily be acquired. Of all senior management at city hall he had only inducted the chief financial officer for New Haven. Frank Newman had suggested to Darwin that keeping more senior staff might be a good idea, but Darwin decided the town needed new blood and a new direction. The treasury was important, and immediate control of the town's revenues was required.

Darwin's introduction to the family was an extravagant event that he designed himself. He wanted the family to understand what it meant to be chosen; that being a member would mean a change in their lives for the better. He had the event catered with elegant wines and champagnes served in crystal

Darwinism

glasses, two tables of fine cheese and meats, cognac and cigars were also made available to any of the men who wished to indulge. On the lighter faire was a table with three kinds of pate all graciously provided from the residents of the New Haven Seniors Center. Each pate had a distinct seasoning which meant marrying it to the correct wine was a challenge. For the children in attendance Darwin had ensured pizza and hot dogs were available along with unlimited pop, candy and popcorn. He did not wish to bore them so the children would be in cinema one watching a children's movie. Darwin also considered the children a liability because he had requested that no child under the age of fifteen be turned until the group could arrive at a consensus on the issue. For the moment the younger children were oblivious to what was going on around them.

"People, could we all proceed to cinema six and take your seat. We are about to begin." Ray announced on the public address system.

Husbands and wives of the various city agencies and services dressed in their finest wear began moving down the corridor to the theatre. Most took a plate of food and glass of wine with them but all were laughing and joking as though they hadn't a care in the world. Fire Chief Patrick O'Donnavan and his wife marched arm in arm together like youngsters in love. Dave Cronin was trying to convince his search and rescue colleagues to try the pate before moving to the auditorium, but they had only been inducted the day before and were still a little shy. The children had all entered cinema one ten minutes earlier and were now enthralled with their movie. The rest of the family shuffled into cinema six and took their seats, eagerly awaiting the meeting they had all been dying for.

A hum of conversation filled the theatre but all the topics seemed to be related.

Have you tried the pate – it really gets me going! When were you made? My husband bit me. Do you know what happens now? Do you like the power – I can barely control myself – I really don't want to either.

The lights of the theatre lowered and a hush fell upon the audience. A lone spot light targeted the floor at the base of the screen and Tim Waters appeared from behind the curtain holding a microphone.

"Hello New Haven! Welcome to tonight's main event! My name is Tim Waters; you might recognize me as one of the employees here at the Caprice. I've moved onto bigger and better things now, as have all of you!" The audience all laughed but returned to silence as Tim raised his hand to the crowd. "In all seriousness, though, I want you to meet the man who is responsible for putting this all together, please would you put your hands together for our leader: DARWIN FOSTER!"

The crowd stood in ovation as Darwin entered the theatre from the rear.

Mark Fuson

As he descended the aisle he shook a few hands along the way like a politician and waving to people who were seated in the middle. Cheers of thanks were shouted at him in all directions and he could feel the vibe of control and acceptance in the room. They were his children.

In front of the crowd Darwin raised his arms in triumph and victory. His followers were enthralled to be in his presence. Darwin lowered his arms and indicated with his hands to be seated which the crowd seemed to understand without verbal directions. Darwin had their complete obedience. He shook Tim's hand and took the microphone and began.

Darwin stood in silence in front of the theatre; he held the microphone to his mouth but kept his lips closed. He panned the crowd as though he was looking for someone but was unable to find them. The silence became discomfiting as the stillness went on. Darwin appeared to have stage fright with the exception that his body language did not imply a confidence issue, rather the opposite. Finally he spoke.

"A long time ago I was a happy boy lost in the wonders of childhood. Life seemed simpler in those days. I know you laugh at that, for me childhood was only a few years ago, for many of you it was a lifetime ago. Think back to that time when innocence was your companion and life was easy. Do you remember that time? Do you remember when it stopped being that way? When was our innocence crushed, when was our childhood destroyed? Everyone has a moment in time where the child they were was ruined. Rebuilding the joys of childhood is an impossibility, when it is gone, it's gone!

I'm not here tonight to tell you we're rebuilding our youth. I wanted to start there because I think we can all appreciate the symbolism. I doubt that anyone of you could say they were never bullied, harassed or picked on as a child. Worse than that, how many in this room were abused, physically or sexually by a friend, neighbour clergyman or family member? You don't have to answer to me, just answer to yourself. How many times throughout your life have you been wronged in someway, while the wrongdoers just continue on the merry little way doing whatever they feel like without consequence. They have zero concern for the feelings they have trampled on. We all know these people, directly or indirectly, you are only lying to yourself if you truly believe there is good in everyone. THERE IS NOT!

Man is inherently flawed. Some only strive to ensure the misery and pain of others. These people, whether they be the school yard bully or the town rapist, they will never change. Our liberal thinking society gives these evil tumours the right and privilege of remaining in our communities, tormenting and violating the innocent without consequence because some therapist somewhere says everyone has the ability to change. And who is the one who

Darwinism

pays the ultimate price for the evil we must endure when these cancers act out? You and me! I am here tonight to inform you, it need not be this way!

Something glorious happened to me awhile back, I think you can guess what. It gave me the clairvoyance to see a new path, an evolutionary change that could bond us together as a community for the common good. No longer will we sit in our homes too afraid to go for a walk because we might get mugged. No longer will our children be too terrified to go to school. No longer will someone hate you because of who you are. Our path is a simple one. Our goal is clear. We are one family, strong and united! We stand together, to protect our own and to improve ourselves. I ask you, are you with me!?" Darwin shouted as the crowd exploded into applause, his rally was taking shape.

"The road ahead is perilous. Like any operation there will be pain. The only way to purge the cancer from our town is to remove it by force. We all know the elements of this town that we could call: a negative aspect. I pose the question to you! If you agree you want to live in a world as I have described it, and you agree the cancer must be removed, who would you remove first?" Darwin pointed to a woman in the third row who put her hand up first. "Yes!"

"The house on Eighth, the one everyone knows is a drug house but the police don't do anything about it. I think anyone caught there should be removed." The woman said confidently.

"YES! ANOTHER – YES YOU!" Darwin pointed to a middle row and man in his thirties.

"I think that crooked Mayor of ours should be taken away!" He said brusquely before sitting down again.

Darwin laughed out loud. "I must be doing something right; I removed her from office this afternoon!" Once again the auditorium erupted into applause. "SOMEONE ELSE!"

"The bank manager!" An unidentified voice hollered.

"Thomas Berry and his clan…they respect no one and threaten and intimidate whoever they want. Those people are rude and just plain ignorant. They come into the grocery store where I work and openly steal knowing full well no one will stop them. You've seen them, they're huge, even my husband is afraid of them" The wife of NHPD Officer Kuntz implored to the embarrassment of her husband.

"I think the New Haven Police should just tell us everyone who's committed a crime, and we should get rid of all of them!" Terri Bailey shouted.

"Thanks Terri!" Darwin winked at his little pup who he had decided to personally bring over. He had gone to her shop a day after Steve's funeral to

Mark Fuson

thank her for attending and he decided to bring her over. She didn't resist, it was almost as though she knew all along what Darwin was.

"I think we can all see that we have plenty of people in this town that should be removed. Having said that, I want to talk to you about the decision making in what will be our new local government. I encourage all of you to submit names of people, residents of New Haven, business owners, churches or religious affiliations – any person or group that you think New Haven would be better with or without. I will consider any name put forward, however I will have the ultimate say in who goes and who stays. With that in mind I may elect to remove people you may or may not totally agree with. You can disagree with me, but you will accept the decision as final once it has been made. No citizen of New Haven is to be inducted into the family without my explicit approval. Anyone who can not follow this basic rule will be subject to expulsion from our organization. This rule exists to ensure our purity. If we turn anyone and everyone we will merely be making a carbon copy of the existing town. As this is not our goal, certain choices will have to be made, some of them may be difficult for you, but know this, it is for the greater good." Darwin paused for the crowd and he could see he still had their loyalty.

"We are not monsters. We have a gift. Some may call it a dark gift, and it is true we do things that as humans we would never have done. With the power of the wolf racing through our veins our judgment and view of the world has changed. We have a mission that we must carry out. In exchange for immortality, and peace –we must feed. This comes as a warning to you, especially those who are reluctant to feed. We must feed or our minds deteriorate. We can survive three months without eating the flesh of man, after that you will kill and you will have no control over who you kill. I am speaking from experience. When I first became the wolf I loved it, the feeling and power, but I resisted the lust for blood for fear of what I might do. A spirit from that after world warned me of my impending demise, I gave in soon after. I ate the search and rescue once I knew what was happening to me. To the search and rescue here tonight, sorry guys, I was hungry!" The crowd chuckled at the black humour. "I hope you never have to experience hunger like I did! I have to tell you though, I could feel my grip on reality slipping rapidly, and it wasn't pleasant. Anyway, once I tried human, there was no going back. We are not monsters; we are an evolved species of mankind. Humans just happen to be our food. And that brings me to the next subject of importance." Darwin again paused, taking a deep breath.

"Those of you who have eaten and killed know the feeling. It is indescribable the feeling that moves through you as you feed. For myself, and others I know, it is very sexual. The feeling in itself is addictive. We cannot go out feeding whenever we get hungry or have an urge. We must remain below the radar, especially while humans continue to live among us. If you wish to feed, we are building a facility at the old mine, Clayburn Nurseries. There you may go and feed in privacy, we haven't decided how often, but due to supply we should limit ourselves to once a month – which is more than enough."

"What do we do if an outsider shows up and starts asking questions?" The question came from a woman in the front row that Darwin recognized as a doctor from the hospital.

"When the exodus of the humans not selected for membership is complete, we can be more casual with who we are around town. No outsiders will be permitted to live in New Haven without being blessed. Tourists will be a fact of life and we will have to be mindful of them, but not many come this way so it should be a non issue. We will have a security perimeter for anyone that does come to New Haven, to alert us. Outsiders will be inevitable. As our plan progresses we will have a more detailed idea on how to deal with these situations."

"Excuse me, sir?" A beautiful woman in row eight put her hand up.

"Yes love." Darwin responded flirtatiously.

"What do we do at full moon?" She asked curiously.

Darwin hadn't considered that. It was still another two weeks to the full moon but she was right, they would need a plan in place, or at least have the humans dealt with by then. "Tomorrow I will be hosting a conference of my council. At this conference we will begin discussing matters such as that. Stay tuned!" Darwin smirked provocatively.

"We have many unanswered questions that as a community we will have to come to some kind of resolution on; for example, the children? The parents of the room will need to decide what's best for the children. I am of the thinking that children should not be turned, but that is only my opinion, and I'm not married to it! As a community we must work together to attempt to make rules that we can live by. I am not your dictator, though I will rule with an iron fist if I am forced to. Follow the basic rules; this is all I ask for everyone's sake." Darwin stopped and cleared his throat before continuing.

"The council will convene tomorrow at Mayor Bollen's estate; I think she's done with it." Darwin humoured. "Some of you will be invited, as observers or as experts, to weigh in on the work ahead. If you are one of these lucky people, you will be notified by myself or by Mr. Waters before this evening is over. It is my hope that by the end of the day tomorrow we will have a roadmap to guide us through the next little while. We have a lot of work to do, and I'm going to need your help to make it work. I want you all to start thinking now about areas you might want to volunteer in to help our community grow. I know Clint Littleford is in desperate need of workers, and that demand is only going to get worse as his population climbs." Darwin again stopped gazing at the crowd looking individuals directly in the eye. "Tonight is a night for celebration. Join me in the lobby for some food and drink; let us get to know each other in our new skins!" The crowd stood in applause and ovation once again.

"This is a brave new world we are creating! We are our own masters; we are our own architects of societal genius. Soon we will live in a world of our own creation. Soon the enemies of our past will be vanquished and we will be free to pursue a life of supernatural fulfilment. Now is our time, our time to lay the foundation for our future. A future that will be the envy of any outsider, it will be engineered to perfection. Through our gift we will create something exceptional and only though our gift will we be allowed to maintain it. Our New Wolf Order begins tonight!

The crowd roared to the words of their new leader. The course had been set, and no one questioned the direction. The crowd moved about and people began to meet each other. The event was social and polite and the atmosphere was pleasant and the ineptness of a typical social gathering wasn't present. Jokes were told and stories were heard. Everyone listened and everyone cared. They were a family.

CHAPTER 23

The Bollen estate was on the bank of the Fisherman Creek. The home was a stately manor that had eight bedrooms, ten bathrooms, movie theatre and an indoor pool. At one time it had been the summer residence of Stanley Andrews, the owner of the New Haven Coal. History surrounding him was vague at best but it was widely held that the estate sat vacant most of the time. Anyone stepping into the home for the first time could see that no expense had been spared in the construction. Solid cherry wood paneling adorned the walls that were polished to a high sheen. The floors in the elegant entryway were Italian marble; and above was a crystal chandelier that would make any maid cringe. Inside to the left of the foyer was a clear view of a sitting room, and ornate fireplace and highly polished wood floors. Large floor to ceiling windows on either side of the fireplace brought in all the light the room required. To the right of the entry was another room for sitting with bookcases filled to capacity and beyond the library a guest could see the arboretum.

The Bollen's had purchased the home twenty years prior and had done extensive restoration work. Mike Bollen was a big shot realtor in town and managed to snag the manor from a foreclosure deal before anyone else had a shot at it. Tara Bollen, at that time, had her own interior design company. The majority of the restoration work she had either done herself or personally supervised. Her company failed a few years later which is when she tried her hand at politics. Evidently she was a better liar than a decorator.

Darwin arrived around eight that morning. Tim and Dave were already

Mark Fuson

at the house cleaning up from the previous evening round up. The police had been there to collect the Bollen children around the same time the rally had been concluding. The Bollen's had two daughters and two sons from age twelve to seventeen. They decided to put up a fight, but with some swift action from the standard issue New Haven police taser that stand off was put to an end quickly. The house was now ready for the council and invited guests. The day would be long and the topics would be dry, but everyone knew it would be important work.

Darwin considered the council only to be an interim one. Tim Waters would be allowed to stay on as his vice-chair, but Dave Cronin was an accident and would be phased out and shuffled into a more administrative position. Frank Newman would be tolerated for the time being, but Darwin was already having some concerns about loyalty. For the moment, Frank would be kept on. Robert Fletcher would not be offered a seat on council, but Newman could keep him on in security if he so chose. What Darwin was really looking for was to diversify. He wanted to add some women to the council, and members from different parts of the community. To achieve his vision he needed to break away from the norms.

Darwin, again, spared no expense when it came to appearances. The day was catered and they would have a chef and aids on site during the meeting. Three meals would be served, starting with breakfast. Every attendee could order whatever they wanted and the chef would prepare it. Darwin had told the chef when arranging the catering that he was to bring only high end ingredients, and to be prepared for all possible requests. Assuming all went well and the job was done to perfection a ten thousand dollar bonus would be given on top of the normal fee and salary charged by the catering company. The chef agreed to the challenge, knowing it would be nearly impossible to anticipate everyone's needs, but the bonus made it a challenge worth taking. Lunch would consist of soup and sandwiches. Three soups made from scratch, of the chef's choosing and a variety of sandwiches on fresh baked bread were on order. Dinner was a secret but it would be something magical. To round off the experience of the day a fully stocked bar was provided which could make most anything desired. In the library off the arboretum was a grand piano that would be played during the intermissions.

The conference was set to begin at eight-thirty and Dave and Tim were running around making the final touches. When Darwin arrived he was pleased with what he saw. The grand staircase in the foyer was titivated with a seasonal garland and illuminated with tiny white LED lights. The piano flowed through the house and could be heard pleasantly in any room on the main floor. The smell of Christmas was evident, cinnamon and cloves flowed through the home like a bakery.

Darwinism

"Good morning sir, may I take your coat?" The young attendant asked as she approached from no where.

"Yes, thank you." Darwin responded removing his overcoat. "Are the other guests here?"

"Mr Waters and Mr Cronin are working in the dinning room and Dr. Gagnon and Evian Pierce are in the arboretum." The beautiful girl replied.

"Thank you, I can find them." Darwin said as he began walking towards the sounds of Silent Night on the piano.

"Care for a drink sir?" A male attendant asked promptly on Darwin entering the room.

"Coffee, with Baileys." Darwin replied as he admired the feel of the room. It inspired the Christmas spirit in him. The attendant disappeared, but only for a moment, and Darwin found a cup in saucer in front of him before he had finished taking in the space.

"Darwin, good to see you." Evian Pierce embraced Darwin with. "You must come into the arboretum; it has stunning views of the creek."

"I'm glad you both could make it. Have you been waiting long?" Darwin asked as the gracious host he was attempting to be.

"It's no trouble Darwin; the atmosphere makes it an extremely pleasant wait. What time did you get out of the meeting last night? "Dr. Gagnon asked as the trio now stood looking through the windows onto the partially frozen creek.

"Well after midnight. Too many questions, I'm afraid." Darwin replied taking a sip of his coffee which made him cringe a little. He was drinking coffee only as an appearance. Darwin had never cared for coffee but he thought having pure Irish Cream on its own would make him look like a lush.

"It's only natural Darwin, we all have questions. This is a new and exciting life you have given us. We all have questions, but you also have a calming effect on us which helps. The idea that you have shared with us was one we could have only dreamed of before. With you we are able to make it a reality. A town that can live in pure harmony, it will be nothing short of paradise. I think our questions are, how do we make it work, how do we make it last?" Dr. Evita Gagnon asked.

"That's the point of today's meeting. Hopefully we can arrive at some form of consensus." Darwin replied, quickly cringing back another sip of his black bitter.

"I thought she was Jewish? What's with the Christmas Trees?" Frank Newman asked as he strolled into the arboretum with Robert Fletcher in tow.

"Frank, Bob, I'd like you to meet Dr. Evita Gagnon and Evian Pierce.

209

This is Frank Newman, head of the New Haven Police Department. And his colleague Robert Fletcher" Darwin introduced with grace,

"Ladies, a pleasure." Frank kissed each of their hands like an old world gentleman before returning his attention to Darwin. "Seriously Darwin, I know she was a liar, but did she lie about being Hebrew too?"

Darwin sighed at his uncultured security chief. "She was Jewish Frank; I had the decorations put up. I happen to like Christmas and I thought this house would look good done up for the holidays. It might make our work today a little easier."

"Well I think you've done a fantastic job. The home is so warm and inviting. I could spend the whole season here. "Evian Pierce assured.

"Mr. Foster would you care to retire to the dinning room, most of your guests are arriving right now." The young girl from the front door informed.

"Absolutely, I'm starving. What do you say, ladies?" Darwin announced putting his hands on his hips for the two older women to put their arms through his. They did so without prompting and the three marched down the long hall to the other end of the home to the dinning room that overlooked the east lawn. Newman and Fletcher followed close behind.

The main dinning room was long and rectangular with a beautiful oval antique table that could seat twenty. The walls of the room had cherry paneling on the lower part of the wall but the upper portion was done in a raised deep green wallpaper. Mid room was another fireplace fully ablaze with windows on either side of the fireplace similar to the sitting room off the foyer. The room length required the use of two chandeliers that mimicked the one in the front entry, still a maid's nightmare. The table itself was covered in a beautiful white linen table cloth, with seasonal floral arrangements down the center of the table. Cutlery was in place and shined of gold. Darwin had requested specifically gold cutlery as he was unsure if silver was a good idea. The gold flatware looked good on the table and Darwin was happy with the result.

The first hour of the conference was mostly for introductions and small talk. The food was simply divine – as Dr Gagnon had insisted. The chef had managed to meet everyone's palate desires without difficulty. It seemed to the chef that the group was big on meat, no vegetarian dishes were ordered, as Darwin had warned prior to their arrival. The chef found this revelation comforting as he was now able to put animal stock into the soup which would make them that much better.

Town treasurer Evian Pierce expressed her gratitude for the opportunity to become a member of the new ruling council. She was an up front woman who had no issues saying she understood she was blessed only because of her access to the town money. She pledged to the attending members that she would devote herself to the cause and prove she was more valuable that just a "bean counter".

Dr Evita Gagnon had been a member for nearly two weeks. Tim Waters had brought her over as the first hospital staff to be inducted. Evita, unlike Evian, was more reluctant to embrace her gift. It took both Tim and Darwin a great deal of persuasion before she came around. She was a healer and the power of the wolf made that skill seem redundant. To be around the blood and organs of a patient was now a problem for her. As the days passed she began to relax in her approach to the gift. Darwin had also touched a nerve with her when he told Dr. Gagnon that her primary job in the new community would be in research. She would be responsible for researching the gift to learn all they could about it from the physical to the metaphysical. She would also be part of the cover story, to help explain away the senior deaths, and anyone else that came through New Haven and found themselves to be dinner by sheer happenstance.

Dave Cronin had bit Vivian Yee from channel six. Since her induction into the family news stories from New Haven had all but dried up. Vivian was blessed while taking time out in the lavatory after having some bad Chinese food at the local ethnic eatery. By all accounts her induction was the messiest yet. Despite the shitty introduction into the family, Vivian was happy to be on board from the get go. Her position was obvious; she would be in charge or directing and deflecting the media from New Haven as needed. She would also be instrumental in keeping the townsfolk calm in the time leading up to the round up.

Clint Littleford was present too, but his decision making on the council would be limited to matters directly related to the facility. As the meeting had a lot to do with the removal and storage of the populace Darwin felt that Clint's presence was required, despite the fact he was still nervous about Clint's past.

Tim, being Darwin's right hand man, and the only one he really trusted, was allowed to bring over two people of his choosing to become advisors to the council. Tim had selected true geeks among geeks. Benny Yates was a Trekkie, but excellent in matters requiring logical thinking. Benny was also well versed in the world of the supernatural.

Tim's second choice was Angela Beckford who Darwin suspected he had picked only for the sexual aspects. But, Tim assured Darwin that he would be impressed with her in time.

Fire Chief Patrick O'Donnavan and coroner Jane Wansee were also requested to attend. The fire chief was present because of the continued and ongoing need for emergency services in New Haven and the coroner would be required to assist in any additional cover up that may become public.

The last in attendance was a complete surprise to Darwin. Darwin had asked Tim to locate someone who would make a good scribe for the meeting. The person should be someone good with words and able to keep up. Tim found Cindy Holmes who he knew to be very good at short hand. Darwin believed Tim had brought Cindy over, but it was Darwin himself who had done the deed. Cindy apparently became infected through the exchange of bodily fluids during their wild sex. Cindy was a clever girl who could taste the power, she knew there was more going on than a random sexual encounter. Darwin had been different, and the hair that seemed to appear and disappear on his chest told her a story. She didn't know that she would become a werewolf, but she knew she liked the taste of Darwin, and she made it her business to drink as much of him as she could.

The real meeting began with a simple question. "What can you tell us about our origins Darwin?" Fire Chief O'Donnavan asked.

"Unfortunately not as much as I would like. I can't even tell you how I was made. I don't know who did it to me. I'm starting to think that I was marked from the time I was born – but I can't say for certain. I know no other werewolves; I am indirectly responsible for everyone at this table and anyone else in town that has been turned." Darwin informed.

"I believe we are here to create a new breed of humanity, one that can know the difference between right and wrong and act accordingly. I believe the world in which we have been living is flawed, and some force from beyond the grave has created us as a way of reinstating the common good that the world is capable of. I believe in my heart that New Haven will become a template for other communities, but for now we are the experiment." Darwin shared.

"Bravo! I like what I'm hearing, but how do you propose we take ourselves from the experimental stage into full scale operation?" Dr. Gagnon asked.

"This is the tricky part. The next several days will be complicated and clumsy. One thing is certain, in my mind; we cannot keep everyone in New Haven. Can we at least agree to that in principle?" Darwin put to the group.

All heads around the table shook.

"How will we select the ones who stay and the ones who go?" Vivian Yee asked.

"That's why we're having this meeting. The selection of new members condemns those who are not chosen to be relocated to the mine. Let me put that in plain English, instead of beating around the bush, those not chosen to be blessed with our bite will become our food." Darwin educated.

"Why so black and white?" Angela Beckford asked.

"When the moon is full we will change. That will never change. If we have humans living in town that we wish to keep, there's a good chance one of us will end up eating them. As an example, maybe you want your mom to stay human living in town. She's important to you, but to the fire chief she's simply food – why should he care. And that scenario would be repeated over and over again, it would become a blood bath. No, I believe the town should be all or nothing. Does anyone disagree with that logic?" Darwin asked.

"Sir, we should consider a small contingent of humans..." Angela said before being cut off.

"Which part of NO wasn't clear?" Darwin scolded.

"Wouldn't it be wise, to have gate keepers guarding the town during the full moon. Since we're all going to be busy...we should have someone protecting the town from intruders." Angela forced her point.

"I think she's on to something. We could choose members of the human community who want to become like us, but maybe they need to earn their way in. They could be our guardians and once they have proven their loyalty we can then bless them." Tim suggested.

"Well okay. We need guardians, how many are we talking? Newman, what kind of security force would we need to look after the perimeter during a full moon?" Darwin asked.

"The circumference of the town is a little more than thirty miles. Once we have the electronic surveillance and alarms installed I think we could do the job effectively with ten to fifteen men." Newman said as though it was fact.

"What happens if the guardians are attacked by one of us during the full moon?" Evian asked politely.

"What's the old saying: You can't make an omelette without breaking some eggs. It's something like that. If we kill them, oh well. That will have to be a chance the guardians are willing to take. If they want our bite, they'll likely take the chance. Besides, I have a sneaking suspicion that finding volunteers won't be difficult." Darwin said with a smile on his face looking to Benny.

"Oh yes, that's true. Lots of people on the internet wanting to become vampires and werewolves...mind you most are a little weird" Benny replied.

"Are you one of those people Benjamin?" Dr. Gagnon asked.

Benny smiled warmly to the good doctor. "Yes ma'am!"

The group chuckled at Benny's admission before moving the agenda forward. For the next hour the group debated the best way to recruit Guardians for the full moon security positions. Several options were considered but in the end the resident geek convinced the council he could subtly locate and recruit followers from the internet. The motion was passed and the job fell to Benny to fill the portfolio before the next full moon. Also decided in that hour was the job description of the Guardians. They had but one function, and that was to keep intruders out of New Haven during a full moon. The decision to turn them would be made by the council on a quarterly basis based on several criteria. Admission into the family would be based on loyalty, work performance and talents offered. A Guardian who went above and beyond the call of duty could be sworn in at Darwin's discretion. And the most crucial element of the Guardian platform was there was no quitting the position. Once the position had been accepted they did the job until they were made, or disposed of. Potential Guardians would be made aware of this policy before joining; however they would be disposed of if they refused the position. Essentially a person who was selected to be a Guardian either did the job and eventually was bit becoming a member or they fed the family.

A short recess was called after the resolution of the Guardian issue. The council members retreated to the arboretum where coffee and tea was waiting along with some fresh baked scones. The atmosphere in the group seemed up beat and relieved. Some progress had been made but some large issues remained. Before lunch Darwin hoped to tackle the issue of membership selection.

"Pumpkin scones with maple butter, these are just to die for!" Jane moaned. "And they're still warm too!"

"I wonder what she'd say if it was a small child." Fletcher jabbed.

"You quit it!" Jane barked with scone crumbs blowing from her mouth.

Chestnuts began roasting on an open fire from the piano and Darwin began nipping at everyone's ears. "On the subject of membership…" Darwin asked.

"What happened to the break?" Newman fired at Darwin.

"No, it's a good question. If we are starting a new – species – I guess we have a chance to leave out certain groups that maybe detract from good wholesome living." Vivian Yee supported.

"But how do we even begin to select who's in, and who's out?" Tim asked.

"Well I for one have no use for Jehovah's Witnesses. The whole coming to your house to preach about God, it's always irked me! For once I'd love to live in a community where I wouldn't have to be subjected to that." Evian confessed.

"I agree, no JW's" Pat O'Donnavan seconded.

"Okay, are we all in agreement then?" Darwin looked around to the group who all shook their heads in agreement. Darwin himself was indifferent to Jehovah, or any other ethnic of religious group, but he knew some appeasements would be necessary.

With that first informal vote the exclusion list began.

Darwinism

The conversation continued throughout the break and by the time they had reconvened in the sitting room Muslims, ex-cons, the uneducated and mentally challenged would be barred from admittance. The mentally challenged group was decided as a matter of safety since no one knew how a human with brain damage would respond to the gift. The question was an interesting one and Dr. Gagnon volunteered to explore the concept further. If the gift cured the mentally challenged of their human condition consideration would be given to removing them from the list. The other three groups were on the list either from bigotry or mistrust. In some cases it was both. The group didn't argue much when compiling the list, it came almost naturally.

"The reality is that the human body is closely related to the pig, inducting Muslims into the family would be sacrilege for them." Dr. Gagnon informed the group.

"You had me at - ban them." Newman spit out a little on the annoyed side.

"What about the Jews? They don't eat pork, right? Is it sacrilege to turn them?" Fletcher asked.

"Jews are more flexible in their faith; I think they'd be alright bending the rules a bit." Dr. Gagnon replied.

"Darwin, what should our policy be on inducting our spouses? Are we required to, or can we opt to send them to special handling instead?" Shelia asked with genuine interest.

Darwin paused for a moment with a complete loss for words. "I never considered it. I suppose it is up to you. If you want to send them to special handling, that's entirely up to you. Anyone disagree?" Darwin put to the group. No one spoke up. No one offered a nod so Darwin carried the motion, knowing it was likely only to affect Jane. "Send him to the camps Jane, if that's what you want."

"GOOD! Cheating bastard! I think I'll eat his balls while he watches… then I'll eat the rest of him, but not until he's sat up there for a few months." The bitter and scorned woman shared.

"On that cheery note I think it's time we discuss the selection process. How do we select the ones we want? We've already said who is not allowed, so we can add them to the exclusion list right away. What do we do with people who meet our overall criteria but still don't make the cut? Do we remove the bad apples first then turn the rest?" Tim asked the group to open discussion.

"From a stand point of security it would be better if we turned the ones we wanted first. If we attempt to do mass deportations with humans around watching it will make our job that much harder. We need to turn the

215

town first, and with our increased numbers the deportations should go more smoothly."

"Agreed." Darwin stated. "How do you propose we bless our selected citizens in a way that will be fast and inconspicuous?"

Dr Gagnon piped up. "A clinic at the legion. We can send letters to the ones we want telling them they've been exposed to a biological contaminant. Then we can get them."

"Good plan, except all the hypochondriacs will show up too, what do we do then? I don't think we can just bite people without someone freaking out. If non-selected people show up, then what? Too risky in my opinion." Clint said.

"True, but what if we have a vaccine, or serum. Maybe we could make a town emergency that requires people to get a shot. We could have two shots, one with our blood for the chosen, and one with saline. All we have to do is check the list and give the correct shot." The good doctor educated.

"Could you take that a step further? Would it be possible to give the rejects a sedative so we could shuffle them off to special handling right away?" Clint suggested.

"I don't see why not?" Dr. Gagnon replied.

"Make it so." Darwin ordered. "There's also the matter of the stragglers. Obviously some people won't show up for a vaccine, what do we do with them – if they were on the chosen list?"

"They could still be turned, we might just have to be more aggressive with them, maybe show a little teeth at their door to gain submission." Bobby Fletcher stated as though it was no big deal.

Around the same time the wood doors to the dinning room slid open and lunch was served. The group retired to the dinning room once again to feast on what mortals would call pure decadence. Cucumber sandwiches on home baked sourdough bread, dill chicken salad on multigrain and Philadelphia Cheesesteak rounded out the top three sandwiches, beating out Salmon and Tuna. The soups were traditional but had been engineered with the love only a chef could give. Beef barley made from beef roasted that morning and accompanied with only fresh and local vegetables, Italian Wedding a very uncommon choice and finally spicy Hungarian goulash soup.

Everything was laid out buffet style along the windows overlooking the east lawn for the group to take as much as they wished. The chef had prepared enough food for thirty guests, but looking at the lack of leftovers he questioned whether he had made enough. He was now rethinking his strategy for dinner.

Conversation over lunch varied from topic to topic but the layout for the selection process was finalized. Current members could turn their families

Darwinism

if they chose. Current members could also put forth their recommendations to the selection committee made up of Darwin and Tim. From these recommendations would come the bulk of the chosen. Darwin and Tim would select anyone they wanted based on the agreed criteria. Newman would provide a list of all known and suspected criminals in New Haven who would automatically be purged from the list. Darwin knew that the afternoon session would be the long and most important part of the day. At one o'clock that afternoon they retreated to the grand fire place in the sitting room to begin drinking cocktails.

"Seven thousand." Darwin stated standing in front of the fireplace as his pack looked on. "That's how many I expect to remove from New Haven. That should leave us roughly the same amount as members. The question I have to the group is, how do we move that many people up to the camp without raising suspicions?"

Robert Fletcher was first to respond. "Lockdown." He stated simply while the group looked at him in confusion. "We need to seal off the town, sever all communications both ground based and wireless and put up a multilayered perimeter around the town to catch anyone who might try to make a break for it."

"That's all well and good but I think we need to get them to want to leave their homes willingly." Jane responded.

"How do you get seven thousand people to want to leave town? Mind you it will be less than that, maybe three to four thousand. We're bound to get at least several thousand using the vaccination plan." Dr. Gagnon put forward.

Newman piped up. "A well crafted town emergency. With communications down and if we cut the power, people should believe whatever we tell them, especially if it's time sensitive – they won't want to stay to see if it's true. A flood might work, or some kind of chemical spill on the main line of the railway."

"Yes, that would work!" Pat O'Donnavan declared. "A few years back we looked at disaster preparedness in this town. A chemical spill was one of those plans. A cloud of cyanide gas or something similar would be enough to enact the town's evacuation strategy. An accident out on the mainline would force the town to evacuate towards New Haven Coal with emergency services funnelling the masses right to where we want them."

"Problem." Benny Yates announced as he sipped on his first ever Long Island Ice Tea. "Do we really want them in their cars? What happens if they start to get nervous; they might try to flee. Plus there is the traffic issue – it could cause things to go much more slowly – this should be done fast. I think we should look at using the old rail line that runs up to the mine."

"Is that an option Clint?" Darwin asked.

"I'm not sure. We have boxcars; they're stored on an old spur line. We could use them but I don't know if the line is intact or safe all the way to town." Clint replied.

"If it did need upgrades, do you think we could get it done in the next week?" Darwin asked looking for only one answer to come back to him.

"Yes sir, I can have it ready." Clint replied with confidence. "We'll also need a locomotive. We can probably rent one from the railway, but I'll have to check into it."

"The railway may insist in using one of their engineers to operate the train if we rent, we should probably consider buying an engine and running it ourselves. Is there someone in town who knows how to operate a train?" Tim asked.

"I think Herman Stein, a patient at the care home, I think he, at one time, operated trains?" Dr. Gagnon said.

"Call over to the hospital right away Evita, have them put a stop order on Mr. Stein until we can determine if he is a railroad man. He may have just beaten Father Time!" Darwin joked to the amusement of the others.

The group discussed and argued on many lewd points throughout the afternoon. The brandy and cognac began to flow heavily around four o'clock and the official plan for the round up was complete. The last major component of the day that had yet to be discussed seemed to be most important. Darwin raised the issue of long-term sustainability with the group and what their future may look like.

"On the issue of sustainability..." Darwin began. "It seems to me we have a few options on the table.

Option one: Keep our holdings in New Haven, and farm whatever comes our way.

Option two: Keep our holdings in New Haven but begin producing food in New Haven.

Option three: Branch out and expand into larger centers, and redirect existing food in those centers to New Haven.

Your thoughts, starting with Newman?" Darwin asked.

"Option one carries the least risks. If we focus on tourists and vagrants we should be able to remain hidden from the rest of the world." Newman suggested.

"But Frank, we must consider supply and demand. If we know that we are required to eat to maintain ourselves then our food supply will need to be significant." Dr Gagnon weighed in on Newman's thoughts.

"If we fed only once a month, and we only killed one human, our supply would be gone within a month. If we shared kills, which would really suck,

Darwinism

we could stretch the current supply out to two months. If we ate only every other month and shared a kill we could last four months. The end result would be the same; we run out of food and face this degradation Darwin has told us about. The only way to avoid catastrophe is to replenish the food source – options two and three." Benny Yates analyzed the situation and told the only answer the group could consider. He was right of course.

"Running out of food isn't an option, so how do we begin to replenish seven thousand, and maintain those amounts?" Vivian asked.

"One of the economic plans Mayor Bollen was working on was a prison that the federal government was interested in building here in New Haven. The popular opinion was opposed to it, but with the change in thinking it might now be possible to draw it here, that could become a source of food. If we told the Feds that we would only take, life sentence and death row inmates, with zero community contact." Evian said.

"A super max is what you are describing. There are watch dogs in place; it might be difficult to keep them out. However if the jail were privatized and prone to violence, we might be able to hide a higher than normal death rate." Newman agreed.

"A prison won't make up a seven thousand per month deficit. It's a good idea but we'll need other options to fill the gap." Darwin returned to the group with.

"Could we send missionaries to the city under the premise they were there to help the homeless? We could put the homeless on a bus with the promise of food and drugs." Tim suggested.

Bobby Fletcher weighed in. "Too much exposure if we put them on a bus and drive them here ourselves. However we could send someone undercover to plant the idea of New Haven in a few street people. If I know drug addicts, they'll flock here in droves if they think there's an easy fix to be had."

The group agreed and added the drug addict solution to the list, but they still found themselves coming up short. The afternoon wore on through six o'clock when dinner was served. Several suggestions were brought forward but the risks in most of the ideas were too great to even be considered. Tour groups from abroad were a great idea in principle except they would be missed if they failed to return. A more robust plan was to infiltrate the Customs and Immigration departments and direct new landed immigrants to New Haven. This idea had merit but would require some work. A spin off to this plan was to lure illegal immigrants to New Haven; they would neither be missed nor counted by the Feds. This plan also had merit but it too required further study. It was around the time the main course arrived that discussion turned to a more unthinkable solutions.

"This pork tenderloin is absolutely fabulous, perhaps the best I've ever had. No, it is the best I've ever had! It's orgasmic." Jane shuttered as her wolf teeth began to show themselves.

All the guests wolfed down their meals which had been made with care and attention. Stuffed bell peppers with couscous and herb garlic goat cheese, roasted vegetables done in a cherry vinaigrette and tenderloin with cranberry-rosemary glaze were all on the plate. To accompany the epicurean food the guests were treated to Boudreaux wine with a hint of oak to compliment the meat. The dinning room filled with the aromas of a five star restaurant and the meat infused the guests with the energy to continue the discussions.

"Thank you for this brilliant treat Darwin, dare we ask who the swine was?" Vivian yarned.

"I believe it was one of the Bollen children." Darwin informed as a matter of fact.

"It is really good; we should think about keeping this chef around, he's very good. I still prefer raw meat, but if I had to have cooked it's still incredibly good." Tim commented to the group.

"Maybe we should turn the help. They're in the kitchen right now eating the exact same thing!" Darwin laughed out loud at his own revelation and he was soon joined by the rest of the group.

"To think, only a month ago I would have found this absolutely revolting, and now I could think of no other way to live. Did you know in my former life I was a vegan?" Jane stated to herself not caring if anyone was listening. She merely looked at her fork and drooled over her next bite.

"Darwin, we never did resolve the issue of the children." Tim reminded.

"Right! Well I have no immediate feelings either way but condemning a child to a child's body for eternity doesn't seem fair. On the other hand, children could become a liability, either through talking to outsiders or, heaven forbid, we kill one during the full moon."

"We are all condemned to our bodies. Being sentenced to live as a child is no different than being sentenced to live as a senior citizen for all time. They all have their pros and cons. I think we should turn the children, but after they are turned our general policy on the subject should be no." Pat O'Donnavan said.

"Are we saying that only to protect our humanity? I think parents should be allowed the choice to relieve their children of this life or give them a new life, but the option to remain mortal should not be on the table. Darwin is correct, we would probably kill them anyway, or they'd blab to the outside world." Angela insisted.

I think we'll let the parents decide on an individual family basis. Turn or kill, but mortality will not be an option. Further to that, parents unable or

Darwinism

unwilling to make that choice will be terminated. I really want to get back to our big problem, sustainability. We have some great ideas but I want you to consider another option." Darwin looked to the group who had all fallen silent, they were ready to hear. "We have decided to bring inmates and drug addicts here, anyone in need for that matter; creating some kind of shelter for the unwanted. On top of that we could create an orphanage to attract more unwanted people. A great stop gap measure to get us through the interim could be cutting off the limbs of humans and eating them a piece at a time to make the livestock last longer. And finally I want the group to consider a breeding program specifically for humans to breed children for our consumption." Darwin threw the boulder in the air hoping someone would catch it; it was a leap into new acceptable behaviours as a wolf. He knew how he felt, how would others?

The room remained silent. The thought had been on everyone's mind for awhile. To kill a child, they could truly call themselves a monster if they killed a child for food. Throughout the day the line had been pushed further and further until finally they had arrived at the conclusion; there was nothing they wouldn't do to sustain themselves. A secret they all carried deep within them was not that they had never considered killing a child; it was that they all longed to do it. It was a temptation they all resisted, but one by one they admitted to each other that the thought was ok, and as it happened, necessary. In reality they were all jumping up and down at the possibility. To have the opportunity to consume pure innocence was about as close to God as they could ever hope to achieve. For the moment, the matter was approved, but constrained to a matter of need, not desire.

The group continued for several hours that evening. The members retired to the sitting room after dinner to continue drinking and telling stories in an attempt to get to know one another. The plan was in place, and within a few days they would be able to proceed. They were engineering death. They were preparing to eliminate those who did not conform to their societal expectations. They were justified and righteous in their actions. They were monsters, pretending to be human.

CHAPTER 24

The coup d'etat was set to begin on Wednesday December 22nd. In the early morning hours on that day a story would begin to circulate in the local media. The town water supply will have tested positive for Microsporidiosis, and although the tests show a low concentration it was belived it was possible that the infection may have existed for a few days. As a percaution the public was being advised to attend a free clinic at the town Legion for preventative treatment and testing. Dr. Gagnon would be on site throughout the day to answer questions and to put peoples' minds at ease.

The infection itself caused nothing more than diherra, but it could be extremely dangerous for indicviduals with a compromised immune system. The plan was to illicit concern among the local residents without causing a panic. Throughout the day the clinic would divert indiduals who were not on the chosen list to a transport that would move them up to the mine. These individuals would be given a seditive in the treatment injection which would allow the medical teams to move them without conflict. The chosen citizens would be given an injection with the gift and a sedative.

The sedative for them would work more slowly and the receipiant would be warned of drowsiness within two hours of the injection. This lead time would allow the newly infected time to go home and sleep through the round up. However, there was a problem with the chosen citizens coming to the clinic too close to the commencment of phase two. In that case the sedative would not be working and it was likely that some of the newly chosen would end up

Darwinism

on the deportation transports. To deal with this issue, Dr Gagnon opted to inject a luminescent dye into anyone chosen from two o'clock onwards so they could be easily identified and sparated from the mine bound citizens when they were received at special handling.

By the afternoon on the 22nd the plan would move into the second phase. The road to the mine would be sealed off through an improtu landslide. Shortly after that, at three o'clock preciscly, the electricity would fail, communications would go down and word would reach town of a toxic cloud moving towards New Haven. The evacuations would begin at three-thirty at the rail station. Twenty boxcars with a capacity to hold one hundred and fifty people per car would mean that one transport could move three thousand people. This would become the tricky part of the operation.

The appearance had to be maintained that the train just happened to be there and ready to go. If anyone began to suspect something was a foot there might be a panic in town and control could become difficult. Speed was essential, as long as the threat of toxic fumes existed it was felt the towns people would be more than happy to over fill the railcars in an effort to evacuate the town quickly. For phase two to succeed it was felt it would need to be carried out within an hour. Anymore time than that would give the deportees time to talk, research and look around.

Phase three of the plan was to begin searching for anyone who had yet to be accounted for on either list. Until all names had been accounted for, the town would remain in lockdown. Unfortunately, keeping the town in indefinite lockdown was not practical because it would draw attention from the outside world. This phase would also need to be conducted as swiftly as possible.

At five in the morning the outer most perimeter of the blockade began tightening its grip on New Haven. Road closure signs were placed on all access roads into New Haven along with armed guards who were not to appear intimidating but should be able to respond if the need arose. Security forces under the banner of the New Haven Police Department would stop all incoming vehicles; those who were not residents were turned away because of a police incident. Area residents were allowed to proceed into New Haven without issue. Any vehicle attempting to leave New Haven would be stopped at a blockade setup two miles before the outer perimeter and turned back to New Haven; they would be told the road was closed until further notice. If anyone tried using an alternate route they would find the same situation. If people began asking too many questions at the blockade they would be detained and sent to special handling immediately. If they happened to be red marked the security forces would bite them on the spot and before sending them back to town after they had been properly motivated.

223

Mark Fuson

On the security line it was bitterly cold in the first few hours of the plan. Traffic had been non existent but they knew it was not to be that way all day. Delivery trucks began pulling up to the border around seven that morning and each were told the road to New Haven was closed until further notice. All other access routes into New Haven had load limits or were too narrow for semi trucks to pass. The first car trying to get into New Haven was a problem. Sam and Gertrude Feltstein were up from Rocky Mountain Springs visiting their daughter's family for Christmas. Security was unable to sway them into turning around.

"Sir, I'm sorry, but all access to New Haven is currently blocked due to a police incident." The security contact informed the elderly driver.

"Sonny, I'm going to see my grand-babies for Christmas. Now you can either arrest me, or let me go, but I'm going to New Haven."

"Let me speak to my section commander, sir." The guard replied.

The old couple sat patiently it their Lincoln Town Car with the backseat loaded with beautifully wrapped gifts. They watched the odd sight in front of them as the security personnel ran back and forth talking to one another passing around a cell phone. The security officer that had initially talked to them returned to the vehicle after a few minutes shaking his head.

"Sir, proceed slowly up the road. About a mile up you'll find a dirt road on the right. Stop there and someone will come and get you. You won't be able to get into New Haven in this car, but you can park it and get it later. Our men will pick you up and drive you to your daughter's house. That's the best I can offer you." The officer stated.

"I guess we'll take it. When will we be able to get our car?" Old man Feltstein asked.

"Probably tomorrow, our officers can call you and then drive you out to get it once the road is clear." Was the answer that security gave.

"That's fine I'm sure my son-in-law can drag his ass off the couch long enough to drive me out here." Feltstein joked. "Why exactly is the road closed?"

"You know, it's kind of complicated. Why don't you drive on ahead, you should be able to see why once you're a little further up the road. It really is quite amazing." The security officer lured the couple in with.

"Thank you, I will. Have a Merry Christmas officer." Feltstein said with a sarcastic tone.

"Same to you sir."

The big Lincoln drove slowly ahead through the perimeter. Feltstein honked as they passed the last barrier and security vehicle. The old couple vanished over the rolling hill on their way to celebrate the holidays with their Catholic son-in-law.

Darwinism

"What happens to them now, sir?" An officer asked.

"They're being taken to special handling. Our orders are now to apply protocol to any out of town visitors who have family in New Haven. We check our lists, and deal with them accordingly. I guess it's easier to bring them in and clean up the mess later than to have them leave and report to the world what's happening here."

That morning saw seventy five vehicles attempting to enter New Haven. All of them had family they were visiting for Christmas. The split was about sixty-forty, with sixty percent of the visitors being sent to special handling. The forty percent was enticed into a private area for induction; all fought and screamed but were eventually brought over to acceptance. Security personnel guarded the new inductees in a barn until it was safe to release them with their new gift. Darwin sent direction that any of the new inductees who were found to not fall within the acceptable norms of induction should be disposed of.

The new werewolves did not go on to New Haven. They remained at the barn where they were fed an alluring meal that helped to properly motivate them. While under the spell of the blood, interrogations occurred to ensure their conformity to the ideals of the group. Two of the new werewolves were found to have criminal records and were lead into the woods where security personnel sliced the heads off of the unintended creations.

Another accident was a family friend tagging along for the holidays who was a Muslim; he too was disposed of in quick action. Rules were rules and Darwin did not want to interfere in the agreed upon laws.

*   *   *

The Legion was set up and ready to receive the first wave of people. There were forty nurses on hand with the hopes of processing in the neighbourhood of five thousand people. The plan now called for a general emergency and anticipation of who would show up to the clinic now became a matter of chance. There was the possibility that far fewer would show up, or far more. The Christmas season also made it difficult to calculate how many residents had left town for vacations and family gatherings.

The fire department began driving the streets at six that morning along with the New Haven Police Department using loud hailers to notify the citizens of the water problem and of the clinic that had been set up. On the television an emergency message was broadcast on a local channel assuring the problem was being taken care of, but to avoid drinking the water. The announcement encouraged citizens to attend a free clinic at the local Legion that would open at seven that morning where they could receive a preventative treatment and information. A paper campaign was also underway with lamp, telephone poles and residential front doors being plastered with the health warning. All bulletins reminded the townsfolk to remain calm.

At seven that morning the line stretched around the block and hundreds of people could be seen funnelling towards the Legion. When the doors opened the people had to give their name and identification to be checked off the list. The lists that had been provided to the check-in tables were in two separate books prepared ahead of time. The red book was for the chosen ones, and the black book was for the deportees. There were twenty check-in stations but the medical staff had the ability to add more if the demand was there. The lists were an essential part of the plan; knowing who had checked in and been blessed or deported made phase three that much easier. Before moving on to the injections the individual was given a color coded card that they were asked to fill in with their basic personal information. Residents would then be directed to an appropriate station where they handed their card to a nurse who would give the appropriate injection. Later a runner would come by and collect the cards so that the names could be computerized into a new list. This was a check and balance approach to keeping track of the population.

The triage room was divided into two, left for red cards, or right for the black cards. For anyone with a black card they could expect a fifteen minute wait time after the injection to watch for adverse reactions in one of two side rooms near the rear of the building. The rooms were off of the loading dock which made transporting the incapacitated people more private. People with the red card were expected to wait in a separate room near the front of the building for fifteen minutes as well, to keep up appearances. After the fifteen minutes had elapsed the people who had the red card injection were advised to go home.

When the doors swung open promptly at seven the crowd began to push through as though it would get them there faster. Panic was present in the crowd and the first twenty people to arrive at the registration table were all from the Cadmore Avenue area.

Wilma Jestins and her four children were the first to be processed that morning. The obese woman was wearing thick rubber boots, a bright flower dress and a Hells Angels leather jacket. With one toddler in arm and three more in orbit she marched up to the desk and slapped down her identification. "So what the fuck is wrong with this town, trying to kill our kids with poisoned water!" She commented so the whole room could hear.

The young greeter took the identification and scanned the black book, first finding the entire Jestins family listed. "Mrs. Jestins and the children please fill in these black cards and then proceed to the triage where you will receive treatment." The calm register informed.

Darwinism

"I'm suing this town for all it's got!" She yelled as she moved on to a table to fill in her black cards.

In the first five minutes of being open ninety-five percent of those seeking treatment were from the black book. Dr. Gagnon scanned the room to find all the seats on the right side of the room now full with only one person being blessed on the left side. Jim Baker, owner of Baker the Baker, was the first that morning to receive the gift. Jim owned the bakery and was considered to be a very kind man whom everyone in the community looked up to. Jim often donated cookies and cakes to local events and his prices were reasonable. The new community would need a baker, and Jim was excellent at it. The decision to bring him in to the family was an easy one for the committee to make.

Wilma Jestins moved her clan towards the waiting room after her injection where she was told there were free coffee and donuts, as well as juice for the kids. Wilma was never one to turn down free food not to mention the children wanted a donut. Dr. Gagnon approached Wilma and reminded her she should hurry and sit down while the medicine absorbed because she will be dizzy in a few minutes. Dr. Gagnon expected an argument, but he could see in Wilma's eyes that she was already getting drowsy. The good doctor asked some of the volunteers to help her into the waiting room quickly. Wilma did not resist.

Wilma fell asleep almost as soon as she sat in the wheel chair. The children hit the floor seconds after that. The standby clean up crew moved in and picked up the bodies and put them onto a waiting truck. By the time the next black booked people arrived the room was again empty. With the help of the second room they were able to juggle back and forth making sure one room was always empty. While one room was being emptied the other one was being filled. Judging by how fast the sedative worked, Dr. Gagnon was concerned people would not make it to the waiting area before passing out. She decided to put a crew of five people on the floor to herd the black book masses more quickly.

At seven twenty that morning there was a good system in place. The ratio of red book to black book was three to one in favour of the black book but Dr. Gagnon perused the line and saw that the initial burst of black book citizens was beginning to level off. From her vantage point the line seemed to be more mixed which would help to take the strain off the black book side of the operation. She listened in to some of the line conversation which drifted from the water problem, to TV to the rumour of the road closures due to an unknown police incident. The mood still appeared calm and upbeat, overall.

"Dr. Gagnon? Do we have any reason to be concerned? My children and I aren't sick?" A concerned parent asked from the line.

"Yes, in the sense you need the shot. We don't know how long the

Mark Fuson

contaminant has been in the water. The water could cause you to have severe diarrhoea. I know needles aren't pleasant, especially for children, but the medicine will eliminate or reduce any symptoms you may experience. I know you want to do the right thing for your children, and what lovely children they are! What are their names?"

"This is Shannon and this is Brendan." The mother responded.

"What beautiful names!" Dr. Gagnon said. "After you get your shot we have donuts for you, if your mom says it's ok, of course."

"Oh mommy! Please!!!" Brendan begged, drowning out his sister.

"Maybe if you two split one. It's a little early for donuts." The mother responded.

"What are your favourite colors?" Dr Gagnon asked with a sly grin.

Shannon shouted out her answer first, beating out her brother by nanoseconds. "RED!"

"Me too!" Brendan said.

"Well it's mine too. I hope today red is you lucky color." Dr. Gagnon patted them both on the head before walking back inside to monitor the clinic.

At eight thirty that morning the line was no shorter. People from around town were converging on the clinic, most not fully understanding why they were attending. In the hour and half since opening, the clinic had processed nearly nine hundred people. Seven hundred and eleven had been transported to the mine and the rest had been blessed. As the morning wore on the trend continued to be heavier on the black book names but the right side of the clinic managed to keep up. At times people from the black book line were seen looking at the left side of the clinic that was mostly empty. The question could be heard being asked among a few of the waiting black card holders - why the left side was not being used, but no one asked Dr Gagnon, at least not until nine that morning.

"The line would move faster if you used both sides." A large gruff man with a beer belly that hung over his belt stated.

"We are using both sides, sir." Dr. Gagnon replied pointing to the three people on the left side of the room receiving injections.

"Bullshit! What's with the red card and black cards?" He jousted.

"Different serums for different body types. As you can see the majority of people with the black cards are obese." Dr. Gagnon offered knowing that it wasn't completely true looking at the group.

"I'm not fat! I'm in excellent shape!" He retorted.

"I don't doubt that sir, but for the dosage to be correct you need to be with the black cards." Dr. Gagnon stated curtly. "I can see you are a busy

Darwinism

man, clearly you are in a hurry. Let me take you to the front of the line, we'll prioritize you."

"That's better!" He stated with a swagger.

*　　　　*　　　　*

Phase one of the plan was moving along well. The clinic had a little more than five hours to continue the injections before phase two would kick into high gear. At the special handling center the processing was happening rapidly. Truck loads of bodies were arriving every twenty minutes or so. The unloading procedure was done by manual labour that Clint had selected. The bodies were then tossed out of the truck like meat at a butchery shop. From there they were hauled inside a warehouse for processing. Their clothing was cut from their bodies and their jewellery and other valuables - including eyewear - were removed. At that time they were placed on the specialized mine trains, sorted by sex, and taken down to housing. Once underground the jailers would ring the bell and ten representatives from the mine colony would surface and come to the gates to retrieve the new intakes. Under a watchful eye the detainees would take the new arrivals below the surface to be introduced to their new life.

Clint had twenty men stationed at the man gates in the mine with sub machine guns. He had ordered the men to not speak to the detainees, and to shoot them on site if they attempted to do anything other than retrieve the bodies. The first load of unconscious victims was the load with the most challenges. The sedative was continuing to work as expected but Mayor Bollen had decided she wanted answers.

"Why are you bringing these people here? Why are you holding us?" She asked in humanity.

The officers stood silently all in black ignoring her question. Clint approached to give her the instructions. Mike Bollen was representing the men's side of the special handling center and was coming through the gate with his selected workers when he spotted his wife and began running towards her.

"Stop or I will shoot." The guard yelled only to be ignored. The officer fired a warning shot into the rock wall which caused the entire cavern to echo as though he had fired multiple times. Mike Bollen stopped ten feet shy of his wife. This was his first time seeing his wife since he had been detained. He looked at her in horror knowing their situation was precarious.

"You will only do as you are told. You will only speak when spoken to. If you fail to comply you will be punished in the harshest possible way. You are to unload these cars and take the bodies down to level two. Do it now!" Clint demanded in authority.

The group looked at each other, and then to Mayor Bollen for guidance. "Can we please know why we are being held?" The mayor pleaded.

"If you speak again I will shoot your son." Clint said to her with blackness and hate filling his eyes.

"I don't understand?" Mayor Bollen stuttered in bravery.

BANG! The cavern filled once again with the reverberation of the gun shot. The boy sighed and coughed up some blood before collapsing to the ground. Mike Bollen began moving towards his son while his mother began to scream in horror.

"Touch him and your daughter dies!" Clint shouted in malevolence. "Empty this train now!"

The remaining prisoners ran to the train and began grabbing the nude bodies and dragging them through the gates. Mike and Tara Bollen looked at each other in tears but remaining silent. Tara mouthed the words "I LOVE YOU". Mike reciprocated before turning away to his forced job.

Work in the mine went more smoothly after the first shipment. Mayor Bollen did not speak to any of her jailers after the death of her son; she only nodded with a bowed head. With her cooperation phase one went more smoothly. Clint knew that the big operation would be the arrival of the first train later that afternoon. It was possible that three thousand people would all be arriving at once. The mine could accommodate the amount but he had some concern over the abilities to process that number in a timely manner. Three thousand people who were not sedated would offer security challenges. It was possible that uprisings could occur and since the plan was not to kill the food but to preserve it for later use safe and efficient processing would be essential. Clint had already determined the only way he could process that number without issue was to lock the boxcars in New Haven and only do one at a time. Darwin was not thrilled with this solution as he felt it would slow down the takeover too much, causing problems for the left over populace waiting for the train to return to the station in New Haven. One component of the plan that remained constant was - it was all subject to change.

"Clint, outer perimeter security is sending another twenty detainees. They should be here in fifteen minutes. And Darwin wants you to call him." One of workers yelled over.

Clint nodded in acknowledgment. "I'm guessing the arrivals are not sedated?"

"Nope, wide awake, and very cranky!"

"Consider it a dress rehearsal for later today. If we can't handle twenty at one time, how are we going to handle a hundred and fifty?" Clint barked back as he climbed aboard the empty mine train to begin the ride back up to the surface. The inmates had moved the entire load through the man gates

Darwinism

and were on their way to level two. Another load would be coming down in the next few minutes, but Clint's attention could be elsewhere.

Clint returned to his home where the bustle of the outside operations was muffled. He sat down in his recliner and dialled Darwin. The phone rang in his ear four times before Darwin answered. Darwin could be heard yelling at someone as he answered his phone.

"Yeah!" Darwin barked into the phone.

"Dude, what's up!?!" Clint greeted in his human façade.

"Clint, can you spare some of your men? I have a situation brewing in town that I need to squash and Newman's men are already stretched pretty thin to handle it on their own." Darwin informed.

"I could spare twenty or so, as long as the live shipments were more staggered, or at least sedated. Why, what's the issue?" Clint inquired.

"The communications office intercepted a phone call to the outside. It was to the health ministry and they began asking questions about our water problem. We cut the call off before anything damaging was said, but we've got a group of dissidents beginning to ask questions, and it's spreading. For the moment we've disrupted communications in that area, and we're using cell phone inhibitors in that neighbourhood to eliminate the problem. But that's only a band-aid solution; we need to quell it now." Darwin said.

"Sure thing dude, where do you want them?" Clint offered in obedience.

"Sixth and Douglas in ten minutes. Make sure they're dressed in civilian clothing; I want them to blend in. Tell them to come armed, they'll be back up for Newman's men should things go sideways." Darwin ordered.

"Yes sir!" Clint replied before hanging up and rounding up his men.

*   *   *

The group was really good at assembling in short order. They were like a small military that could march throughout the night and enter battle the next morning and still fight like warriors. Special Handling had sent twenty guards at random by transport down to Sixth and Douglas. The group dressed in the back of the truck as they sped towards the scene. Eleven men and nine women dressed in basic casual wear which consisted of jeans and/or slacks and a sweater. Each of the personnel had a Glock in the belt line of their pants which they were ordered not to use except in intimidation.

Three women dressed in business suits accompanied by two police officers were waiting at the corner of Sixth and Douglas. One of the women was holding a clip board but all three had badges affixed to their clothing. Only one of the guards approached from the truck to receive their orders.

"How many are you?" The lady with the clip board asked.

231

Mark Fuson

"Twenty, including myself." The young female guard replied.

"Good, 617 Douglas is where the people are gathering. We estimate there are at least ten in the house. The plan is to go to the door and tell them they've all been exposed to high doses of the bacteria and they need immediate treatment. We're telling them that the source of the contamination was found on this street. We want you out walking on the sidewalks, if things aren't going well we might have you move in to assist. Get a few of your people in behind the house in case they try to run. There's an alley behind the house, post them there. The key here is to minimize the attention we draw. Ideally they will let us in to the home and we can sedate them inside." The health official reported.

"What if they don't let you in?" The guard asked.

"We'll cross that bridge when we come to it. Right now we need to deal with the immediate problem. Let's get to it!" She demanded.

The health officials and the two male police officers turned and began walking down Douglas Street. On Sixth Avenue twenty people began walking around attempting to look inconspicuous. The men and women paired off holding hands as though the street had filled with lovers. The leftover group of two men just walked together as though they were friends enjoying the day. The effort to blend in was forced and from a distance the streets looked as though a poorly laid sting operation was in progress.

As the female health officers marched past 613 and 615 they could feel the eyes watching them through the curtains of the neighbouring houses. Their every move was being watched and getting inside the house was now more important than ever. The group rounded the open gate and goose-stepped their way up the cobblestone path to find the front door of the modest sized bungalow opening.

"What's this?" The short stocky man asked.

"Mr. Apcot, I'm Helen Maginot of the New Haven Health District. As you may have heard we have a bacterial contaminant in the water and we believe we've isolated the problem to this street. We believe anyone living in this area may have been exposed to a rather high dose of the contaminant. We'd like to examine everyone in your household and offer free treatment. If you have been exposed you will become very ill in a short time." Helen stated in as much of a professional tone as she could muster.

"We're aware of the clinic downtown. If I want treatment we'll go there. Thanks for stopping by." The man slammed the door but not before rolling his eyes.

Helen slapped the door with her palm and shouted through the wood. "Sir I don't think you understand the severity of the situation!"

The door swung open and the little man was again in the doorway. "I believe this is still a free country. My family and I are refusing treatment. Something stinks about this. The fact that you brought the police with you tells me something's wrong with this whole thing. Now GET OFF MY LAND!" Once again the door slammed shut.

Helen thought to herself for a moment. She turned and looked to the street to see more and more heads popping out from the curtains. "We need to regroup, this isn't working."

"Excuse me ma'am. Did I hear you say the contamination is from this street?" A woman in a house coat hollered from the next house.

"Yes, you really should get your family down to the clinic." Helen replied as she turned and began walking away from the dissidents' home. She pulled her cell phone out to call Darwin but found she had no signal. The woman in the housecoat retreated in doors and could be heard yelling to her children to grab their coats.

"What do we do now, Helen?" Her colleague asked.

"I need to call Darwin, we're drawing too much attention with this plan. We may need to initiate phase two earlier than planned." Helen marched back to Sixth Avenue accompanied by her group. The sound of the residents talking about the problem could be heard spreading throughout the street. Was the talk about the water or was it the same belief of 617 that the water problem was a scam? The family in 617 stayed inside and did not appear to be spreading rumours, but the security kept a close watch on the situation.

Helen had to drive four blocks away to use her cell phone. At Tenth and Pine her signal returned and she dialled Darwin's direct number. Darwin answered on the first ring

"Helen, report." Darwin ordered.

"They're not budging and we've drawn a lot of unwanted attention. For the moment the street seems to be buying the water story, but 617 isn't."

"Have they tried to flee or talk to anyone else since you arrived?" Darwin asked.

"No, they've stayed inside, except for my brief conversation with Apcot." Helen replied.

"Do you think we can keep them under surveillance until three o'clock?" Darwin conferred with his ground troops.

"I don't see why not. Other than our lack of man power we should be able to keep them inside for another three hours. If other issues in town arise though, we might be in for some real trouble. I'm wondering if we should initiate phase two now, sir?"

Darwin remained silent for a moment as he pondered the possibility. "Is that really necessary? The clinic is working well; we've processed more than three thousand already and initiated another fifteen hundred. I'd like to keep the pace up until three if we could. Phase two is going to be a challenge, the fewer people left on the streets the easier our job will be. Tell Special Handling to maintain ten of their people down there, if they need to react then do it. Communication in that neighbourhood is severed; I don't see what damage this guy Apcot could do to us." Darwin hung up not waiting for Helen's response.

"Problems?" Benny Yates asked.

"Nothing serious. We've got it under control for the moment. Just some guy who questions authority trying to bring in outside parties to investigate the water story. We cut communications to that area and his house is under surveillance, everything should be fine." Darwin mumbled to himself as he slouched into Mayor Bollen's leather chair. City Hall was deserted and he and Benny Yates were the only two in the building both acting as coordinators for phase one.

Darwin got up from the desk and moved to the window. Through the curtains he could see the line of people up the block waiting for their treatment. The people in the streets around city hall and away from the Legion seemed to be thinning out, the town was becoming dead.

"How long do you think communications will be down after phase two begins?" Benny asked as he plugged away on his lap top.

"I don't know, hopefully no more than that fifteen or sixteen hours. I'd like to be back up online by morning."

"Damn, I'm going to miss my show tonight." Benny replied still working away on his computer.

"Which show?" Darwin asked still watching the street.

"Prison Row. I think it's a fun show; pretty insane." Benny chuckled to himself.

"You can always record it and watch it when things are calmer." Darwin calmly replied.

"I'll have to wait for the DVD to come out. I'll buy the whole season. I guess I'll just have to miss out today." Benny replied quietly.

"Just record it, how hard is that?" Darwin replied. "Look, Santa Claus is in line, wonder if he's red or black?"

Benny jumped from his desk and came to the window and began laughing at the sight. "Santa as a werewolf that would be awesome; of course he might taste good too!" Both Darwin and Benny chuckled a little more before Benny returned to Prison Row. "I can't record my show, the cable will be out."

Darwin looked at Benny and realized his error. "Right, the power will be out."

"And the cable." Benny replied.

Darwinism

"I'm sure we can get a generator and you can still watch your show." Darwin offered, attempting to be a good employer.

"Darwin, the cable will be out. Communications remember?" Benny stated to Darwin like he wasn't being heard.

It dawned on Darwin what Benny was saying. "Internet on cable! FUCK ME!" Darwin ran to his desk and picked up the phone dialling frantically. A moment later the line was picked up. "This is Foster, cut the town's cable, and pull the records for 617 Douglas– billing name Apcot. I need to know if they have internet on cable and what they've been up to in the last hour."

The room hung in silence and a voice in could be heard speaking to Darwin. A moment later Darwin said "Thank you." And he hung up.

"Benny, we need to initiate phase two. Call Tim and have him detonate the explosives at the earliest possibility. Get a hold of Newman and O'Donnavan and put them on standby and advise Clint to prepare to receive new intakes en masse. Also contact Vivian and have her get over to her station to put out any rumours in her media circle." Darwin ordered as he threw on his jacket.

"What happened?" Benny asked in shock.

"Our friend Mr. Apcot has been sending emails around town. He's also trying to contact other health agencies and the media." Darwin said.

"Where are you going?" Benny yelled as Darwin moved to the door.

"I'm going to the clinic to get Gagnon ready for the switch over. Then I'm off to the rail yard." Darwin informed as he ran from City Hall. Phase two was beginning, more than two hours ahead of schedule. Everything was in place, but the numbers they would be dealing with were higher than expected, and processing would take longer.

CHAPTER 25

It took twenty two minutes to get everything into place. At three minutes past one a large explosion occurred ten minutes east of town. It was large enough for most residents in downtown New Haven to hear it. Moments after the explosion the fire department turned on the sirens and raced towards the growing column of black smoke that could been seen in the sky. The residents in line at the Legion for their shots all marvelled and wondered what the commotion was about, but no one seemed overly concerned. At seven minutes past one a second explosion occurred and with it came the simultaneous disruption to the electrical grid. With the power gone the residents now seemed more concerned, knowing the explosion had something to do with the electrical outage. The injection line up did not waver, but everyone remained fixated on the cloud of black smoke.

Inside the clinic Dr. Gagnon was rushing the last of the registered patients through to get them on the truck so the road west of New Haven could be closed. Registration at the front door had now stopped and people in line were told there would be a minor delay until they could determine if their services were required at the hospital. Concern outside the clinic began mounting as people began to realize that the cellular network was not working. One person after another began yelling down the line, asking if anybody had a signal but the answers all came back as a no. The lack of answers put more and more people on edge.

Dr. Gagnon emerged from the darkened clinic at fourteen minutes after the hour to begin comforting the restless masses. She walked up and down the line telling people she was waiting to hear from Chief O'Donnavan, but that she felt the situation was probably better than it looked. A blown transformer or a car accident that hit a power pole; it was all possible. Dr. Gagnon's presence on the line eased some of the nerves but people at the rear of the line began to leave.

"Excuse me, Doctor?" A tall and beefy man asked. He was wearing a black leather jacket and he had a salt and pepper beard. Around his head he wore a bandanna and he was clearly a biker from the good doctor's perspective.

"Yes, may I help you?" Dr. Gagnon asked.

"My family came down here this morning for their shots, but I haven't seen them since." He stated politely and obviously concerned.

"What were their names?" The Doctor replied.

"Wilma Jestins and our four children." He said almost in tears.

A siren could be heard approaching at an excessive speed. The crowd including Dr Gagnon could see the Fire Chief burning up the road towards the clinic. As he drew closer the siren grew in intensity causing the children to cover their ears. Chief O'Donnavan slammed on the brakes and came to a halt near Dr. Gagnon. The old chief bolted from the vehicle and ran over to the doctor whispering something into her ear; seconds after that they both retreated inside the clinic. The chatter in the line edged its way up to a dull roar.

Dr. Gagnon and Chief O'Donnavan talked about the plan privately for a moment. In less than a minute a general emergency would be declared and all citizens were to be told to evacuate to the west of New Haven. Around the same time of the announcement it would be learnt that the road running west from New Haven had been blocked by a land slide. After a few minutes of discussion on how to deal with the emergency the suggestion of the old mine railway would be made. If all went well the masses would accept that solution like sheep and the evacuation could commence. The next hour would tell the tale.

"How many did we get?" The chief asked.

"We deported a little more than four thousand. The blessed was around two thousand." The doctor said.

"You did well considering you had less time than originally planned. Do you think the next part will go smoothly?" He asked.

"How can it, more people, we're rushed and stretched pretty thin. Plus we have some residents who've noticed their loved ones are missing. If they start talking to others people may begin to question the story." Dr. Gagnon said worried.

"People want to believe Evita, do you really think anyone could put together the truth, and stop us? Anyone that gives us trouble we can deal with."

"You're right, I guess." She replied in a more sombre tone. "I guess it's show time!"

The two New Haven officials returned to the street. Chief O'Donnavan got into his car and turned on his public address system to inform the people nearby of the situation.

"Ladies and Gentleman, this is an emergency. As Fire Chief for New Haven and the surrounding areas I am declaring an emergency and ordering a general evacuation of New Haven. A cloud of toxic smoke is drifting towards downtown New Haven. This smoke, we believe to be cyanide, is lethal in prolonged exposure. Currently all roads east of New Haven are impassable, residents are advised to proceed west to stay ahead of the cloud." Chief O'Donnavan dictated.

"Chief!" Another fireman yelled as he ran up the road. The fully suited up fireman stopped at the window of the chief's vehicle and whispered something very quickly before looking to the chief for a response.

Again on the loud hailer the chief spread the word. "Folks, I've just been informed the road just west of town is now impassable due to a rock slide. I want everyone to remain here; we will find a solution in short order." The chief assured.

Darwin surfaced from the depths of the crowd to play his role in the lie. "HEY! CHIEF!" Darwin yelled as he ran over to the car. Darwin spoke loud enough for people nearby to hear him to make his story look good. "My friend owns Clayburn Nurseries at the old mine. He's got the rail line working…it runs west! I think the train is over at the old station right now!"

"Ladies and Gentleman everyone head over to the old rail station! We believe there's a train in operation that can take everyone west towards the old mine. That will get us around the road closure…we can have busses come get us from there. That should buy us plenty of time!"

The frenzy began and the mob moved like a herd of cattle all stampeding towards the old station. The rail yard was in a derelict industrial area about five minutes away from downtown. In this part of town were old auto shops and junk yards. The railway had died a slow death; the mine had been the main reason for the railway. When the mine closed the railway operated for a few more years but due to profitability issues it was closed. When the railway left New Haven the industrial area died too.

The old white train station had been built around nineteen hundred to service the bustling immigration trade of the day. As travel trends changed the passenger service ceased and the building became just a railway office. The building now stood as a testament of a different era. The once proud

Darwinism

building that greeted the colonizers of New Haven would now be their farewell image.

Herman Stein was wearing his traditional stripped railway coveralls as he walked around the FP9-1750 inspecting the last little details of the locomotive. Herman had been a railway man more than thirty years earlier but with the gift now in him he had the energy and the drive to do all the work himself and it was as though the knowledge had never left him. He had enjoyed picking up the locomotive and driving it to New Haven from Beaverton City some two hundred miles away. When Herman arrived at the rail yard to pick up the antique locomotive the sellers could hardly believe how spry the old codger was. The ninety year old newborn werewolf drove the engine back to New Haven and did all the prep work for the big day on his own. Hooking up the box cars brought him back to his youth and he felt like a big kid with a toy train set. Herman knew the plan had been moved ahead and when he heard the roar of people coming he knew it was his time. Herman had the train stopped along an old dock that forklifts could drive directly into the cars from. The plan was to have the townspeople walk into the cars and fill them to capacity in urgency to avoid the toxic cloud.

"What the hell is going on here!?!" Herman shouted with his rejuvenated vocal cords.

The crowd ran past Herman and began filling the box cars without saying a word to the driver. The sound of the crowd was deafening with the screams and tears of the children. The panic they had hoped to create seemed to be present. The sheep dog pulled up next to the station and approached Herman, again for appearances.

"Sir, I'm Chief O'Donnavan. We have a serious emergency and we need to get these people out of New Haven. I am ordering you take them up to the mine as soon as these cars are full!" The chief recited his well rehearsed lines.

"Of course. I know the plan, I ain't retarded." Herman said dumbfounded.

The chief bulged his eyes realizing that Herman had nearly spilled the beans. The chief opted to not correct Herman instead focusing on getting the plan moving. O'Donnavan returned to his car and got back onto the loud hailer.

"People! Once the cars are full Herman Stein has agreed to take us up to the mine. We probably will need to do two trips, so the faster we are loaded the faster Herman can come back for the rest of us." Chief O'Donnavan repeated his message again to keep the crowd moving.

Frank Newman and the security crew arrived on schedule at the station

Mark Fuson

to help maintain order. The wolves watched their prey follow direction and command without resistance. The whole situation seemed all too easy.

"Daddy, where are we going?" One child asked her father as they marched onto the rapidly filling box car.

"We're going on a train ride! Won't that be fun?" The father reassured his youngster.

"Where's mommy?" The child asked.

"She'll be waiting for us when we get there. I promise."

Other conversations in the crowd did question the situation but it didn't seem to stop anyone from continuing to follow the majority. If one jumps off a bridge, they all jump off.

"I know that man driving the train, Herman Stein, I swear he was in palliative care last week." A young woman urged her boyfriend to believe.

"He's on death's door last week and now he drives trains? Not likely! Come on, let's get on before there are no more spots." The boyfriend insisted.

The presence of an escape route actually seemed to calm the crowd. The loading dock was abuzz with people but they quickly disappeared into the cars. Within ten minutes the train was full to capacity and all problems were kept to a bare minimum. New Haven security made the call to begin sealing the box car. Each slid shut with a shudder and a crack. The people caught on the dock ran from car to car trying to find a spot only to be greeted by people struggling to stay in the car without being bumped out.

The panic came not from the box cars, but from those trapped on the dock in New Haven with the impending cloud approaching. When the train was sealed completely Herman climbed into the cab of his engine, blew the horn three times and the train lurched into motion. As the train rolled away people screamed and hollered, begging for the train to stop, praying it would take them as well. The last car rolled past the dock and on down the tracks to the New Haven Coal spur line. When the train was out of sight those left behind had nothing more they could do but wait.

Security tried to assure the stranded that the wait would not be long, and that the wind was cooperating and the cloud was still far enough away from town that the threat was relatively low. People from around town kept arriving at the station from all directions. Some of the evacuees had even found time to go home and grab a bag. Members of the New Haven emergency services were driving around town informing people of the impending doom and where they need to go for salvation. It was perfection.

*   *   *

"Does anyone else feel like something's wrong?" Was the first question asked in box car number three.

Darwinism

"What do you mean?" Was the question that came back from somewhere in the car.

"I don't know anyone who was sick. Do you?" The man asked in general to the whole crowd.

Their car filled with the same answer. NO.

The questioning man continued. "How did they get the clinic set up so fast? And a friend of mine went this morning. He said the clinic was really weird, like people were being segregated. He told me they had red cards and black cards and most people were getting black cards. He also said the shot made him feel funny."

"But what does that mean?" The lady next to him asked.

"I don't know. Something in my gut just says this whole thing is really weird. Too perfect. Then this big emergency and the railway hasn't operated in years, but there's a train, like it's waiting for us. What does a nursery need with a train anyway?"

A man behind the questioner responded. "Why are you on the train then?"

"I went because everyone else was." He responded realizing he was right to be worried.

Further down the train a similar story was unfolding. In the last box car the evacuees were also talking conspiracy with a comical twist.

"We're all screwed now! Big Brother has got us right where he wants us!" A geeky man with glasses announced.

"And we all fell for it! See how gullible we all are. We deserve whatever is coming our way!" His wife confirmed.

An older woman next to them spoke up. "Excuse me; I think your sense of humour is tasteless. There are children; you'll frighten them."

"I meant no disrespect ma'am. I was just trying to lighten the mood." The geek reaffirmed.

"Who is Big Brother?" The old lady asked.

"That's just a term some people, conspiracy theorists mostly, use to describe the government. Big Brother is watching, cameras, police, freedom restrictions...some people believe one day the government will come and round up all the unwanted people and send them away to camps. Crazy shit like that."

"Such a colourful way to describe it. Why would they want to round us up?" She asked in genuine interest.

"I don't know. That's probably why it will never happen." He replied with a smile on his face.

"And yet here we are, on a train, crammed in like cattle. Big Brother

241

may have got you, and you didn't even realize it." The old woman chuckled in delight to herself.

"I don't believe it. Besides, why would anyone want to round up people and send them away? It's ludicrous; it serves no purpose." The young geek rationalized.

"It obviously serves the needs of the ones in charge." She retorted.

"The government would never round up the people and put them in to camps, they wouldn't!' He shrieked in ignorance.

"You're right. They would never do that. Why would anyone?" The old woman lied to put the issue to rest. She closed her eyes and listened to the sound of the tracks clip by under her feet. The car remained quiet for the rest of the trip.

CHAPTER 26

Clint had all available officers on hand to greet the incoming shipment. The train would pull up alongside building one and the extraction team would open the door on the first box car. This was the component of the plan that was left to chance. Clint knew that there was no guarantee that the new arrivals would comply with direction. Machine guns would be pointed at the detainees and discharged in a safe direction if necessary, but shooting the arrivals was counter productive.

Herman stopped the train with precision at the end of the line. Without delay a team of fifteen officers approached box car one with a ramp and snapped the latch back, sliding the door open. The compacted group of travelers were greeted to men in black with machine guns pointed at them. On seeing it for the first time, everyone knew the story they had been told was a ruse.

"Everybody out, follow the yellow line. You will not be harmed if you obey." A man on a loud hailer shouted.

The train car of people looked on in shock and refused to move. The guards looked to each other to determine their next move. One of the young protégés of Clint walked up the ramp and grabbed a young boy no more than five years old from the arms of his mother. The officer promptly shot the child in the face.

"MOVE NOW!" He yelled to the car load of disbelievers.

The screams began along with the bawling but the car unloaded. The citizens of New Haven marched over the child's body making every attempt to not look at him, but everyone saw him. His lifeless body continued to spurt blood from his face in weaker and weaker streams. His blood streamed down the ramp in a river causing several New Haven citizens to slip and fall. The car was empty within a minute. For the plan to succeed they would need to move faster.

Building one of the complex was nothing much to look at. Clint had it converted specifically for special handling which really didn't entail much. The building was nothing more than an empty warehouse now but in the mine's heyday it had been the machine shop. As the first load of people arrived into building one they were instructed to disrobe. The group was reminded of the child and what could happen to more of them if they chose to resist; quick compliance was recommended. Once the group was naked and their clothing was piled into several carts to be moved later. Jewellery, wallets, purses and any other personal items were placed into a separate pile. When this critical phase was complete the new arrivals moved on to identification. The group was kept together at gun point, and resistance was no where to be found.

Identification occurred in a separate area of building one. This part of induction was essential to phase three. The hope was to have all bodies accounted for which would eliminate the worry of escapees. The order was a tall one, but Clint would attempt to catalogue all of his inventory to achieve the goal. While group one was in identification box car two was unloaded. The guards made a special point to show the child which appeared to help reduce resistance. Screaming and whining could be heard throughout the rest of the train but there was little else those detainees could do.

"NAME?" The guard shouted from behind the laptop.

"What the fuck is going on?!?" A young man in his early twenties shouted making no attempt to cover his nude body.

A guard came up from behind him and hit him as hard as he could with a hickory stick club on the lower back. The man hit the ground instantly, gasping in shock.

The guard behind the computer asked once again. "Name?"

The young man gasped and coughed stumbling to his feet attempting to put on a brave face. "Allan, Allan Bromberger." He said in absolute distain.

The guard plugged away the information into the computer. A second later his colleague tapped him on the shoulder and stated "Red."

"Good news Mr Bromberger, follow this officer here and he will get you into something more comfortable." The guard behind the computer said with a sarcastic grin. "Next!" He shouted.

Two guards approached Bromberger from either side and grabbed him. He resisted but the officers were stronger than he was. A moment later he was

Darwinism

in a private room and being bit by the officers, beginning his journey into a new life.

"Name!" He shouted.

"Janice Copeland and this is my husband Richard." The timid woman said while holding onto her cowering husband.

"Black," A guard stated.

"Special handling! Next!" The machine at the computer yelled.

Thirty stations were in full operation inside building one. Every thirty seconds a station was processing a new intake and separating them from indoctrination to special handling. The system was working at peak efficiency and within thirty minutes the train was completely unloaded. Only one other detainee was shot and that was a woman attempting to send a text on her cell phone. Cell phone inhibitors were in operation and her attempts were pointless but one of the guards took exception to her lack of interest in following direction. He shot her in the stomach and then strung her up for the next train to see. He hoped she would still be alive when they were finished so he could experiment with her.

Herman backed the train up slowly down the tracks towards New Haven. The remaining people in building one were being processed at identification. While that was happening the first group was arriving at the man gates in the mine. For security purposes the men were bound two by two at the wrist and ankles making resistance more difficult. As a matter of practice the arriving men were Billy clubbed at random to ensure compliance. The men knew as long as they were targeted the women might be left alone. Of course, that didn't stop some of the men from acting out when they arrived on level one.

Some of the men struggled, screamed and refused to walk towards the man gates. The officers present decided to make an example of one of these men. They decided if he didn't want to walk then he no longer needed his feet. The disrespectful detainee and his obedient counterpart were removed from the line and pushed to the ground. The officers put their boots across their necks and applied pressure. Both prisoners then had their ankles placed on the mine track and the mine train was instructed to pull ahead slowly. The wheels of the mine car crushed the bones of the first man in a slow snapping sound. The sound that came from his voice was extreme regret and terror. The second man watched as the wheel approached his own ankles, he knew that soon he would experience a lasting impression of evil. When the train had crossed both men it stopped and the two were pulled from the tracks. They yelled and sputtered in agony. The agitator now had two bleeding stumps and his innocent partner had one still partially attached foot that was hanging by some tissue. His other foot was severed completely.

"Let me help you with that." The guard said to the man who was in anguish and in minor convulsions. The officer grabbed the partially mangled foot and tore it off. The injured man gasped and coughed before passing out. "I'm going to go have a snack; I'll be back in a minute." The guard joked to his friends as he walked away holding the foot.

The bell had rung three times on both the men's and women's sides of the detention center. A delegation from both sides arrived to meet the nude and in shock arrivals. Two young men with tattoos on their neck were instructed to come and retrieve the footless men which they did without issue; they knew all too well the consequences.

*   *   *

In New Haven the streets were nearly void of all life. Most homes remained lifeless but the odd one had smoke rising from the chimney. Newman was driving the streets with his crew rounding up the remaining citizens, still playing the cover story of evacuation. When the last train departed town they would shift to phase three, physical round up with no care for cover story. It was just before two thirty that afternoon, most everyone had fled to the station and was awaiting evacuation. Newman kept up the urgency on his cruiser's loud hailer but to him it appeared that everyone was planning to leave without encouragement.

Out on the town perimeter several townspeople had attempted to flee east even after being told it was impassable. Most of these escapees failed to recognize the gravity of their situation and instead found themselves driving directly into the net. They had known well enough that the situation was a scam but were not smart enough to attempt to avoid capture. In the final hour of phase two some vehicles wised up and began driving through the country side and across farm fields to avoid capture. Newman had put two helicopters in the air to monitor the off road activities. The first was a Ford Bronco gaining airtime off the rolling hills as he hurried away from town. The eye in the sky watched the vehicle's progress knowing the snow would slow it down and possibly stop it all together. Each helicopter had thermal imaging and a shooter on board that would open fire if the escapees began making too much progress. The Bronco was aware of the helicopter which seemed to encourage a more erratic driving pattern. The driver increased his speed which made his jump off the next hill longer and sloppy. The vehicle came down hard and was unable to regain control. It flipped and rolled into a ditch, tossing out one of the passengers before bursting into flames.

On the other end of the town perimeter three people had abandoned their late model sedan and were making their way out of town on foot. In the cold of winter it made hiding, even in dense trees, nearly impossible to escape thermal imaging. The copter hovered just above the tree lines and the

Darwinism

shooter prepared to open fire. If he could land even one shot the ground troops would be able to track the smell of blood and pinpoint their location more rapidly. If they failed to capture the runners here, in another two miles there was ground level motion detectors they could rely on. The motto among the security was, sooner was better.

On the imaging screen the shooter could see three heat signatures running through the trees. In the real world it was much harder to pinpoint them, but based on the heat signature he attempted to estimate where one of the runners would appear. He took aim in a clearing hoping he was right. In the blink of an eye he saw movement in his scope. He fired, nipping his prey in the shoulder. The individual hit the ground and the copter moved in to make the kill shot. The gunman again took aim this time he could see the young man clearly in the scope, the shot was ready and he began to pull the trigger when he noticed it. The man was changing. His eyes were full of color and he was growing canines. His faced darkened with fur and razors sliced through his gloves. The gunman watched as the new partially transformed werewolf got up and growled at the helicopter in anger. The gunman decided to use the new ground troop to do their work. Returning his attention to the monitor he found another runner. Once again he took aim through his scope hoping to catch a quick glimpse of the next runner. One shot and some blood would be enough for the new member to lose control and chase down his former friend. On the other hand the second runner might also be a werewolf. The gunman was anxious to see which story was true.

The copter circled around a bluff where they found two women huddled together next to a boulder. The gunman took quick aim and fired a shot into one of the women's legs. Blood sprayed from the wound marking the other woman, but the two stayed together crouched by the rock. The helicopter maintained position but did not fire another shot. The shooter could see the injured woman was not changing from the pain of the gun shot. He prepared to finish off the two, unsure if the former friend would make an appearance, but at the last moment the new creature leapt from above. Even over the roar of the rotors the screams could be heard as the females realized what had happened to their friend who was still partially dressed. The monster approached the two girls and tore them apart within seconds. They didn't even resist, which the shooter found to be very erotic. With a growing lust of his own and a set of teeth to prove it, he waved the pilot on to continue patrolling. He was jealous of the new wolf and the fine meal he had just had.

On the dock at the train station the crowd waited nervously. Jim Baker had woke from his slumber, groggy but feeling good. Dr. Gagnon had pulled him aside when he arrived at the train station for evacuation and forced him to feed from her. Once he understood what he was he became part of the plan.

Mark Fuson

Jim went to his shop and loaded up all the baked goods he could and brought them over to the dock to help keep people at ease. A Christmas choir was also on hand to create a festive mood that the children seemed to enjoy. The horn blasted on the train which alerted the excited children of the impending ride. Darwin could see the Christmas theme on the dock was working very well to create a calm atmosphere, which he wished they had utilized more of in the early part of the day. Overall everything had gone well and there had been fewer problems than even he had anticipated. In a few minutes the final train would be full and they could do a final sweep of the town looking for the stragglers.

"Have you heard from Clint?" Dr Gagnon asked Darwin as he munched on a relatively fresh donut from the bakery.

"No, that's the problem with our plan. All communications are down, and it affects us too. That's why everyone has a part to play, and they're expected to do it with out direction from me. I guess since the train is back it went well. I was hoping it would have been here sooner, but the crowds seem to be relatively calm. Your baker and choir idea was brilliant, it really helped!" Darwin said in admiration.

"Thank you sir." The doctor humbly accepted from her master. "I've been meaning to ask you. Your original plan was for roughly a fifty-fifty split between red and black, but it seems to me we were closer to thirty-seventy red-black. Am I wrong?"

"No, you're not wrong. We decided to cut back on the chosen because the selection in the town was limited, more so that even I thought. On top of that, life will be easier with fewer mouths to feed and more food in storage." Darwin stated as the boxcars came to a screeching halt. The children cheered along with the adults.

The boxcar doors were opened by the anxious people. As the doors slid open the dock emptied in quick succession. The second train would not be full, that much was clear within a few seconds.

"Is that all?" A New Haven police officer asked in the direction of Dr. Gagnon and Darwin.

"Seal them." Darwin ordered in view of people in boxcar six who seemed puzzled why the young man was giving direction to the police, but no one said anything until it was too late.

"WHAT THE FUCK IS THIS!" Echoed along the dock from one of the cars.

Security ran to car six along with Darwin and the doctor to find people trying to leave the car. Security forces began forcibly pushing the residents back into the carriage.

Darwinism

"Time is short, people; everyone must be on board the train needs to leave!" One officer implored.

"IT SAYS IT'S A TRAP! A TRAP! WHAT THE HELL DOES THAT MEAN???" The frantic woman screamed wielding a note in her hand. "And there's blood on the paper, and on the door in here! It's fresh!"

"Someone's idea of a sick joke, no doubt. Please people, we need to get moving!" The officer again begged.

A young woman charged the officer from the side and stabbed him in the eye with a nail file. He screamed in pain as the wolf in him began to emerge. He hit the woman with the back of his hand propelling her back into the car. He roared at her exposing his teeth and eye, but only for a moment. The sight was enough to cause car six to panic as everyone pushed to the far corner of the car to escape the man with the protruding nail file. Newman ran up from behind and pulled the officer away, and the door quickly slammed shut.

News of the trap spread from car to car down the train, but all doors were sealed and the train began rolling towards the mine. They were too late. They departed New Haven, leaving the membership on the dock to gloat in their victory. Those present shook each others hands and patted each other on the back in a job well done. Even the werewolf with the nail file in his eye took a moment to celebrate before mustering the courage to pull it out. The plan had been executed in an exceptional time that exceeded everyone's expectations. The lack of problems and swiftness that issues had been dealt with pleased Darwin immensely.

All that remained was to go house to house and remove the few people in town that remained. Perimeter security would function at full capacity throughout the night or until Darwin declared the removal complete. His gut feeling was the final phase of the round up would be complete by midnight. As dusk approached the group pulled out the champagne to begin the early celebrations.

"Here's to phase three, may it go as swiftly as the others!" Newman raised his glass in honour of the work they had completed.

"I want to thank all of you for showing the courage and strength to be able to do this work with such professionalism and speed. I owe each and every one of you a debt of gratitude for allowing this plan to come to life. I know it must have been hard for you to see people you may have known, knowing full well where they were going. We are superior to them and not everyone can be like us; never forget that. Those who have been selected for special handling should be pitied. This world was not for them. Now that we have removed the cancers of our town we may begin to thrive and build a civilization that will be the envy of any outsider. Our power will give us the wisdom to flourish and perhaps in time we can expand outwards. We build a better world on the backs of those who sought to ruin the previous one. What we do here now is the purest good known to humanity. We are faced with challenges that we tackle and resolve. We don't run and hide or plead ignorance. Today is the birth of our world, from here on out, we are gods!" Darwin declared to the delight of his followers.

"In celebration of our victory tonight I declare phase three to be a feast! Put on your best face and seek out those who attempt to defy us. Use you power to hunt your prey as nature intended us to do. Eat until you can eat no more. LET THE HUNT BEGIN!" Darwin announced to great fanfare.

There on the dock the group began to change, throwing down their champagne glasses and howling in freedom. They ran through the streets that night in celebration of their new world.

All civilizations end but on this night theirs was beginning.

CHAPTER 27

The depths of the coal mine offered no warmth. The walls, floor and roof were all black and the air was old. The lights strung along the wall just amplified the blackness of the surroundings. If the situation wasn't so bleak the caverns themselves would be enough to drain the people of their fight.

Six thousand-five hundred women and children were now living on A2 and A3 of the women's facility. The last shipment of people had arrived the day before and now all activity on A1 seemed to have ceased. In the early hours of the populating Mayor Bollen struggled to keep order and calm. As a natural leader she expected the population to band together, to settle in and make sense of the situation. The flood of arriving detainees did not seem overly interested in what Mayor Bollen had to say as she stood at the gateway of A2. Even her three colleagues on the city council appeared to have little interest in working to establish order; they all sat in housing, victims of extreme shock.. The torrent of screaming children and mothers behaved like refugees gravitating towards the basic needs. Those arriving ran to the arms of people already housed in the ghetto that they knew or recognized just so they could be embraced with compassion.

Distribution of the clothing and shelter was done in quick fashion. No one argued what they were given, they were merely happy to no longer be walking around in the nude. All residents of A2 wore the same clothing, hospital pajamas, all in light blue. For footwear they were provided wool socks but no actual shoes. Tarps were given so the residents could set up tent

Mark Fuson

communities along the walls in the offshoot corridors of the mine. No shower facilities were available nor were toilets. Water was only available in the form of bottled and the supply was limited. Food was available in large quantity but it consisted only of crackers and canned meat – but no can openers were provided.

After the first twenty four hours Mayor Bollen realized that sanitation would become a huge issue. The children were urinating and defecating wherever it happened which was creating a sewer like stench in the old air. It was apparent that the adults were following the children's lead. The corridors were filling with a salty humidity that had a hint of ammonia to it.

"Excuse me. Mayor?" A young woman stopped the mayor as she walked the corridors of the mine.

"Yes." The mayor replied.

"I'm Caroline Lutz. Do you have a minute?" The woman asked in sincerity.

The mayor had nothing but time. Most of the inmates did not want to speak to her, or they didn't know who she was. For most of the day the mayor had felt useless. Finally having someone approach her made her feel as though she had a sense of purpose. "Yes of course, I'm still trying to make sense of what happened."

"When I was at the train station yesterday I saw something. I'm not the only one who saw it, but I can't explain it." She said confused, looking at the ground.

"Well, explain it to me the best way you can." Tara Bollen replied.

The woman shook her head a little and looked back to the Mayor. "We were all waiting for the train to come back to get us. There were baked goods and a choir, it was all really festive. The evacuation just didn't seem all that urgent."

"Tell me about the evacuation. Most people down here haven't been willing to talk about it. I've been down here for awhile now; I wasn't there when it all began. What happened?" The mayor asked as though she only wanted to be included.

"It was all day." Caroline said. "It started with the contaminated water. The police and fire department were out urging people to go downtown to a clinic for treatment. I didn't go."

"I heard about it. That was a ruse too. They put people to sleep and brought them here. Some of the ones who were willing to talk told me about red and black cards at the clinic. All the ones here received black. Do you know what that meant?" The mayor interrupted.

"No. As I said, I didn't go to the clinic. I don't drink tap water so I wasn't worried about infection." Caroline replied.

252

Darwinism

"What happened next?" The mayor asked becoming completely caught up in the story.

"That afternoon there was a large explosion east of town. The fire chief declared a state of emergency saying a cloud of poison gas was coming towards New Haven. It was very confusing, for some reason we couldn't leave town by car. They told everyone to go to the train station and that's where they put us into boxcars and brought us here." She continued.

"Who brought you here?" The mayor asked.

"It looked like all of New Haven police, fire and medical services were in on it. Also I saw this young guy at the train station. I don't know him, but he appeared to be giving orders to the police. I heard him yell – seal them! I'm sure he meant the boxcars" She informed.

"Is there anything else you can tell me?" The mayor asked.

"What I wanted to tell you. It's crazy, I don't even know if I believe it." She paused for a moment as she thought back to her last moments in New Haven. "One of the women in our car found a note; it said the train was a trap. She told everyone and they freaked we even noticed some blood in the car that looked pretty fresh. We tried to run from the car but security was already at the door pushing us back in. They kept trying to keep us calm and remind us of the gas cloud. They didn't even seem interested in what we were saying. I don't know what made me do it, but I grabbed a nail file from my purse and I stabbed one of the guards in the eye. I guess my instincts told me we were in trouble. I was so angry that they wouldn't listen to us or let us go. That's when it happened. I only saw it for a moment, but I know what I saw. The man changed. He had fangs and his eyes; I'll never forget his eyes. He let out this god awful roar. I've never heard anything like it. Whatever he was he knocked me down and when I got my eyes focused back to the door it was closed." Caroline stopped.

"Do you really expect me to believe that?" The major responded.

"Look around, do you believe this? Have they even told you why we're here?" Caroline asked in disbelief.

"Newman said we were - the treat. He didn't elaborate." The mayor said to herself now beginning to piece it together. "We should find the others who were in your boxcar, do you know who they were?" The mayor responded as a leader.

"No, but I might recognize the woman who found the note." She replied.

"Well Caroline congratulations, you've been drafted. I need help down here and you seem to have a decent head on your shoulders. I think we need to find others willing to help put up a resistance. We don't know for sure why were here or what we're dealing with, but I think it's safe to say we're in real danger." The mayor concluded.

"What should we do now?" Caroline asked.

"We need to establish some form of order down here. We'll look for the others from your boxcar but we also need to establish some basic rules. Waste needs to be dealt with properly otherwise we'll all die from disease despite what's waiting for us on the surface." The mayor and Caroline continued their conversation searching the masses for people who were willing and able to fight.

*   *   *

On A2 of the men's domain rudimentary order had been established quickly. Luxuries of shelter were not as important as establishing a hierarchy and a plan of attack. Meetings were held almost continuously to discuss the situation and how they could fight back. Inventoried food and water and been declared sufficient to sustain the roughly four thousand men for up to six weeks if they rationed. Distribution of the supplies was closely monitored by the elected committee of the New Haven Fish and Game Club who were the self proclaimed leaders of the testosterone ghetto.

Like all men the bathroom facilities were the first area to be established. An entire corridor in the furthest reaches of A2 was designated the toilet area. No man was permitted to use buckets in the living quarters to store waste as water was in limited supply and the bucket could not be cleaned. The rule was sensible and although some of the men initially opted to defy the resolution, ghetto justice was quickly reined in. The situation in the caverns made physical violence an undesirable solution. The first man caught urinating outside of the designated area was surrounded, pushed to the ground and then urinated on. Another man found with a bucket of waste in the living quarters found his head submerged into the bucket multiple times until he repented.

The men of A2 were separated from the women. They knew the women were in a separate chamber but no one could be sure where that was. The men knew they had an easier situation to contend with compared to the women. The youngest of the four thousand men was fifteen year old Sam Brighton who looked mature for his age. There were a handful of other teenagers in the men's side who appeared to be there only because they had a more mature appearance as well. Boys from the same grade were sent to the women's side because they appeared as children to the induction officers. The lack of children made the men's area quieter and it also gave them more time to calculate their situation.

Mike Bollen was a member of the Fish and Game Club and held a position of authority in the cavern. Rudy Weiss, Carl Daven, Helmet Schmidt

Darwinism

and Alexander Johnson all made up the ruling committee in the men's cave which the four thousand men as whole did not seem to mind. Rudy and Carl had also been sitting members of the New Haven City Council which brought more credibility to the cavern council. There was no where in the cavern where all four thousand men could meet but they seemed to be pleased that a small group of hard working men were discussing the problem and working on a solution. Word spread among the entire population in short order every time a decision had been made.

"I say we stroll right up to A1 and march on out of here. Do we even believe these people?" Carl put to the group who was huddled around a battery powered lantern. The men were sitting on boxes under a tarp which came as close to a meeting room as they could muster.

"I knew some of those guys. Good men. I don't understand what's happening here. I tried to talk to one of them; he just acted like I was subhuman, I didn't even exist." Helmet stated.

"Whatever this is, they planned it very well. The – police – came to my office; they said they needed to ask me a few questions. Once we were in my office they threw me up against the wall and cuffed me. They took me out the back door and tossed me into the back of a van. I was taken right to the mine. I don't think it's because I'm important, I think it's because they already had Tara and I would cause problems as soon as I realized she was gone. That night they got our kids too. Brandon told me they killed his brother at the house." Mike began to sob openly and could not continue. Alexander put his arm around Mike.

"So people, we know we are being held here against our will by good men, or at least men who were good at one time. Why?" Rudy put to the group.

The council sat in silence while Mike blew his nose, attempting to regain his composure. Silence consumed the group for minutes as they combed their minds for a rational solution or explanation.

"Have you ever heard of the theory of Occam's Razor?" Carl asked the group to which he received no response. "It's complicated, but it boils down to – the simplest explanation is usually the correct one. Now if we think about our situation in the simplest of terms can we explain why we are here? What do we all have in common with each other that condemns us to this place?

"I've thought about that, but I can't see any connection. There are poor, wealthy, powerful, working class, young and old and I see no one faith being singled out…I just can't see a connection to any of us." Helmet assured.

"There has to be a connection! Everyone here who was drugged received a black card. We know there was a red card but yet no one here was given a red card. We can safely assume red card holders were spared." Carl hypothesised.

Mark Fuson

"Can we, Carl? Perhaps red cards were sent somewhere else?" Alexander rebutted.

"True, but I think it's a safe bet they weren't detained. If we go on that assumption what can we say about people who were given a red card? Surely someone from the clinic must remember who was in the red card line up." Carl said with confidence.

"I know Albert Hess told me he saw Andrew Collins and his family in the red line. And I haven't seen him here" Mike answered now able to speak again without bawling.

"What's special about Mr. Collins?" Carl asked.

"His family is no different than any other family. Andrew works for the city and his wife is a butcher." Mike answered.

"What does Andrew do for the city?" Carl shot back.

"I think he works at the waste treatment plant, but I wouldn't swear to it." Rudy replied.

"I couldn't help but notice that some of the kids that are here with us are what some call the bad apples. There's quite a few teachers here too and I think I saw the principal from Ridgemount." Alexander threw out to the group.

"There's no one here from emergency services, but most everyone from City Hall is here, but there are a few select people missing. I think we need to go around the mine and make a list of who is here; maybe if we make a list the red card people will be more obvious." Carl suggested.

"What do we hope to learn from this?" Mike asked.

"Knowing why we are here might help us defend what we are up against." Carl replied.

*   *   *

Knowing what time it was in the mine was impossible. No watches or clocks were available and the lights of the mine were always on. The women had considered unscrewing some of the bulbs making sleeping a bit easier but a fear existed that once the lights were extinguished they would not be able to turn them back on. Hours and minutes were as one in the mine which was quickly wearing down the inhabitants.

On the afternoon of December 24 Mayor Bollen was inspecting the various areas of the mine. She was in the depths of A4 which seemed to stretch on for miles upon miles. Deep in A4 it appeared to her that it was nothing more than extra space to accommodate more people. The walls, the corridors the lighting were all indistinguishable from the levels above. Only one thing made A4 an interesting place to visit. The mayor had received a report of a barricade at the furthest reaches of A4 that was new and seemed interesting.

Mayor Bollen and Caroline arrived at the gate after a long walk. The

Darwinism

barrier existed as it had been told to them. The new fencing was flush to the walls, floor and ceiling. Interwoven in the fence was razor wire and one lone sign in the middle of the fence indicated the fence was electrified.

"Where do you think the passage goes?" Caroline asked.

"They don't want us to go down there, that much is clear." Tara responded. "I wonder if they really did electrify it?"

"It looks like it. The wiring for the lighting seems to connect with the fence." Caroline said pointing to the wires. "I bet there's something down there they don't want us to see."

"Like what?" Tara asked.

"A way out." Caroline responded as a matter of fact. The light breeze in the cavern lightly rippled past them, through the fencing into the blackness of the forbidden place. The women stood at the fence holding themselves as they began to shiver.

The siren blasted through the grotto as a loud whooping sound which no human could ignore. The sound muted all other noises and it continued uninterrupted for a solid minute. Tara began running as fast as she could towards the ramp that would take her to the above levels. She knew she had ten minutes to reach level A1 but she also knew that it would take closer to fifteen minutes at a flat out run to reach it. It was a lesson learned for Tara who now knew that she could not venture to the depths of the mine. The only thought that raced through her mind was what would be her consequence.

*   *   *

At A1 Mike Bollen and Clint stood looking at each other in complete distain for one another. Clint taunted Mr. Bollen when ten minutes had come and gone and Tara had not appeared. He suggested that the Bollen daughters be disposed of in retribution but the idea was quickly dismissed in place of a more diabolical plan.

"Your wife must work on her cardio." Clint said mockingly. "This delay is unacceptable, especially for our first meeting. I had planned on giving you all a special treat for Christmas, but now I think I should forget the whole idea." Clint approached Mike rubbing his fingers on his soot covered face.

"Go to hell, you bastard!" Mike announced under his breath.

"My friend, you know the rules, no speaking to me unless I ask you a question. Give me your hand." Clint demanded calmly and calculated. "NOW."

Mike raised his hand towards Clint's midsection. When his wrist was snapped Mike wasn't even aware of it. His hand was now pointed in the wrong direction and it was the sight of this that caused Mike to feel the first bolt of pain. He collapsed to the ground traumatized by his disability. He said nothing as he broke out in a feverish sweat.

"Remember this. Next time I'll sever your arm and make you eat it. If you care about your family you will behave, are we clear?" Clint asked with a smile to the shivering body at his feet. "That was a question for you, you may answer."

"YES!" Mike shouted in hatred.

"Now where is that whore you call a wife. She really is starting to piss me off! Maybe we should hit the siren again. Does she suffer from selective hearing as so many wives do?" Clint taunted which he was growing to love. The pain and fear he inflicted brought him a rush that he could not explain.

Clint's ears perked as he heard the patter of feet rushing towards the man gate. The sound of laboured breathing soon became clear and within a few seconds the small figure of a woman running along A1 towards the man gate could be seen. Clint began applauding the marathon woman and cheering her on.

"Bravo! I hope we didn't catch you at a bad time!" Clint shouted to the woman who was stumbling and working very hard to keep moving. When she arrived in front of Clint she made no excuse for her tardiness. Clint looked her over and he could smell the blood running from her feet which began to stimulate him. "Do you find the stockings inadequate for your living quarters?" He asked the woman who refused to look at him.

Tara would not raise her head and she could not answer him. Through her peripheral vision she could see her husband had been injured and she knew that she would soon face punishment for her inability to follow the rules.

"I asked you a question dear, are you too afraid of me to answer? You shouldn't be; I'm not a monster." Clint stated to the delight of the other guards present in the tunnel with him. "If you don't want to answer me, that's fine, I really don't care if you don't like your footwear." Clint chuckled to the timid woman who was still waiting for her punishment. "I hope you are finding your accommodations satisfactory. I wish I could have done better for you but this was put together on short notice. Actually I could give two shits what you think...I'm a real dick today!"

Again the men in the cavern laughed at the expense of the inmates. While the men were distracted Tara looked up to see if she could recognize her captors. In the brief two second glimpse she recognized one of the guards as the daughter of Evian Pierce, town treasurer. She returned her eyes to the ground waiting for the hit to come, but it didn't. She had gotten away with this glance.

"I have called you here in celebration of the holiday season. Tara, as a gesture of good faith I want you to select twenty children for immediate

Darwinism

release. Mike, I want you to select forty of your members for immediate release. Mike, you may pick anyone you wish, including yourself, but Tara remains here with me. You have twenty minutes to make your selection, I will wait here. Please don't disappoint me. I really want you to renew my faith in the human spirit of cooperation. Go now!" Clint demanded. Tara and Mike turned to their perspective gates for the trip back to A2. "One more thing. Because it is Christmas I'll forgive your little infraction, Tara. But if it happens again I will rape your daughters while you watch, are we clear on that?"

Tara said nothing and continued marching to her hell as her eyes welled up with tears. As she ran along A1 she looked to her side as Mike ran next to her on the other side of the A1 partition. Mike was holding his wrists and openly crying but neither said a word to each other.

*   *   *

Caroline was waiting at the entrance to A2 when Tara came running down the ramp to her. The mayor was sobbing opening when she collapsed into Caroline's arms. "They want twenty children." She gasped out.

"For what?" Caroline asked in concern.

"They said they want to release them for Christmas." Tara said openly crying now as other residents began to circle around the two women. Tara whispered into Caroline's ear what was to be kept a secret. "I think they're going to kill them. We have twenty minutes to pick them. Do you understand?"

Tara looked into her new friend's eyes and she understood the work they now had to do. Caroline announced to the women who were surrounding them. "Listen up people. They want twenty children to for release. They've given us twenty minutes to choose which ones. I suggest we pick the sick children and children with medical needs we can't meet down here. Mentally ill children, diabetic kids, kids along those lines! Fan out, and bring them here. The first twenty kids here are the ones who go. If we don't do this fast they may change their minds, or worse." Caroline sold the story and women scattered like ants.

"They're going to kill them. I know it." Tara mumbled into Caroline's ear.

"I know." She replied.

*   *   *

On the men's side of A2 Mike arrived back at the council room to inform the others what was required. He was ignoring his broken wrist but the sweat pouring from his face showed everyone the agony he was in. Under the privacy of the tarp Mike Bollen informed the men what they needed to do.

"They want forty men to go up to A1 within the next twenty minutes." Mike started with.

"For what?" Helmet asked.

"I think they plan on killing them. They told us it was for release, but I don't buy that. I'm certain anyone we send up there will be dead tonight." Mike replied.

"That's impossible. Those men up there were citizens of New Haven! We don't behave this way." Alex insisted.

"Things have changed my friend, things have changed." Mike replied.

"I trust your judgement Mike; if you think that's what they're doing. What happens if we don't select forty?" Carl asked.

"I don't know. The head guy told me he'd make me eat my own arm next time I got out of line. This time he broke my wrist. Fucker is strong too. He told Tara he'd rape our daughters while she watched. I believe what they say, when it comes to the punishment. Whatever these men are, they're not the men we use to know. I think if we don't give them forty our situation may become worse that it is now. I think it's in all our best interest to give them what they want." Mike informed.

"You want us to send forty men to their deaths?" Rudy asked to clarify their position.

"I wouldn't ask this of you unless I thought there was another way. I think we should pick the old men, ones who have had a good long life. At least we could live with ourselves knowing we sentenced someone to death who would have died from natural causes sooner or later anyway." Mike rationalized within the emerging ghetto law.

"How do we pick them?" Helmet asked.

"Go around and find elderly men who look frail and sick. Tell them they are wanted on A1, we don't know why, but we think they might be released. Leave it at that. Remember we only have a few minutes, make the selections quickly." Mike insisted.

*   *   *

Rumour of the impending release of children spread rapidly among the women and a child's medical status was no longer a concern. The problem was not having enough children; the problem quickly became which children to send. Mothers rushed the landing at A2 begging the mayor to select their children. The mayor and Caroline were taken back a bit. The sight of panic among the women seemed surreal as none of the begging mothers seemed to be considering that the release was a lie. The mothers had decided that any chance for escape to the outside world was better than an existence in the mine. It was a group panic scenario and it troubled the two women in the know that the mothers were begging to have their children slaughtered. They also knew telling the mothers the truth would make things worse for everyone.

"The first twenty only; this offer expires soon, we must bring them up top or none will be taken." The mayor shouted with all her lungs' capacity.

The two women directed children to move up the ramp towards A1 and to stop part way up. Mothers hugged and kissed their children in a hurry wanting their children to be selected and not miss out on the opportunity for escape. Within a few minutes all twenty seats had been filled with more mothers still running towards the entrance with their children in arms. Mayor Bollen began her march up the ramp to A1 directing the children to follow. The kids were all very excited to be leaving and many looked back down the ramp to wave at their moms telling them how much they loved them. The mothers blew kisses and cried watching their children being saved. Soon they were gone, left to nothing more than a memory.

*   *   *

On the men's side of A2, selection of the senior males was progressing. The pressing time constraints forced the council to begin selecting anyone with grey hair. At one point Rudy Weiss selected a man in his forties who he knew had been having an affair with his wife. It was revenge, but in his heart he felt like he had done the right thing.

Mike Bollen marched the forty men who all had smiles on their faces. The group was mostly elderly but a few younger men were in the group. Mike didn't really care. There was no one among the forty that he personally knew and it gave him a sense of calm knowing that the immediate threat to him and his people was, for the moment, over.

"Would you look at that, they're all back in seventeen minutes. I must say I'm impressed. Was it difficult making the selections?" Clint hollered to the approaching groups.

"You know, you people must really work on your communications skills. I ask you a question and you ignore me. Do you have any idea how that's affecting my self esteem?" Clint chuckled in demonic fashion. "I assume you told them the truth, Bollen family?"

"They were told they are being released; just as you have promised." Tara said to Clint as she approached with the children.

Clint looked at Tara knowing she had just lied to him, but he let it go, instead choosing to greet his children. "Hello boys and girls! Are you ready to go home?"

"YEAH!!!!" They all screamed in joy.

"Well ok then, everybody climb on board the train and we'll get you out

Mark Fuson

of here! We've got hot cocoa, cookies and candy canes for all of you on top! YIPPEE!" Clint hollered luring in his victims. The children screamed in joy and happiness and they all climbed aboard without issue. The doors were sealed by the guards and Clint then turned his attention to the men.

Clint looked the group over and commented to Mike. "Interesting choices. I wondered how you would make them. I can see you were going for an older clientele, but a few young ones slipped in there. Did you start to panic, or did you pick them for a more selfish reason?" Clint whispered into Mike's ear. "Gentlemen, climb aboard, let's get you out of here!"

Clint looked at the group realizing they were frozen in place. They had collectively all realized that they would soon be dead and that release would not be happening for them.

"You are reminded your cooperation directly benefits those you have left behind." Clint manipulated.

One by one the men climbed aboard the mine car, most beginning to weep at the realization what was happening to them.

"You bastard, you knew this was going to happen didn't you!" One of the men yelled at Mike who could do nothing but look away in shame. He did, after all, know in his heart he was condemning these men to death.

"I'm sorry." Was all Mike could say as the frustrated and scared men climbed into the train car. Only one man hung back, a senior who seemed defiant.

A guard approached him and told him quietly. "Get on board; you don't want to frighten the children, do you?"

"I have no family or friends in this town. I don't care what happens to them. Why should I die, those assholes in the mine are no better than me." He stated surely.

"Don't be selfish. Through your sacrifice you save someone else. That should bring you great pride!" Clint said to the man calmly.

"I don't want to die!" The man exclaimed in cowardice.

Clint leaned in and whispered into his ear. "Well you're going to, so stop bitching about it. Now you can put yourself on that train, or we will, and I assure you, it won't be good for you if we do it. I'll make it my personal goal to ensure you live your final hours in utter anguish. Are we clear?"

Senior defiance crumbled and the man was lead away by a guard. He was placed on the train which departed right away leaving Clint with the Bollen's once again.

"Well I think that went rather well, don't you?" Clint looked at both representatives who had visible tears streaming down their face. "You're mad at me, aren't you? I want you to know if it were up to me this whole thing would have been handled much better. I don't think we need to conduct

Darwinism

ourselves as monsters. If it makes you feel better, I'll make sure that no one suffers, except for the old man – he really pissed me off!" Clint said with a bit of anger in his eye. "Is there anything I can do to make your Christmas a little more comfortable?"

"Yeah you can…"

"I'm sorry, except for that, good try though Mikey!" Clint interrupted knowing the man was going to suggest release. "I was thinking a long the lines of some hot rocks to warm yourselves with. I can have the guards warm them in a fire on the surface and they can bring them to you, does that sound nice?" Clint asked being a complete ass.

"Blankets would be better…sir!" Tara responded coldly.

"I'm sorry." Clint asked as he approached Tara sticking his face into hers. "Did I hear you correctly? I could have sworn you turned down my hot rocks and requested blankets instead. Well if that's going to be your attitude you can forget the whole thing. You may go now!" Clint marched off to another mine train engine and hoped aboard. His driver put it in gear and chugged away saying nothing more to the detainees.

The guards ushered the Bollen's through their perspective gates back to their hell. As the two marched side by side separated by their mutual barrier Tara attempted to talk to Mike.

She whispered her first statement almost at an inaudible level. "They'll kill all of us."

"I agree." Mike said quickly.

"Can you get to us? Dig a tunnel?" Tara asked.

"Maybe, but where do we dig?" He replied in question.

Tara tried to limp so it looked as though she needed to move slower. "Does your ramp go straight down? No turns?"

"Yeah." He replied quickly

"A4 landing, straight across, should link with ours." Tara offered quickly as the ramp to the lower level appeared for both of them. They said nothing more and returned to their subterranean hell. Tara could only guess if they had successfully created a workable plan. If she knew her husband, he would begin work right away.

*　　　　*　　　　*

Christmas Eve for the women was mostly exciting knowing that some of them had been released. It was beginning to circulate among the group that they were being held for ransom and that soon the police would come to their rescue. Tara and Caroline had no idea who started that rumour but they went along with it and at one point they even convinced themselves that it was true. In the hollow chambers of the women's ghetto they sung Christmas carols and rejoiced in the knowledge that there was a purpose to their captivity and that soon it would be resolved.

Mayor Bollen knew that the situation required a plan of action and that if anyone in the mine had a chance of survival it was through their own attempts at escape. Spending Christmas with the knowledge they would all be slaughtered was a huge burden for the mayor, but she kept silent with the exception of her new confidant. Together the two women sold the concept of ransom which helped give everyone hope.

In the back of Caroline's mind she kept thinking back to the level four gate. Her gut told her this was a way out. She would make it a point to explore this area of the mine further. In the meantime she would sing carols and tell the story of The Night Before Christmas as best as she could recall for the children who were around her. She only choked up once when the —visions of sugar plums danced in their heads. Both Caroline and Tara put on a brave face; they were the only warriors who could fight for their survival. Their heart ached for the children who had been sent to their deaths. They wondered how many more would die before they could escape.

Chapter 28

New Haven was flourishing with excitement on Christmas Eve afternoon. The town was getting ready for a celebration and inauguration of their new world. New Christmas lights were being strung from the lamp posts and every tree in downtown was to be adorned with clear twinkling lights. Christmas wreaths were to be hung in every store window and doorway accompanied with seasonal lighting to match. New Haven would bring its pride in celebration of the holiday season to a new level. Downtown would be a model community that all other towns would strive to be. The atmosphere had to be perfect.

In the evening a celebration in the town square would occur. Roasted chestnuts, snowman making, carol singing and a grand winter ball were all on the agenda. New Haven was to come out in spirit and celebrate the ending of evil and disassociation and begin a new world revived in community spirit and vision. Through the holiday season the ruling council hoped to ignite the town to embrace the new platform, to sell that vision to the world. By example New Haven would become the template for other communities around the country, continent and eventually the world. Societal perfection could only be achieved through a common understanding and likeminded values. The gift was the bridging force that allowed the reinvented people of New Haven to see and welcome the tides of change.

The dark elements of New Haven were gone, purged from existence with lightening speed. It had been necessary; without their removal the relaunching of New Haven would have been impossible. Those who had been selected for the blessing understood fully the ideas and expectations. It wasn't that the new members had no feelings for those who had been taken away. The blessed of New Haven cared very deeply for those who had not been selected. With the gift in their veins they understood that those not selected could never have been a part of the vision, they were simply incapable of ever being anything more than the flawed individuals they had been. For the vision to work it was essential all identified problems be eliminated, whether that be because of substance abuse, criminal behaviour or merely because they abused or took advantage of their fellow man. The chosen of New Haven understood that those not selected were not necessarily bad people; they just weren't suitable candidates for the vision.

Only a few days had passed since the last of the people had been transported out of New Haven. Power and communications had been restored and the registers office was satisfied that all citizens had been accounted for. Vivian Yee had kept New Haven off the radar during the lockdown and once again the roads into New Haven were open for all, not that anyone would come to the out of the way town. If an outsider arrived now they would find a town getting ready to celebrate Christmas like few towns did anymore. Security around the town was still in place but more covertly, if someone did attempt to drive to New Haven they would be stopped as a matter of routine. Once security knew the destination they were headed for the vehicle would be allowed to proceed but the information would be forwarded to town to be on the lookout. The idea was to not interfere, unless absolutely necessary.

On Main Street a block from the Caprice a crew of volunteers were quickly wrapping up the lamp poles with extra lights and affixing a red bow below the lamp. A brass band dressed in red suits were standing outside the bank tooting away the melody of "Oh Come All Yee Faithful". Newly blessed children were running up the street throwing snowballs at each other in good fun. One of the children was nearly run over by a horse drawn sleigh, but at the last second the horse veered away missing the young pup by a foot.

"Woo there! Be careful little one, I don't want to hurt ya!" The sleigh driver said as he brought his sleigh to a halt.

"You can't hurt me!" The boy exclaimed with a devilish grin.

"Just the same child, I'd hate to see you wreck your clothes. Why don't you head on over to the park, I think they're barbequing up something tasty for lunch!" The sleigh driver reported.

"Yeah! Lunch! I'm starving!" The boy yelled running off with his snowball buddies.

Mr. Sleigh-man continued up Main Street waving to the townspeople as he went. The bells around the horse jingled alerting everyone to his arrival. The sleigh would be there to give celebrators a traditional ride around their

Darwinism

winter wonderland that night, all for free of course. For the moment he was shuttling supplies around town and dropping people along the way if he could.

In preparation for the festivities vehicle use was prohibited downtown. The roads were to be left unplowed and all of Main Street was to be an open air mall with entertainment and party tricks for all. The feeling of excitement would lead the community to the town square where the feast and celebration would occur. The whole party would end with a fireworks display that would mark the beginning of the new era.

At the town square a committee of women were decorating the park, taking hints and suggestions from every decorating magazine they could. The theme at the square was to be nothing short of fantasy. When a visitor first set foot inside the magical whimsy their breath had to be taken away. The park had to be a gateway back to their youth when Christmas had a power over them that ignited their imagination and excitement in their heart. Lighting of every type, ribbons of every color, tinsel, garland, presents larger than life and carollers all had to be present in the park to create the vision. If Santa Claus was real, it was his home that you would be walking into, warm and inviting.

"Suzie! Should we put stars or angels on the tree tops?" Marybeth Gilden asked.

"Oh, I don't know, what's more appropriate?" Suzie replied.

"Well I'm more of a traditionalist; I think angels would be better, but maybe that's too religious for this type of gathering." Marybeth pondered.

"Think Rockwell. That's the template we've been asked to use. I think as long as we're not overtly religious I think some angels would be just fine." Suzie suggested.

"Suzie, the food is here, what should we do with it?" Debbie Poundstone asked interrupting Suzie's progress on her tree decorating.

"Oh no, it's too early, I wasn't expecting it until later. If we put it out now people might eat it all. Can you find somewhere to stash it?" Suzie asked.

"I can put it in the fridge over at the grocery store, they won't mind." Debbie suggested.

"Thanks babe!" Suzie replied with a warm smile. She returned to her tree which was starting to assemble into a masterpiece of silver and gold.

"Excuse me; I'm looking for Suzie Templeton?" Tim Waters asked standing in the sea of ribbon ornamented women.

"That's me!" She announced still attempting to hook a bow at the highest part of her tree.

"I'm Timothy Waters, New Haven Governance. I just wanted to pop by and speak to the head of our Heritage Committee. By the looks of things you really have achieved the look we were going for. Is there anything that I can assist you with to help your work along?" He asked in typical politician fashion.

"Mr. Waters, no thank you, everything is moving a long well. We'll be ready before sunset, that's a promise." She replied still working on her tree.

"Excellent!" Tim replied. "Do you know if the audio has been set up yet?"

"Ah, yes, that was done this morning." She replied putting the final touches on her ribbon.

"Who needs a manager when you've got dedicated workers like yourself? Carry on!" Tim stated walking away marvelling at the emerging wonderland. Even in the light of day, under construction, the magic was beginning to appear.

Santa Claus appeared on scene with a bag loaded with all kinds of treats for the busy citizens. He tossed out every kind of holiday treat all neatly wrapped in red and green cellophane. Some received cookies, and others received holiday favourites like rum balls and Nanaimo bars. All were graciously prepared by none other than Jim Baker himself but the man behind the Santa Claus remained a mystery.

Norman Rockwell could not have created a better image of small town life at Christmas. Everyone was overjoyed and worry free, it was the happiest anyone had been in New Haven for years. The joy of the day spilled over into the twilight hours and the transition from daytime set up into evening celebration almost seemed indistinguishable.

The lights all came on illuminating Main Street around four thirty that afternoon. The sun had gone behind the mountain and the magic of Christmas was on the horizon. Singing, laughing and cheering were all sounds of the street. The roasted chestnuts were dolled out to keep peoples' hands warm – no one actually liked eating them. A choir dressed in Victorian era garments gathered at the entrance of the square where they began singing all the songs of Christmas. At the far end of Main Street the brass band played on making special attention to avoid playing the same song twice. Along the street were puppet shows and games that you might find at a carnival. A candied apple booth was set up in front of the Caprice that allowed children to dip their own apples in as much sugar and caramel as they wanted. Next to the candied apples were fresh fried miniature donuts that people could help themselves to. Further down the street one whole block had been dedicated to a snowman making competition for all ages. The winner would receive a special treat. Every corner of Main Street was filled with life and joy, and every citizen of New Haven was in attendance.

At six o'clock sharp the town bell at city hall rang which was unusual

Darwinism

for the townsfolk to hear. The bell had not functioned in many years, but Darwin made it a priority to have it repaired to signal the beginning of their new world. With the tolling of the bell everyone knew it meant the assembly in the park was about to begin. Families walked hand in hand signing and laughing in harmony as they made their way down to the park. Main Street emptied quickly while the park began to overflow.

The Victorian Choir rounded out their singing greeting with "Santa Claus is Coming to Town". Santa himself marched into the park waving and stopping to hug the children and parents who stood along the candy cane lined path to the stage. The crowd all began singing the carol and the whole park filled with love and joy. Santa opened his bag of goodies and began tossing ornately decorated packages to the children. The children all begged and screamed to be given a tantalizing gift. Santa assured the children there was enough for everyone who wanted one.

"WELCOME CITIZENS OF NEW HAVEN!" Darwin yelled into the microphone to the delight of the entire crowd. "How's the celebration so far?" He eagerly asked.

The crowd hollered in approval and clapped with delight.

Darwin continued. "I want to thank all of you for making this night become a reality. I always knew that our fair town was capable of so much more. I stand before you tonight to proclaim that this night will not be our last!" Darwin was interrupted as the crowd erupted into more applause. He raised his hands with a smile ad the crowd calmed again. "Our destiny has been told to me; our path is the right path. Through our intuition we are able to see the potential and the good in all. Everyone here tonight knows the evils that this town has been poisoned with throughout the decades. I ask you, could this night have been possible last year?"

"NO" The crowd shouted in unison.

"Why is that? It was because the criminals would steal lighting at ground level for the copper. It's because the vandals would trash the town decorations long before the party began. It's because the previous town did not want to fund celebrations that would unite a community and make us closer to one another. My friends, I'm here tonight to tell you that today is the beginning of our history. This night is only the first of many. Our new world which we have created will be based on love and caring of our own kind. Community will no longer be a foreign concept. Gone are the days of disappointment of civic celebrations being cancelled because some special interest group is offended. Gone are the days of funding being pulled to host such important events. Our goal in this new world is to ensure our community remains strong and that our bonds are solid. Through our actions we will create the world that we can all see just beyond the looking glass. The future of New Haven is bright,

Mark Fuson

our future begins today!" The crowd once again erupted in enthusiasm. "We have a lot of work ahead of us, and I know a lot of you have questions. We will answer all of them in time. For tonight, I want everyone to celebrate and rejoice in this fantastic world we have created! Let the entertainment begin!" Darwin announced.

Darwin was not a political person. In his new role it was unavoidable. Darwin was young with little life experience but the one thing he knew about politics was to keep the speeches short and to dump the political correctness. Darwin wanted to enjoy the evening as much as anyone else. In his position it made mingling in the crowd difficult because everyone wanted a moment of his time. Being the graceful leader he knew that he would have to spend sometime humouring the crowd.

"Darwin, I want you to meet the Giesbrecks! This is Rudy and Helen, they own that quaint little craft store on the corner of Elm and Main." Suzie Templeton insisted.

Darwin extended his hand and shook Rudy's before moving on to Helen whom he gave a big hug too. "Welcome. It's so nice to finally meet you both. How are you finding everything so far?" Darwin asked in sincerity.

"It's been wonderful! You have no idea how nice it is to be able to go outside without being afraid of getting mugged. I'd like to see those bastards try it now!" Helen informed.

"Did you have problems before, Helen?" Darwin asked.

"Oh yes, horrible problems. Our shop was broken into four times this year alone. My neighbour was raped in her house just last May; I was terrified to go out." Helen told the story like an old pro.

"I hope your neighbour was ok." Darwin said.

Helen stopped for a moment thinking. "Well she always was a bit of a wench; I think she got a black card. But the possibility of getting raped in my home just frightened the hell out of me."

"Well Helen we're glad to have you, you're a fine addition to New Haven." Darwin stated as he smiled and began to move on to the next group that was waiting to meet him.

"Mr. Foster, I'm Roberta Torrance, of Roberta's Hair and Nails. I just want to thank you for this lovely evening. You've managed to take our town and make it look like a Frank Capra movie. Never have I seen New Haven so beautiful. I'd love you to come into my shop sometime, it would be an honour to do your nails, or hair, or both!" Roberta stated almost with star envy.

"Which nails do you want to do?" Darwin asked comically.

For a moment Darwin's joke fell flat until the crowd finally got what he meant. Everyone in ear shot finally clued in to the joke and they began to laugh almost forcibly.

Darwinism

"Mr. Foster, what happens at full moon?" A man wearing an elf hat asked.

"I guess I'm the only one here who's been through it. You'll love it. It's not like the blood transformation, or even anger – if you've had that. The moon has an incredible pull on you. Your whole body will feel like it's in orgasm; it's all very erotic." Darwin assured.

"That sounds fantastic!" The elf replied. "Do we just run around town and do whatever?"

"We have another week to discuss it. I think all options are on the table. I think what's more important is that people are ready for the full power the wolf will have over you. The power can be very addictive." Darwin said as his mind drifted to the last full moon he saw.

"Darwin, we're just about to eat, come and grab a plate! You're the man of the hour!" Tim shouted to his friend.

"How do you think tonight is going?" Darwin asked Tim who seemed enchanted by the atmosphere.

"It's perfect Dar. I'm really beginning to see your vision. There's no evil here. No one wants to hurt us. We are all fighting for the same team. You were right, it's perfection." Tim stated as he patted his friend on the back. "I hope you like the selection. I brought that chef in you liked so much from the conference, actually I bit him. I figured you enjoyed his food so much we should keep him around. I hope you don't mind?" Tim asked, grabbing a plate for Darwin and himself.

"You know the rules Tim, I approve all inductees. But in this case you did good, thanks dude." Darwin perused the selection and the aromas got his heart going. "This looks fantastic. Fresh baked rolls – my favourite and assorted deli meats and cheese are essential at Christmas. Is that prime rib at the end of the table?"

"Sort of, you'll like it though!" Tim replied. "Try the cabbage rolls; I had the chef make them special."

"What's in them?" Darwin asked reluctantly.

"Kinda like lamb, I guess." Tim looked at them unsure how else to describe the fare. "Oh, and there's more of that pate you really liked."

"Awesome, you did really good Tim. I couldn't have done all this without you. I just want you to know that." Darwin stated as he took one of the recommended cabbage rolls.

"Hey don't get all sappy on me man; we've still got a lot of work to do. You're a leader now; your work is only just beginning." Tim replied.

"Our work." Darwin countered to a smiling Tim. "When do you want to give out the prize for the snowman competition? I think it's safe to say Rosetta

Gonzallas won hands down. I had no idea a child could mould snow into a statue of the Virgin Mary, it was remarkable."

"Geeze I thought you were going to be a traditionalist. I thought Bobby Green's version of Frosty the Werewolf would have won your vote?"

"Believe me, he's a definite close second. I just really liked Rosetta's, more detail in it. But for creativity, absolutely, Bobby wins that one." Darwin replied as he cut a hunk of prime rib for himself.

"You could award both of them prizes." Tim suggested.

"Why, not! They are both excellent. What amazes me most is that the contest was open to all ages and yet it was the children who won – and not because I'm being nice. Come to think of it, none of the children's entries were bad. Maybe it's not such a bad thing we decided Children could be turned. I really struggled with that one."

"I know you did Darwin. But how would you expect parents to be loyal to you if you made them kill their own children. As you so often remind us, we're not monsters!" Tim smiled to his master who moved to a table reserved for him and the council.

Darwin bit in to his cabbage roll first and sighed at the wondrous taste. The flavours brought out his little nubs as he ate in enjoyment. "These are probably the best cabbage rolls I've ever had."

"Told you!" Tim replied biting into one of his own. A moment later he had his own little nubs showing. The two friends and leaders relished their meals for what it was.

The party continued for hours and the conversations in the crowd were all friendly and caring. Old time polkas started after dinner and the crowd danced their dinners away. Games resumed on Main Street and so did the little donut machine. The community thrived and it was though everyone knew everything about everyone. Nothing was forced, and nothing was staged. It was all very real.

At nine o'clock, when the bells tolled, the prize for the snowman competition was revealed. Darwin handed out the honour himself and everyone in the crowded hushed waiting to find out who had won the secret prize.

"After much debate the judges have decided to award two prizes to two different entries! Put your hands together in congratulating Bobby Green and Rosetta Gonzallas!" The crowd erupted into cheers and applause once again. "Bobby made Frosty the Werewolf – wonder where that idea came from! And Rosetta did that beautiful rendition of the Virgin Mary."

With both children on stage Darwin shook each of their hands in congratulations. He looked at both children who were eagerly awaiting the prize. Darwin finally said "What do you want?"

Darwinism

"I thought there was a prize?" Little Bobby asked innocently.

"The prize was meeting me." Darwin stated to a stunned crowd. Knowing he only had a moment to drop the hammer he broke the news to the kids. "You got me! Yeah we have prizes for both of you!" A wave of relief swept over both children. "Rosetta, for your attention to detail you are awarded this treat!"

With those words spoken a man strapped to a dolly was wheeled out on stage bound and gagged. The man struggled but was unable to move. "This is yours to do with as you wish. You can eat it here or take it home to share with your parents!"

"Hell no, I'm hungry!" Rosetta shouted out in joy.

"Well ok then, take her around back to have her snack! Happy eating Rosetta!" Darwin exclaimed to the adoring crowd. "BOBBY! What would you like for your prize?" Darwin asked skilfully.

"Can't I have a man too?" Little Bobby asked in innocence.

"I don't know Bobby, do you think you've earned it?" Darwin asked in earnest. "What do you think people, should we give him something to eat too?"

"YEAH!" The crowd shouted as one.

"Bobby, the crowd has spoken! Give him what he wants!" Darwin shouted. Another man strapped to a dolly was rolled out. This was the old man who didn't want to die; who didn't care about the other people. He was the worst the town had to offer. He was a man who thought he was good but did nothing to help his fellow man. "Bobby, I need you to do me a favour."

"Sure!" He replied in joy.

"This one is really bad. It didn't care about anyone. It's the kind that would only look out for itself. So what I want you to do, and this is very important, I want you to do him really slow. Make him watch every little thing you eat. Can you do that for me?" Darwin asked luring the innocent monster in.

"Sure thing mister!" The child exclaimed in glee.

"Then take him around back! Enjoy your treat Bobby!" Darwin announced to the whole audience. "Ladies and Gentlemen, Boy and Girls – the fireworks!" Darwin raised his hands to the sky to the sight of red and green explosions over head. Hidden in the explosions were the screams of the two men being torn to pieces by the puppies. In all, the night was a success, and Darwin felt good about this first night of the new age.

As the fireworks went on it began to snow. A white Christmas was a good sign.

Chapter 29

Christmas in New Haven had been one long celebration the entire community had participated in. Tobogganing and ice skating at McCarran Park filled the days while in the evening families and friends gathered around cozy fires and just talked. Everyone was relaxed without a care in the world. The world that had been was no more and as the days passed the former world morphed into nothing more than a distant memory.

New Haven continued to function even with the severe reduction in the number of its citizens. The streets were cleared, the garbage was picked up, most of the shops were open and the beauty of the town was maintained. In the town square the magical wonderland had been left for all to enjoy, even the sculptures from the snowman competition had been left as a mid street art show. The town was renewed and the citizens revelled being out and about in their new world. It was charming, it was safe and it was home.

The new town had significant differences that were evident. Darwin and Tim walked down Main Street together and noted the amount of people saying hello to each other. Citizens held doors open for each other and wished one another a Happy New Year. There was no anger in the air; there was nothing but pure love and affection for each other. A month before the town seemed jaded and hard towards everyone and everything. Personal gain at the expense of others was rampant. Moreover the biggest difference was the façade the other town had developed. Happiness, joy and friendliness were all staged to create the illusion of community. The question of how you were doing was

Darwinism

so often asked but the answer simply didn't matter. Civility was a matter of routine in the old New Haven which was nothing more that a program that played itself out over and over again. In a little more than a week since the launch of New Haven the old ways had all but disappeared. With a common interest in all of the citizens understanding and acceptance was second nature to all of them. Darwin and Tim found their new rolls to be far easier than they could have ever hoped. The sense of cooperation in the town was so great that Darwin was letting the town more or less run itself.

Darwin and Tim were meeting at city hall on December 31 to finalize the remaining details for the evening's events. It was the first of the full moon and everyone's first night transforming and experiencing the full power of the wolf. For Darwin, this would be the true test to how the plan would work. Would his creations run amuck or would they run the woods having fun? Many unanswered questions existed but Darwin knew time would resolve them; for right now he was about to meet his Guardians.

Benny Yates had spent the last few weeks combing the internet chat rooms looking for the cyber geeks and dweebs that would make up his moonlight security force. Finding a volunteer was not difficult, finding reliable candidates was. Benny had found people all around the world that claimed to want the blessing of the wolf, and they all had their reasons. The first priority for Benny was to weed through all the children and young teenagers, secondly was to eliminate people who were mentally unstable. Spending countless hours online Benny realized most people in the dark arts chat rooms had some kind of mental dysfunction. He found the key to finding appropriate people was to find those with a positive outlook on werewolves, who enjoyed talking about werewolves but who didn't take it that seriously. Once he had found people like that he groomed them with a job offer, a very tantalizing offer that they couldn't resist. The candidates were told nothing more about the job other than it involved security and it paid very well. Benny put the offer out to more than thirty people and he told them if they were interested to show up in New Haven at noon on the 31ˢᵗ for orientation.

Twenty interested parties showed up that afternoon. The group was mostly men but a few females were present as well. The group appeared largely overweight with acne ranging from mild to extreme and none were dressed in anything trendy. The youngest applicant was seventeen and the oldest was forty-two and one look at the group as a whole told you they didn't get out often.

Darwin and Tim entered the council chambers to find the group being antisocial and not talking to one another, a symptom of where Benny had acquired them. Darwin sat in the mayor's seat at the head of the council chamber and Tim took a former councilman's chair. Darwin looked to the

Mark Fuson

group and chuckled to himself. What he saw in front of him was a geek squad and he wondered how these selected people could ever hope to effectively guard the town.

"Welcome to New Haven, thank you for coming. I'm Mayor Foster and this is Tim Waters. First let me say the job that we have available for you pays very well." Darwin said.

"How much?" A fat guy in the front row yelled.

"Well, if you'd let me finish, I would tell you." Darwin said annoyed. "This job is security, night time, three nights a month. What we are looking for is a squad of people who can guard the town and keep people out. I understand a part time job is not the most desirable but this is why we will compensate you to the amount one thousand dollars per night."

The crowd perked up and became restless. A lot of low level chatter could be heard but all members of the audience seemed to be talking to themselves.

"What's the catch?" A young looking lesbian asked. "There's gotta be a catch."

"Of course there's a catch. The catch is anyone with any doubts or reservations about the job is requested to leave right now. If you choose to stay there's no going back. You will have to decide what you want to do. I give you one minute to decide. If you are still in the room after one minute then we will proceed to orientation." Darwin stood from the mayor's seat and exited the chamber with Tim following behind. The group was left to look at each other for guidance.

"This sounds like a scam if you ask me. Three nights a month! That's what I get for taking a job offer in a chat room, and the guy isn't even here." One naysayer commented.

"I was invited in a chat room too, which one were you in?" A younger job seeker asked.

"Full Moon Forum." The naysayer replied.

"Anyone else approached like that?" The young seeker asked the group as some looked to be getting up to leave. But then the answers began coming back, and the group began to realize they had all been approached in a chat room, dealing with monsters and werewolves."

"I think we should stay, this could get interesting. Three nights a month and we were all approached in forums dealing with werewolves. What's the worst that could happen?" The young go getter job seeker assured the questioning group.

Darwin entered the room with Tim again to find half of the group standing with their coats on but no one had actually left the room. Darwin sat in his seat again to continue with the group. "Everyone stayed, that's good."

Darwinism

"Are you werewolves?" The young job seeker came out and asked.

Darwin and Tim both belted out sarcastic laughs. They were both more shocked that someone was ballsy enough to come right out and ask the question. "Do you believe in werewolves?"

"I want to?" The young man replied.

"If you could become one, would you?" Darwin replied with a sly grin.

"I'd give my left nut to be one!" He replied.

"What's your name?" Darwin asked politely.

"Scott Spencer." He said.

"Well Scott Spencer, you came for a job interview and now we're talking about werewolves. How did that happen?" Darwin asked as he leaned forward from his bench.

Scott shrugged his shoulders nervously knowing he had made a fool of himself. He sat himself down and said nothing more on the topic.

"The doors have now been sealed. You are now a member of our Guardians." Darwin announced as the locks on the doors could be heard bolting from the outside. The group looked slightly nervous but no one ran for the door. "From this moment forward you will work for this town. You are now sworn to secrecy. What happens from this point forward will not be discussed with the outside world. You may not quit this job or abandon your post. If you attempt to do so you will be slaughtered along with your family and friends."

The jaws of the crowd dropped in disbelief. Was it a joke? If it was it had been done in extremely bad taste. The group remained tight lipped, unsure of how to proceed.

"You will be compensated one thousand dollars per night of work. You will work three nights a month, in a row. Tonight is your first night of work; your shift starts in roughly six hours." Darwin informed.

"It's New Years Eve; I have a party to go to." Another fat man yelled from the back row.

"Really?" Tim shot back at the man who had likely never been invited to a party.

"I refer you my previous statement. You are expected to be on post. Failure to comply will result in your death as well as that of your family and friends. Young Mr. Spencer was right. You have been selected to be the Guardians of werewolves. Your job is to ensure outsiders do not enter New Haven during a full moon. You will establish a perimeter and keep out all unwanted attention. You may use as much force to achieve this goal as needed, including death. You will be compensated for your efforts, in cash, on the morning after the third full moon. In addition those who show extreme loyalty and devotion to

Mark Fuson

us will be granted our blessing. I commit to you right now that I will bite one of you in three days to show how committed I am to you."

"Bullshit! I'm outta here." The fat party goer announced getting up to find he was no match for the locked door. "Open the fucking door you freak!"

Darwin placed his arms on the desk in front of him and brought out the wolf to give his Guardians a demonstration of his bullshit. His body twitched and began to spasm. Darwin opened his mouth to show his forming and extending teeth. He puffed his chest out bursting the buttons on his shirt and tearing the fabric. His chest was growing thick with hair as was his face. Darwin leapt from the desk with his feet bursting from his shoes. He bolted to the door and grabbed the fat man by the neck lifting him off the ground. Darwin looked up to the cowering man who seemed more amazed than scared. "Still bullshit?" Darwin growled out of his wolf mouth.

Struggling for air the fat man managed to sputter out one word. "Awesome."

Darwin dropped the two hundred and fifty pound man to the ground and walked away reverting back to his human form. When Darwin sat down behind the desk again his human features had reasserted themselves. Darwin's chest still hung out of his shirt but he made no attempt to tidy himself, he just looked at the group who all smiled and chuckled in nervousness. "Anyone else think this is bullshit?" Darwin asked the group who shook their heads in delight, even the fat man picked himself up and applauded his new leader.

Darwin and Tim spent the next hour giving the Guardians an overview of the expectations. They understood that every month Darwin would personally sample their blood to inspect their purity. Guardians found to be in non compliance with any of the rules regarding secrecy would be terminated along with their families. The Guardians understood it was either by death or by blessing that they would leave the Guardianship and this concept seemed to excite them all.

Darwin led the group outside to a Ridgemount school bus where Frank Newman was waiting to take them to their field orientation. The group scrambled onto the bus without question and waited patiently to be taken on a tour of the town perimeter. Frank approached Darwin in disgust when he saw the security detail.

"What the fuck are those?" Frank said disapprovingly.

"Those are the people who are going to watch over us. You should treat them with a little respect." Darwin replied.

"I don't get why we need a bunch of faggoty ass geeks to look after us. Why can't we just do it ourselves once we change?" Newman said.

"We need a human voice to speak for us. We could handle some intruders

Darwinism

on our own, I agree, but if a flood of them showed up…it would be better they turned around." Darwin insisted.

"What's the point of this power if we aren't going to use it?" Newman said hastily as he climbed aboard the bus refusing to speak further to Darwin. A moment later the bus rolled away leaving Darwin and Tim standing on the street wondering what had happened.

"A little disobedient, isn't he?" Tim said.

Darwin mumbled an answer in affirmation but said nothing more. One thing that Darwin knew about leadership was sometimes a leader had to shake up his organization to maintain loyalty. He would give it some thought but with the moon fast approaching Darwin knew there were more important issues to finalize.

"How are you feeling, Tim?" Darwin asked with his mind still clearly elsewhere.

"It's coming. I can feel it growing inside of me. I can hardly wait, dude!" Tim said hungrily.

"A few more hours. Have you thought about what you want to do tonight after you change?" Darwin asked.

Tim thought about it for a moment and then realized he didn't actually have an answer. "What do you think I should do?"

"Hell, I don't even know what I should do. I use to drug myself or go out to the woods. Now I can do whatever, where ever; it's kinda cool. I might just change where ever and do what comes naturally." Darwin said plainly.

"We should go up to the mine, we could have a real feast!" Tim exclaimed.

Darwin laughed out loud at the good idea. "As fun as that would be I don't think we'd be too popular with the rest of the family."

"That reminds me, what does Clint do on the full moon nights? He doesn't get - all you can eat- does he?" Tim asked.

"No. It's a weak spot for us. No one is guarding them. Clint will evacuate all his staff at six tonight. We only hope the fences and electrified wires hold – should they attempt anything while we are busy. But I think the fear Clint programmed into them should prevent them from trying anything." Darwin informed Tim with a hint of depression in his voice.

"What if some of us get hungry? Anything in place to stop us from breaking in?" Tim asked.

"I hope it doesn't come to that. I think everyone will have some level of control. We should be ok." Darwin replied to Tim while the two returned to the warmth of City Hall.

*   *   *

The waiting was the hardest part Darwin had found. As the sun set that afternoon and the lights of Christmas blazed the town in a warm glow Darwin could feel his heart rate increasing in anticipation. He had wanted to work on a few town transitional issues before the change but he found his mind wandering from place to place. He looked out the window of the mayor's office into the sky, looking for his moon which had yet to begin its ascent. Behind the hill he could see a bright white glow and he knew that it was near. NHPD drove the streets on the loud hailer reminding people how much time left they all had.

"One hour seventeen minutes, one hour seventeen minutes." Was all that was said because everyone knew what it meant.

Darwin continued looking out his window watching time slip away. The streets of New Haven emptied and Darwin found himself to be the master of the emptiness.

"Is this as you envisioned it, young Darwin?" His mother asked.

Darwin turned from the window to find his office was now his mind. In the office was Steve, Zack and his mother all appearing as they had before. The inner most part of himself was not a cavern; the messengers arrived in his real world and stood before him. Darwin replied to his mother's question. "It's nearly perfection."

"Perfection is subjective." Zack offered.

"It is, but never before has there been such joy and love in this town. What I have created here is perfection." Darwin insisted.

"Perfection is subjective." Steve said coldly.

"What do you want?" Darwin asked.

"What does the Darwin require? Purification is complete; you must begin the next phase or face annihilation."

"I don't understand!" Darwin shouted in anger. "I lost Steve to you but I continued with the purification. It's done! What more is there?"

"Through your gift you have created life. You are the one. Only once you have conquered the inferior species will you truly be free." Zack replied.

"The Darwin does not understand. He is too young to understand. Have we chosen poorly?" His mother asked.

"Only once you have let go of your humanity can you truly be free." Steve said lovingly.

"Darwin!" It was Cindy Holmes that found Darwin in his office alone.

Darwin turned to the large wood doors to find Cindy standing in the doorway. He ran over and gave her a hug rubbing her back as he did so. He pushed his body up against hers and began to grind a little bit. "I'm glad to see you. How have you been?"

Darwinism

"I've been ok, and you, you looked like you were in a trance or something." She said quietly into his ear.

"Or something. Are you ready for the big moment?" Darwin asked, pulling himself away from Cindy's intoxicating smell.

Cindy went over to the sitting area and sat herself down, patting the seat indicating Darwin was to join her which he did without dispute. "I came by because I wanted to thank you for letting me keep the gift."

"It's not like I can take it away, Cindy." Darwin said a little confused.

"You could have killed me, I was an accident." She said rubbing his leg. "Would I have gone to special handling with my family if the mistake hadn't happened?"

Darwin thought for a moment. He never gave a lot of thought of who he sent to special handling. He had a list of people which amounted to a hundred or so. Darwin had insisted that Cindy's brother go to special handling, he would deal with him personally after Teddy had suffered underground. He was still thinking what revenge he would inflict on Teddy but he knew when it happened it would be vicious and long lasting. "You know your brother was going. There was no way I'd ever back down on that. I always liked you Cindy, but I never thought much about whether I'd bless you or not. I'm glad you're like me, though."

"My brother wasn't a bad person." Cindy said almost sad.

"I can never forgive him for what happened to Steve, I'm sorry." Darwin said looking into her eyes.

"You loved Steve, didn't you?" Cindy asked in innocence.

"More than anything in this life." Darwin welled up. "Steve was mine; it was the love I never knew until it was gone."

"That's the worse kind." She replied softly. "Are you gay?"

Darwin wiped an escaping tear that was fast rolling down his cheek. "I don't know what I was when I was human. The wolf makes me tri-sexual I think."

"Tri-sexual?" She asked

"I'll fuck anything once." Darwin laughed and Cindy joined in. "I enjoyed having you, so I'm not completely gay."

Saying nothing more she pressed her lips to his and thrust her tongue into his mouth. For several minutes they wrestled in each others' mouths grunting and slurping. Cindy threw her leg over Darwin and sat on his crotch riding him like a horse. They panted and huffed as she dry humped his bulging member. Forgetting civility Darwin tore Cindy's blouse from her body exposing her soft breasts and hard peaks. The animal in Darwin traced his tongue down her body until he found one of her breasts. Instinctively he bit down drawing a small stream of blood from her nipple.

*   *   *

Elsewhere around town the locals made their final preparations. The clock was fast running out and even the street announcements had ceased. Families and friends gathered to be together when the moment occurred. Others stayed in their bedrooms opting to change privately. A group of labourers decided they would go bowling and change there. It was New Years Eve but the clock was counting down for a much better New Year than anyone could have ever imagined.

The Guardians were in place throughout the perimeter of New Haven. Newman had given them a brief instruction but more or less they were told they were on their own until morning. Newman made it a personal point to frighten the humans reminding them it was entirely possible they themselves could get attacked. One could never be too sure of these kinds of things. The group of geeks stood five miles away from the action, nervous and excited at what their new future would bring. Newman had armed the geek squad, as he called them privately, with the shotguns and stun grenades. The shot gun would scare off the wolves if they approached the Guardians; at least, that's what he told them.

At ten minutes past seven Kenny Beckman was about to roll his first ball in a new game. The others had argued starting a new game was stupid but Kenny had argued they could always finish the game the next night. Kenny rolled the ball and got a strike to his amazement. "No wonder you guys don't want to play anymore, I'm on fire!" He said in victory.

"Kenny, that was just a lucky roll! Step aside!" Jeremy Busche taunted as he stepped up to roll his first ball. The men at the bowling alley were feeling good, really good. As Jeremy picked up his bowling ball his member stiffened under his jeans as did all the other players, but no one commented on the occurrence. Taking aim Jeremy swung the ball back and forth calmly waiting for the perfect alignment. He pulled his arm all the way back and then released it like a winch snapping. The ball flung through the air and landed two lanes over. The other men laughed at the horrific bowl. Jeremy turned around to yell at his friends but his orgasm had begun. He rolled his eyes up into his head, collapsed to his knees and began to change. The other bowlers looked in amazement and one by one the moon reached them too.

At the home of Suzie Templeton a small group of friends gathered to celebrate New Years Eve. Suzie had remembered at the last minute to turn her oven off and remove the stuffed jalapeno peppers that she had been baking. As she ran back to the kitchen she began to feel warm and tingling growing inside of her. The sensation came on fast and strong barely leaving her enough time to kill the oven but she did. One of her party guests yelled to the kitchen that

Darwinism

it had begun, but Suzie already knew that. Now on her knees she trembled in pleasure as her claws pushed over her nails.

Terri Bailey and her postman were watching an evening trivia show on television when the power took over. Both Terri and her new lover endured the pleasure of the change continuing to watch the TV as though nothing had happened. When the show went to commercial break the two werewolves found a new interest in each other. Sex in raw animalistic fashion began between the two and it didn't stop until morning.

Cindy had been riding Darwin's cock for the second time that evening. During the first session Darwin's chest hair fuzzed up briefly and then disappeared. Cindy did not experience any excess hair growth during their love making but she was wild. Darwin had been given a pair of scratch marks on his shoulders when Cindy had climaxed the first time. Darwin and Cindy were now both traveling fast and hard to their next orgasm, both panting and gasping trying to reach the climax before the moon gave them one. It happened and neither would ever be sure if they climaxed at the same time or if it was the transformation. Darwin pumped his load inside of Cindy in a torrent as she let out a long and sensual moan that would have been the envy of any porn star. The two young lovers changed together never missing a beat of their sexual urge. When the change was done a few minutes later, they went right in to their third sexual session of the night.

*   *   *

In the women's side of A2 Mayor Bollen and a group of women were talking about the gate on A4. At the urging of a growing number of women Mayor Bollen was tasked with exploring the gate in more detail. Some of the women had gone down and looked at the gate and one in particular suggested the gate was blocking a way out. The woman who suggested it was Beatrice O'mally who had done a fair amount of caving in her spare time. Beatrice acknowledged that even though they were in a mine, the draft blowing down the tunnel on A4 suggested to her there was an exit in that direction.

"What do we do about the electricity that feeds the fence?" Was asked.

"I think we can cut the power without issue. My concern is I don't know if that will trigger some kind of alarm. If we do try something and we set off an alarm, we might escape, but what about the men?" Jillian Annhower put to the group.

"I think we need to wait until the men dig through at A4. Once they can come to our side we can cut the power to the gate and all escape together." Mayor Bollen stated.

"What if the men are never able to cut through? We're not even sure how far the dig would be. How long do we wait? It's clear the police aren't coming anytime soon." Ellen Tate said.

"Maybe we need to be more proactive. Should we start digging across to the men's side? It might save us some time, and it would give us something to do." Caroline Lutz asked.

"Is there any reason to escape? They're letting us go a few at a time. If we get caught they might punish us. I think we should stay put." A mother yelled from a spot within ear shot of the meeting.

Mayor Bollen and Caroline looked to each other contemplating letting the other women in on the secret. "I think for the moment Caroline is right, we will begin work on a tunnel on this side of the cave. Just because we link up with the men doesn't mean we'll escape, but it might be nice to have the company." The mayor offered as conciliation. "We should talk to Betty Ransom, I'm certain I saw her here. She's got an engineering background; she might be able to help us with the tunnelling."

"I know her; I think she's down on A3. I'll go get her." Caroline replied.

She ran down the ramp to A3 and continued on to A4. Caroline wanted to get away from the group, she'd begun feeling strange an hour before, and now the feeling was swelling fast. She didn't feel horrible, but she knew something was not right.

CHAPTER 30

When the sun rose on the morning of January 1st the town had an eerie calm throughout. All through the night it had snowed heavily leaving the streets impassable for the average car. Overall the town had faired well with damage that could be considered nothing more than light. The window to the florist shop was broken in and Suzie Templton found herself alone in a nest of flowers on the shop floor. The men at the bowling alley never left the building, instead finding new and amusing ways to occupy themselves utilizing primal indoor activities. The men wrestled and fought each other with their new found strength, smashing display cases and tearing away at the dated wallpaper that adorned the smoke laden walls. The children had instinctively gathered at the various parks around town and had apparently played with each other throughout the night. In the morning the pups awoke in human form laying on top of each other in an attempt to keep warm.

For the citizens of New Haven the fog of the animal was thick and their first view of the world that morning brought a certain disbelief to it. They were hung-over, but yet they felt fantastic. The images in their mind seemed like a dream but as they awoke they soon realized their dreams had been their actions. Completely liberated of their human limitations the newborns got up to greet their new reality with open arms. In their hearts the excitement was already building that the change would soon happen again. New Years Day would be a long one.

Darwin awoke in his office without his she wolf. He remembered his

Mark Fuson

night well, better than the other citizens who were awaking into various situations around town. Darwin and Cindy had fucked for most of the night. There was no love making in it, it was pure, raw sex. The heavy wood doors to his office were open, and Cindy was no where to be found. Invigorated, the young mayor picked himself up from the floor taking a moment to inspect the office and although he remembered extremely rough intercourse, the office had come through the night more or less intact. One end table and a tiffany lamp had been smashed when Darwin had decided to chase Cindy around the room in an attempt to penetrate her anally, which he eventually succeeded in doing. As the she wolf was railed from behind her claws dug into the arms of the leather sofa causing some tears. Darwin could see from his office the damage should have been worse.

He put his clothes on which were saved by the pre-lunar sex. Darwin poked his head out the window of the mayor's office to see more and more nudists running around town in the deep snow. Darwin shouted to the people below "Happy New Year everyone!"

"Same to you!" A man yelled as he ran up Main Street holding himself tightly.

"The night was cool, but this blows!" Another young man shouted as he ran up the other side of Main Street.

Darwin laughed in amusement remembering his experience stuck in the woods the previous month. He agreed; it did blow. "It gets easier. You'll learn to control it so you can change back somewhere warm."

"I hope I live to try it again!" The young man replied still running away.

"Don't worry, the cold can't kill you!" Darwin reassured.

"No but it-it-it FUUCCKINGGG hurts!" He hollered back as he rounded the corner out of sight.

His puppies were alive and well and now they could see the world as he did. The reality for them would never be the same. In the days and weeks leading up to the moon they had only experienced a small part of the wolf. Now that the wolf had burst through their human skin it would dominate their personality and decision making for eternity. For Darwin the reverse had been true. He had changed into the monster but he had failed to complete his transformation until he ate human flesh. His creations had already eaten human, before the wolf had consumed them, and Darwin felt a bit of envy towards their rapid development. He considered his own maturation to be an embarrassment and something that should be ridiculed. The past to him seemed unreasonable; his thoughts towards his gift had been skewed. His puppies understood that they were the next evolution and the consumption of the inferior was necessary, and as it happened, extremely enjoyable. Darwin had come to that realization slowly, and he was ashamed to admit there was a time he resisted, but that time had passed.

It was a little after eight in the morning which gave the town roughly eleven hours until the wolf returned and Darwin had several items he wanted to address before the moon rose. Firstly, he wanted to have something to eat, and pancakes weren't on his mind. He thought as a treat for himself he would travel to special handling and select one person he could eat. Darwin knew he really didn't need to eat a whole detainee so he began toying with the idea of amputating only a portion to eat now. As long as the bleeding and shock was addressed he felt the detainee could be consumed over several days, instead of all at once. It was a worthwhile experiment that Darwin wanted to try right away. Darwin knew after the full moons were completed he would need to work rapidly on replenishing the food stocks as it was becoming very clear that the want for human meat was going to exceed the need for it. The amputation project seemed like an ideal place to kill two birds with one stone.

Also in his preliminary plans for the day was an inspection of the town and discussion with the citizens. How did they feel, did they have any thoughts, feelings or concerns about their lunar curriculum. It was part of his leadership role that he knew he had to attend to.

The Guardians also had to be spoken to. Did they experience any problems? Were some of them killed? Had a few tried to run away? Darwin had wanted to leave the Guardians to Frank Newman but he was concerned Newman was being too critical with the young novice security officers. As their leader, and future father, Darwin thought he should make his presence and appreciation known to them.

The day was young but the clock was counting down to the transformation and that sensation of -needing to be somewhere but not being able to get there – seemed very real. Mayor Foster was torn between the tasks because each seemed important but he kept coming back to the idea of special handling. After nearly half an hour of debating in a trance he gave into his lust and went to special handling.

Darwin hopped into one of several four wheel drive vehicles that were available in the parking area of New Haven City Hall. Though the snow was deep the clearance on the vehicle seemed sufficient to make his way up to special handling without difficulty. If all went well Darwin expected the snow ploughs would hit the streets before nine that morning. His expectations were that life after a full moon would resume uninterrupted and that an outsider would be none the wiser of the lunar activities. The first full moon or two would be a grace period as the town adjusted to their new reality, but the haze of existence should settle enough for the citizens to get on with a daily

Mark Fuson

routine. They did, after all, have a great deal of work to do to bring New Haven up to speed.

When Darwin arrived at special handling he was surprised to find activity. The gates to the compound were open and several of the guards in uniform were walking towards the mine entrance. Darwin was relieved to see his creations attending to their duties without prompting from him and he would make a point of commending Clint on the job he was doing.

Clint was coming down the steps of his home when Darwin stopped his city vehicle. The warden of special handling was professional in his duties, wearing a full dress uniform and matching cap. Clint had the uniforms specially made insisting that a separation and distinction be maintained at all times between the detainees and the staff. It was felt that those residing in special handling would lose their will if their captors appeared superior and an intimidating look was the best way to achieve this effect. The uniforms he had made were, in part, modeled on various military regimes throughout history. Many authoritarian states had used black uniforms in their campaign of intimidation; some were ornate but others more simplistic. The guards who worked one on one with the detainees were kept in a reasonably simplistic getup that still looked coercive. They wore black cargo pants with a black long sleeve shirts made from a spandex style material that could stretch should they start to transform out of anger. Each man wore a beret style hat also in black but no where on the uniform were markings of any kind.

The camp warden, on the other hand, opted to ensure that all who saw him knew his importance and power. Clint had created his uniform from German SS designs from the Second World War. He wore a proper dress uniform and cap with slick black boots. His jacket was ornamented with platinum wolf's head buttons that he had custom made. On his cap he had a full moon with light clouds fading off of it for his symbol, also custom made and done in platinum. The final element of his ensemble was a ring, also with a wolf head, that sat proudly on his ring finger. Darwin had no feelings either way about how Clint had elected to run the facility but he had to admit the uniforms did make the operation look intimidating.

"Wasn't expecting to see you out here this morning, boss." Clint said as he adjusted his cap while descending his steps.

"Thought I'd do my rounds and see how everyone is doing. I'm glad to see you are up and running. Did anyone break into the mine over night?" Darwin asked.

"We sealed the main entrance before the moon rose. Getting in would have been difficult for us. From what we can tell it worked, all the gates and security systems are still in place. We are assuming the detainees are none the wiser of what happened last night." Clint said as he walked Darwin towards

Darwinism

the mine entrance pointing out the large sliding door that they used to keep the wolves out at night.

Darwin switched the conversation over to what was now consuming his every thought. "Bring me Teddy Holmes. I'll be in hallway ten, room one."

"Hungry?" Clint said with a smile.

"Get him up here now. I want to run a little experiment with him." Darwin suggested as he walked away from Clint towards a building that had been marked as a potential area for future projects. Darwin and Clint had discussed in general terms what those projects might look like, but the specifics had been left to interpretation.

The building had two floors and at one time had been an administrative area of the mine. The old derelict building was now a contrast between abandonment and revitalization. The exterior walls on the buildings inside were ripped apart down to the studs. Limp and pathetic aluminium wiring dangled from the studs begging to be replaced. The old single pane windows along the walls were dusty and some had a few cracks in them. The interior part of the building was a stark contrast to what existed only a few feet away. New drywall, wiring, light fixtures and doors had erased all of the elements of the building's outer shell. Each room was a mystery but Darwin was aware of two rooms on the main level of hallway ten that were functional and ready for use. Darwin had insisted that private rooms, modified for sound dampening and equipped with an array of tools be available for the elite and the medical staff to explore their hidden desires. The majority of the rooms under construction would be plain stainless steel lined rooms with a showerhead that detainees would be brought to and devoured in. The system wasn't fun, but for the moment it would allow his citizens to explore their basic needs in privacy and in relative safety. The stainless steel shower component would make for efficient clean up and sterilization so the room could be put back into use for the next client. Waste water was then directed to sector C of the mine where it could seep into the ground harmlessly.

Hallway ten was at the far end of the building, tucked away in what amounted to a secret corridor. Average New Haven citizens would never be aware of the hallway or the significance of the two rooms that existed here. Hallway ten was forty feet long with one room one on either side of the hallway. The entry to the rooms was by plain steel doors at the end of the hallway and each door was directly across from one another. Overall the feeling was that of a sterile medical clinic. Dull fluorescent lighting that lit the hallway washed away any life the corridor may have exhibited; it was lifeless. Darwin considered adding paintings and color to the bare white walls to put detainees at ease as they were brought to this place, but for the moment the stagnant environment would suffice.

289

Mark Fuson

Darwin entered the room to find it as he had envisioned. The room looked like a surgical bay with a table in the center of the room with thick leather straps dangling off the side the length of the table. Along the far wall of the room was a steel table that ran the length of the room and on the wall above that table were tools that hung on the wall. Saws of various sizes and differing teeth lengths hung ominously in a row, which was the first sight a detainee would see, after the center table of course. In other rows along the wall were mystery tools, some long and cylindrical, while others were clamp shaped. At the far end of the room was another steel table with straps vertical on the wall that was reminiscent of stirrups. A cabinet with vials of fluids that lined numerous shelves was next to the fake birthing table. What made the room most interesting was the steel rods, metal hoops and cables that were all neatly contained on the ceiling that kept a mysterious question about the room. Finally, next to the door, were a commercial refrigerator and freezer. Darwin admired his creation and he knew his imagination and revenge could run wild in this place.

Within a few minutes of waiting in the room he could hear the familiar and hated voice struggling on his approach to the room. Darwin had left the door open specifically so he could listen to his old foe beg and plead for his safety. It amused Darwin to know that Teddy Holmes could experience fear like anyone else. As the young man drew closer to his courtroom it was clear he was being dragged. The pathetic judge of moral character must have known that his past was about to confront him.

"Teddy! Hi, remember me?" Darwin shouted to the balling young man as the two officers brought him in. Teddy looked up at Darwin and knew him right away. "Strap him to the table, please." Darwin commanded to the guards.

"I remember you." Teddy said harshly as the salt water streamed through the coal dust on his cheeks. "You're Cardwen's fudge packing buddy." Teddy said as a matter of fact while he was being strapped to the table.

Darwin boiled at the comment but he took a deep breath trying to calm himself. It was important to Darwin that his interactions with Teddy were kept calm and civil. During the procedure Darwin wanted professionalism and civility to rein strong. He wanted Teddy to understand the absolute hatred he held for him and the best way to show it was through lack of concern for his pain or well being. "No Teddy, I'm not that person. I am Darwin Foster, friend to the late Steve Cardwen."

"Whatever, freak! Why are we being held!?!" Teddy shouted in anger, now strapped to the steel table.

"Along time ago something happened to a young boy. It was just an accident – you understand. I admit it must have been embarrassing for

Darwinism

yourself, but in your quest to take the shame away from you, you demonised him." Darwin said flatly to his captive as the guards departed leaving the two in private. "You killed him, you know?"

"Who? Cardwen! He spunked all over me in the shower! How the fuck is that my fault?" Teddy replied coldly.

"You lead a campaign to persecute Steve. You never let it drop. Your hatred of him fuelled others to hate him. Steve was never given the chance to live, all because of an accident." Darwin said standing over the bound man.

"What the FUCK is this!?! Why are we being held? Why are you here!?! What is this place? ANSWER ME!" Teddy shouted in fear as he realized something horrible would soon happen to him.

"This is room one of hallway ten. You're in special handling. And this is the place where I will help you understand a little bit about yourself." Darwin said calmly. "I must admit, I'm a little new to this, so if you have any suggestions for improvement after we're done, I'd love to hear them."

Teddy said nothing more as he began to tremble. Darwin walked over to the cabinet and began looking through the various vials that lined the shelf. After a few moments he selected one, pulled a large syringe from a drawer and he returned to the table. Darwin rolled a small hospital table over and he began preparing an injection. Again Teddy said nothing choosing only to look on in fear.

"I'm fucking your sister."

"What?" Teddy said nervously.

"Cindy and I are fucking. Never thought that would happen, did you? You want to smell my cock, it probably still smells like her ass!" Darwin chuckled to himself as he put down the large needle on his mobile tray table. Teddy did not comment to Darwin, instead he only watched intently as Darwin began looking over the tools that hung on the wall. After a few moments of contemplation Darwin made his selection. The choices had been many but Darwin finally selected a small scalpel that allowed Teddy to relax a little bit.

"Look. Darwin, I'm sorry. What I did to Steve was wrong." Teddy offered in his final plea.

Darwin looked at him in the eyes at close range. "I'm sorry too." Darwin grabbed Teddy's hospital top and tore it effortlessly from his body. The young man began to sob as his skin became exposed to the cold air. Darwin then took hold of his pajamas and ripped them from Teddy's body leaving him completely nude on the table. Darwin took the fabric and tossed it on the floor as though there were more pressing matters to attend to. He took the needle from the side table and then he leapt on top of Teddy, straddling his

Mark Fuson

mid section. Darwin raised his hands over his head with the needle poised to hit Teddy in the general area of his heart.

Teddy froze in panic. "Please." He said pathetically.

"Now if I'm right I should hit your left ventricular chamber. A dose of 0.5 mg should stave off the shock." Darwin began swinging lightly.

Teddy stuttered one more question. "What are you doing?"

"An injection of pure adrenaline into your heart should help you avoid shock and stay awake throughout the procedure. I've never done this before so I hope I do it right. I admit I'm skipping a few steps, but hey, I'm not a doctor!" Darwin said nothing more and for Teddy it came instantly and without warning. The needle plunged down and impacted through Teddy's skin to which he gasped. Darwin pushed the plunger down as fast as he could before quickly removing the needle and tossing it to the floor.

Teddy's eyes bolted open and he broke out into a light sweat. Darwin sat back on Teddy's groin waiting to see if he died or if he could proceed. After a minute it was becoming clear to Darwin that Teddy was very much awake and although the adrenaline had probably not been good for the young man, it appeared as though he would survive the dose.

"WOW! Holy shit!" Teddy said as he began to buzz.

"I thought you'd enjoy that. It was necessary because this is something I want us to share together. I think technically I'm suppose to give you the adrenaline after shock sets in, but I thought we'd be pro active." Darwin looked into the face of the wide eyed subject. Darwin slapped him lightly on the cheek and began the procedure.

Dr. Foster slid a tourniquet under Teddy's thigh which Darwin tightened as much as possible until the leg began to go pale white-blue. He then took the small scalpel and began slicing into the flesh of Teddy's leg, just above the knee, which at first he did not seem to notice despite the fact he was watching the incision being made. After creating a four inch long gash, Darwin pushed the cutting instrument a little deeper as he attempted to cut into the muscle. He sliced deep into the wound and then he pulled the blade back out and cut the flesh a little more. He repeated this cutting action throughout the procedure. The smell of iron began to fill the room as the blood began leaking and spurting onto Darwin, Teddy, the table and floor. Looking into the ever widening wound Darwin found himself transfixed on the tissue and muscle fibers that were separating with ease. Every moment or so he would get a glimpse of white that he took to be a bone, it fascinated him. Darwin completed his butchery on the outer leg and he was still unaware of the death curdling screams that Teddy Holmes was emitting. The young patient was not making any intelligent remarks only raw unadulterated agony. Darwin jammed the scalpel into the inner leg, creating another incision. The doctor began the same sawing technique until he met the first incision. When the two cuts met, Darwin had created a three inch deep cut that almost completely encircled the leg. With the cutting complete Darwin tossed the medical instrument carelessly across the room not watching where it went.

Teddy sputtered and cried as he tried to breath. Darwin looked to Teddy only to find his eyes were winced closed and almost completely flooded with water. As he looked at his foe he felt nothing in the area of remorse or pity, he did however, feel satisfaction.

"I'm sorry, Teddy where are my manners?" Darwin grabbed a handful of white granular powder and tossed it into the wound, which brought about a sustained and ear numbing scream from the patient. "I'm reasonably certain salt is good for the wound; prevents infection."

Teddy began to vomit large white chucky material that had been bread a few hours before. The slimy mush exploded for his mouth sending splatters of material to the floor. Darwin took a brief instant to make sure Teddy could still breathe, which he was. A dead Teddy would serve no purpose; the point was to bring him to the edge of hell without actually pushing him over.

Darwin prepared Teddy for the next phase of the procedure. Teddy was succumbing to shock despite the adrenaline but he hoped he would stay awake long enough to experience the finale. The tough leather straps that secured his legs individually to the table had to be removed from the operated leg for Darwin to succeed in completing the procedure. Once the leg was free, Darwin put the calf under his arms and he quickly jolted the leg making it perpendicular to the secured body. At the extreme angle the patella and tibia snapped away from the femur. The tissue and cartilage began to cleave and stretch like a turkey leg being ripped from the carcass. The leg now swung effortlessly from his side but a small amount of tissue would not allow the leg to detach completely. Darwin tangoed back and forth in an effort to break the leg free but it was no use. Darwin switched his tactics to blunt force and he began pulling on the severed leg hoping the remaining fibers would shred and snap off. At the foot Darwin began tugging as hard as he could. Like pulling on an elastic band the leg began to stretch away from the stump until the last fiber finally gave up and tore away. Darwin stumbled back clumsily and hit the wall still holding his prize. With a dumb look on his face Darwin held the leg up in triumph hoping Teddy would be looking, but he wasn't.

The tourniquet was working but the artery was still leaking a lot of blood, which Darwin knew he would have to address right away. He had several options available to him to stop the bleeding. A very simple method was a hemostatic agent that was common in the military. Darwin had several varieties of hemostatic agents available, but he was thinking something more inventive would be in order.

Darwin grabbed a large dressing that he could slap onto Teddy's stump. He quickly tucked the dressing under, around and inside the wound. Once Darwin was satisfied the wound was covered he grabbed a bottle of rubbing alcohol and poured onto the dressing liberally. The patient hollered a little more when the alcohol touched his exposed nerves but the strength and the will to fight had left him. The doctor grabbed a barbeque lighter from a drawer and wasted no time in igniting the gauze and with a quick blue flame the candle stump burned forth. Darwin admired the crackling of the wound as all the exposed veins, nerves and arteries were sealed in an instant.

"Teddy. I want to thank you for being a real good sport. I look forward to having breakfast with you again." Darwin said as he looked into the eyes of Teddy, who was trying to be someplace else at that moment.

Darwin gabbed his breakfast and walked over to Teddy. Darwin bit into the calf muscle and like a dog he tossed his head from side to side until the muscle fiber broke away. Darwin was working himself up but he kept his wolf at bay. With a mouth full of meat he looked directly at Teddy who could not avoid the sight. Darwin swallowed the muscle without chewing. With his mouth still full Darwin told Teddy one more thing. "I'll have Dr. Gagnon come by and make sure I did everything ok. Thanks for the leg!"

Darwin left Teddy alone and abused in hallway ten where he remained for several hours before Dr. Gagnon showed up. His torture was only just beginning.

CHAPTER 31

Around two that day Darwin found himself driving the newly cleared streets of New Haven. It was New Years Day and most of the shops were closed but Darwin was pleased to find a lot of locals out walking and taking in the day. Normality was obvious in the small town just as he had hoped. Even the window of the florist shop had already been replaced which was a pleasant surprise. As Darwin drove past the bowling alley he found a crew of men running in and out of the building carrying ladders and paint and removing rubble. The fun of the previous night was being cleaned up and Darwin was proud of his people for taking such care to their nocturnal actions. He was hoping to stop and speak to a few of the local residents but everyone seemed to be getting along fine. Occasionally a person would take note to his presence and wave to him, but for the most part the town just motored on in bliss.

Darwin turned onto Clairmount Boulevard partially thinking about Steve. His mind was drifting back to a time when he was just a kid riding his bike up and down the neighbourhoods or running through a yard on a hot sunny day dancing in a sprinkler. There had been happy times, even if there weren't many of them.

A loud thump on the front of the vehicle lured Darwin from his brief vision. Instinctively he slammed on his brakes coming to a halt. Darwin jumped from the car knowing he had hit someone or something. He bolted to the front to find nothing and then along the passenger side to still finding nothing. From under the car he could hear a slight growl which brought him to his knees to look. Under the darkness of the car he found two small orbs of piercing light that leapt out from under the car. Darwin grabbed the back of the child's coat and lifted him from the ground as he emerged into the daylight. He had run the boy over but the gift had saved him. The small wolf boy was angry but aside from some quickly healing scrapes on his face, he was ok. Darwin looked into the child's werewolf eyes and thought a message of peace and calmness. The child growled and hissed, but only for a moment. He soon heeded his master's request and the boy's monster teeth and hair retreated. Darwin put the puppy on the ground and gave him a pat on the back side sending him on his way. The child ran off giggling to himself and Darwin was left alone wondering in the street.

He felt alone in the world despite all of his achievements in the previous month; he felt more isolated than ever before. The town around him was happy and in great spirits. Mothers and fathers were spending time with their children, neighbours invited neighbours over to play cards or to simply be neighbourly. Young men and women were falling in love and experiencing sensuality they never thought possible. Everyone was everyone's friend. Darwin was liked and respected, but he was kept at a distance. The towns' people around him knew he was responsible, but Darwin was an elitist, someone to be feared, not befriended. Darwin had their loyalty, but he could never have their friendship.

Still next to his city vehicle Darwin became upset at his situation. For a moment, he nearly began to cry, but his personal emotions were shoved aside when a text message came across his phone, the first of the year.

The text read: *Need to talk in person ASAP. Come to outer perimeter station one. Tim.*

The text was short on details but Darwin sensed some kind of urgency in it. He had planned on making his way out to visit with the Guardians and now he had a reason to go sooner. The image of the town was depressing him even though it was everything he had hoped for. Work might help distract him until the moon rose and then he could let loose a little.

Darwin sped away from the happy town as he drifted deeper into his own depression. The darkness of his feelings was something he had no control over. He had no reason to feel sad but yet he could feel himself sinking into a very dangerous place. Darwin was beginning to feel the more he changed the more his situation stayed the same. The town was purged of all the evil that had existed, pure good remained but his feeling of being an outcast persisted. He wanted to have friends and someone to love; his gift had yet to deliver these basic needs. The cold road out of town was as empty as Darwin's heart, he saw no one, and he passed no one.

As he neared the perimeter he began to realize all he could ever be, all he could ever have was his job and his creations. His curse was to never know happiness or love, and it angered him to know this.

The Guardian station was nothing more than an old farm house off the main road. Tim was outside speaking with one of the Guardians when he rolled up the drive. He left his vehicle a leader, and now was his time to work.

"Thought you were ignoring me. I didn't get a text back from you. I'm glad you didn't text though." Tim stated as Darwin approached.

"You're glad I didn't text?" Darwin asked to clarify.

"I think we have a problem with Newman." Tim said bluntly.

"Ok, you've got my attention." Darwin said still coming across unconcerned.

"I think Newman might be monitoring communications." Tim replied.

"Yeah, of course he's monitoring. We're still keeping an eye on everyone to make sure the gift has been embraced. We can probably pull back on the monitoring now." Darwin replied.

"No, you don't understand. I think he's monitoring the council?" Tim said with a distinctly staid tone.

Darwin seemed taken a back for a moment but he quickly regained his thoughts. "What proof do you have?"

"This is Tina Redding, she's one of our Guardians. I'll let her tell you." Tim said.

"Sir." The woman in her early thirties began with bowing her head. Darwin made no effort to tell her it was not necessary; the respect humbled him. "Last night Frank Newman gave us our – tour -. Let's just say he was unpleasant the whole time and he showed little respect towards us. That's fine, we get that, he's a cop and we're just geeks and dweebs. It got later and later and he just kept going on about what useless sacks of shit we were and that he'd make sure we didn't last the night."

"What did he do?" Darwin asked.

"Frank never left. He said he wanted us to experience real fear. He went outside because he said he wanted the challenge to be fair. He shouted and screamed at us until the moon rose, and then it happened. He changed. As he changed he said he'd get rid of us and then you. He said Darwin, by name." Tina relayed.

"How did you survive the night?" Darwin asked.

"We're innovative but we didn't all survive. Frank got one of the guys early on. He pulled him through one of the windows we hadn't secured. And Scott Spencer got bit, he's ok though."

"He didn't lose his left nut did he?" Darwin asked in inappropriate humour.

Mark Fuson

"No, he was bit on the arm. I guess he'll need to go into town tonight, lucky bastard." She said in jealousy

"Why are you all still here?" Darwin asked.

"We all know there's a risk to this job, but if it gives us the chance to become a werewolf, I don't think anyone of us plans on running, this is all too cool!" Tina said almost thrilled.

"So what happened? Did he stalk you all night?" Darwin asked.

"Yep. Little fucker wouldn't let us out of the house. We never did get to do any patrols. All the shotguns were in the bus, we had nothing to fight him with. We tried Molotov cocktails, that scared him off for a bit, but he always came back. Finally around four this morning he wandered off into the woods. I don't know if he knows what he said when he was changing, but we heard him say your name. He wants us out of the way along with you." Tina informed loyally.

"That makes sense Darwin, he was acting strange yesterday." Tim said in agreement with the Guardian.

"But why? I gave him the gift; he was part of the planning. Why would he go against us, especially in such a crucial phase?" Darwin asked in disbelief.

"Dar, have you heard from Newman today?" Tim said.

Darwin thought for a moment. He had been too consumed by his inability to focus; his mind kept drifting into a void of nothingness. "No."

"What if Newman intends to take control of New Haven, with you out of the way he could be in charge – he has his own army." Tim suggested.

"Do you think his men would be loyal to him, and not me?" Darwin asked blankly looking at the ground.

"Darwin, all of us with the gift feel a kinship to you. We are loyal not because you have some mystical power over us. We like you, we like what you offer but I think every one of us has free will if we choose to fight the bond. What if Newman is just fighting the bond? He might be offering his men something too irresistible for them to refuse. More food, more often?" Tim said.

"Again it comes back to the - what - of the question?" Tina interjected.

"He wants us out of the way because we know his secrets. Maybe you forgot Tim, but we know about his dirty dealings. Get us out of the way and he protects his image and he still has an image in the outside world. If he eliminates us maybe he takes control of the council...or worse, gets rid of it." Darwin considered.

"How did I get dragged into this?" Tim asked.

"I think the situation is worse than we think Tim. It's not me. He wants the power and the blood and he'll get rid of anyone who gets in his way. If he acted out last night and killed a Guardian then there's a good chance he's working today to finalize his plans, he'll move ahead quickly because he knows I'm bound to find out what he did. I think we need to be sensible. There's no time to sit back and wait for him to make the first move, we need to mobilize and remove Newman and his men, and we need to do it now." Darwin declared.

"How did we get here so fast? I said I thought there was a problem. If Newman did attack the Guardians last night why hasn't he come back today to smooth things over? And now you're suggesting we remove a professional police force from power? How do propose we do that?" Tim asked.

"Special handling. We'll pull security from the camp and we'll draft a few of our trusted locals to help us out." Darwin replied. "There is an element of speculation here, I realize that. You're right, why hasn't he turned up today? Why hasn't he tried to cover up what he did? Maybe because he doesn't remember. To him, in his mind, the things he remembers are fragmented. You changed last night Tim; do you remember everything you did?"

"No" Tim replied quietly.

"I've had a bad feeling around him for a little while now. What you're telling me makes sense. I think he might be planning to take us out. The point is we needed him in the early stages, we don't need him now. If we eliminate the NHPD we can hand security over to Clint who's doing a bang up job in special handling. In all honesty I trust Clint and his boys more than Newman; replacing Newman might be the right move at this time, whether we're right about his intentions or not." Darwin rationalized.

"Does that mean we take out the entire force?" Tim asked.

"Probably. I suppose we can cross that bridge when we come to it. If we think some can be saved we could incorporate them into the special handling crew, but I think the NHPD needs to be dissolved. It is a symbol of the past and as long as it exists any police officer working there will always remember it as such. Loyalty might always be an issue." Darwin said.

"So how do we fight immortals?" Tim looked to Darwin for some real guidance.

"Silver?" Tina asked with naivety.

"I think we'll have to do it the old fashioned way." Darwin said without alluding to the real answer before his phone began to ring. Darwin excused himself from the discussion while he took the call.

"Dar!" Clint shouted as soon as Darwin picked up the line.

"Clint, I need to talk to you." He replied.

"Did you authorize Newman to remove eighty men from the camp?" Clint said quickly,

"No! Why?!?" Darwin shot back.

"He's here with some of his goons. He said to me that he's making a

Mark Fuson

withdrawal on your orders. I played along, but I thought it sounded strange. I figured if it had been true you would have mentioned it this morning." Clint concluded.

"Clint, don't get in Newman's way. We're coming over with some back up…" Darwin said with authority before the call was disconnected.

Darwin returned his attention to Tim, the battle was on and it was happening faster than Darwin thought possible. "Tim we've gotta get up to the camp now. Newman's on the move. He's at special handling making a large withdrawal. Tina we need you to round up the Guardians; looks like we've got a battle to go to and we're going to need all the help we can get."

"Why is he up there?" Tim asked.

"I don't know, but he's taking out eighty men apparently. We can't afford to be losing that many to such a small group." Darwin said as he began walking to his car.

"What's special handling?" Tina asked to the horror of Darwin and Tim.

Darwin returned to Tina's side knowing that she deserved the truth. "Special handling is where we store our food. Part of being a werewolf is needing to eat. We store humans underground. When we are hungry we go there and eat; you will too one day." Darwin said softly placing his hand on her arm.

"Where do they come from?" She asked, now appearing a little concerned.

"We have a doctrine that we follow. Some people are destined to go there; Criminals and drug addicts, the general scum of society mostly. Is it fair, no, I admit that. It is what it is. You want to be a werewolf. The power and gift makes treatment of humans a non issue. I'm better than them; you'll get that once you're embraced."

"I'm not judging." Tina replied simply.

"Well alright then! Let's get your people and move out!" Darwin told the adoring woman. "And bring me Scott Spencer, he can ride with me." Tina ran into the house like an excited school girl, leaving Darwin alone with Tim.

"He's making more werewolves, isn't he?" Tim asked.

Darwin took pause for a second. The idea had entered his mind and somewhere inside of him he knew it would be true. Darwin had placed his faith in loyalty all based around the concept that his gift had a power over people. He had been wrong. He held no supernatural power over anyone. Darwin was their drug dealer; he provided answers and solutions to their needs, that's why they followed him. Newman had found out early that Darwin wasn't needed and using Darwin as the template he would dispose of his enemies effectively placing Newman in charge. He was a strong and merciless leader who would offer the drug of life to all those who followed him. Newman's concept would be impossible to resist for most, order and civility would collapse as consumption would run uncontrolled. The idea had been in his mind and he knew it to be true. Darwin shook his head in affirmation but he said nothing. Darwin went to his vehicle and waited for Scott Spencer to join him. He had a lot thrown at him and now he would need to educate a new pup less than three hours before his first change. It was only one more problem in a growing string of issues.

A minute later the Guardians began to exit the farm house in a torrent of excitement. Darwin thought it was such an unusual sight to see. Looking at the group of geeks Darwin wondered how they could be so happy and excited to be part of such an exercise. Many would soon be dead, some might even become werewolves but all would lose their innocence, if they ever had it to begin with.

Scott Spencer was only seventeen but he looked younger than his age. He was tall and lanky with light blond hair and he had the palest of blue eyes. The boy just looked awkward as he approached the vehicle holding his arm which was in a poorly made sling. He kept his head down as he rounded the front of the vehicle. He opened the door and hopped in without looking Darwin in the eye. "I'm going to change soon." He said bluntly.

"Yeah but you got to keep your left nut, so quit your complaining!" Darwin said with a slight chuckle. "You're not depressed, are you?" Darwin asked, as he began backing out the driveway with the Ridgemount school bus, revving up its diesel engine preparing to depart.

"Will it hurt? In the movies it always hurts." Scott asked with genuine concern.

"You wanted this, now you've got it, and you're worried if it will hurt. Kid, it doesn't hurt, it actually feels amazing, better than sex." Darwin assured.

"I've never had sex." Scott replied.

Darwin rolled his eyes in frustration. "You jack off though!"

Scott almost looked embarrassed to admit it as though he had never told anyone before. "Yeah, a couple of times."

"Holy fuck kid! Everyone jacks it. Most guys do it daily, so stop thinking you're weird. Anyway, turning is a lot like when you cum, except it's your whole body that has the orgasm, it's pretty fucking sweet." Darwin realized he could show Scott better so he bit his finger drawing some blood and he promptly shoved it into Scott's mouth.

Scott fought it for a moment but soon he wasn't pushing Darwin's arm away. Scott grabbed a hold of Darwin's arm and drew in the finger deeper into his mouth. He sucked as much blood as he could draw from the small wound but it was enough to induce the feeling that Darwin had promised.

Darwin drove away with the bus of dweebs not far behind. Scott had his euphoric episode that would have been the envy of any human on the bus and Darwin just drove on wondering how to defeat Newman.

"Ok, that was pretty fucking awesome." Scott said to Darwin who seemed to be in a metamorphic trance.

"That's only a taste of what's to come." Darwin's automated reply spoke. Scott went on talking about his feelings but Darwin tuned him out, merely shaking his head in agreement occasionally.

His mind was becoming a flowchart of possibilities but he knew he was about to go into battle against professional men; the odds were not in his favour. Darwin was planning on exterminating Newman and his men but the thought left him with a real problem. How do you kill a werewolf? Ancient lore and Hollywood spoke of silver but Darwin had no idea if any truth existed in the legend. On top of his doubts was the reality that he had no silver and with time growing short finding silver wasn't a practical option. Other considerations that Darwin thought might be workable were fire and decapitation. Slicing the head off worked well during the takeover but those were new werewolves who didn't know how to bring about the change. Newman and the NHPD were stronger; could they get close enough to cut off their heads? As hard as he tried he could think of no way to make fire a usable option, which brought him back to a physical assault as the only viable choice.

Darwin had sampled Newman's blood, he knew the man, and he knew what he was capable of. The power of the werewolf had consumed him and Newman would stop at nothing to feed his thirst. He was an accomplished liar; Darwin would have to be ready for that. Newman would attempt to talk his way into a tactical position that would allow him the chance to eliminate Darwin and the New Haven council. For Darwin there would only be one chance and that meant he could not listen to Newman. He would have to attack first and hit hard. Success would be hinged on confronting Newman before he embraced the detainees which Darwin had now concluded was his plan. If Newman had finished making his army Darwin felt he would still have until the full moon before the situation became critical.

Chapter 32

The phones were down completely. Darwin had tried to call Clint again but he was met with an automated message stating the cellular customer was unavailable. Darwin tried phoning anyone in New Haven that might be able to help but no calls were going through. With communications down Darwin knew that the situation at special handling was far worse than he had first thought. His last hope was to swing through town to quickly tell anyone he might come across about the potential putsch.

As the city vehicle rolled through the streets of downtown all signs of life appeared to be hidden. The shops and restaurants were all closed and even the bowling alley was deserted. There simply was no one to ask for help. Street after street was desolate. For a moment Darwin considered driving up to a house with lights on but he was afraid of wasting precious minutes and decided it was more important to get to special handling. He told Scott to keep an eye open for anyone they could pull alongside of to give the warning to but despite their best efforts they found no one. Darwin moved on up the road to the mine driving as fast as he could. He could only wonder what would await him when he arrived at the gates.

"I feel strange." Scott said.

Darwin broke from his trance to hear the question of his new pup. Knowing what Scott was referring to and needing a distraction Darwin answered. "The second full moon is the strongest. We change a little earlier than we did last night. That feeling in your gut is the start of the change. It's a little like butterflies, it will get stronger in the next hour or so. We'll change just before seven."

"I watched Newman change last night. It was fantastic! When the clothing tore from his body and his muscles enlarged with the hair on them…that was shit right there! Where did you change last night?" Scott asked.

"In my office with a girl. We were fucking. It was pretty cool." Darwin said with a grin still watching the road as he continued to accelerate towards the mine.

"She's a werewolf too, or did you change and kill a human?" Scott asked.

"I made her a few weeks ago. We changed together; it was intense. Then we fucked some more while we were the wolf. Hey you should take your sling off; your arm will be healed by now." Darwin said in much higher spirits than he had been all afternoon.

Scott looked to his amateur first aid realizing Darwin was right; his arm had stopped hurting an hour after he was bit. Wasting no time he tore the sling away and ripped the bandage exposing his perfectly normal skin. He rubbed it in awe. "This is really happening to me."

"Yes it is. Twenty four hours ago you were a geeky human who was drafted to look after a town of werewolves with the promise of becoming one yourself. A day later you've been given the gift, by accident, but you are still one of us. Soon you'll change for your first time and I'm guaranteeing you will make your first kill tonight. That's a lot to go through all in one day. How do you think you'll handle it?" Darwin asked fatherly.

"I wish I could change now. The anticipation is killing me." Scott replied with a level of confidence. "I've always wanted to be a werewolf. I love werewolf movies. I never understood why the werewolf thought it was a curse. I've been a werewolf for less than a day and I'm already looking forward to killing someone. It's like being hungry, really hungry, and you don't care what you eat. That blood you gave me really helped me see things more clearly."

"Human blood works even better." Darwin replied as he slowed the vehicle down as he could see special handling speeding towards their eyes. With the main gate approaching rapidly Darwin had to make a decision, park at the gate and conduct surveillance or drive right in. He looked at his watch and decided time was a luxury they did not have.

Darwin's armada, if you could call it that, sped towards Clint's house hoping and praying that things would work out. The geek squad was about to confront the elite, the only remaining bullies of New Haven. In another time or place they would turned and ran away. They would have found a quiet hallway or secluded corner to wait for the hunters to lose interest and move on. Darwin knew he was making a stand for every high school assault and shower room rape that had ever occurred. A line would be drawn in his mind;

no longer would someone push him without consequence. Gone were the days of people hurting him or the ones he cared about. Darwin would no longer stand by idly while the strong manipulated the weak for their own purposes. Frank Newman and the NHPD were nothing more than bullies. They stood for everything Darwin hated in society. These men were the adult version of his own tormentors and he felt foolish for actually believing Newman could be trusted.

As he rolled up to the main house Darwin's heart began to race; he was nervous. The fluttering of his cardiac muscle made him feel susceptible to an involuntary change. Doubt and unease drove his concerns; he wanted the clarity of his human mind for as long as possible, but he knew sooner or later he would change out of anger.

"Darwin." Newman called out before emerging from the shadows of the intake building.

"Frank, I'm looking for Clint, have you seen him?" Darwin asked, trying to keep his cool.

"Yes I have." He replied calmly as he began to slowly approach. "Why are the human geeks here?"

Darwin hesitated for a moment but came up with a decent lie. "They asked about our food. I thought honesty would be the best policy; they will be like us one day."

Newman didn't say much to Darwin's answer, he only huffed a bit. He could smell a lie like a decaying corpse. As a cop he might have been crooked but he did have a few skills that were legit and detecting the truth was one of them. "You're a bad liar Darwin. I knew that about you even before you bit me. You were right though, I was going to arrest you. The sad thing is you actually did commit those murders, so I really wasn't wrong about you."

"I knew I was right. I could feel it." Darwin said bluntly.

"You know, this whole thing exists because of me." Newman said with smugness.

Irritated, Darwin struggled to ask nicely what Newman meant. "How do you figure that?"

"Well you may have started it…but hell do we really need you? I admit a lot of what we have is of your imagination. But let's face it Darwin, you're just a stupid kid. Because you came up with the idea, you are the leader! Give me a break! If I hadn't made you a suspect you would have continued on your merry little way with your faggoty friend Steve. None of this would exist!" Newman said with a growing impatience.

"What did you say?!?" Darwin asked with his blood coming to a boil.

"You heard me. You think it's any secret you and Cardwen were fudge-packing. What kind of a leader pulls all of his security to hunt down his gay lover. Do you really think I would do that? I thought there was a chance that you might actually be a good leader once Cardwen was out of the way. I mean, don't get me wrong, you could never have been anything more than a figure head, but there was a chance it might have worked. Once Cardwen was gone I could really seen how pathetic you really were. Maybe I could have stopped him, but a voice inside of me told me not to." Newman said wrinkling his nose in contemplative thought.

Darwin lowered his hands to his sides extending his fingers as wide as they would go. Slowly claws began to extend from his tips as his rage began to boil over. "What do you mean, Newman?" Darwin asked in slightly more hoarse voice than before.

Newman laughed at Darwin's changing face as he began to slip into the wolf. "I knew where he was. I even had a pretty good idea what he was about to do. I saw him with the jerrycan of gasoline entering the school. I was close enough to see him bawling; and to me he had all the signs of someone who was suicidal. I could have stopped him, but I thought the world would be a better place with one less fag in it! I gave him a good lead before coming to get you."

Tim Waters came alongside Darwin to take some of the heat away. "Who the fuck are you to decide that Steve would be better off dead?"

"Ever heard of respect for your elders kid?" Newman said dismissively.

"We made you for fuck sake! Without us you'd be nothing!" Tim yelled in hatred as Darwin trembled next to him.

"Without me you would both have been in jail last night awaiting trial for murder. You would have changed in a cage and your secret would have been out. This morning you would have been in some government research facility being dissected. You know it and I know it. You should bow before me and give me thanks for everything I did for you!" Newman said in narcissism.

"So what are you planning Frank?" Darwin asked, still slowly changing.

"I can do better than you. You put some good men inside that mine. I'm pulling them out and giving them their rightful place among the chosen." Newman said as a matter of fact.

"What about our doctrine; if you had an issue with it why didn't you speak up?!?" Tim shouted.

Newman again laughed dismissively. "Fuck your doctrine! You're just a bunch of kids with some big ideas. You might be werewolves, but like all young people, you are both idealists. The world is full of bullies Darwin. You're either a bully or bullied, that's just how it is. If you want to be the strongest, you need to surround yourself with the strongest. Abused and bullied fags and geeks were the wrong approach. We must be strong and as much as this pains you, the people you hate are the ones you are trying to be. If you want to be tough, then hang around them! Be them!"

Darwinism

"I will not sell out my beliefs! I am not them, and I never will be!" Darwin said he prepared to lunge at Newman.

"Cutting off a leg and eating it seems pretty barbaric. Did he really deserve that? You seem a bit hypocritical in your approach." Newman said casually attempting to push more of Darwin's buttons.

Instead of reacting Darwin remembered what he had thought to himself before the confrontation. He had been listening to Newman which he knew was dangerous. Newman was stalling and Darwin was being suckered in. Newman had hit every button on Darwin and the knowledge that Steve could have been saved was the trigger that Darwin latched on and used to release his wolf. In mid air Darwin let go of his humanity and his rage landing on Newman. Darwin snapped his teeth dripping saliva into Newman's surprised face. Newman pushed back beginning to change himself. Darwin could see the throat he wanted to tear into but he couldn't reach it. The wolf in Newman ripped through his human exterior and the strength Darwin was fighting became equally matched. Darwin held his ground and kept Newman pinned but the fight was becoming a stalemate. In a momentary lapse in concentration Darwin felt a distinct and familiar crushing feeling between his legs. His stomach seized as a throbbing tsunami over took his wolf body. Darwin fell off to the side as he struggled to turn his pain into extreme rage as fast as he could. Newman was getting up and coming towards Darwin and he knew he had seconds to act or he would face his end.

Scott Spencer came from behind smashing Newman in the head with a shovel. The metal spade rang his skull like a broken bell but it made no impact on Newman. Newman turned in fury and hit Scott with the back of his hand throwing the young man back twenty feet colliding with a diesel tanker truck. Scott fell to the ground limply for a moment. The other Guardians stood by in horror, unsure of what they could do against the paranormal strength. Tina Redding ran over to Scott but by the time she was next to him he had begun to change. She knelt down to him and looked into his coloring eyes as he body began to grown in size and strength. The nerd in Scott washed away forever and his new life took hold. Scott jumped from his spot and charged back to Newman with his new razor claws out and ready to carve up some meat.

Wolf Tim was now out and Newman was facing a three on one battle just like all good bully fights. Darwin grabbed Newman's arm in an attempt to restrain him and Tim strapped himself to the legs. When Scott arrived he knew exactly what to go for. With one fell swoop the new comer slit Newman's throat releasing a torrent of blood to the ground. Scott howled in joy at his success. Newman's fight waned as he attempted to hold his wound and keep his blood in.

The flash and zaps came almost simultaneously. In three successive bursts

307

Mark Fuson

Darwin, Tim and Scott all yelped and collapsed. Newman's henchman had arrived with their police toys and now the trio of werewolves were surrounded by a much larger pack. The Guardians hung back in disbelief, really not accomplishing anything more than creating a live audience. They wanted to help but with nothing more than shot guns available to them they knew their effectiveness was limited.

The entire New Haven Police Department now surrounded the ill prepared army. Darwin looked around at the men he once considered his security force and he realized he was now deposed as leader. What was more disheartening was Clint and his special handling crew were also standing nearby. Darwin and his dream of New Haven were being systematically destroyed.

"Good effort." Newman coughed out as he stumbled back to his feet still holding his throat, the wound now almost completely sealed. "I guess you lose."

"Clint, why?" Darwin asked now in human form now weeping.

"Newman is a prick, but he's right. You're too young. You might be smart, but you're not a leader, you never could be. It's better this way." Clint replied softly.

"Without Darwin none of this would exist! You can't just kick him out." Tim begged.

"Who said anything about kicking you guys out? We feel that keeping you around would just cause us headaches in the long run. And letting you go might give you some dangerous ideas. Sorry guys, you've got to go." Fletcher informed.

"You should feel honoured Darwin; you're like Caesar, in a way." Newman reassured attempting to appeal to Darwin's vanity.

"What are you going to do with the Guardians?" Tim asked.

"Well we can't exactly let them go about their business. You know my stance on them; we don't need them. I'm on the fence right now as to what to do with them but I think we'll keep it simple." Newman suggested.

"I hate dragging this stuff out. Take our three werewolf heroes over to hallway ten. Let's use this opportunity to learn what kills a werewolf. Put the dweebs onto the bus and guard them; we'll have them tonight." Newman ordered his men and without further prompting the resistors were shuffled off to their predetermined areas. The humans offered some verbal resistance but were lead away without firing a shot. Darwin, Tim and Scott found themselves being restrained by six men each making a struggle impossible. All three fought without success and soon they found themselves in room two of hallway ten.

Chapter 33

Room two was similar to room one; the medical feel dominated the appearance. The significant difference in room two was it had four gurney style tables evenly spaced in the room with thick leather straps hanging from the edge. Darwin had this room designed for Dr. Gagnon as a place where she could monitor and conduct the same experiment on multiple people at the same time. Now, on the room's maiden voyage, the three young werewolves were being strapped down including a thick strap across their neck. Once secure, they were left alone in the room to wait for their torture to begin.

"How long until we change?" Tim mumbled with the air he could muster.

"Less than an hour. I think we're fucked." Darwin admitted.

Scott wheezed. His neck strap was tighter than the others making it much harder to speak. "Don't....give....up." He said.

"Suggestions." Darwin gasped.

The three remained silent. There were no options. Darwin thought he could break through the leather when the moon rose, but he expected Newman would have him killed before that. He could not move. There was no way to loosen the straps and it seemed to him he had no friends left that might be able to help him. He had begun to realize as death approached that his attitude had been too green. Darwin had been ill prepared to take on the challenges of leadership; he regretted not taking his position more seriously. Time and circumstances had made his importance in the community an essential component which he had taken for granted. Steve had made it impossible for Darwin. Whether Steve lived or died Darwin's human emotions would have been a distraction. If Darwin had ever hoped to be an effective leader, love would have been a luxury he had to live without. He understood that now.

Newman and Clint entered the room after a long while of silence and reflection had passed between the heroes. Darwin had given up in his mind; there was nothing more he could do. Tim and Scott appeared to be at the same conclusion.

In Newman's hand was a small case which he placed on a steel table along the wall. He began working right away with his back turned to the young men. It remained a mystery to the three captives what he was doing.

"Newman, it doesn't have to end this way." Darwin choked out with all his air.

Newman shook his head from side to side as though it was true but he continued working with the case. "It doesn't have to, but it is."

"What if I'm the first?" Darwin said quickly.

"What if you are? It doesn't change anything." Newman replied. "Clint, loosen his neck strap so he can talk better. He sounds like a stuttering moron."

Clint went over to the Darwin's table and undid the strap by one hole. It was enough relief for Darwin to talk more freely. "I might be the first, if I am, killing me might make the rest of you become mortal again."

Newman and Clint both laughed freely at the suggestion. "You're grasping at straws boy. We don't even know the rules of our gift. All we have to go on is lore and Hollywood. I doubt killing you will make any bit of difference to our own condition. Anyway, it's a risk I'm willing to take." Newman said cheerfully as he spun around wielding a needle.

"What is that?" Tim asked nervously.

"Silver Nitrate. If there's any truth to the silver legend this should work just fine. Who would like to go first?" Newman looked to the three tables as though he actually expected someone to volunteer. After a few seconds of silence he decided to correct his mistake. "How about my little accident from last night?"

"Please, no." Scott begged.

"This won't hurt a bit." Newman assured, taking Scott's left arm and inserting the needle into the first available vein. Once the syringe was buried into his arm Newman depressed the plunger quickly.

The boy shuttered and his eyes opened wide as the poison began to flow through his heart. Beads of sweat rushed to the surface of his skin until his face glistened. Within seconds his clothing began to soak through with his salty perspiration that flowed from him in a stream. Scott let out a human-

Darwinism

wolf howl as his body began to change. The pants filled out and began to tear along the seams at the same time his torso was growing. The sound of growling and tearing fabric was all that could be heard in the room. Scott was changing into a full out werewolf without the help of the moon. The force of his growing body against the leather straps was too much and one by one they began to buckle and break. Newman took a step back and looked like he was about to flee when he realized the silver was not working as he had hoped. Free from the straps, Scott was almost completely changed when he sat up. The new werewolf looked around the room but made no effort to move. His head drooped and his breath was heavy. The large claws of Scott Spencer moved to his neck as though he was choking. A large mass erupted in his throat, like volcanic pillow lava, it grew bulbously from him and began to stretch to the floor. Scott made no more noise; his animal vibrated in pain as more dermis erupted throughout his body. Moments later the cracking and stretching cartilage stopped. Scott fell back onto the table an infected mound of hair and skin. He was dead.

"Wow, that was cool!" Clint said. "For a moment I thought it wasn't going to work."

"Me too!" Newman replied. "I think I'll up the dose for the next one; that took longer than I had hoped." Newman filled a second syringe with twice the dose of the first needle and then handed it to Clint. "Try it! It's fun."

Clint took the needle from Newman and walked over to Tim. Wasting no time Clint jabbed the needle down and pushed the fluid out. Clint walked back to Newman for the second needle not waiting to see Tim die.

"I want to do Darwin." Clint requested.

"Why didn't you do it with the last needle?" Newman asked annoyed.

"I wanted him to squirm a bit. I'd really like to do him too." Clint asked.

"Fine!" Newman replied handing over the third needle.

Clint walked over to Darwin and looked him in the eyes. "I'm sorry my friend. Maybe one day we will meet in Hell?"

Darwin took a deep breath clenching his teeth. "Get on with it." Was all he said before closing his eyes on his world.

Darwin felt no prick on his arm, no pain rushing to his heart like he expected. All Darwin heard was a quick thud and a pant of shock. A moment later he could hear fabric beginning to tear and the straps on his arms were coming off. Afraid to open his eyes Darwin waited for the pits of Hell to open up and take him. He found the sensation of death to be very different than what he expected. Darwin felt his body was alive, even his member had begun to stiffen. Death felt good to Darwin.

"Darwin, get up!" Clint shouted.

Mark Fuson

Darwin opened his eyes to find what he took to be Frank Newman on the floor convulsing in a rupturing pile of puss. "Clint! What happened?" Darwin asked as he jumped from the table.

"I'm doing what I can to get us out of here. I'm sorry I couldn't save Scott. You're my friend, I wouldn't let anything happen to you." Clint said quickly as he ran over to Tim and undid his straps. Tim was returning to his human shape, his clothes still only partially torn.

"Tim! You're alive." Darwin shouted in excitement.

"Clint stuck the needle past my arm and shot the fluid onto the floor! I saw Clint wink so I tried to sell it. I changed as much as I could to buy him some time." Tim said now free of the table.

"I jabbed Newman in the neck when his guard was down. We've got to get out of here." Clint said filling another syringe with silver nitrate.

"Where are your men, Clint?" Tim asked.

"They sided with Newman, even before I had a chance to talk to them. I guess the promise of constant flesh was too much for them to resist. I went along with it until I had a good opportunity to help you guys. We've got bigger problems now. Newman's building his army in the intake building; they're over there right now. The moon is going to be up in twenty minutes. The three of us can't fight them, but I have a plan that might work."

"We should try and save the Guardians as well." Darwin said.

"We should be able to get to them, I saw only two men guarding the bus. If we use this silver nitrate on them we should neutralize them quickly." Clint said filling a second and third needle.

"How do we stop Newman's army?" Tim asked.

"Ammonium Nitrate. I'm not an expert, and this might not work, but it's all we've got. When this place was a nursery I kept a whole shed of different fertilizers on hand, including ammonium nitrate. The feds use to give me shit for storing too much of the stuff. It can be very volatile especially in a fire. I have ten thousand pounds of that stuff next to the induction building, if we use the diesel fueling truck we should be able to get a decent fire going. With a little luck it will detonate and wipe out our competition."

"How large of an explosion are we talking about?" Darwin asked.

"Large enough that it will destroy most of special handling. I'm guessing anything within a hundred feet of the explosion will vaporize. It should flatten every building on the site." Clint replied handing a needle to both Darwin and Tim.

"How do we set the bomb off and how much time will we have to get away before it explodes?" Tim asked.

"I think if I run the fuel truck up to the shed and begin dumping the fuel for a minute or two, a road flare should be enough to start the fire, but again,

Darwinism

it's only a guess. I don't think it will be long enough for us to make a break for it." Clint replied moving towards the door.

"Is this a suicide mission?" Darwin asked.

"If we had more time before the moon rose we could make a run for it. I think the only way this can work is if we run into the mine instead. The blast will seal us in, but we can escape through that entrance I told you about, the one a few miles from here." Clint shot out as he left the room at high speed. Tim and Darwin were close behind realizing the plan had been adopted even though they weren't one hundred percent sure of what was about to happen.

"Clint, are you sure there's no other way? Why save the Guardians then, if they're in the mine with us we might kill them." Tim shouted up the hallway as they raced to outside.

"No Tim, I think we can control it. I've controlled it before. Besides we can always feed on the detainees. When you are the wolf just hold on to that thought, as long as you know you can eat, you should be able to choose who you eat." Darwin assured. "Fuck my cock is hard!"

"Yeah mine too!" Tim shouted back.

"We're running out of time. Tim, Darwin - go over and take out the guards by the bus. Get the Guardians to the mine as quick as you can. I'll go start the truck and get that fire going. I can't wait for you so move as fast as you can! Just get inside that mine!" Clint demanded as he ran off into the night.

Darwin and Tim both looked up to the cloudless sky and a bright white moon that began singing to their souls. The white orb was mesmerizing to the soon to be lycans. Their members pulsated to the lunar vibrations which brought about tremors in their testicles.

"I think we have less time than we thought." Darwin said.

"I think you're right." Tim agreed.

"The bus is over there. Can you see where the guards are?" Darwin asked as he crouched down, shuffling his way over to the hostages.

"I think there's one at the side door and one at the emergency exit at the rear, that's what it looks like anyways." Tim replied.

"Ok. I'll get the guy at the front; you get the guy at the back. Just jab him with the silver and don't wait for me, we gotta be quick." Darwin insisted. Not waiting for a response he ran as quietly as he could leaving Tim behind.

As Darwin approached the bus he became aware of the sound of the snow under his feet. The snow was a powder but it made a scrunching noise as he walked that seemed to get louder with every step. Some of the Guardians became aware of Darwin's approach and spontaneously began making a distraction on the bus.

Mark Fuson

"Hey!!! HEY!!!!" One of the Guardians began to shout and smacking the windows attempting to get the guard's attention. Soon others on the bus began hitting the windows which gave Darwin the chance he needed to cover the distance to the front of the bus quickly.

"What the fuck is it!?!" The guard yelled at his human captives as he stepped onto the bus.

"Make us. Please! We want to be like you!" Tina Redding pleaded.

"Not happening! In a few minutes you're going to be my dinner. I'm starting to change, it won't be long; I can feel it." He replied. "Don't go anywhere!"

"We're expected elsewhere." Darwin whispered as he stuck the needle into the Guard's leg.

"Darwin!" Tina yelled running over to him and embracing him.

He was taken back by the greeting but was pleased to know someone was happy to see him. "Everyone, we've got to move now! We need to get to inside the mine as fast as possible. Let's move!" He commanded.

"Why?" A voice from the group asked as the Guardians began pushing their way off the bus.

"DARWIN! WE'VE GOT TO GO NOW! THE FIRE HAS STARTED!" Tim yelled from near the rear of the bus as he stood over a steaming mound of hair.

"EVERYONE FOLLOW ME! BIG EXPLOSION COMING." Darwin informed the group in broken and nervous English.

Darwin and Tim lead the way towards the mine taking a moment every few feet to make sure the Guardians were in close proximity. From the direction of the fire Darwin could see the silhouette of someone running towards the group. The figure was alone and he could only hope the man was Clint. The tunnel entrance was a hundred feet away when the first explosion started. A deafening thud and a fireball roared into the night sky illuminating the entire compound.

"MOVE PEOPLE! MOVE, MOVE, MOVE!!!" Darwin demand as the group became distracted by the pyrotechnique display. The first explosion caught the attention of the growing army in the induction building. A flood of confused and disorganized men ran around looking for a way to hit the fire but it was too late for them.

Darwin stopped at the entrance of the mine making sure everyone made it. Tim lead the group in at a full out sprint. A few seconds later the silhouetted figure arrived and it was Clint but he had also found some unwanted attention. Five men were in chase but were too far away to be a concern. The bright flash and air compression knocked Clint and Darwin like feathers into the shaft; the ceiling and entrance closed like a zipper as they flew deep into the mine.

Darwinism

They traversed an incredible distance before they came to a rest tumbling along the railway tracks. The pain that rolled through their bones would have killed a mere mortal but for Clint and Darwin it only brought out the wolf.

The lights in the mine tunnel extinguished leaving everything in complete darkness. After a few moments the lighting slowly returned. "Batteries." Clint barked through his fangs of anger. "We're off the grid now."

"Your little explosion worked better than I thought. How long will the batteries hold?" Darwin asked as his wolf retracted under his skin for a few more minutes.

"Thirty-six hours. We'll be out of here by then." Clint replied getting up off the tracks and dusting himself off. Darwin laughed to himself at the sight of Clint taking the time to brush off dust from clothing that would soon be torn to shreds but he said nothing.

"Darwin, Clint! You made it. Come on, I've got the gates to the woman's side open...that's the way to the other exit, right?" Tim asked with giddy anticipation.

"Yes. Where are the others?" Darwin asked.

"They're making their way down to A2." Tim replied. "I told them what to expect, they're ok with it I think."

"Should we change here or go down to A2?" Clint asked honestly.

"Let's start walking. We change wherever we change." Darwin suggested as he began walking down the track.

The three monsters marched onwards with the thought of killing becoming all consuming. The trio said nothing to each other but they knew what each other was thinking. The sound of beating hearts echoed in the cavern, thousands of them. The song enticed the young wolves; it would be a celebration of their victory over Newman and their continued existence. They would slaughter as many as they felt they could. Nothing mattered anymore.

The divided corridor beyond the man gates was void of people. The Guardians were gone and the place was dead. The three men continued walking towards the ramp to A2, their penis' danced and poked at their pant fabric on the verge of release. Their time was nearly over.

"STOP!" A female voice shouted from the ramp to A2, running towards the three intruders.

Darwin put his arms up his side, indicating to Clint and Tim to hold back for a moment. Amused at the strong willed woman, Darwin asked her what she wanted. The woman stopped a few feet from the men without replying. "What are you hoping to accomplish?"

"I know what you are, and I won't let you kill my friends." The woman said.

"How do you propose to stop us?" Tim asked with a dismissive tone.

"I'm like you. I'm a werewolf. I changed last night. I can feel it, I'm about to change again." She replied.

"A werewolf? How did that happen?" Clint asked.

"One of your goons scratched me at the train station. It was small. I didn't think anything of it at the time." The woman replied with a deep breath and a moan as the change approached.

"What's your name, chicky?" Darwin asked as his orgasm began.

"I'm Caroline Lutz. And like I said, I'm not going to let you hurt my friends." The woman restated as she collapsed to the ground letting out a scream of joy and release.

"We'll see about that!" Darwin grumbled as his shoes split from his feet.

The four humans screamed and hollered in enjoyment as their bodies began to reshape into something better. Clint ripped his shirt from his body long before he was big enough to burst through it but he was already covered in a light coating of hair. Tim was the tallest by far, over seven feet, but still maintaining most of his human features aside from a scruffy beard. Caroline dropped her hospital gown as her body took on the musculature of a man and then on to a powerful animal. Hair washed across all four lycans and they howled and snapped at each other waiting for the change to conclude.

The three males fanned out attempting to encircle the accidental female. Clint dove in first nipping her arm and drawing out a bit of blood. Caroline hit back, reaching deep with her uninjured claw, she grabbed a hold of Clint's grapes and shook them around vigorously stunning the animal momentarily. Darwin charged at her but was hit by a fast and repetitive move on her part. Caroline again aimed low landing her claw on Darwin's wolf balls but this time she picked up her attacker and flung him towards the dividing fence. Darwin collided with the electrified wire sending an explosion of sparks and smoke throughout the chamber. The lights flickered and dimmed for a moment until Darwin landed on the ground away from the fence. Darwin's wolf lay in rest while the other two continued their assault.

Tim moved in for a face to face attack which Caroline appeared ready for. Like a mother protecting her young she was poised to push her strength to the limits. No attack the three monsters could throw at her would faze her. Her instincts were tough, she was resolute; these men would not pass.

With a lash of her claw she sliced through the thick cave air severing Tim's jugular before he was even able to make a move. Tim collapsed to the ground holding his throat. He would not die from his injury but what fight he had in him was now gone. Clint approached the bitch from behind; he hoped to break her neck and dislocate her cranium. The sly female had already sensed

Darwinism

Clint's approach. Hitting the ground she rolled backwards knocking the creature over. Clint had barely come to a rest and Caroline was jumping up almost hitting the ceiling. With one set of claws extended like a gun Caroline came down with her razors targeted to Clint. The warden of special handling would never see his prison more clearly than he did in that moment. Caroline jammed her claws deep inside his orbital socket causing the male werewolf to yelp in defeat.

She howled in victory loud enough that every area of the mine could hear her. Her primal sense told her that she did not need to worry about continued attacks from the three. She had proven her worth and dominance. They would retreat to a dark corner and sulk in their defeat until morning. She would stay on guard, just in case.

CHAPTER 34

The three men woke the next day lying in a pile on top of each other attempting to stay warm. The cavern was cool and damp and despite the heat their bodies were radiating, they knew they would soon be cold. They climbed off of each other realizing they had no clothing and they were not alone.

"My eye!" Clint shouted in horror as he realized Caroline had burst his eye with her claws. His gift had only allowed for the wound to heal over but the eye itself did not regenerate. "I'm fucking blind!" He cried.

Tim rubbed his own neck remembering that it had been slashed the night before. His wound was more or less healed though he still could feel a scar running across. "How are you feeling Darwin?"

"I can still smell burning hair and I think that fence left a griddle mark on my back." He stated in disgust. Darwin turned so Tim could inspect him and it was true he did have a pattern of fencing tattooed into his back which made Tim chuckle.

"Boys will be boys, I guess." A nude and confident Caroline approached. The woman looked stunning in her new and reshaped body. She had curves and not an ounce of extra fat to be found anywhere. Her breasts were supple and perky once again, like they had been when she was eighteen. "Are you ready to start talking?"

"What's there to talk about?" Tim replied.

"I could think of a few things. Maybe…why are we being held here?" Caroline simply asked.

"You know the answer to that." Darwin replied.

"But I want to hear your answer. What's your name?" She replied cunningly.

"I'm Darwin Foster, leader of the group. You are the food. We are werewolves and you are kept here so we don't have to hunt." Darwin replied bluntly.

"Ah! Some truth. Maybe you'll be happy to share a little more with me then." Caroline said standing face to face with her demonic leader.

"Why not!" Darwin said sarcastically.

"Not everyone in town is here. I saw people pulled from the line when we arrived here. Where did they go?" The woman demanded.

"We turned them." Darwin answered.

"How did you select those who came here and those who were infected?" The interrogation continued.

The answer to the question was complicated and from her point of view no answer could ever justify how she ended up on the dinner plate. Darwin considered his words carefully but Tim came to his rescue.

"It was a hard choice. Some people were selected because we simply didn't like them. I admit that. They were bad people, some of them. I was raped in the shower at school with a golf club – they ended up here because I wanted them here. But that's not everyone." Tim offered softly.

"It's revenge?" Caroline asked in clarification.

"In part, yes. But we also knew we needed people to run the town, special skills and trades. They were selected to receive the gift." Darwin said with a hint of remorse under his breath.

"And the rest?" She asked.

"By lottery. Was it fair – no. Most of you weren't picked for any reason other than just plain bad luck on your part." Darwin replied on the verge of tears.

"Why can't you just turn all of us? One big werewolf town! The, gift…it is amazing!" Caroline confessed.

"How do we feed that many people?" Clint interjected.

"Why do we need to eat human? I haven't and I'm doing great!" Caroline replied as though it was the biggest revelation the world had ever known.

"You must feel it inside of you?" Darwin stated shaking his head. "The urge to kill is in you, you won't be able to control it forever. Eventually you will give in to your desire and consume human flesh. Admit it! Even now, hearing me talking about it is starting it get you excited. You are thinking about it. You can't even take your mind off the idea of a piece a meat tossing around inside your mouth. Your teeth shredding the muscle fibres and the shots of blood that coat your mouth, it's much more than a fantasy. It will continue to grow in your mind until you can't help it any longer. You will kill; it's only a matter of time."

"I don't know what you're talking about." Caroline replied in disbelief.

"You're a fucking liar!" Tim grumbled.

"Caroline?" A timid voice from the ramp shouted.

"I'm ok, Tara. You can come on up." Caroline replied.

"The newcomers weren't lying, were they? They are werewolves." Mayor Bollen stated as she approached the group.

"This is Darwin Foster, the apparent leader of the werewolves. He was just telling me why we're all here. The wolves arbitrarily made a list of the naughty and nice and sent the unwanted here to be their food source." Caroline informed.

"You killed my children YOU DIRTY MOTHER FUCKER!" Tara jumped on Darwin beating him in the face and shouting indistinguishable curses. Darwin just laid there and let the angry woman release her pain. "WHY?????" She bellowed in anguish as her hits slowed and then stopped.

"I've made some mistakes. I admit that. There's nothing I can do to bring your children back and for that I am truly sorry." Darwin said with tears streaming down his cheeks.

"The children you took from the mine, they're dead aren't they?" Tara asked in grief.

"Yes." Darwin replied softly. "Please don't ask why, there's no answer I could give you that you would understand. We're monsters; that's all you need to know. That's the only thing that will make sense."

"There are only three of you. Naked and unarmed. Do you really think we're going to be compliant with you? I'm sure several thousand of us could tear you apart." Tara said defiantly.

"We could slaughter a lot of you before that happened. Does it really need to be like that?" Darwin asked.

"I don't see anyway around it." The mayor replied as though she had really been considering other alternatives.

"Tara - go and find your husband, and ask him to join us. Maybe it's time we bring this to an end." Darwin said, looking to the ground.

"Why not just open the doors and let us go?" Caroline asked.

"Did you hear a loud explosion last night; maybe you felt some shaking too?" Darwin said.

Both Tara and Caroline shook their heads in acknowledgment. The sound had rumbled throughout the mine at the same time the lights had gone out. There was no denying that something big had happened only they had no idea that the explosion had been on the surface. They also had no idea how severe the damage was. Darwin informed them that main entrance had been sealed

Darwinism

and now their only hope of escape was through the women's side of special handling. It was a long walk to the escape hatch and it could take days to get everyone out but it would work. The only snag was the hatch was sealed from the outside and the best chance to move it was with the power of the wolf. Tara and Mike would have to agree to remain civil to their captors until they were outside if they wanted their help to escape. Once free of the mine a decision would have to be made, but Darwin would not make that call.

*   *   *

Darwin and his Guardians took the lead of the group with a stream of refugees behind them. The smell in the cave was thick with feces and body odour. The slums of special handling had enveloped all three levels of the living quarters. Garbage and toilets were indistinguishable from the beds. Darwin thought at one point he actually saw a bed made from shit, almost like a nest. The people that he saw in the mine reminded him why he had them placed there in the first place. Were they a product of their environment or was what they were becoming merely an amplification of something they always were?

Clint managed to disable the electrified gate at the far end of the tunnel on A4. The wiring was actually very simple to bypass, which made Darwin wonder why the barrier had ever been erected in the first place. Clint said the wiring was alarmed in the guard post so they would know if someone was attempting to pass through the gate. The basic premise behind the fence was to make sure the detainees were never aware of the escape hatch, even if it was unlikely they could ever hope to move it. It was just one more piece of enhanced security that Darwin loved about the operation.

An hour beyond the barrier, Clint arrived at the ladder that was bolted into the rock. The ladder entered a hole in the ceiling and continued on into the darkness that, according to Clint, would be blocked by a solid concrete slab.

"If this is going to work we're going to need Darwin, Tim and myself at the top of that ladder. If we can get angry we might be strong enough to slide the lid off." Clint informed the group as the cavern began to fill with a brigade of malnourished zombies.

"And if it doesn't work?" Tim asked.

"We're royally fucked." Darwin said plainly.

"It's going to be tight up at the top of the ladder, hope you guys are ok sharing your personal space." Clint laughed as he began ascending the ladder still completely naked.

Becoming angry at the top of the ladder was not a challenge. The rungs drove into their feet causing cramping and a bit of a Charlie horse in Tim, who was already a wolf, when they butted their shoulders against the slab.

Darwin and Clint began to change as they pushed against the frozen block. As their muscles formed and expanded the strength of the three began to shift the block. The move was slow but daylight punctured the darkness, giving them the courage to continue. Fresh air blasted down the shaft at the moment Tim was able to reach out with his arm, feeling the freeness of the day. Using his hands Tim was able to wiggle the block further, allowing Clint and Darwin to get their arms into the outside world as well. With six paws pushing on the block it finally slid open enough that people could pass through. They were free.

Darwin took in the splendour of the cold January day. Not a cloud in the sky but a breath of wind was in the tree tops; it was very relaxing. The world around him was much different than he had envisioned it. He was different.

In his heart he had allowed himself to become a monster, fuelled by injustice of his past and the perception that the world as a whole was holding him back. Darwin was learning that he was the master of his own destiny and the abuse and torment of his past did not need to dictate who he was. He had been given a gift that he still had no idea where it had come from, but that gift had proven to him that he had worth. His gift had given him confidence and a realization and acceptance that good and evil was all but a matter or perspective.

Darwin had been beaten down in the world to the point of suicide. It had taken Steve and now all Darwin could think to do was make a world a place that Steve would have been proud of.

"Freedom!" Mayor Bollen shouted as she emerged from the ladder with Caroline Lutz close behind. "So what happens now?"

"We head back to town. Tomorrow we'll have to clean things up. Remember tonight is the last full moon, not much we can do about anything now." Darwin said.

"The world doesn't look the same anymore." Caroline commented.

"It isn't the same and it never will be." Darwin replied.

"Darwin!" Tina Redding yelled as she emerged from the hole.

"Are all your people up?" Darwin asked.

"I'm the last, just prisoners behind me. Does this mean I'm out of work now?" Tina asked with a hint of sincerity mixed with sarcasm.

"Hell no! Seal the hatch; we've got work to do!" Darwin said with an evil grin that stretched ear to ear.

Tim and Clint slid the stone block over the hole to the screams of the people below who knew their situation was not about to change. The last attempt of escape was blocked when the stone fell onto an arm that was reaching for freedom. The stone severed the limb in one fantastic snap, leaving the forearm and hand resting helplessly in the snow.

Darwinism

"Another bite to eat, Mayor?" Darwin asked out of courtesy. The mayor respectfully declined, leaving her blood urges to fester inside her new reality. Darwin shared the hand with Tim and Clint on the long walk back to New Haven.

The evolution of the species had only just begun.